June is known as "Brides Month." And what better way
to celebrate matrimony than with wonderful love
stories filled with rich romance?
Join us as three beloved Arabesque authors celebrate
the joining of two hearts.
After reading our first Brides Month collection,
you will be hearing

WEDDING BELLS

BOOK YOUR PLACE ON OUR WEBSITE AND MAKE THE ARABESQUE ROMANCE CONNECTION!

We've created a customized website just for our very special Arabesque readers, where you can get the inside scoop on everything that's going on with Arabesque romance novels.

When you come online, you'll have the exciting opportunity to:

- View covers of upcoming books

- Learn about our future publishing schedule (listed by publication month and author)

- Find out when your favorite authors will be visiting a city near you.

- Search for and order backlist books from our line catalog

- Check out author bios and background information

- Send e-mail to your favorite authors

- Join us in weekly chats with authors, readers and other guests

- Get writing guidelines

- AND MUCH MORE!

Visit our website at
http://www.arabesquebooks.com

WEDDING BELLS

GWYNNE FORSTER

FRANCINE CRAFT

NIQUI STANHOPE

BET Publications, LLC
www.msbet.com
www.arabesquebooks.com

ARABESQUE BOOKS are published by

BET Publications, LLC
c/o BET BOOKS
One BET Plaza
1900 W Place NE
Washington, D.C. 20018-1211

First Printing: June, 1999
10 9 8 7 6 5 4 3 2 1

Printed in the United States of America

CONTENTS

Love for a Lifetime by Gwynne Forster   7

A Love Made in Heaven by Francine Craft   105

Champagne Wishes by Niqui Stanhope   229

LOVE FOR A LIFETIME

GWYNNE FORSTER

Ginger Hinds stepped out on the balcony of her hotel room in Harare, Zimbabwe, gazed up at the red, blue, and purple streaked sky and took a deep, restorative breath. *Free at last!* Four years of marriage behind her, and she didn't know a thing about life. But, beginning today, she planned to make up for lost time. She smiled at the birds— at least two dozen of them in every color—resting on the edge of her balcony, unafraid of her. *That's for me,* she told herself. *Free as a bird.* She raised her arms toward the heavens and let the breeze swirl around her body. For the next two weeks, she was going to live. She ducked back inside, got dressed, and made her way to the dining room to see what the Zimbabweans served for breakfast.

Waiting for the elevator, she wondered how she'd let things get out of hand. For four years, she'd withstood Harold Lawson's constant harassment and nagging. If a man wanted his wife to be a carefree playgirl and to tag along when and wherever he chose to go without regard to her own interests, he shouldn't have married an attorney with a host of clients and fixed court dates. She had thought him obsessed with her until she figured out that he was attempting to control her with his nightly passion. He hadn't realized, and she hadn't had the guts to tell him, that he'd wasted a lot of time. She had compromised until she risked losing her identity—and she'd lost more than a few clients.

When he wanted them to spend the summer hiking through the Tennessee Smokies and then start a family, and she'd refused because they had neither substantial funds nor a house, he'd told her he wanted out. She'd quickly recovered from the blow to her ego and let him have his wish. Her sister, Linda, had encouraged her to clean the slate and start over. Three months later, here she was where nobody knew her, where she was on her own, and New York was over two thousand miles away.

She slid her tray along the shining chrome and inspected the steam table. Sawdust–like sausages, violated eggs that someone had labeled "scrambled," crisp, greasy bacon, porridge, hard rolls, orange juice, and the most exquisite fruits she'd ever seen. Might as well live dangerously. She filled her plate with eggs, bacon, fruit, and rolls and found a corner table. A waiter brought coffee and the local paper.

"Good morning."

Ginger glanced up from the paper and quickly looked up again. The fork she'd held in her hand clattered against her plate as she stared into his gray mesmeric eyes. Tall, handsome, and a clean–shaven, golden beige complexion. Butterflies danced in her belly, and she tried to break the gaze, but he held her transfixed. She had the presence of mind to bite her bottom lip or it would surely have dropped and left her gaping at him. She picked up the paper that had fallen to a spot beside her plate and dropped it again when she realized she was about to fan herself with it. A smile lit his unbelievable eyes, and her heart seemed to roll in her chest.

"We seem to be the only Americans in this place. Do you mind if I join you?"

"What? Oh. Uh . . . no. I don't mind."

He took his food off the tray, put his plate, knife, fork, spoon, and napkin in their proper places, and took the tray back to the counter. "Thanks," he said when he returned. "My name is Jason. Who're you?"

Considering her unsettling experience just looking at him, she hadn't intended to shake hands, but he gave her no choice. "I'm Ginger," she told him and submitted to the electrifying current that coursed up her bare arm when he took her hand.

"Glad to meet you, Ginger," he said, and she noticed that his deep baritone carried a Southern lilt. "What brings you almost to the end of Africa?"

He could smile all he wanted to. She wasn't going to tell this good–looking stranger her business. "I needed a change, something drastically different. What about you?"

He took a sip of coffee and leaned back in the chair, and it struck her that this man knew and liked who he was. "That about says it for me, too. I got here last night, so I haven't seen a thing. Been here long?"

She told him that she'd also arrived the night before.

"What do you say we spend the day together?" he asked. "It's no fun sightseeing alone. How about it?" He frowned. "Unless you're with someone."

If he wanted to know whether she had a man with her, he'd have to ask. She was about to decline, when she remembered her vow to live life to the hilt for the next two weeks, to let the sun shine on her, the water flow over her, and the breeze blow around her. To be a whole woman. "I'd love company," she said, knowing she sounded less than convincing.

As if unaware of her seeming reluctance, he stacked their dishes in her tray and rose. "Meet me at the desk in half an hour?"

She nodded and sat riveted in her chair as he sauntered off. Her intuition told her that she was in for a rollicking ride, but after four years of standing still, so be it.

* * *

Jason Calhoun stood at the reception desk waiting for
Ginger. When she'd looked up from her newspaper, he'd
had a wallop to the gut. He'd lived for thirty-four years,
been married, in love and out of it, and for the first time
in his life he knew what it was to have a woman dull his
senses with a single glance. Her eyes had telegraphed a
need that started a twinge in his belly, that had melted
something inside of him.

"Ah. Here you are." She hadn't kept him waiting, and
he liked that.

They settled on a tour and headed for the bus. Jason
hadn't expected to be so at ease with her, not after the
eviscerating experience he'd had when she'd looked up
at him. "I assume you like animals," he said, looking for
a conversation opener.

"Animals? I like puppies. But I can't stand anything that
crawls. Even the picture of a snake scares me."

"Good," he teased. "When one swings out of the bush,
you'll grab hold of me."

From the look on her face, she wasn't joking. He
changed the subject. "Did you leave a husband at home?
Or a fiancé?"

"Jason, if I had either of those, you wouldn't be holding
my hand, and you *are* holding my hand."

He released it. "Aren't you going to ask about my marital
status?" As she stepped on the bus, he put a finger to her
elbow, then followed her to the seat she chose.

She looked up at him. "I figure the less I know about
you the better off I'll be."

"What do you mean by that?"

"We're strangers, Jason. Let's enjoy each other's company today, and no more personal questions. That way,
we'll be as free as the birds."

He came close to asking what she was running from,
and bit it back. "What are you scared of, Ginger? You're a

grown woman. How old are you? Twenty–seven'? Twenty–
eight? What happened to us back there at that breakfast
table when we met—and something *did* happen—won't
erase itself no matter how much we deny it. We clicked,
and I don't plan to pretend otherwise." She raised an
eyebrow, and he added, "Pretense is a waste of time."

"Suit yourself," she said, trying to shake off the effect
of his words. "I'm going to enjoy myself, and I doubt that'll
be possible if I have to worry about what could be or might
have been between you and me. No point in our getting
enmeshed in a libidinous snare when we know we'll say
good–bye tomorrow."

"So you admit the possibility?"

"Why should I deny it? You're a smart man. Let's just
have fun. And, to answer your other question, I'll be thirty
my next birthday."

He mulled over her words, so different from what he
would have expected of most women he'd known, women
who didn't put a distance between him and them, who
didn't want to be independent, but who lassoed and clung.
He did what came naturally to him—extended his right
hand to her and waited.

"All right, Ginger. Let's agree that this day is ours, that
we'll enjoy every second of it . . . together. You game? One
day . . . for a lifetime."

Her gaze shifted from his hand to his face. He didn't
know what she saw there, but he'd never seen a more
serious expression on anyone. She might well have been
judging, measuring him by what she found in his eyes.

Stunned at her suddenly tense, prayerful expression,
her umnistakable appeal to his decency, he squeezed her
fingers. "Ginger, I'm an honorable man. No one has ever
doubted that."

Her eyes widened, as though he'd surprised her by reading her so well and, at last, her damp fingers clasped his
palm. Reluctantly. As tentatively as a baby taking its first

step. "All right," she said. "No promises. No confessions, and—"

"And no regrets," he finished. "Just one day together."

He thought she flushed with embarrassment, but why would she? He hadn't suggested anything unseemly. "Ever been here or anywhere else in Africa before?" he asked for want of something more interesting to say. After all, he couldn't talk about them without getting personal. She'd vetoed that.

"I was in Kenya once, but I didn't see much of it because the rain never let up, and there wasn't much joy in walking around in a downpour. I did get to a place where some gnarled, old men sat carving clusters of people on a single piece of ebony wood. I bought one carving for ten dollars. Can you imagine the talent and work that went into it?"

"Yes. I can. Let's check out the museum when we get back to Harare. Look, I want to go to Victoria Falls tomorrow. Can't you stay one more day and take the trip with me?" Why was he pursuing a relationship with this woman when he knew they would go their separate ways tomorrow or the next day? She didn't move her hand from his but leaned against the window, turned sideways, and looked at him. She had the most penetrating gaze, and such lovely, light brown eyes punctuated her dark face. Everything about her beckoned to him.

He liked the way she looked at a man, too. Straight in the eye. No coquettish nonsense. "I've heard that the Falls are unforgettable. We'll see."

He should have relaxed into contentment, but instead he got an unfamiliar jolt of ill–defined anxiety, and he didn't like it. But if she decided to go, he'd welcome her company.

By noon, she'd had enough of lions, cheetahs, and alligators. Even her lunch included alligator croquettes. She ate it with relish and wouldn't have guessed what it was if the waiter hadn't been so proud of the great delicacy he had placed before them. She resisted telling him that she'd rather he'd told her it was ground turkey breast. They finished the meal, walked to the door of the rustic but attractively decorated lodge, and looked out at the darkened sky, almost black at one o'clock in the afternoon. A great roar rattled her eardrums, and she felt his hands on her, lifting her.

Holding her tightly to his chest, he sprinted off the porch. "We'd better make a run for the bus. These storms can last for days."

Her arms found their way to his neck and locked themselves there. Strangely, she had the urge to rest her face in the curve of his neck and no doubt would have, if he hadn't said, "Open the door. Quick!" as they reached the tour bus.

Thanking God for presence of mind, she managed to slide the door open, and he jumped inside with her. "You can put me down now," she told him as he continued carrying her until he reached their seats.

He settled her on her feet. "Yeah. Looks like the other tourists got stuck in the lodge." He sat beside her, and her shoulders tensed as his left arm curled around her and she could feel the heat of his fingers through her blouse.

"I thought that noise was thunder."

"It was the rain announcing its arrival. Might as well relax, Ginger. We could be here for hours. The driver is in the lodge, or at least I hope he is. This rain brings out all kinds of crawling things. *Look over there going up that—*"

"Will you please change the subject. I told you I was afraid of—"

His hand tightened on her shoulder. "Gee, that's right. I forgot."

What she'd intended as a quick glance settled on his face just before he laughed, and—without thinking about it, she let her elbow give his chest a lesson. He laughed harder.

"What's so funny? Are you sadistic or something?"

His shoulders shook as he tried but failed to control his mirth. "Me? No. It's just that . . . you were actually scared. How on earth could anything out there get in this bus? Besides, I'm sitting here with my arm around your shoulder, and you actually thought I'd let that thing get to you. What kind of guys have you been hanging out with?"

"I haven't been hanging out with any guys, and would you please give me back my shoulder?"

"Sure, so long as I can keep your hand. You wouldn't begrudge me the comfort of your hand, would you? I could be scared of . . . of . . . let me see . . . I could be scared of . . . of all this rain."

"If you ask me, you're a smart aleck."

He let out a long breath, and she wondered about that until he followed it up with quiet, deliberate words. "Better for me to tease you than to do what I'd like."

Her senses whirled dizzily, exciting her. Exhilarating her. Recklessly, she dared him to say it. "I had the impression that you're man enough to do whatever you want."

His rapt stare, powerfully and wildly masculine in its challenge, rocked her. "And you were never more right," he said as his right index finger tipped her chin.

This thing was moving at the speed of sound, and she should move away, put out her hand, anything to stop him, but her traitorous mouth went to meet his lips, and both his hands locked behind her head as he warmed her from her head to the bottoms of her feet. She had never trembled for a man, but the tremors rolled through her, and her heart bounced out of control in her chest.

He stopped kissing her and, still cradling her head with his hands, stared into her eyes. "If I ever get into serious trouble, it will probably be due to my failure to pass up an exciting challenge. Daring me can be the same as begging me, Ginger."

I don't know this man, she reminded herself, regrouping as best she could. "Now that you've gotten it out of your system," she told him, "you don't have to think about it anymore. Wonder what time that museum closes?"

This time, his laugh held no mirth. "You're kidding. The way you responded to me? Woman, all that did was whet my appetite."

She withdrew the hand that he'd reclaimed. "Your imagination is out of control."

A wide grin revealed snow–white teeth and sparkles in his gray eyes. "Really? Well, I won't dispute your word, but I'm willing to test it, see if I'm losing my perceptive skills. What about you?" His arms mateuvered around her shoulders again, and he leaned toward her.

"All right. All right. So I knew you were here," she admitted, shielding her emotions with the remark. "That kiss only proves I'm not dead."

His laughter curled around her like a protective blanket comforting her on a cool evening. As quickly as the laughter came, he sobered. "I could like you. Really like you, Ginger."

She could only shrug, because she already knew she wouldn't soon forget him. "I've decided it must be a case of forbidden fruit." She slapped her hand over her mouth, her nerves a riot at the thought that she might have reminded him of what that fruit did for Eve.

The rain slackened, and the driver and five other tourists boarded the bus. "I'm going to have to head back to Harare," the driver told them. "If the rain continues, the roads will be muddy, and we could get stranded out here. No refunds, though."

Ginger listened for grumbles, but didn't hear any. She wasn't sorry to get away from Jason and to work at getting her head straightened out. She hadn't thought of herself as being vulnerable, but Jason had lowered her defenses from the minute she'd looked up and seen him holding that tray of fruit, porridge, and two cups of coffee.

"Have dinner with me?" he asked as they entered the hotel lobby.

She shook her head. "Thanks, but I'll have a bite in my room. After that huge lunch, I don't want much dinner."

He rubbed his right index finger across his chin and looked into the distance as though alone with his thoughts. Then he set his gaze on her, and the muscles in her stomach tightened as his grin crawled over his face.

"It's been great, girl of my dreams. Have a good life."

"I . . . thanks. You, too." She scampered away from him, wanting to get a last look, but not daring to tempt herself.

She rested, wrote some letters and ordered dinner in her room. She'd seen half a dozen women in the hotel who appeared to be unattached, and she didn't doubt that some of them would be glad for his company. What woman wouldn't want the company of such a handsome, intelligent man? She answered the door, and a porter handed her a bouquet of calla lilies to which an attached note read, *Thank you for a day that I shall never forget. J.*

How could he know that she loved calla lilies? She broke off a petal, put it in one of the little plastic Ziploc bags that she always carried in her luggage and pressed it flat. It might be all she'd ever have of him. She would keep it forever, though she'd be better off if he hadn't sent them. Just one more reason why she could never forget him.

She was tempted to ignore the telephone, but after it rang a full two minutes she lifted the receiver. "Hello."

"You knew it was I, Ginger. Let's not say good-bye yet. I still want to see Victoria Falls. The flight leaves at noon, and we'd get back just after nightfall. What about it? It's something special that we'll have to remember."

The brochure lay open on the desk before her. She looked at the picture of the Falls and thought how much more wonderful they must be in reality. Her gaze drifted to the bouquet of calla lilies, thoughts of what they would always represent swirled in her mind, and something deep inside of her wouldn't let her say no.

"All right. But no sweet stuff, Jason."

"A woman doesn't have to tell me no," he growled. "She only has to shake her head once. Get it? If I get sweet, you'll have to suggest it. You going?"

"Okay. And don't be so self–righteous. The saints are all in heaven."

"Whatever. Meet you at breakfast? Say, around nine?"

"I'm eating early. I want to go to the soapstone museum. See you on the plane. And Jason, thank you for the beautiful flowers. I love them."

"My pleasure."

She hung up and considered kicking herself for agreeing to join him on that trip; she wanted to see the Falls, but she knew she wanted to see him more.

The soapstone museum proved to be an outdoor factory and a tiny room in which the carvings were displayed in glass cases. All were for sale. She bought two small heads, one of an old woman and the other of a man with eighty years of toil and grief etched in his face. She paid the few dollars without bargaining, ashamed to have them for such a pittance. When she turned to leave, she faced Jason, who held his own purchases—an ebony free–form that would have been at home in New York's Museum of Modern Art, a statue of mother and child, and one of an old man bowed beneath the weight of the heavy bag on his shoulder.

He pointed to the latter. "This is for my father," he said, affection abloom on his face as he caressed the figure.

He loves his father, she thought. A second sense, or maybe it was a premonition, warned her: fate was shadowing her. She forced a smile, and told him he had good taste, but she could have said that in that short sentence he'd said a lot about himself and his background. They ate a lunch of roast chicken sandwiches, French fries, and iced tea at a nearby hotel and waited for the limousine to take them

to the airport. Sunset found them at the Zambezi River
looking at the falls.

"Want to take the cruise up the river?" he asked, the
urgency in his voice pulling at the woman in her and
pushing aside her common sense.

She remembered her trip on Maid of the Mist at Niagara
Falls and nodded. "I . . . I'd love it."

Her response seemed to energize him, for his wonderful
face lit up with the sparkles in his eyes, and he threw an
arm around her, lifted her from her feet, and spun her
around. "I can hardly wait. Let's go get our slickers."

They rented hats, boots, coats, and pants of heavy, yellow
plastic and joined the cruise.

"From what I can see," he teased, "we're the only couple
here that isn't honeymooning."

She glared at him and pointed to one couple. "They're
kissing because the gal is scared, and he doesn't want her
screaming."

Jason doubled up with laughter, put his arms around
her wet slicker, and hugged her. Well, the whole thing was
crazy. She hugged him back.

The Sundowner cruiser took them along the spray at
the entrance to the great gorge and into the ever-changing
rainbows that flexed their awesome beauty against the rays
of the setting sun. He didn't expect ever to see a sight that
compared to it. He looked down at the woman whom he
had folded to himself and whose hands gripped his biceps,
hoping for the look of recognition that would tell him
he'd found a kindred soul. He didn't want to speak and
spoil the moment, so he tipped her chin up with his right
index finger and gasped when he saw the tears that cas-
caded down her cheeks. He wanted to kiss them away, but
he only held her close to him. Who knew what memories,
if any, the sight before them had triggered in her? The
short cruise ended before they reached the river's bend,

and they watched the sunset. It didn't surprise him that
no words passed between them. What could anyone say in
the presence of such beauty?

He thought he understood her silence as the Fokker 12
flew them back to Harare. Once more, he didn't want to
say good–bye, and they would both depart the next day.
At the elevator, he took her hand. "Have dinner with me
this last night. I'm just not ready to say good–bye."

He held his breath as he waited for her answer. "Yes."
The word came out slowly, as if she were giving birth to
something. "That would be nice. What time?"

He let himself breathe. "Seven?"

She nodded, and he let go of her hand. "See you right
here at seven."

Ginger dressed carefully, knowing that she played with
fire, because Jason could be the tornado that wrecked her
life. Butterflies flitted around in her belly, and perspiration
made ringlets of the hair at her temples. *If you go down
there, you'll regret it,* her mind warned. But she ignored all
caution, slipped a dusty rose, sleeveless, chiffon minidress
over her dark brown skin, bare but for bra and bikini
panties, dabbed some Opium perfume where it counted
most, brushed her hair around her shoulders, and left the
room.

Good Lord, what a man! Elegant in a white linen suit,
white shirt, and red tie, he filled her vision as she stepped
from the elevator, his face wreathed in a welcoming smile.
If he had opened his arms, she wouldn't have hesitated
until he'd wrapped her securely in them.

You're beautiful, he told her in unuttered words that
seemed to come off the wings of his breath, but spoke
loudly in his smile and demeanor. "I wish the place was
crowded," he said, "and hundreds of people could see
what a lucky man I am."

He had ordered jacaranda blooms, the national flower,

for their table. "What would you like?" he asked after
she'd read the menu.

*A healthy helping of this wonderful man sitting across the table
from me.* "Roast duck, and whatever goes with it," she said,
knowing that he'd taken her appetite.

She made herself eat it and noticed that he appeared
to force down his veal scallopini. The rapport they'd had
in the afternoon had deserted them. They looked at the
few other tourists in the dining room, sipped their wine,
and made insignificant small talk.

At last, she had to stop pretending; "This is . . . I enjoyed
the meal, Jason, and you're wonderful company. I'd better
say good–bye."

She attempted to push back her chair and stand, and
he rushed to assist her. Impulsively, she kissed his cheek
and headed for the elevator as fast as she could without
actually running, but it was his hand that pushed the button, his hand that grasped hers and led her from the
elevator. At his room door, he took the key from his pocket,
held it in his hand, and gazed into her eyes in a wordless
entreaty for permission to open it.

"This doesn't make sense, Jason."

"I know. Nothing has made sense from the minute I
laid eyes on you. Will you come in here with me?"

She nodded, and he opened the door. Before it closed,
he had her in his arms, where she wanted to be. At last,
she could feel his fingers on her bare flesh, caressing,
teasing until bolt after bolt of hot want tore through her.
Why didn't he kiss her?

"I don't play at this, Ginger, and I don't make love
lightly. I'm already fifty percent gone. Will you kiss me?"

"I don't think I understand what you mean."

"Then kiss me. Put your arms around me and kiss me."

The trembling of her lips betrayed her as she reached
up to him, fastened her hands at the back of his head,
and parted her lips. The force of it shook her, pummelled
her loins like pellets of hot steel rocketing from a smelter's

fire. His tongue grazed her lips, and she took him into her mouth and knew the heat of his passion as he loved her until her strength ebbed, and she let him take her weight. His fingers went to the zipper at the back of her dress, and she froze. In five years of marriage, she hadn't once wanted her husband as she wanted this man. She'd slipped up somewhere. She was a rational woman, and women who used their minds didn't let themselves go wild with a stranger, one they'd never see again. The Ginger Hinds she knew wouldn't make love with a man she hadn't known for two whole days, no matter how much she wanted him. She couldn't change into another person just because she was in Zimbabwe and not at home on New York City's Roosevelt Island.

As though he sensed her misgivings, he put an arm around her shoulder and drew her close. "You've changed your mind?"

Was he going to be angry and unruly? No matter, she couldn't do it. "About what I want? No, Jason. I want to be with you, but I can't move so far out of character. All my life I've toed the line, lived a conservative life. I wanted nothing more than a piece of the American dream, and I worked hard for it, but it burst all around me. I came here to begin a change. I realize now that I set out to do something reckless, wild, unlike myself, and I can't go through with it. I know I've disappointed you, and I'm sorry. You made a dent in me, and I didn't know how to handle it. Will you forgive me?"

He rubbed the back of his neck and took in a long breath. "I don't hold it against you.

"I'd better leave."

His smile held no humor, and his gray eyes didn't twinkle. "You won't forget me, Ginger. Not in this life."

He walked to the door, opened it, and brushed her cheek with the tips of his fingers. "No. You won't forget me."

"I don't expect I will, and don't you be surprised if I show up in your thoughts sometimes. All the best, Jason."

"The same to you, Sweetheart. Get home safely.

The door closed, and the most intriguing and wonderful man she'd ever met was out of her life. The next morning, she took Swissair 1102 to Lagos, Nigeria, en route home. She wasn't bubbling over with happiness, but she wasn't ashamed of herself, either.

Jason Calhoun closed the door of his hotel room and considered packing his bag and going home. Ginger— maybe that wasn't even her name—had made the right decision, but for the rest of his life he'd wonder what he'd missed. He could get a woman any time he wanted one, but he didn't care for casual sex, and he hadn't wanted that from Ginger. He had needed to explore something in himself that hadn't been there before he met her, to blend his soul with hers, for he suspected that, with her, he would have known at last who he was. He'd heard that newly divorced individuals had to deal with vulnerability. Maybe that explained his awful need for Ginger. He'd been restless since his divorce, but he hadn't thought himself particularly vulnerable. He unlocked the bar that stood beside the dresser in his room, opened a bottle of ginger ale, and got rid of the dryness in his throat. Six billion people inhabited planet earth, and one of them had a piece of him—maybe the most important piece—and he'd never get it back.

Ginger walked into her eleventh floor apartment on Roosevelt Island, closed the door, and looked around. Same place, she thought; just a different woman. In the short span of six weeks, she'd gotten a divorce from one man and came dangerously close to falling for another one. She kicked off her shoes, walked barefoot to her bedroom and called Clarice.

"Hey, Girlfriend, how'd it go?" Clarice asked.

"Full of adventure. You should have come with me."

"You don't mean that. If I'd been with you, you wouldn't be moaning about that gray–eyed man."

Clarice's psychic ability made Ginger uncomfortable, but she tolerated it because she valued Clarice's friendship. "Girl, I don't want to hear one word about your visions of that man. You got lucky with the color of his eyes. Now, let's drop it. Do I have any mail?"

"Yeah. You want me to bring it to you?"

"No. Thanks for keeping it for me. I need to get a nap so I'll feel like working. I've got a court date day after tomorrow."

"I'll ring your bell and hang it on the doorknob."

Ginger didn't object, because Clarice lived in an apartment several doors down the hall from her.

She told herself that she hadn't met a man named Jason, that he was a part of a surrealistic dream. A minute later she swore at herself for demanding his agreement that they not exchange any information about themselves, including last names. Was he married? Did he have any children? Where did he live, and what did he do for a living?"

The doorbell rang and she waited ten minutes before opening it and getting the bag of mail. She loved Clarice, but right then she didn't want to see her or anyone else. Except Jason. Thumbing through her mail, her gaze caught the schizophrenic handwriting of Steven Roberts, her client and the first party to a divorce. The trouble with Steven was his lack of familiarity with his own mind. She read his letter, rolled her eyes in disgust, and dialed his number.

"Mr. Roberts, this is Ginger Hinds," she said after hearing his clipped hello. "I'm afraid it's too late for you to drop your suit, because Mrs. Roberts has entered a countersuit. I received the notice in my mail today. She's asking for half of your property and one–third of all you earn in the future, plus full payment of two hundred and eighty-two thousand dollars in loans that she made to you. Your case will be considerably weaker if you drop your demands.''

She could imagine that his eyes widened, as they did when he received a surprise. "Well, she sure is a bag of laughs," Steven said. "Last time she tickled my funny bone like this, she didn't want quite that much: just a little old house on Cape Hatteras where the dozen and a half hurricanes that stop by there every year could blow my three hundred thousand dollar house smack out into the Atlantic Ocean. She needs to get her head screwed on right.''

"Now, Mr. Roberts, let's just work on the things we can control," she said. "And please don't talk like that when we're in court. It won't do your case one bit of good.''

"But you listen to me, Miss Hinds. I have never borrowed one cent from my wife.''

They'd been over that before. She took a deep breath and counted to ten. "Can you prove that?"

" 'Course not. When you're in love, you don't keep records on things like that.''

"Evidently, she did. Let's concentrate on your charges. You say she's only interested in sensual gratification, won't work with you to build a home, acts like a teenager, wants to party all the time, and refuses to speak to you if you don't join her, while you want to strengthen your relationship with her, save, and build a future. Right?''

"Right. And I want irreconcilable differences thrown in there.''

She stifled a laugh. Nobody who'd been through one would think divorce amusing. "That much is obvious, Mr. Roberts. This is the second time you've indicated a change of heart about this divorce. If it happens again, get another attorney. Some counseling wouldn't hurt.''

"Look, maybe I've been too hard on her. She's got a

right to enjoy life. Maybe if her mother had stayed out of it ... damn. I must be crazy. I just had a weak moment there thinking about how it was, how perfect it used to be. I never thought it would come to this. See you in court."

Tell me about it. She hung up and checked her court hearings. Nancy Holloway was suing her stock broker for fraud, and she figured they had an eighty percent chance of winning. Not so with Jake Henderson, a sculptor, who was suing his landlord for having shut off all services in the hopes of forcing him out of his rent—controlled apartment.

She called her sister, Linda, to let her know she was back at home, showered, put on some work clothes and headed for her garden. She always had to explain to people that there were two hundred and fifty individually owned out-door gardens on Roosevelt Island—her little village in the middle of the East River, twenty minutes from Times Square—along with a rose garden that was the pride of the community. Her garden was clear of weeds, which she guessed was Clarice's handiwork. With nothing better to do in the blistering heat, she walked back to Andy's Place, the Island hangout for company, food, drinks, coffee, or whatever, and waited to see who'd come in. Minutes later, she was rewarded with Clarice's company.

"Hey, Girl, what kind of weather is this for April? I thought I'd die out there yesterday getting the grass out of your garden. Sure could use some of Andy's good old iced tea."

Ginger hugged her friend. "You can get the folks out of the south, but everybody knows where they come from. Don't tell me your strange mind told you I was here."

Clarice beckoned the waiter, ordered iced tea for herself and ginger ale for Ginger. "Nobody has to ask you what you want to drink, Ginger. You take your name seriously. Now, about those gray eyes. Where'd you leave him?"

Ginger pushed back the irritation she always felt when Clarice discussed things she wasn't supposed to know. "He's in Harare."

Clarice let her have a look of disdain. "Is that so? You and your principles. I got principles, too, Honey, but they wouldn't let me walk away from *that* man. What are you going to do?"

Ginger looked long and hard at Clarice. If the woman was such a great psychic, shouldn't she know what was going to happen? She shrugged. "What's past is prologue."

Clarice's giggle stunned Ginger, because her friend prided herself on her refinement. "From the sound of that, I'd say you're capable of *seeing* a few things yourself?"

Nervous at the turn of the conversation, Ginger gulped down her drink. "I'd better run. How're things over at the United Nations? Maybe you can tell the Secretary-General whether our country is ever going to pay the UN all that money we owe it." She slid out of the booth, picked up her garden gloves and trowel, and looked down at her friend. "Please don't pester me about Jason, Clarice. It's over, and I want to forget."

"Whatever you say. Just don't say I didn't—"

"Clarice, *please!*" She waved at her friend and walked out into the heat. So much for her attempts to push Jason out of her thoughts.

Jason paid the taxi driver, picked up his bags, and started into the building at Fifth Avenue and 110th Street, the lower edge of Harlem, where he lived in a two bedroom duplex condominium. He walked with legs that fought with his mind, seemingly wanting to go elsewhere, nodded to the concierge, and strode rapidly toward the elevator.

"I have a bundle of mail here for you, Mr. Calhoun," the concierge called after him. "Ring me when you're ready for it, and I'll bring it up."

Jason thanked him but didn't pause, because he didn't want conversation or anyone's company. Except Ginger's. Unable to stop thinking of her, he cursed himself for not at least having gotten her last name. *No promises, no confessions, and no regrets.* They had agreed to remain strangers. And in spite of the soul–searing intimacy they'd shared, they knew nothing of one another. Nothing, that is, except that their need for each other had almost overpowered them. He opened the windows to rid the apartment of stuffiness, then quickly closed them as the oppressive heat assaulted his body. He turned on the air–conditioning units, emptied his suitcase, and dumped the clothing into the hamper. After stripping down to his shorts, he got a Coke from the refrigerator, propped himself up on his bed, and telephoned his father in Dallas.

"I didn't expect you back so soon, son," his father said after they'd greeted each other. "How'd it go?"

"All right, I guess."

He had to be careful, because his dad had a sixth sense about him, and keeping secrets from him was hard work.

"Didn't you like Mother Africa?"

He kept his voice even. "Yes. What I saw of it."

"Something or somebody got between you and it. Right?"

Jason enjoyed the last swig of his Coke, set the bottle on the floor beside the bed, and answered, "You could say that."

"It's not a good idea to get involved when you're on the rebound. I know you think you're master of all you survey, but don't forget that Napoleon met his Waterloo."

"Right. Come up July fourth and go fishing with me in the Adirondacks."

He heard the low growl of a laugh that, for as long as he could remember, had given him a sense of peace and security. "All right. I'll butt out. Glad you're back safe."

He hung up, went to his computer, and began a search for travel agents who booked tours to Zimbabwe. By midnight, he had collected the names and phone numbers of one hundred and forty–seven such agents, and he gave up the search when he realized that there could be a thousand more. Maybe he ought to hire a private investiga-

tor—but who could he tell the man to look for? Churning
heat violated his belly, and sweat dripped down his bare
chest as the scent of her perfume came back to him, a
ghost bent on torture. They'd been magic together, flint
and dry grass, and he refused to accept that he'd never
see her again.

Ginger hadn't seen groups of youth congregating in
the streets of Harare. When she'd asked one of the hotel
clerks what the young people did for entertainment, she'd
learned that the people looked primarily to their families
for that, as well as for social life and economic support
and that they rarely made close ties with individuals who
were not members—first of their family, and second of
their tribe. That information had been the germ of an
idea for a mother-daughter club on her beloved Roosevelt
Island, and she decided to start the club with Saturday
morning movies for mothers and their adolescent daughters. Fired up with the idea and its potential, she telephoned Clarice.

"Think I can pull it off?"

"You can try, Ginger, but if these mothers had enough
control over their daughters to bring them to a Saturday
morning movie, would the girls be hanging out in the
street at midnight in the first place?"

She'd thought about that. "Girls will go to free movies.
I'm going to start with something like *Sleepless in Seattle,*
and maybe I can get some of the older boys who have
good manners and values to speak to them once in a while.
What do you think?"

"The boys will certainly bring them out, but if you want
a crowd, get that gray–eyed hunk you walked out on in
Harare. Now, they'd stand in line to listen to him."

She subdued her rising hackles, took a deep breath, and
warned Clarice, "Listen, Girl, if we're going to be friends,
you have to stop prying into my life with your . . . your

so—called psychic gifts. Only God knows my future, and you stop painting your crazy pictures of things you can't possibly know."

"Want me to describe him?"

Ginger stared at the receiver. When Clarice got started with her soothsaying, she gave her the willies. "No, I don't."

"Okay by me, Girlfriend, but I wouldn't have turned *my* back on a six—foot, two inch guy with a washboard belly, a complexion the color of fresh pecans, long—lashed gray eyes, silky black hair, and a smile to die for."

Thank goodness Clarice couldn't see her surprised face. "Maybe he was rough around the edges."

"Honey, if that man got any smoother and any sharper, you could use him to chisel stone."

Pictures of him flashed through her mind, and her blood sped through her veins, dizzying her. She had to sit down on the edge of her bed, but she wouldn't give Clarice the benefit of triumph. "Go feed the pigeons."

Clarice's merriment greeted her ears like the mockery of a conqueror, as though she knew Ginger was doomed to remember Jason forever. "I've already fed them. See you down at Andy's Place about four o'clock?"

Ginger agreed and hung up. She didn't usually work on Saturday afternoon, but she had to make up for the two weeks in Africa, not to speak of the time she'd wasted daydreaming about Jason since she'd returned home. Unable to concentrate on the case she was preparing, she decided to take some clothes downstairs to the dry cleaner. She dipped her hands in the pockets of the linen jacket she'd worn on the trip with Jason to Victoria Falls, and her fingers brushed a piece of folded paper. Part of a menu.

She unfolded it and read: *Thousands of miles may separate us when you read this, but our souls will never be apart.*

"I will not shed a tear over him. Not one," she said and wiped drops of moisture from her cheeks. The man hadn't

been made who could cause her to shrivel up in mourning
like a dried up, inedible prune. She brushed more moisture from her face. "Drat you, Jason who-ever-you-are, I
could love you to the recesses of my womb," she whispered,
"and I could hate you, too. You have no right to torment
me this way."

Jason fared no better than Ginger. In the month since
his return home, he'd managed to get one case postponed
and had gotten a mistrial in another by proving jury tampering. He had a divorce case pending, but couldn't
develop an enthusiasm for it, because the suit reminded
him too much of his own divorce. That Saturday afternoon,
disconcerted by his inability to do any serious work, he
put on a pair of white Bermuda shorts, a yellow, knit
T–shirt and sneakers and took the Lexington IRT subway
down to SOHO, where his younger brother, Eric, a sculptor, lived.

He walked around an unfinished form that stood in the
middle of Eric's living room. "What's this supposed to be,
Eric, a modern Aphrodite?"

"No idea. She just tumbled out of my head. I was working
on her a couple of days ago, looked up at her, and couldn't
believe my eyes."

Jason paced around the figure again and again. "Did
you ever meet a woman named Ginger?"

Eric looked up from the spatula he was cleaning. "Ginger who?"

Jason shook his head. "I couldn't even guess, but this
figure you've done here reminds me of her. Something
about the set of the shoulders and that 'I'll cry tomorrow'
smile. It's eerie, Man."

He must have sounded foolish, because Eric stopped
cleaning his tool and stared at him. "And you don't even
know her last name?"

"You insinuating something?"

"Uh uh. No indeed. I'm saying you wanted her, you still want her, and you don't know who or where she is. Where'd you meet her?"

Jason walked to the other end of the room and back. "In Harare. If I knew where she was, I'd be there right now. And that's all I want to say about it."

Eric's hand rested on his brother's shoulder, and he spoke in a voice heavy with concern. "I'm sorry, Jason. Man, I really am sorry."

Jason shrugged. "I've been through floods, hurricanes, the rigors of a law degree, and a nasty divorce. This won't kill me, either."

Eric resumed cleaning his tools. "Maybe not, but it hurts you like hell."

"Tell me about it. How about putting that thing away and we go down to Dock's sidewalk café and get something cool to drink?"

Eric's raised eyebrow was proof of his disinterest. "It's too hot. I've never known it to be this hot in April."

"Me, neither. Put on something cool and let's go."

It seemed as though Ginger took possession of his thoughts whenever he was indoors. He could only surmise that she left him free of her memory when he went outside, because nothing could compare with the beauty they witnessed together at Victoria Falls and in the environs of Harare. He stuck his hands in the pockets of his shorts and trailed Eric out of the apartment. When had he known such emptiness that he wanted company, crowds of people around him, so that he wouldn't think? He loved Eric's company, but didn't want to talk with him, only to sit with him in a crowd with such a din that it made conversation impossible. *Ginger! In the name of heaven, where are you?*

G.A. Hinds, as Ginger was known to her clients and in court circles, stepped into the judge's chamber and froze, rooted in her tracks as though struck by lightning. *It couldn't be!* She forced herself to take one step closer, willing him to turn around so that she could see his face.

"Good morning, Ms. Hinds," Judge Williams said—and then *he* turned to face her.

"*You!*" she shrieked. "It can't be. It . . . My God, it's *you!*"

As if coming out of a thick fog, he stared, shaking his head as though mute, his feet taking him slowly to her. When barely a yard separated them he grabbed her, lifted her from her feet, spun her around, and squeezed her to him. "*Ginger. Ginger. Ginger!* I can't believe it. I'd given up all hope of ever seeing you again. I—"

"Uh hmm." Judge Williams cleared her throat. "I hope this isn't what it looks like. Attorney Calhoun, I assume you didn't know your client's husband was being represented by Attorney Hinds. This is unusual, but if you aren't married or lovers, I suppose we can continue." She looked at Ginger. "Well?"

Ginger didn't know how she found her voice. "We've never been lovers, Your Honor."

"Mr. Calhoun, do you agree?"

His eyes sparkled with merriment, and he rubbed his chin contemplatively, like a wise man seeking the truth. He told her, "Yes, ma'am, Your Honor. I certainly do."

Ginger saw no reason why Her Honor should smirk. "Good," Judge Agatha Williams said, adjusting her wig. "You may unhand her now, Mr. Calhoun. And if I ask you two that question at any time before this case is closed, your answers had better be the same as now."

"Yes, ma'am," they replied in unison as Jason released Ginger.

Judge Williams cleared her throat, louder than Ginger thought necessary, shuffled some of the papers on her desk, and resumed her official demeanor. "Ms. Hinds, your client is bringing the suit, so I want to hear his charge first."

"Basically," Ginger began, "my client's wife is immature,

interested only in sensual gratification, parties and fun and—because he works hard trying to make a good life for them—she accuses him of putting his career before her."

"And he does, Your Honor," Jason broke in, presenting the wife's countersuit. "He's a workaholic, saves money because he hates to spend it, and pays her absolutely no attention."

"That's not true," Ginger declared. "A person has a right to expect complete cooperation, to have a true partnership with his spouse, not a firefly who wants to run out every evening at sundown."

"And my client has a right to expect some joy in her life with her husband, not to shrivel up with a dull spud who comes home at eight or nine o'clock every night, wolfs down whatever she's cooked, and passes out in front of the TV."

Judge Williams banged her gavel. "I see I don't have to worry about the two of you shacking up any time soon. I had agreed to hear this case with the principals absent, but I've changed my mind. Case recessed for today. Bring those two adolescents in here Monday morning at ten sharp. And go your separate ways."

Jason stood on the top step of the Municipal Building at 60 Lafayette Street in lower Manhattan and made an effort to settle his nerves. In the course of half an hour, he'd had as many shocks as a man ought to have in his lifetime. He'd found her. She proved to be an accomplished woman, and he liked that. But she was his adversary in court and, worse still, she might beat him. He took comfort in the way she'd behaved when her gaze lit on him; she had surely missed him every bit as much as he'd missed her.

He looked back toward the door, hoping to see Ginger stroll through it. After the way in which they'd greeted each other, she couldn't expect him to walk out of there and leave her, no matter what Judge Williams said. And if the judge had meant they shouldn't see each other, she needed to learn something about the behavior of men and women when a sizzling chemistry hooked them together.

After what seemed like half an hour, she walked out of the building, and he rushed to her; he couldn't have restrained himself if his life had depended on it. He had to touch her, to assure himself that she was really Ginger. "What took you so long?" he asked her.

The warm and welcoming lights in her wonderful brown eyes made a mockery of her effort to maintain a cool, professional façade. "Hi, Jason. I figured you'd get tired of waiting and leave. I'm not in the habit of ignoring a judge's orders."

He took her hand and walked with her toward the steps, still wondering whether he could be dreaming. "Ginger, that judge is not stupid. She said what was required of her, but she'd think us both insane if we obeyed."

Her fingers tightened around his, but her words denied her gesture of affection. "I don't disobey judges, and that's that. I'm glad to see you, though. I really am, Jason."

The tone of finality in her voice gave him a feeling of anxiety, and he stared in shocked disbelief as she dropped his hand, ran down the remaining steps, jumped into a cab, and rode away. He went back to the clerk's office.

"Hi, Ann. Could you give me the phone number of the lawyer for my client's husband?"

"Your reasons, Mr. Calhoun?"

"I'm going to try for a deal." She didn't ask what kind of deal, and he didn't see a need to tell.

"Sure." She flipped through her files, wrote two numbers on a scratch pad, and handed them to him.

He thanked Ann, and headed for the street. "Ginger, Girl," he said to himself, "you won't get away from me this time," and strolled down the steps whistling Marty Stewart's number one hit, 'Till I Found You." He spotted a florist, went in, and asked for a Manhattan telephone directory. An address for her matched the phone number that Ann gave him, so he ordered a bouquet of calla lilies and had them delivered to her.

Ginger told herself she'd done the professional thing, but she'd used as much fortitude as any woman ever had when she walked away from Jason Calhoun. Calhoun. She liked his name. She hadn't guessed he'd be an attorney, though she had realized he was a man of some accomplishment. She didn't let herself imagine what could come next. Maybe he had a wife. The taxi driver pulled up to West View, the building in which she lived, and she paid and got out.

Who was that man? she wondered. Every time she saw him he had a thick, hardcover book in his hand. Something about his demeanor, his clothing, and his carriage suggested academic life. Always a book, even while he ate his meals, which he took at Andy's Place. She supposed he was retired. Oddly, he seemed as curious about her as she was about him, but neither had bridged the gap and spoken. She thought that strange, because Roosevelt Islanders spoke to each other whether they'd been introduced or not. She made up her mind to put an end to it first chance she got.

With the afternoon free of court duties, she changed into casual dress and went to Andy's Place for lunch. One of the local clergymen walked in and was soon joined by the mystery man with his book. Seeing an opportunity for an introduction, she left her table, walked over, and greeted the minister.

"Hello, Ginger," the Reverend Armstrong said. "You know Amos Logan, don't you?"

"I've been wondering who you were. I'm Ginger Hinds,"

she said to Amos, who rose to his feet and extended his hand.

"Same here, Miss Hinds. How do you do? I figured you were either in banking, education or law. How far off was I?"

"Law."

"Why don't you join us old folk?" Reverend Armstrong asked. "Amos retired last year from his cushy job as a law school dean."

Amos raised both eyebrows. "About as cushy as running a church." He regarded Ginger with the penetrating stare of a judge. "What kind of law do you practice?"

"Criminal, but right now I have a divorce case, my first, and I'm not sure I'll take another one."

"Why?" Amos wanted to know.

"Because my client can't make up his mind. He's called me twice to indicate he may be making a mistake, but he has no choice now, because his wife has entered a countersuit."

"Smart woman," Amos said.

The Reverend Armstrong pulled air through his teeth and strummed his fingers on the table. "If they'd only go for counselling and work out their problems."

Amos shrugged. "A lot of them do . . . just before they file for divorce."

She ordered bean soup and a green salad and finished it quickly. Amos had come too close to her life, to the crumbling of her own marriage, and she wouldn't put it past the good Reverend to pounce on it in the presence of this stranger.

She gulped down the last of her ginger ale and stood. "See you Sunday, Reverend Armstrong. I'm glad to know who you are, Mr. Logan."

Amos wiped his mouth with one of Andy's paper napkins and stood. "Call me Amos. Perhaps we can have a cup of coffee together sometime. Not many people around here want to talk law."

"I'd love it," she said, and headed back to her apartment. Amos Logan was an interesting man.

She stopped by the mailbox, collected her mail, and hastened to the air–conditioned haven of her apartment. Who ever heard of ninety–one degrees in April? That and the equally high humidity had sapped her energy in the short walk from Andy's Place to the building in which she lived. The first letter confirmed her sister Linda's wedding date in late May, a month away, and she hadn't shopped for the dress she'd wear as maid of honor. She looked at the long list of things that Linda couldn't find in the small town of Easton and wanted her to purchase in New York, and made some notes as to where she might find them. Anything except settling down to her work, because the minute she tried it, the face of Jason Calhoun mocked her from the pages before her.

The sound of the doorman's buzzer irritated her, because she didn't want company. "Delivery, Ms. Hinds."

"Thanks, Allan. Please send him up."

Minutes later, she stood in the doorway of her apartment and stared at the bouquet of one dozen calla lilies in her arm, winded as if she had run for miles. She closed the door, found the note, and read, *Fate has caught us in her net. What shall we do about it? As for me, I'm overjoyed. Jason.*

She kissed the flowers, placed them in a vase, and sat staring at them. She had found him, and he was more man than she had thought existed. And he wanted *her!* She hugged herself and danced around and around until she collapsed on the sofa, giddy with joy. She didn't want to work or do anything but think of him.

Suddenly, she sobered and, annoyed at her frivolity, got up and went to her desk. "I'm not going to let him control me this way," she admonished herself, opened her file on Roberts versus Roberts and got down to work. Until Steven's wife contested the divorce, she hadn't worried about the reasons Steven was giving for wanting one. An uncontested divorce posed no problem. But in her view, her client's grounds were no better than his wife's charges and, from the judge's order that the contestants be present at the trial, she suspected that Agatha Williams meant to raise some tough questions. Well, she could only represent her client as best she could with the flimsy reasons he'd given her. She worked until dinnertime, called the Chinese take-out shop, and ordered her dinner. Minutes after she'd finished it and destroyed the evidence, her phone rang.

"Hello, Ginger. This is Jason."

At the sound of his voice, a sharp, unfamiliar sensation shot through her, but she spoke with a calm voice. "Hello, Jason. I don't remember giving you my address or my home phone number."

Laughter tinged his words. "Of course you don't. I have my sources. If you had remembered giving either one to me, I'd start worrying about your truthfulness."

"Jason, we're not supposed to be consorting socially. You know that."

"What do you think we can do through these telephone wires? I spent weeks cursing myself for letting you get away without a clue as to who you were or where to find you. God let you back into my life and, unless there is a compelling reason for me to do otherwise, I am not, I repeat *not,* letting you get away from me again."

She grabbed her chest to still her heart's pounding, but she was doggoned if she'd let him know how he excited her. Coolly, she told him, "We don't know each other well enough for you to say things like that."

"Speak for yourself, Ginger. I let you walk away because you wanted to go, and because I'd never had a one-night affair with anyone and agreed that it wasn't wise. But after you'd checked out of the hotel the next morning, I saw the hole you'd left me in, and I knew that if we had made love you wouldn't have been a one-time fling. In those two days, you got so deep in me, Sweetheart, that you'll be with me forever. I don't know what it means, but I want to—"

"Jason, please don't. You can't say things like this to me. We're adversaries, and the judge said—"

She heard him pull air through his front teeth. "Hang that woman. Alma Roberts and Steven Roberts are adversaries. You and I are not, and don't you forget that."

A flush of blood warmed her face. "What are you talking about? You practically bit off my head in that judge's chamber this morning."

"You were taking your frustrations out on my client, and I wasn't going to stand for it."

She looked toward the ceiling and rolled her eyes. Another self–satisfied male chauvinist. "Jason, a wife isn't somebody you stash away at home to eat chocolates and watch the soaps. Women have brains, and they can use them for something other than sterilizing baby bottles."

She figured from his long silence that she'd hit a tender spot, and she was certain when he said, "Women who think like you are the reason for half of society's problems. A man has no rights in a marriage, as far as you're concerned. You never heard of fifty–fifty. A woman can work if she wants to, but nobody should force her to do it. Women who stay at home, though, are less likely to get a divorce than those who work outside."

She pulled her hair away from her face and got comfortable. "Spoken like a true Republican, a species for which I have no use. And don't forget—Alma Roberts stayed at home and didn't work."

"You probably love Republicans about as much as I love Democrats, especially the so–called liberals." When she didn't respond to that sally, he asked, "Ginger, what in the devil are we fighting about?"

"You're asking me? It all started because you went after me in court this morning with all your guns blasting."

"Come on, Ginger. That's between Calhoun and Hinds. It's got nothing to do with Jason and Ginger."

Images of his gray eyes lit with merriment, of the way his smile sort of hung on the right side of his mouth, danced before her eyes, and she slapped her forehead to dispel them.

"What was that I heard?" he asked.

"Don't change the subject," she said, increasingly wary of the force of her feelings for him. "I'm not a schizophrenic with two personalities and two minds, so don't expect me to split myself into DayGinger and NightGinger. No socializing until this case is over."

"When it's over, lady," he growled, "I'm going to delight in reminding you of the way it feels to slump against me in submission when my tongue is deep in your mouth loving you and teaching you who you are. Have you forgotten how close we became?"

When awareness slammed into her, she would have enjoyed throttling him for tampering with her brain and shaking up her sense of self. "For that, you would need my cooperation, mister," she shot at him.

"And I'll make sure I get it," he drawled.

"I'm going to hang up, Jason."

"Ginger." His voice was no longer assertive with self—confidence, but carried an urgency, a need that found its destination in her heart. "Ginger, I am serious. I called to ask if we can be friends. It got personal today, but I want us to be as we were in Zimbabwe. I need that woman in my life. I've never known anyone like her. For two days, she lit up my horizon, brightened my world. While I roamed those hills, preserves, parks and streams with her, the world strutted brand new all around me, every place I looked. You and I were ourselves, then, not the products of our training, not public personas acting out the roles that society and the people we know have set for us. I want you back with me, Ginger."

Stunned, she parted her lips but no words came out of them.

"I mean every word I'm saying," he went on. "I missed you more than I can describe, and I can't believe that feelings this strong, this deep, are one—sided. Will you walk away again from what we found together in Harare? Or maybe I'm wrong. Can't you tell me you reciprocate what I feel?"

She had forgotten how direct he could be. "Jason, surely you know that you touched me. I didn't forget you. I didn't even try. But I have to do my best for my client, and that won't happen if I'm moonlighting with you. So let's be glad we found each other and let the future take care of itself—after this case is over."

"Well, thanks for that much, Ginger. I'd better tell you, though, that I don't leave my life to Miss Future's whims. I do whatever I can to shape it the way I want it, and I want to get to know you well enough to find out where you fit in my future. You ought to want the same."

"I do, Jason, but right now I want you to give me some room. You needn't worry. You won't be out of my mind. Can I count on that?"

"You can always count on me, Ginger. No matter what. I'll be there for you." His tone turned sheepish. "You wouldn't give a guy a goodnight kiss would you?"

The thought of kissing him sent her emotions into high gear. She didn't recognize the sultry voice that said, "I'm parting my lips."

His silence shouted to her through the wires. "Jason?"

"I . . . I'm loving you. Goodnight, Ginger."

"Jason! Thanks for the beautiful calla lilies."

"My pleasure, Goodnight, Sweetheart."

He hung up, leaving her to stare at the receiver. After a few minutes, she shrugged. No point in wondering why he'd done that, because she doubted he'd tell. She wanted to be with him, to know again the strength of his arms around her, to loll in his sweetness. She rubbed the goose-pimples on her forearms as thoughts of how she'd felt believing she'd never see him again crowded all else from her mind. She reached for the telephone, remembered that she didn't have his phone number, and laughed. Thank God she didn't have to decide whether to be stupid or heated to the boiling point. But one day soon she'd have to choose whether to call him when she needed him, because he would surely give her his telephone number. Of that, she was certain; Jason Calhoun had served notice that he didn't wait for things to happen to him. He acted.

What a woman! He walked out on his balcony that covered part of the roof of the building in which he lived, and looked out over Central Park. Sprawled out on a chaise lounge, he reached into the bar that stood beside it and got a bottle of iced tea. At sixteen stories above the street, the traffic below was barely a hum and, though he wouldn't have minded hearing the nightly jazz that floated up from the club around the corner on Fifth Avenue, he preferred the more serene atmosphere of 110th Street. He mused over his good fortune in finding Ginger. He understood himself and his needs, and he knew right down to his gut that Ginger Hinds was the woman for him. He hadn't meant their first kiss that day in the tour bus to be serious, but she had responded to him honestly, giving all of herself. He didn't even want to think about that night in his hotel room. For a while, he looked at the lights that made New York famous and conjured up pictures of himself showing Ginger what lay behind so many of them. He wanted to show her the world. Several hours later, raindrops awakened him, and he went inside, dried off, and climbed into bed.

Jason rose early the next morning, went down to the exercise gym and did thirty push–ups and half an hour on the treadmill. After swimming a few laps, he went back to his apartment. dressed, and took the elevator down to Hilda's coffee shop on the ground floor of the building.

"Your usual, Mr. Calhoun?" the waitress asked.

He nodded, and within minutes she returned with cheese grits, buttermilk biscuits, fried country ham, red–eye gravy, scrambled eggs and coffee.

"I tell you, you Southern fellows do love this ham, grits, and biscuits, and I'm sure glad you do."

"Yeah," he responded, sampling a biscuit, "when I get homesick for some real food, I make a beeline for this place." He tasted the ham and grits. "Midge, this stuff is good."

Her smile struck him as being a little too sweet, and he stopped eating and stared at her. "Well, I'll be damned," he said to himself, when her olive-toned face turned crimson. Best to pretend he hadn't seen it, because he was doggoned if he was going to give up the best breakfast in New York City. He laid beside his plate a tip that was much too large, went back home, left a message on his secretary's answering machine, and called Ginger at her office. When he got the answering service, he called her at home.

"Hello, Ginger, this is Jason."

"Jason? But I thought you promised me last night that—"

"This is strictly business. I'll be out of town 'til Sunday night, and I wanted to make sure you didn't want a conference with me or our clients before we see Judge Williams Monday morning."

She resisted asking him what good he thought that would do, and asked whether his client was going to withdraw her countersuit and stop wasting their time. He countered with the remark that her client was a cheapskate for refusing his wife a small monthly allowance.

"Now, you wait a minute," she fumed. "A woman who refused to work and help her husband build a life for them, who wanted to go out to dinner every night to expensive restaurants because she hated the sight of the kitchen, now wants a pile of alimony so she can sit on her lazy behind for the rest of her life? Give me a break, buddy. A man with modern ideals wouldn't represent such a parasite."

"And a lawyer with humane consideration for her fellow human beings wouldn't—Ginger, for heaven's sake, what are we doing here? This is ridiculous!" He took a deep breath, hating the feeling of defeat. "Ginger, I didn't have that case on my mind. I really called to wish you a happy weekend and to tell you that I'll be down in Dallas with my dad. See you Monday morning."

"Oh, Jason. I'm . . . sorry I flew off the handle, but you made me so mad with—"

"Don't say it. We're both sensitive about this case, and I wish I knew why. See you."

Jason telephoned American Airlines and reserved a seat on the twelve–forty flight from LaGuardia to Dallas International, packed a few personal items, and left for the airport. In Dallas, he rented a Ford Taurus and headed for the brick Tudor thirty miles from Dallas that he'd bought for his father the year before. He couldn't have said why he wanted a couple of days with his father, but when he saw Aaron Calhoun he was immediately enveloped in that peace his father always exuded.

"What brings you here, Son?"

"Everything. Nothing. I have to get away from New York City every so often so I can stay human, and I hadn't seen you for a while."

Aaron took him at his word, as he always had, and didn't probe. "Fish been jumping that high." He held a hand five feet above the floor. "We can still get a mess of catfish 'fore sunset."

Jason grinned as pleasure stole over him. "You cleaning 'em?"

Aaron's left eyebrow shot up. "Don't I always? Want a bite before we head for the lake?" The local people called it a lake, but it was actually the wide, bowl shaped area of the river.

"Thanks. I ate on the plane. Let's go. I haven't fished in months."

They walked to the river, put their gear in order, and cast their lines. "Eric said you'd found a girl and lost her," Aaron began, while they watched their little red and white floaters bobble with the rush of the river.

"That's right, but I found her again. I still can't believe

I've seen her and talked with her. When I saw her in New York for the first time and realized I'd found her, we were in the judge's chamber. Ginger's a lawyer, opposing me in a case. You wouldn't believe how totally unprofessional I acted."

"I can imagine what a shock it was." Aaron grabbed his line. "Oh, oh. There goes my fish."

"Would you believe that judge told us not to see each other socially until the case is settled?"

Aaron stopped lighting his pipe and looked at the son who, even as a child, disliked taking orders from anyone, including his father. "And you're doing it?"

Jason had to laugh at the look of incredulity on his father's face. "I don't have a choice. Ginger believes in obeying authority."

Aaron Calhoun threw back his head and enjoyed a guffaw. "Well, I'll be doggoned. You love her?"

Jason ran his left hand over his silken curls, a move certain to alert his father to his bemusement. "I don't know, Dad. I haven't seen much of her."

"Pshaw. Sometimes, it only takes that first glance, one minute, and you're in for life."

"That didn't happen with Louise and me."

Aaron took a few puffs on his pipe and furrowed his brow. "You can say that again. You two backed into it, and it should never have happened. You were about as well-suited as a donkey and a thoroughbred race horse."

"I don't think much of that analogy, and I hate hearing you say, 'I told you so.' "

"And I didn't say it, either. Soon as you can manage it, I want to meet your Ginger."

He wished she was his Ginger. "If she's the one, I'll bring her down here."

"Whether she is or not, I want to meet the woman who shook you up like this. Never thought I'd see the day it happened to you. Louise didn't know who you were, but this one's got your number."

"You've got a fish, Dad," Jason said, glad not to have to comment on his father's arrow–straight observations.

Aaron pulled in a big catfish, looked at his elder son, and grinned. "We can go now.

"Wait a minute. Not until I get—" The line jerked in his hand and, when he began to reel it in, the big fish fought him, jumping high out of the water, until Jason managed to get him in the net.

Jason looked down at the fish, still wiggling and trying to jump. "We don't need both of them," he told his father. "I'm throwing him back in."

Aaron got up from the rock on which he'd been sitting and dusted off the back of his trousers. "When your mother was living, we used to say you must be the strongest soft-hearted man on this planet. Go ahead and throw him back."

"You wouldn't make some hush puppies to go with this fish, would you?" Jason asked him.

"That and some stewed down collards, too. Doesn't take much to make you happy, son, but what it does take isn't one bit ordinary."

Jason slung an arm around his father's shoulders as they began the half–mile walk back to the house. Peace. He hoped he'd someday give at least that much to his sons. A stream of fear streaked down his back. What if Ginger wouldn't consider having children? He'd seen many women lawyers in court, but not one of them looked as if she might be pregnant. No, it didn't take a lot to make him happy, but children were a must.

Ginger dressed with extra care that Monday morning. She had to look smart, businesslike, and feminine too. She had Jason on her mind, but she also wanted that judge to take her seriously, so she settled for an electric blue linen suit and knotted her hair at her nape. Hot as it was, it didn't much matter how she wore it, but at least her neck

would get a little air. As she'd expected, Jason arrived
dressed to kill in what had to be a Brooks Brothers suit
and a red tie guaranteed to keep the judge's eyes glued
to him. She smirked at the sight of Alma Roberts in a
clinging, red miniskirt dress and long, dangling earrings—
a walking confirmation of her client's accusations.

"You may begin, Ms. Hinds," Judge Williams announced
at precisely ten o'clock.

She looked toward Jason and wasn't surprised to find
his gaze fixed on her. Her respect for him climbed a notch
when she noticed nothing personal in the way in which
he observed her.

"Good morning, Your Honor. Mr. Calhoun." Thank
goodness she hadn't forgotten that; Jason had a way of
disarming her without trying. "Your Honor, my client,
Steven Roberts, is seeking a divorce from Alma Roberts,
his wife of seven years, on the following grounds." She
repeated the statement she'd made at the preliminary
hearing.

Jason greeted the judge and Ginger and followed with
his client's countersuit. "If it pleases the court, my client
rejects Steven Roberts' charges as nonsense and wants
them thrown out. A wife has a right to expect affection
and companionship from her husband, but all she's gotten
from this man is a constant diet of her own company. All
by herself, Your Honor."

"Your Honor, my client has had to work so that this . . .
his wife could live comfortably and he could still provide
for their old age. Did she help him? No, ma'am. She spent
what he earned trying to be a teenager. Pop records, clubs,
parties, shopping sprees, and lunch two or three times a
week with the girls, while he wanted to build a home and
a future for them."

Jason dropped his court manners and pounded his right
fist into his palm. "A man has no right to expect his wife
to work," Jason growled, "not even if he has to hack two
jobs. A guy is supposed to pamper his woman. Besides,

how's she going to have children and raise a family if she has to punch a time clock every morning?''

"Mr. Calhoun,'' the judge said in a tone just short of sarcastic, "are you saying a woman's place is in the home?''

Jason stuck his hands in his pockets, paced, and then turned to the judge with a half—smile at the corner of his mouth and his smooth demeanor intact. "Your Honor does me a disservice.''

"Glad to hear it,'' Agatha Williams replied. "For a minute there, I was afraid you hadn't made it into the twentieth century.''

"Wasted worry, Your Honor,'' he shot back. "At times I get the feeling there aren't many of us in it. If I may proceed? My client deserves restitution.''

Ginger couldn't believe he'd risk flippancy with that straightlaced judge. She looked at the woman on the bench. Doggoned if he wasn't getting away with it. Maybe she wasn't the only female with whom that red tie and those gray eyes paid off.

She glanced at her notes. "Restitution?'' She stuck a hand on her left hip and glared at Jason. "Your Honor, a person can only take so much. You work yourself to death giving one hundred percent, and find out you're the only one giving. You're struggling to build a home and a future, and all that wonderful person you married is interested in is having a good time. My client deserves a partner who shares his goals.''

Jason propped both hands on the bar and gave the impression of someone whose patience was fast eroding. After a second, he leaned toward the judge, his voice low and soothing like cool water lapping softly over and around you on a hot summer day. Ginger braced herself for a smooth job of conning.

"Your Honor,'' he began, his face glazed with childlike innocence, "shouldn't a young woman have the company of an energetic man rather that a burned—out Joe who straggles home late every night and conks out on the sofa in front of the TV?"

Ginger had to marvel as a smile brought sparkles to his eyes. "You'll agree, I'm sure," he continued, "that a woman should be able to enjoy her man when she's young, and not have to wait until she's over the hill."

Who did he think he was? As if driven by a nest of hornets, Ginger bounded to within two feet of Jason. "Why don't you men stop letting your libidos take the place of your common sense? A levelheaded man doesn't try to have his cake and eat it, too. He plans for his family, makes certain that his wife and children will have a good life, and *then* he has a good time. Deliver me from the guy who wants his wife to start having a family the day they get married."

She ignored the storm brewing in his eyes and the sparks that seemed to fly from them as he glared at her, his expression thunderous. "I suppose your client gets his ideas about family life from his mother. That's usually what undermines a marriage isn't it? A spouse who hasn't gotten three feet from the womb? A smart attorney would have advised Steven Roberts to seek counselling."

She stepped closer to him, the presence of the judge and the divorcing couple forgotten. "I *did* advise it. And, anyway, what business is it of yours what I do or don't say to my client? You obviously approve of your client's adolescent frivolity. She's too immature for marriage, a crybaby who doesn't appreciate a solid, hardworking man. I would never have expected that of you."

Bang! Bang! Bang! "Mr. Calhoun. Ms. Hinds. Those statements do not appear in the briefs you gave me, and I can only conclude that the two of you are either stretching the truth or you've gotten personal. I think you've gotten personal, and I won't have any more of it."

Ginger didn't hear the judge's words and, from the expression on Jason's face as he stared at her, she suspected that he hadn't heard them, either.

Steven Roberts stood. "Your Honor, could I please say a word?"

Ginger whirled around, and a gasp escaped her. She hadn't seen Steven move across the room and sit beside his wife. "You're supposed to consult with your attorney first," she told him.

"Let me hear what he has to say," Judge Williams interjected, "because up to now I don't see any grounds for divorce. Marriage isn't a game for the entertainment of adolescents, Mrs. Roberts."

"Your Honor," Steven pleaded. "We just decided we don't want a divorce. After we heard Ms. Hinds and Mr. Calhoun going at it, what we thought was so important just kinda sounded childish."

Ginger restrained her impulse to shake her fist at him. Hadn't she told him that half a dozen times?

"I'm glad to hear it, Mr. Roberts," Judge Williams said, "because childish is precisely what it is. And Mrs. Roberts, take my advice and grow up. Case dismissed."

Ginger stuffed her papers into her briefcase, locked it, and turned to leave the judge's chamber. "Thank you, Judge Williams," she said in the mandatory gesture of politeness, nodded in Jason's direction, and headed for the door.

"Just a minute, Ms. Hinds," Agatha Williams called after her, "I want to speak with the two of you. If you're having a problem, straighten it out. Better still, avoid cases in which you're working against each other. And do something about this thing between you that's so hot you forgot yourselves and behaved unprofessionally." She grinned at Ginger. "Surely you can handle it, Ms. Hinds."

"I'm not so sure," Ginger replied and left Jason and the judge gaping as she walked away.

She took a taxi to her office on Broadway just below Houston and walked into the refreshing softness of blue walls, tall ficus trees, desert cacti, and warm mahogany furnishings that always seemed so inviting. Whenever she

raised her gaze from the papers on her desk, she looked
directly into the vision of artist Edward Mitchell Bannister,
of whose calming seascape she never tired. Feminine, yet
professional. Elegant, like the Turkish carpet beneath her
feet. She sat down, wrote a summary of the trial's conclusion, and buzzed her secretary.

"I didn't know you'd come in, Ms. Hinds," her secretary
said. "Mr. Calhoun called. He said it was urgent. May I
ring him?"

A shiver jetted up her spine. If only she knew what to
expect of him. "Yes. Then I want you to take some notes
on Roberts versus Roberts."

"Yes ma'am."

Minutes later, his voice soothed her ears like a liquid
prelude from a master flutist. "Ginger, this is personal, so
if your secretary is on the line, ask her to—"

"No one's on but me. What is it?"

"Look. We sat alone on that tour bus looking at rain
as thick as ocean water pouring all around us, and with
lightning streaking around in it like naked dancers frolick-
ing through time. We sat there dazed by it, and it made
you shiver, pulled at your insides until you turned to me
with your lips parted and ready for my mouth. Now, you
act as though it never happened. What about Victoria Falls
in that little boat in the middle of the Zambezi River, when
we stood at the stern with our arms around each other
and watched a sunset that made you cry? You held me
then, Ginger. And I mean you held me so close to you
that everything you felt—your longing, your desire for me,
and your fear of it—seeped down into me, trashing my
will to avoid getting involved with you."

She couldn't find words to respond, though he waited.
Then he let out a long breath. *"Woman, what is it with
you?* I am the same man you wanted to make love with
that night in Harare. You were honest, then. Talk to me."

She clutched the phone until her knuckles stretched
the skin on her right hand. He didn't have to remind her

of what she would never forget. She searched for a safe, impersonal answer, couldn't find one, and settled for the truth.

"You want to know what's going on with me, Jason? Well, I'll tell you. I'm scared, Jason, and I have been from the moment we met. I kissed you less than six hours after I first saw you, and I still marvel that I had the sense and strength to leave you that night, because it wasn't my conscious self that did it. The woman who walked away from you was the woman I am the other three hundred and fifty-one days in the year taking over. Do you think I ever did anything like that before? You bet I'm uneasy around a man who gets between me and my common sense just by showing up and smiling."

"Ginger. Ginger. Honey, did it occur to you that we might be each other's salvation? Destiny? If you've never responded to a man as you did to me, shouldn't you go for it, see what it holds for you? Do you think *I'm* in the habit of taking strange women to bed? No way! After two days of the happenings between us, you were no longer a stranger, but someone I needed. And, mind you, I didn't say *want.*"

Goosepimples popped out on her arms and her pulse jumped into a wild gallop. How could he say he needed her? In four years of marriage, Harold hadn't used the word. "These are strong statements, Jason. Be careful what you say."

"I always choose my words carefully, Ginger. We have a second chance now, and you know who I am. The case is closed, and I want to see you. Can I bring this champagne or not?"

The thought of being alone with him again burned her brain with anticipation. Unwanted. Yet, uncontrollable. She didn't want a repeat of her life with Harold, and if this man was wrong for her and she let him into her life, she'd pay a heavy price. She remembered her feeling of desperation when it seemed certain that she'd never see him again.

"Jason. I'll have to think about whether we should continue what we started—"

She'd bet those gray eyes shot fire as he said, "Sorry. I'm not giving you that luxury. You promised."

She wanted desperately to be with him, but she didn't think she could handle him. Her experience was limited to her ex–husband, and he hadn't needed handling. After having spent time with Jason, she suspected that the chemistry between Harold and her had been as weak as steam in a tunnel of trapped air. Well, if she spent the remainder of her life protecting herself, she might as well shrivel up right then.

"I promised we'd have champagne," she said in a voice that bore an unfamiliar weakness. "So come over about six–thirty, and we can drink it sitting at the river bank."

"Watching the sunset again? Sure you want to hazard that?"

"Watching the boats. Six–thirty."

Jason waited for the city bus at the corner of 110th Street and Fifth Avenue, in front of the building in which he lived. He loved Harlem, but preferred to live close to it rather than in it. Every few minutes he glanced at his left wrist. Time seemed to be playing a game with him, crawling along with all the deliberate speed of a snail. He put his watch to his ear and satisfied himself that it hadn't stopped. He walked to the corner, turned, and walked to the other end of the short block, didn't see a bus, and walked back to the bus stop. He'd gladly hail a taxi, but if he stood there until Christmas he probably wouldn't see one. He didn't want to admit that the prospect of seeing Ginger in her home, of being alone with her again, had his blood flying through his veins. The bus arrived, and he took it as far as Seventy–ninth Street, got off, and hailed a cab.

Fifteen minutes later, his right index finger pressed her doorbell.

The door opened, he looked at Ginger and lost his breath. With her hair down below her shoulders, her softened, guileless appearance pulled at the man in him, and he had to check his spiralling desire.

"Hello, Ginger."

"Hi. Uh . . . come on in while I get the glasses and some snacks."

He eyed her closely. A bag of raw nerves or his name wasn't Jason Calhoun. "I can wait out here, if you'd rather."

Her eyes widened and then blinked rapidly. "Oh. It's okay. Come on in."

He figured he'd scored some points by offering to wait in the hall. At least, he hoped so. He handed her a dozen calla lilies, and joy suffused him when she made no attempt to hide her pleasure in receiving them.

"Calla lilies have been my absolute favorite for years. Thank you. They're so beautiful."

"My pleasure. Beautiful lilies for a beautiful lady."

He followed her into the living room, anxious for any clues to her personality. Curtainless windows and track lights beside them told him nothing. He took in the burnt orange chairs and antique, gold–colored sofa that sat on a soft, beige–patterned Tabriz Persian carpet. Tall, live plants stood near the windows, and a James H. Johnson reproduction dominated one beige–colored wall. Her good taste didn't surprise him. He'd expected it. His gaze swept over her books. History, biography, politics. A rack beside the piano held—*a piano*. He stepped closer to see what she played. Handel's *Largo*, Duke Ellington's sacred music, and Bix Beiderbeckes's haunting "In a Mist," a jazz classic from the nineteen twenties. He shook his head. Where was she in that mélange of interests? He shrugged off the question. With such catholic tastes, at least she wouldn't be narrow–minded.

Her footsteps announced her arrival. "I see you play the piano."

She glanced toward the door. "Yes, but I don't often have time these days."

Maybe if she played, he'd find her through her music. "Play something for me."

"I uh . . . She looked at the bag he'd rested on the coffee table. "What about the champagne?"

He picked up the bag, stepped closer, and handed it to her. "Put it in the refrigerator. I want to hear you play."

He could see that he made her ill at ease, and he didn't like it. Might as well get it out in the open. "Ginger, relax and get used to me."

Her smooth. dark skin took on a reddish caste from a rush of blood to her cheeks. He'd give a lot to know what went on in her mind, but he didn't want to play games, so he didn't query,

"Why do you think I'm not relaxed?"

He believed in straight talk. "If a bird chirped behind you right now, you'd jump. You're scared to death that I'll shake your sugar tree."

"Jason!"

"Don't act so surprised. You know the truth when you hear it. Play something, will you?"

"Anything special?"

He shook his head. "I only want to hear you play."

A soft, barely audible whistle slipped through his lips as he watched her slow, lazy glide across the room to the piano and the easy grace with which she slid onto the bench. Her fingers moved over the keys with practiced skill as she coaxed from them Duke Ellington's haunting "Mood Indigo." She threw back her head, closed her eyes, and teased the music until it surrounded him, flowing to him from every corner and nook of the room. He thought he'd lost her to the music until she opened her eyes, fixed them on his, and let their soft, brown beauty tell him that he was the most special of men.

With her soul still open to him, her soft, mezzo–soprano gave life to the words of Ellington's great song, one that he'd loved since listening to his parents' records when he was a child. With every breath she took and every note that flowed from her lungs, he lost a little more of himself.

At last no sound could be heard in the room, and she stared down at her hands lying in her lap. "Did you like it?"

He longed to touch her, but controlled the urge for fear of destroying the moment. "The last time anything moved me so deeply, I was holding you while we gazed at the sunset and your tears dripped over my hand. You sing and play beautifully. Everything about you is beautiful."

She diverted her gaze and lowered her head. "I'm glad you like it so much. I . . . I don't know what to say."

He figured he'd better get them out of there before he did something stupid and got on the wrong side of her. "This seems like the perfect time for champagne. Ready to go?

When she stood immediately, he got the impression that she wanted to get out of there as badly as he did and, he suspected, for the same reason.

She returned from the kitchen with the champagne and a small wicker basket. "Ready when you are."

She seemed nonplussed, but he told himself to stop second–guessing her. She'd said she was scared, and that made sense, because anybody who was headed for what he knew they faced would be foolish to barge into it fearlessly. Giving yourself to another person wasn't all that the muses claimed; it could ruin your life.

Ginger laid a red–and–white checkered cloth on the concrete seating ledge beside the East River facing Manhattan and opened the basket.

"What's in there?" Jason asked as he eased the champagne from the confines of its bottle.

"Some sandwiches."

He poured the bubbly wine into the long–stemmed glasses she'd brought, linked their right elbows and looked into her eyes. Her pulse raced crazily, and her senses whirled with the giddiness of a moth dancing around a flame. She fought the old, habitual caution that threatened to drag her back down to reality, back to the staid, conservative Ginger—the Ginger who didn't take chances. This man meant business. If only she could ignore his mesmeric gray eyes, his tempting lips, and his air of power and authority, and concentrate on who and what he seemed to be— the real man.

"Here's to the woman who, with a single glance, rocked my world."

She raised her glass, smiled at him, and let the cool liquid caress her throat while he stared at her, stripping her bare with the naked desire in his eyes.

"Don't I get a toast?" he asked.

She clicked her glass to his own. "A man such as you will always get his share in life and so much more."

His face clouded, though not, she knew, with bemusement, but impatience. "Try not to talk over my head, Ginger. All I'm seeking right now is some assurance that you'll give us a chance. Nothing more. That doesn't mean commitment, just openness. How about that toast, so I can enjoy my drink?"

She tipped the glass toward him. "Here's to the man with whom I have dreamed."

She didn't think she'd ever seen a man change so quickly. The heated desire of minutes earlier dissolved into a kind of warm sweetness, and something else that she was scared to name.

That smile. Lights danced in his eyes and his face bore such a gentleness, a softness that she wanted to hug him to her breasts. "Sail with me, Ginger, and I'll make silver sails for you. If you'd rather we flew, I'll give you golden wings, and if you'll walk with me, I'll put the spring of joy and life into your steps. Come with me, and your eyes will see only things of beauty, your ears will hear heavenly music, and you'll dine on food prepared for the gods. What do you say?"

Her breath had lodged in her throat, and she had to gasp for air, but his magnificent gray eyes refused to release her from his spell. He unlinked their arms and smoothed her cheek with his fingers, something he'd done twice in Harare, as though his fingers communicated what words could not. She wanted to drown in him.

"Well?"

"I'm speechless, Jason. You offer me a world I never heard of. One day at a time?"

"All right. You said you weren't married, living with a man or engaged. I don't have any of those ties, either. You know I'm an honorable, law-abiding man, so I can't understand your reluctance to let us get closer. I understood why you walked away in Zimbabwe. You didn't know anything about me. But now you do."

Male logic. He couldn't see a reason, so there wasn't one. "Jason, would you walk into a roaring fire without an asbestos suit, or jump into the Atlantic Ocean knowing you couldn't swim? You swept me off my feet in Harare, and I don't like not being able to control my behavior. We're a couple a thousand miles from there, and . . . and—"

"And you still want me? Do you think you didn't sweep me off *my* feet? Honey, this is a mutual thing. You turned me around every bit as much as I unsettled you. Maybe more, from the looks of things. If we're honest with each other, we don't have anything to fear." A full smile bloomed on his face. "Problem solved. What kind of sandwiches you got in there?"

She uncovered the food. "Ham, smoked salmon, and cheese. Some grapes in here too."

His grin couldn't have been broader if she'd said she had a basket of diamonds. *I could love this man,* she admitted to herself when he lifted the bottle, winked at her, and said, "A loaf of bread, a jug of wine, and thou beside me singing in the wilderness."

A barge floated by with the aid of her favorite tugboat. "I named that tug Midnight," she told him, "because it moves by my bedroom window all times of night. I welcome it when I can't sleep." What she didn't tell him was that those sleepless nights had begun after her return from Zimbabwe. Lovers barely into their teens strolled by holding hands, and a man and woman stopped a few feet from them and kissed with such passion that she had to close her eyes. She opened them to find Jason's gaze locked on her and didn't have to wonder as to his thoughts. They had once kissed each other like that. They finished the sandwiches and champagne, and Jason put the glasses, napkins, and tablecloth in the basket.

"Where's that garden you told me about?"

"Not far. Want to walk down there?"

She delighted in showing him her handiwork. Although it was still April, scallions, turnips, spinach, and lettuce grew six or more inches above the soil, and blooming jonquils, crocuses, and evening primrose beautified the small plot. He rested his arm around her shoulders and, as though programmed to do so, she moved closer to him. When his arm tightened around her, she snuggled nearer still, and savored once more the perfect peace that she'd known only with him.

"Don't move," he warned, his voice hoarse with passion. "It won't take more than a deep breath for me to wrap myself around you and get lost in you right here and now."

Her skin tingled, but she refused to be caught up in the web that he spun. She'd walked blindly into a life of unhappiness with Harold, but not again. Still, she knew that Jason was different, that he offered her more. So much more.

"You're moving too fast, Jason."

He squeezed her shoulders. "But you're moving with

me, Sweetheart. It's a tidal wave, and nothing we do is going to stop it."

He asked her not to move, but shivers shook her and she settled against him.

The wind picked up velocity, and a whiff of perfume from the purple crocuses teased her nostrils. "This wind's bringing a storm," she told him, "and it's getting darker. I think we'd better get out of here."

"Yeah. Let's run for it," he said, picked up the basket and grabbed her arms as the first big raindrops spattered them.

"There's the minibus. Come on," she urged.

They boarded the red Island Transport bus as torrents of rain fell around them.

What does this remind you of?" Jason asked her.

She put two quarters, one for each of them, in the fare box and pulled her damp shirt away from her body. "You didn't let me get wet in Zimbabwe. You're slipping."

He shrugged. "We're on your territory now, Sweetheart, so *you* should have protected *me.*"

They got off at the second step and dashed into West View, the building in which she lived.

She couldn't speak, because conflicting emotions clogged her thoughts as her desire to be one with him wrestled with her fear of losing her very soul.

She pressed the elevator button and turned to him. "I'm crazy, Jason. Everything about you appeals to me, but right now I feel like putting a couple of miles between us."

A half–smile curled around his lips. "Okay to feel like it, so long as you don't do it."

At her apartment door she noticed that he stepped back, leaving the decision to her. Marbles rattled around in her belly when she turned and looked into his turbulent eyes.

"Come on in."

"You sure?"

"No, I'm not sure," she said, able to laugh at her own foolishness, "but come on in, anyway. You can put that basket in the kitchen while I get out of this wet shirt. Be right back.''

He wasn't wet, but he didn't sit down. He had to get control of the longing for her that had begun to drive him like a locomotive sucking the wind in its headlong plunge out of control. The sensation of being propelled to her by some supernatural force had begun that morning in Harare at breakfast and hadn't slackened; if anything, it had intensified. He had dissected it, analyzed it and prayed about it, but he still needed her.

"Why didn't you sit down?" she called out in a tone of gaiety that he knew was forced.

Well, he wasn't going to string it out. Quick steps took him to her, and she stared up at him with want blazing in her eyes. Hot energy shot to his belly, and he pulled her into his arms. Her breasts nestled snugly against his chest, and when their hard tips rubbed against him, he lifted her from the floor, parted her lips with his tongue, and knew heaven at last. When she took him into her warm, sweet mouth, desire vibrated through him like atomic waves. She asked for more of him, and he gave, visiting every nook and crevice of her mouth, sampling the sweetness he found there. He thought he'd explode as the fullness of his manhood nestled against her belly. What sense he could muster told him he'd better ease up, but she wouldn't release him and clutched him to her as she groaned in pleasure. He wanted to burst within her, but if he did, he'd regret it. They both would. What they needed wasn't a quick fix standing in the middle of a room, but a place and time to savor, to revel in each other's bodies.

With one hand, he loosened her grip on him. "Ginger, Sweetheart, if we can lose ourselves in each other as we just did, nature is telling us something. I'm not going to see any other woman. Will you cut any romantic ties you have, and let's see if we can make it together? We haven't spoken about our lives, things we experienced that might affect us now, but it's time we did that. I'm in deep, here and so are you. Right?''

She nodded. "All right. I won't see any one else until we know where we're going.''

He hugged her to his heart. "You want me to leave?''

"I don't think we ought to make love right now, if that's what you're asking. Oh, I know I would have, but I believe we can have more if we do as you suggested.''

"I know we can. See you tomorrow evening?''

"I'd like that, but I have to prepare for a case, and I don't know anything about the business involved. I need to do some research at the Schomburg Library, and it doesn't open 'til noon. We can talk when I get home, though.''

"Okay. I'll call you about nine–thirty. Right now, I'm out of here before things start to heat up again. Kiss me?''

His heart turned over when she raised her mouth to his, and he knew he'd never be able to live without her. Her lips brushed his, then parted for his tongue, but he resisted her invitation. No point in steaming himself up again.

"Goodnight, Sweetheart.''

" 'Nite.'' She opened the door, and as he walked through it she reached up and kissed his cheek. " 'Til tomorrow.''

He had to control the temptation to follow her back into that apartment.

Ginger grabbed the nearest chair and barely missed sitting on the floor. No use lying to herself; he made her come alive, and she couldn't wait to know the ultimate about him—how he'd make her feel and whether what churned inside of her was strong enough to last a lifetime. But maybe he wouldn't want that. With his steel-like will-power, he could dance on the edge and walk away without a backward glance. Well, she wasn't bad at that herself. She jumped up, crossed her arms, and stroked her shoulders. Laughter poured out of her, and she whirled around and around. *Work,* her conscience reminded her, but who could think of work when the taste of him still lingered in her mouth?

At seven the next morning, she took a brisk walk along the river, after which she went to Andy's Place for breakfast. Amos Logan sat at his usual table in the corner reading *The New York Times.*

"You want to read, or may I join you?" she asked him.

He put the paper aside. "I can read any time. How'd that case go?"

She gave the waiter her order of half a cantaloupe, toast, eggs, and coffee. "The opposing attorney and I got into a hassle over the charges, and that apparently inspired the couple to make up. At their request, the judge dismissed the case."

"You got into an argument with the attorney of your client's wife? In front of the judge?"

She took a few sips of coffee. "Yes, and yes. Judge Williams called us on it too."

"Agatha Williams?" Ginger nodded. "Can't say I'm surprised. I taught her. She's just the type. Agatha can split any kind of hair. What did you argue about?"

She told him, and had to experience the discomfort of a knowing look from a man of the world.

"Ginger, if I may call you that. Sounds personal to me."

"It *was* personal. The problem is that I don't know in what respect."

"You'll find out," he said and beckoned the waiter for more coffee. "I expect he'll let you know pretty soon, if he hasn't already done so. Keep me posted."

They talked of the local political scene, of the candidates running for different posts and what they thought of them. "A lackluster bunch," he pronounced.

I'd better be going," she said as Clarice walked in dressed in white slacks and a yellow T-shirt that proclaimed, "Pray

for Spring. Summer is killing me," and brought a gale of
laughter from Amos.

"You two know each other?" Ginger asked.

They didn't, so she invited Clarice to join them and
soon made her way back to her apartment to dress for
work.

Her afternoon and evening at the Schomburg netted
her the information she needed on the nightclubs in Harlem and on The Cat's Pajamas in particular, and she left
there shortly after eight o'clock to begin preparing her
case against the city, which had begun closure proceedings
against the club. The club's owner had a right to bar from
entrance anyone who had ever been evicted from the prem-
ises legally for drunkenness, use of drugs, or similar unde-
sirable behavior. If the owner rejected the offender's
apology, that was his right. Too many Harlem establish-
ments had been closed for a first violation of a city ordi-
nance, and the owner of The Cat's Pajamas wanted to
avoid that penalty. She stopped by Andy's Place, got a
hamburger and soup, and took it home with her.

Exhausted but fulfilled after a productive day, Ginger
finished her supper, took a shower, and prepared for bed.
With an eye to the clock and nine-thirty—when Jason had
said he'd call—she found Donna Hill's book, *Pieces of
Dreams*, and got set to find out what happened to Maxine,
the girl Quinn Parker had left behind. Trouble was, she
hated to put the book down once she'd started it, and
Jason would call at any minute.

By ten minutes to ten, she had stopped wanting to hear
his voice and had developed an urge to tell him what he
could do with his silver sails and golden wings.

When the phone rang at seven minutes after ten, she
was tempted not to answer it, but decided to hear him out.

"I thought you'd decided not to answer," he said after
a greeting that she was certain would have been more

affable if she'd picked up on the first two or three rings. "I called as soon as I could. After dinner downtown, I took a taxi home and would have been here in plenty of time, but the taxi driver elected to drive through the park and went right into a police check. So there I sat for forty minutes, while the police investigated the driver's green card and driver's license, and the cab's inspection certificate. And trust me, they took their time doing it."

In her impatience for his call, she hadn't considered that he'd have good reason not to keep his word. "I admit I was annoyed, and I know I should have waited for your reasons. I'm sorry."

"If your dander got up because you couldn't wait to hear my voice, I won't find it hard to forgive you."

"And if I tell you that's not why I got annoyed—"

"Then you'd be lying, Honey. His low, sultry laugh warmed her soul. "We promised honesty, remember?"

"You're pretty sure of yourself, mister."

"I've learned it never hurts to give that impression."

"What about that honesty you were talking about a second ago?"

A teasing laughter colored his voice. "That was seconds ago. I'm sure you're familiar with the saying, 'Never look back, something may be gaining on you'? Say, I love the woods in spring. You've got the rest of the week to get that brief together. How about going hiking with me in the Catskills Saturday morning? Some of those trails are magnificent. We could go fishing, too, if you'd like."

She loved the outdoors, though hiking wasn't high on her list of fun things. Neither was fishing. But if that's what he enjoyed, she'd learn to love it if it would enrich their time together.

"I've always been able to take both or leave them, but I might enjoy hiking and fishing with you. All right, I'll go."

"Great. All you need is a pair of sturdy shoes and a sweater."

She couldn't resist the jab. "Good heaven, Jason, that's what you wear in the woods—shoes and a sweater?"

"Your imagination is telling tales on you. If that's what you want to see, we don't have to go to the Catskills."

A picture of Jason in shoes and sweater flashed through her mind, and her amusement at it manifested itself in a hearty laugh. "Hmm," was all she said.

"What's so funny?"

"My imagination is both mental and visual."

She supposed that he'd settled back for a good set-to when he said, "Like what you saw?"

Catering to the wickedness that always hovered near the surface, she shot back, "Well, I suppose I've seen worse."

"You bet you have. Give me a kiss, huh?"

She made the sound, and added, "Sweet dreams."

Letting her know that he was as devilish as she, he said, "Oh, I'll dream. Be sure of that, because I'll doze off with a picture of the two of us gamboling through the woods in our shoes and sweaters." He hung up before she could tell him what she thought of his observation.

Ginger got up early Saturday morning, fried some chicken drumsticks Southern style, made buttermilk biscuits, and put the food in a thermal bag. She put a box of ginger snaps and some bananas and apples in her wicker basket along with linens and cutlery. If she were going to walk herself to death in Jason's fairy tale woods, at least she'd be able to eat when she got hungry. She dressed in a cotton shirt, jeans, and low–heeled leather boots, and dropped a sweater on the wicker basket.

At seven sharp, the doorman announced Jason's arrival.

"Hmm," he said, after a quick kiss on her mouth, "do I by some rare piece of luck smell buttermilk biscuits?"

She nodded and picked up the basket, ready to leave.

A look of incredulity masked his face. "Wait a minute. You just made buttermilk biscuits?"

What was so unusual about that? she wondered, but she

answered, "Yes," and pointed to the thermal bag. "I put some in here. Come on. It's after seven."

He cocked an eye and stared at her. "If you just made them, that means they're still hot. You'd need a towtruck to get me out of here before I sample some of those things."

So much for getting to the Catskill Mountains by eleven o'clock. "All right. All right. Just have a seat. She pointed to a dining room chair, but he followed her into the kitchen, sat on a stool, and watched her. She put four biscuits in the toaster.

"Any butter and jam? Just give it to me right here," he said when she started toward the dining room. "I grew up eating in the kitchen."

She poured a mug of coffee for him and learned that he drank it straight. Minutes later, he stood, patted his stomach, and extolled her virtues as a biscuit maker. "A woman who can make biscuits that taste like that," he marveled, shaking his head. "Ginger, you have so many talents. You're a fine attorney, a pianist with a wonderful voice, a gardener, and now, a biscuit maker. Before I start to feel inept, tell me about some of your shortcomings."

"Don't worry, I've got my share of them. For one thing, I'm notoriously lousy at judging men."

"At judging ..." As though frozen, he stopped unlocking the door of the Buick he'd rented and stared at her. "What do you mean by that?"

He had to know some time, and the sooner she could test his reaction the better. "Just what I said. And that's one reason—maybe the main one—why I'm so indecisive about you. With my record, I've gotten cautious." She wished he wouldn't look at her as though he could see through her.

"We need to save that for serious conversation, for that time when we get down to the business of sharing everything about ourselves." He threw the keys up, caught them, and looked into the distance. "Ginger, I don't believe in saying important things in a casual manner, playing down

their significance. Besides, when I'm driving, I don't like
to concentrate on anything else."

She wished she hadn't let those words slip off her tongue,
for she hadn't meant to diminish the importance of Harold's request for a divorce. She had poured one hundred
percent of herself into the marriage, while he'd merely
watched her do it. She'd been devastated. In her reckoning, it was she for whom the marriage had not been fulfilling and when, without warning, he'd said he wanted his
freedom, the wounds that his demand inflicted on her
pride had scarred her deeply.

Jason took the New York State Thruway to Elmsford and
crossed the Tappan Zee Bridge without slowing down.

"I knew this was too good to be true," Ginger said when
he came to a complete stop on Route Eighty–seven behind
what seemed like miles of stalled traffic.

He shook his head. "Beats me. At this rate, it'll be dark
before we get to Stone Hollow. You dead set on it?"

Was she breaking her neck for the opportunity to expose
herself to ticks and poison ivy? She let a look of concern
cover her face. "I would have enjoyed it. Yes. But I'd be
contented if we just found a place to have a little picnic."

He pinched her nose in what she recognized as a gesture
of approval and affection "Great. If I drive along that zebra
for about a quarter mile, I can get off this highway. There's
a nice park and lake not far from here. We can go there.
What do you say?"

"Sounds good to me. All we wanted was an outing together, and we'll have that."

He moved onto the white–striped lane and was soon
able to turn into Route Nine W. He stopped, turned, and
faced her. "Are you always this agreeable?"

"To anything reasonable that doesn't inconvenience
me, why not?"

He moved onto the road and headed for the park. "That
has not been my experience with most people, and certainly not with the women I've known. The lake's about a

mile from here. I think I'll pull over there and get some soft drinks. Come in with me and have a stretch."

They entered the shabby building and rang the bell.

A woman stopped mopping the floor, wiped her hands on the sides of her skirt, and looked them over. "We don't have no rooms right now. Come back in a couple of hours."

Ginger knew she gaped at the woman, but Jason stuck his balled up fists to the sides of his hips and glared. "Run that past me again."

And run it past him, she did, adding, "It'll cost you seven–fifty an hour."

He ran his fingers through his silky curls in an air of frustration. "But that sign says . . . All we want is a Coke and a bottle of ginger ale. What kind of place *is* this?"

The woman went back to her mopping. "Rooms by the hour. The drinks are next door." She nodded to her left. "Be sure and tell 'em Effie sent ya."

Jason took Ginger's hand and stepped outside. "I'm sorry about that. Wait here. No misunderstandings like that one. I'll get the drinks."

"For goodness sake, don't mention Effie," she called after him.

He walked back to her. "You think I'm crazy?" A grin played around his lips as he flashed a set of white teeth, and mischief sparkled in his eyes. She knew she could expect some of his special brand of deviltry, and he didn't let her down. "Of course, when I turned Effie down, I was only speaking for myself. If you want to go back in a couple of hours, I'm not totally opposed, though I'd prefer something elegant, more worthy of you."

She punched her finger in his middle. "In your dreams, Buster."

She loved his laughter, and he gave her a good sample of it before going to get the drinks. As he walked away, she asked herself if she cared for him but refused to hear her heart's answer. They ate lunch by the lake, with their bare toes cushioned in the grass.

"Time flies when I'm with you," he told her. "We've been here three hours."

She sat on the grass with her back resting against an old tree, and he lay supine on a blanket with his head in her lap. "I could spend forever right here with you."

His hair held a peculiar fascination for her, and she yielded to temptation and stroked it with the palm of her right hand. "Worse things could happen," she admitted. "What would we do? Forage for berries and nuts?" She let her thumb caress his lower lip. "What would happen when it got cold? Oh, *I* know. We could scoot back to New York and hibernate."

Suddenly his hand gripped her wrist, and she realized she'd been stroking his neck. He sat upright. "Do you know you've been making love to me for the last twenty minutes?"

"I . . . no, I wasn't."

"Deny it all you want." That grin again. "If you're that skilled at it when you're not thinking about it, I can't wait to have your undivided attention."

"Jason, you're starting to get a one–track mind."

"Don't blame me, Sweetheart. It's your influence. I think we'd better start back."

"How about stopping by my place while I change? Then I'll return the car, get a cab, and take you home. You change, and we can have dinner and take in some jazz down at The Village Vanguard. Would you like that?"

You're going to his place. If it gets out of hand, are you prepared to make love with him? She was, she admitted to herself, though it didn't matter. If she said she wanted to leave, she knew he would take her home at once. Nonetheless, the little mental exercise had been useful: she'd made an important decision.

"You're pretty quiet, lady."

"I was thinking. Sounds good, but why not drop off the car before we stop by your place?"

He shot an inquiring glance in her direction, so she

hastened to explain."That way, you won't have to look for a parking space."

After an Italian meal in a mom–and–pop restaurant on Thompson Street, they wound their way to the city's hottest jazz spot. From the minute they entered, Ginger wished she hadn't been so agreeable. A waitress barely out of her teens sauntered over to their table, her face an open invitation.

"Hi, Jason," she cooed. "Haven't seen you for a while."

For a second, she thought he'd stand up and kiss the little flirt. "I was here, but you weren't. How's everything?"

"You know my situation, Jason. Seeing you is the only good thing that's happened to me this week."

Ginger thought she'd burst. He could at least introduce them or, at worst, glance at her to let her know he remembered her presence. The waitress took their orders and left, and she took great pains not to look at the man who, only hours earlier, she had admitted to herself that she loved. To exacerbate her displeasure, he seemed oblivious to her quiet manner.

If it weren't enough that she had to tolerate the waitress, the comedian who performed during the band's intermission delivered the final insult.

"My wife doesn't understand me," he proclaimed. Then he looked at Ginger. "You'd understand me, wouldn't you, Baby? Soft, pretty thing like you." He looked at the audience, then back at her sitting beside Jason in front of the stage. "Man, look at those warm, brown eyes. Ain't no black chicks supposed to walk around with eyes like that. A lot of our women have big black eyes, but this beauty here—"

Jason grabbed the mike from him. "You say one more word to or about this woman, and you'll wake up a lot smaller than you are now. Got it?"

The comedian looked up at Jason. "I was just teasing,

man. Can I have my mike back? Thanks. I have to tell you, though, if she's yours, you can afford to be cool. She's choice."

Jason glared at the little man. "I thought I told you—"

"Okay. I heard you. No offense meant."

Jason sat down, and she could see the furor boiling up in him. "Would you like to leave?"

So he had a short fuse. She'd have to remember that. Certain that he felt as badly about the incident as she did, she covered his hand with hers and told him, "It never happened. What I want to know is who that child is who waited on us and called you by your first name?"

He leaned back and raised both eyebrows as though he hadn't understood her. "Mindy? She's the wife of one of my clients. She left him and calls herself teaching him a lesson which, I'm sorry to say, he isn't getting. Don't tell me you thought I was foolish enough to bring you to a place where you'd run into . . . " He stared at her. "Ginger, if you don't learn to trust me, we aren't going anywhere together."

She stared right back at him. "If you had introduced us, maybe I wouldn't have thought anything of it."

"I would have, if I'd known what to call her. She isn't using her husband's name now, and I don't know her maiden name. I certainly wasn't going to introduce the two of you as Mindy and Ginger. Okay?"

His light touch warmed her arm. "If we put ourselves to it, we can fight nonstop, but these misunderstandings will cease when we become closer and we're not so uncertain about each other."

He squeezed her fingers with affection, and she couldn't help leaning from her chair and letting her shoulder brush his. "You're positive that we'll be closer?"

"I am. It's something that I can't afford to doubt, Sweetheart. Yes, I am absolutely positive." He moved his chair until it touched hers, and she had again that peculiar sensation of peace when his arm stole around her shoulder. They sat that way through the show.

"I don't think I'd better go in tonight," Jason said at her door.

As far as she was concerned, he'd wasted his breath. "I'm not kissing you in front of my neighbors should any of them walk by, and I'm not letting you go without giving me my kiss."

She'd known that her words would amuse him, but her heart still took a dive when the lights danced in his eyes and his face bloomed into a smile just before he laughed. He held his head with both hands and told her, "If I don't hold it, there's no telling how big it'll get with you saying things like that."

She walked into the foyer, dropped the wicker basket on the floor, and turned to him. "I waited all day for this, Jason."

Gone was his laughter, his lighthearted demeanor, as his face took on the somber caste of a serious man. He took a step to her. "Come to me, Sweetheart."

She'd been anticipating the explosive passion that he'd unleashed Tuesday, the first time she'd been in his arms since they'd found each other. But he brought her to him with a gentleness, a tenderness that seeped into her soul the way a long, breaking sunrise robs you of all but your deep spiritual self. He looked into her eyes, and she searched them for whatever truth he offered her. Her heart quickened at the adoration, the sweetness that she saw there—an openness that said, *Trust me and I will be all good things to you.*

"Jason, don't . . . please don't mislead me."

He continued to look at her, his eyes telling her that he adored her. "Whatever you see, Ginger," he said at last, "comes from inside of me." He pulled her closer, as if he wanted to lock them together, and lowered his head.

Surely he felt her tremors when his lips finally touched hers in a shadow of a kiss. Feather–light, it was, until she held his head to intensify the pressure. He capitulated, but only for a second, and placed soft kisses on her mouth until she thought she'd scream for more.

"We can't go to the brink as we did last time, Honey. We're not ready for more, and if we get that far again, I'll have a hard time stopping."

She let him take her weight when he squeezed her to him and brushed her lips with his kiss. His hand was already on the doorknob. With a wink, he left.

She stuck her hands on her hips and, for want of a human target, glared at the door. "Tell me about the next time," she said. "I guarantee you, you won't stop."

She put away the wicker basket and threw the linen into a hamper while her mind went to work. After Harold obtained the divorce, she'd sworn off men. When she first met Jason, he intimated something about the virtue of being alone. Now they'd both backtracked, and she didn't see herself changing course unless forced.

Jason walked to the bus stop, leaned against it, and waited. Somewhere in the last five weeks, his vow to avoid involvement with women had gone down the drain, and he didn't regret it. Unless Ginger showed him something that he hadn't imagined or anticipated, he was in deep with her for the indefinite future. He knew she cared for him. But did she love him? If he'd learned anything that long day, it was that she meant more to him than any woman ever had. He thanked God that they'd found each other again. It couldn't have been luck or coincidence, and he didn't intend to treat it as such.

When he got home, he stopped by the mail room and found a letter in his box. Mr. and Mrs. Roberts requested the honor of his presence at the renewal of their vows. Would Mr. Calhoun please stand with them. He couldn't help laughing. That case had been both a miracle and a nuisance.

He stepped into his apartment and telephoned Ginger. "Sweetheart, would you believe this? The Roberts are actually getting back together, and they want me to stand with them when they renew their vows. Did you get an announcement?"

"I haven't been to my mailbox. I'll check it."

"If you got one, call me." He made the sound of a kiss and hung up.

Sure enough, she had received a similar announcement and request, but Roberts had added that Judge Williams would preside over their ceremony. She told Jason she wasn't sure she liked that, but he thought it amusing and said he could hardly wait until the four of them strolled into the judge's chambers for the ceremony.

Marriage filled Ginger's thoughts in the days to come. As she awaited the impending marriage between her sister, Linda, and Lloyd Jenkins, she had begun to wonder if she would ever know true love. Everlasting love. She set aside a weekend in which to do Linda's shopping. On the following Monday she put on her electric–blue linen suit and joined the Roberts and Jason in Judge Williams' chambers.

"Well, well," the judge observed, "If this doesn't beat all." She put on her glasses and looked from Ginger to Jason. "I suppose I can count on you two not to go at each other's throats?"

Ginger noted that Jason seemed taken aback, but since the occasion had no legal implications. she decided to get some of her own.

"Yes, Your Honor," she replied, "but that's all you can count on our not doing."

Agatha Williams removed her glasses and stared at Ginger, and Jason cleared his throat several times, obviously in the hope of quieting her. She ignored them both.

"A lot of water's flowed under the bridge since we last saw you," she told the judge.

"I can imagine," Judge Williams replied. "That water was rushing pretty fast while you were arguing this case. Now, if we may begin . . ."

As the judge read the ceremony, Ginger looked up to find Jason's eyes on her, and their gazes clung. His lips formed words that she couldn't hear, and his eyes pierced the distance between them, drawing her into the orbit of his being.

The words, *Till death do us part* reverberated in her head, and her right hand reached involuntarily toward him. His smiling eyes promised her the world, and she knew without doubt that she wanted his universe, to have her being in Jason Calhoun. If only he wanted the same.

Jason invited the Roberts to lunch with Ginger and him, but the couple barely had time to make the plane that would take them on the start of their second honeymoon.

"Think they'll make it?" Ginger asked Jason.

"I'd bet on it. You don't go to that much trouble a second time unless you're certain."

At that, her antennae zipped up, and she wondered what he'd left unsaid, but she didn't voice her thoughts. She couldn't, because she had her own dark chasm to cross. During lunch she told him she'd planned to rent a car in order to take to Easton, Maryland the things she'd purchased for her sister. He offered to drive her, and when he wouldn't be dissuaded, it occurred to her that he might relish the opportunity to meet her only close relative.

"She's getting married, and I'm standing up with her." She had almost said *matron of honor*, but it wasn't the time to go into all that, though she suspected they'd soon have to tell each other of their pasts.

"When's the ceremony?"

"Saturday night. That's why I have to leave here Friday morning."

His glance held no annoyance, but his voice did the job

for him. "Good thing you told me, so I can pack something other than jeans and sneakers."

"Sorry. I'm not thinking straight, but I'm glad you're going with me."

They held hands as they left the restaurant. "I'm not going to see much of you this week, Honey," he told her. "Taking Friday off means cramming five days work into four days and nights. Okay?"

"All right. It's the same with me, and I also have to get my dress fitted."

Still holding her hand, he pressed a quick kiss to her mouth. "We'll talk. Prepare to leave home at seven–thirty Friday morning." Another kiss fell soft on her lips. "And stay out of mischief."

Jason parked the rented Ford Taurus in front of Glenwood Street's only yellow brick house at ten forty–three that morning. He didn't usually speed, but there had been no traffic, and he'd had the wind at his back, so to speak. He busied himself collecting parcels from the car trunk, all the while wondering why he didn't follow Ginger into the house and meet her sister.

A man paused in passing and stopped. "Man, you need any help with those things?"

He swung around defensively, remembered that he was not in New York, but a small Maryland town, and accepted the offer. Together, they lugged Ginger's packages to Linda's front door.

The stranger spoke as he rang the bell. "You down for the wedding?"

"Yes." Why did he feel as though he had to pick his way through a briar patch? "I drove Linda's sister."

The man's face brightened as footsteps could be heard approaching the door. "Well, glad to meet you. I'm Lloyd, Linda's fiancé." He extended his hand. "I live right across the street, so be sure and come over anytime."

"Hi, Sugah," a tall, good–looking woman very much like Ginger crooned when she opened the door and saw Lloyd. "I thought Jason—" Her gaze landed on him, and she flung her arms around his neck. "Jason! I'll never believe she really found you. I'm so happy to meet you. I tell you, the Lord was with her. Lloyd, honey, you and Jason bring those things on in."

He soon learned that Linda organized people. Three women sat on the back porch peeling potatoes, wrapping cutlery in linen napkins, and making party favors, and in the garden a man painted silver stars and crescents to form mobiles. Linda evidently didn't believe in letting a person feel useless. She walked into the dining room where he stood talking with Ginger.

"Ginger, honey, could you take Lloyd—he's gone home across the street—and run down to Dillard's and get me two rolls of silver ribbon about four inches wide? They have it. And Jason, honey, you come in the living room and help me practice my song."

He blinked. "Your song?"

"Yes. I'm singing. Why should I let some other woman sing to my man at my wedding when I can do it, huh?" She had his hand, leading him to the living room. He didn't say, *Whew*, but he thought it. A real steamroller. She played and sang "For You Alone," and her voice brought back to him the moments when he'd been lost in the web Ginger had spun around him as she sang "Mood Indigo."

He applauded her. "You and Ginger have beautiful voices, and very similar, too."

She thanked him. "Just think. After tomorrow, I won't be in this big house all by myself. We're going to live here and rent out Lloyd's house."

He had wondered why she lived alone in such a big house, and voiced his thoughts.

"It's our family home. Our parents died, Ginger went to New York, and I was left." She got up and walked to the window, let out a deep breath, and spoke with her back to him. "I'm a very lucky woman, Jason. Lloyd and I were engaged once before, and a couple of weeks before we were to marry we had an awful spat. It was my fault. I'd always been insecure, and I saw this beautiful woman crawling all over him at our annual NAACP dance. I went nuts. He didn't push her away, so I decided there was something between them. I guess he'd gotten tired of my foolishness, because he walked out of there and left me. When I called him, he said he didn't want to spend the rest of his life accounting for every blink of his eyelids. I begged forgiveness and he gave it, but two days later the same woman came into church and sat beside him. He moved over to make a place for her. I couldn't keep my mouth shut about it, so I strutted out of that big, crowded church.

"As you may imagine, I didn't crawl back, and he didn't ask. Several days later, I heard he'd left town. That ended it, but for the next three years, I was perpetually depressed. I loved him so much that not an hour passed that I didn't long for him. One day I decided to find him. I wrote a letter telling him what I felt and what I knew I'd lost, and asked his forgiveness. Then I hired a private investigator and gave him the letter to give to Lloyd. The PI found him in Denver, and Lloyd called me. I asked if I could go out there to see him. He met me at the airport, and nothing that happens to me in the future will ever supercede in my heart that moment of reconciliation there in his arms in the Denver airport. That was about eight months ago. He moved back here and bought that house, got a job teaching at the University of Maryland in Princess Ann—about thirty miles from here—and we've never looked back."

She turned and faced him. "I grew up, Jason, and I now know what's important between a man and a woman.

"What?"

"Love, trust, and fidelity. I learned the hard way what it means not to trust."

Analyzing events and situations was his business, and he thought about all she'd told him without any provocation on his part. "You arranged this opportunity for us be alone. Why?"

Her light brown eyes, so like Ginger's, appraised him carefully. "My sister was practically a basket case when she got back here from Zimbabwe. She'd found more with you in two days than she'd had in her entire life, and she'd let it slip through her fingers. I hurt for her. As with Lloyd and me, a second chance is not to be taken lightly. The angels aren't happy when you throw their gifts back at them."

He wouldn't argue with that. "What do you do, Linda?"

"I teach math at the University of Maryland."

He nodded absentmindedly. "Two talented, accomplished sisters."

Linda had a right to be concerned for her sibling, but pressure of any kind had never sat well with him and, though she did it subtly, she was nevertheless leaning on him. Not that he blamed Ginger; it wasn't her idea that he drive her down there. As the day wore on, he saw similarities to the life he'd known in Dallas: privacy was non–existent. One neighbor after another greeted him and gave him and Ginger their blessings, assuming that they also planned to marry. Linda hadn't arranged a bridal supper, but a party at her home for neighbors and friends, and he soon had a surfeit of the neighborly well wishes.

He sat on the bride's side of the church the next evening and looked back as Ginger, breathtakingly beautiful in a mauve pink silk evening gown, preceded her sister to the altar. His head did battle with his heart as he watched the proceedings, wanting to the pit of his soul to take that man's place and stand there with Ginger beside him, but at the same time struggling against the irritating thought that the whole town was trying to shove him into it.

At the end of the ceremony, he kissed Linda and was

about to shake Lloyd's hand, but he recoiled when Linda's new husband addressed him as brother–in–law.

A glance at Ginger told him she'd seen the action and understood his reason.

As they left the church, she said, "Jason, I appreciate your driving me down here and helping us, but I have the feeling that you're fed up, that you'd rather be somewhere else. I can rent a car and drive back, so you can go on home. This long-suffering of yours is unnecessary. I'll be in touch."

He grabbed her shoulders, but he hadn't meant to do it so fiercely. "You listen to me, woman. I brought you down here, and I am taking you back home. You're not dismissing me as if I were your third grade pupil. I'd think you'd also have gotten tired of these people telling us what a great couple we make; what beautiful children we'll have; how lucky we are to have each other, and hoping you'll come back home so you can be married before the altar at which you were christened. All that, and not a soul told them we were getting married. Damned straight I'm fed up."

He had to hand it to her. The woman was as cool as spring water. With her regal head high, she didn't miss a step as they walked toward the cars that waited for the bridal party.

"Fed up is written all over you, Jason. If you want to leave, you have my blessing."

"When I leave, you're going with me."

"I won't fight with you in public."

He took her arm as they reached the car that had been assigned to them. "Ginger, we are *not* fighting. I'm going to turn in early, so I'll be out of the way, and I'd like to leave around noon tomorrow, as planned. All right?"

When she nodded, he relaxed, leaned over, and kissed her on the mouth. "The bride is beautiful, but she can't hold a light to my Ginger." The smile on her face warmed his heart. He needed her badly. Right then. *Some day soon,*

he promised himself, reached for her hand, and counted
his blessings.

In spite of the warmth they'd experienced in the car as
they left the wedding, they began the drive back to New
York with relations between them strained. She knew it
was useless to broach anything of importance to Jason while
he drove. Several miles before they reached the Delaware
Memorial Bridge, the dark clouds exploded into a heavy
downpour, forcing Jason to drive into the rest stop.

As streaks of lightning flashed in the sky, Ginger drew
herself up and pushed back her lifelong fear of thunder-
storms. Not for anything would she let him see her afraid
and needing him. "Why do you think the rain has showered us almost every time we've been alone together? Do
you think it's trying to tell us something? It's like an omen,
hooking us together."

He leaned back in the seat and closed his eyes. "Hardly.
I suspect it's something about lightning that turns you into
sweet putty." His half–smile seemed forced. "Ginger, we
have to settle some things. I had promised myself I was
going to treat women as if they carried the plague. And
then you came into my life. When you met me, I was
looking for equilibrium. Peace. Trying to straighten out
my life. I was married for almost six years. I wanted a family,
a real home that felt like one. I didn't want a place where
people dropped in for cocktails, and I didn't want to go
out to dinner or a club or a movie every night. I could
have handled some of that, if my wife hadn't sought coun-
sel from her mother about everything in our lives. I put
my foot down finally, and she went home to mama. There
was a lot more, but a man doesn't tell tales about his
marriage, not even after it's gone sour. Her mother told
her to bow out, and she did. I did not give up that relationship easily, but I managed to do it, and I'm glad.

"You're nothing like her, Ginger. You go after what you

want. I like that. You and I will always be able to meet on some common ground, to have an understanding, because you speak your mind and stand up for what you believe rather than sulk passively in a corner. I believe that if we give ourselves a chance, we can make a life together." He opened his eyes, stretched his right arm out on the back of the seat, and turned to her. "What haven't you told me that you think I should know?"

She took a ginger snap out of the wicker basket and chewed without tasting what she ate. He'd chosen an odd time for them to bare their souls to each other—sitting in a strange place in a rented car while rain drenched it and lightning danced all around it, but she was glad he'd opened the door.

"As you spoke, Jason, I marveled at the similarity of our lives. I, too, was trying to find myself when we met in Harare, but unlike you I wasn't looking for peace. I had spent my life as my parents had taught me. I married as a virgin, went to church on Sundays, worked hard and tried to save for the future, for the time when I could have a family and either stay at home, work part–time, or do consultancies. My husband wanted everything right then. Everything. He saw no reason why we couldn't start a family, though we only had a one bedroom apartment. I wanted to save for a home and the expenses of a first child. I thought we could buy a house with my savings as a down payment, but when I mentioned it he wanted us to take over half of my savings and go on a two–month jaunt through Italy. I should leave my clients that I had worked so hard to get, close my office, and go have fun. He earned a good living as an engineer, making as much money as I, but even though we shared expenses my savings quadrupled his. He loved fun, parties, eating out, and, especially, traveling abroad. We bickered constantly. When I refused to take the trip to Europe with him, he asked me for a divorce. I didn't contest it.

"You met me when I was trying to discard my conserva-

tive behavior and outlook and do something wild for the
first time in my life. I meant to have a fling with you, to
get Harold Lawson out of my system, but I found I couldn't
do anything so completely out of character. Besides, I'd
fallen for you, and I couldn't pretend that I hadn't. Jason,
I thought my world would end when I got back here,
realized what I felt for you, and had to live with the knowledge that I'd never see you again."

He enveloped her hand in his own. "I know the feeling."
Chuckles suddenly spilled out of his throat, and he released
her hand and nearly doubled up laughing.

"Jason, what's the matter? Jason, are you hysterical? Talk
to me."

He began to hiccup, and she pounded him on the back.
"Jason, for Pete's sake, what is it?"

"Ginger," he managed to say at last, "I just figured out
why we got so personal with each other when we were
arguing that divorce case. Don't you realize now that we
had stopped arguing that divorce case and had begun to
argue about the foibles of our own spouses, that we'd
slipped into a debate of the problems of our own failed
marriages?"

She looked out at the rain–washed highway and the
scores of cars idling along the road waiting to continue.
"Yes. But I was so ashamed of myself for having a judge
call me on the carpet that I've been pushing it out of my
conscious thoughts."

He laughed again. "We were so harsh with each other."

She moved closer to him. "I was not mean to you."

"Were so."

She leaned her head on his shoulder and kissed his
neck. "Was not. Was—"

He settled it when he gathered her into his arms and
let her feel the touch of his tongue on her lips. Wild
fires raced through her, and she parted her lips for the
sweetness he'd give her and for which she yearned. His
velvet tongue dipped into her mouth, finding its home,

claiming her. She didn't care if he felt her tremors, if he knew how she longed to belong to him.

He folded her to him and whispered, "We need to be together, Ginger. And soon. The rain's stopped, but I want a few minutes to get off this high before I can drive. Understand?"

She did and forced herself back to her seat. He'd just about reached the limit of his control, and she couldn't wait to exercise her advantage.

He started the engine, checked the traffic, and headed for New York. She'd whetted his appetite, and he wanted, needed, to know more of her, to strip away everything between them but their clothes. "Ginger, were you ever happy in your marriage? I mean . . . Did you . . . did you love him at first?"

She answered without hesitation, and he liked that. "I loved him. The trouble was my naiveté. I don't blame Harold. I was twenty–six when I got married. What man could imagine that a person could live that long and not know any more than I did about human relations? I assumed that if you behaved honorably and had good values and worthwhile goals, everything worked out. I didn't know that the same could be true for my spouse, and that instead of cementing our marriage. the fact that we each had strong goals and values could drive us apart. I didn't want the divorce, but I didn't care to live with a man who desired his freedom."

Maybe he ought not to probe, but there were things he had to know, because he'd committed himself to her with that kiss at the foot of the Delaware Memorial Bridge, and he had to know what he was up against.

"Did you have any problems you haven't told me about, that would help me to steer our own relationship on the right course?" At her hesitancy, he slowed down so as to be able to concentrate on her words.

"A couple of things, but you'll know those when the time comes."

He thought of some of the problems in his own marriage that had centered around Louise's unwillingness to grow, and didn't press Ginger for an explanation. Some things were best discussed in an atmosphere of intimacy. But at least they were talking, sharing themselves.

She had questions for him, too, he learned. "Do you have any hobbies, Jason? What do you do when you want to get away from law?"

"Recently, my problem hasn't been to get away from it, but to stick with it. Before you started fooling around in my head, I used to spend hours playing the flute or the coronet. On Sunday afternoons, you'd find me either at Lincoln Center, the Metropolitan Museum of Art, or at JoJo's down in the Village gigging with some fellow musicians. We're all amateurs, but some great jazz blows around in that place. I do other things, but they're less important to me. What about you?"

She smiled in a mysterious way that piqued his curiosity. "Me? Cross off JoJo's, add gardening and the Thursday night community sing–along on the Island, and you've nailed me. "I'm trying to start a mother-daughter club on the island to bring girls closer to their mothers. Maybe that will heal some of the friction in the homes, and start a decline in out of wedlock pregnancies. So far, I'm not having overwhelming success, But I have hope."

His eyes shone with approval and affection. "You keep working at that mother-daughter project. It'll be a success if you only recruit one family. You know, it's amazing how much alike we are."

"Alike? But you're a Re*pub*lican."

"Yeah. And you needn't pronounce the word as if it's got a vile taste. Don't forget. You're one of those Democrats."

"Are we going to fight about that?" she asked.

He felt good—light and airy like a Chinese kite dancing in a March wind. "You and me fight about politics? Honey,

I hope so, because from where I sit right now we agree on practically everything else. Too much of that would bore both of us to insanity.''

When she spoke again, it was as though she stepped among eggs, fearful of crushing them. ''Jason . . .'' She seemed to hesitate. ''Uh, what happened to you in Easton? You wished you were somewhere else, didn't you?''

He hated to say it, but honesty and straight talk was what they needed now. ''You're right. Those people crowded me, all but set our wedding date. Anybody would have thought they'd been waiting to pounce. I don't let people push me around. I don't care how well—meaning they are. I didn't want to hurt you, but I got pretty steamed up. I know how I feel about you and what I want out of our relationship, and that's between nobody but you and me.''

''I see. Haven't you ever lived in a small town?''

''I've lived in Dallas and New York, except for the two years I endured in New Haven getting my law degree at Yale.''

''Endured?''

''Yeah. I got sick of that cult of indifference. You couldn't believe the pretense. Nobody leveled with anybody.'' He took a deep breath, flipped on the cruise control, and put Yale out of his mind.

He noticed her head tilting forward and put a cassette into the tape deck. She soon slept as the soothing notes of ''Lover Come Back To Me'' pealed out of Benny Carter's saxophone.

It was after six—thirty when they passed through the Lincoln Tunnel and drove into New York City. ''Since we're near Hertz, I suggest we return the car and take a taxi to your place.''

Her ready agreement sent a flash of excitement zinging through him. He didn't look at her, because he didn't want her to see the hunger that he knew blazed across his face. Half an hour later, he held out his hand for her door key, opened the door, and walked in with her.

"Why don't I call down to Andy's Place for dinner?" she asked him. "The take–out won't remind you of Twenty-One, but it's edible."

They finished the meal, and while she put away the remains of it and straightened the kitchen, he prowled around the living room. What he needed was a swift, three-mile run or a half–hour of push–ups. The treadmill. Anything to get rid of the wild energy that wanted to burst out of him. He looked up and saw her standing in the doorway of the kitchen, biting her lip.

"Jason, would you sit down? Put on a CD, or something. I'll be back in a couple of minutes."

He raised an eyebrow and regarded her, temptation gnawing at him, urging him to make a move on her. But he hadn't nursed her feelings for him for nearly three months only to have their relationship fizzle because of his miscalculation. He sat down.

What was keeping her? He was a patient man, he reminded himself, and it didn't make sense to wring himself dry like a sheet in the spin cycle of a washing machine. He stopped shaking his left foot, felt in the breast pocket of his shirt for a package of cigarettes, and remembered that he hadn't smoked in eleven years.

"She's an itch," he told himself, "an itch that's grating every nerve in my body." He stood. Home. That was it. Go home and get out of trouble's way, because she hadn't given him one clue that she wanted any more than a kiss. He looked up to the ceiling, took a deep breath, and threw up his hands. *A kiss!* Who was he kidding? He looked around the room to see where she'd put the overnight bag he'd carried to Easton, and his gaze fell on her walking toward him with two glasses of white wine. He hadn't even seen her go through there to the kitchen.

"You in a hurry or something?" she asked. "I thought

we'd have a glass of wine and wind down. It's been such a—''

At his wits' end, he took the glasses from her and put them on the coffee table. "I can't handle any small talk right now, Ginger, and I don't want to hear anything that smacks of superficiality."

She sat down. "Neither do I. What is it, Jason? What's the matter?''

It was a reasonable question, but she might as well have pulled him into her. The fiery tentacles of long denied need of her singed his nerve ends and plowed straight to his loins. Her open, inquiring look grabbed at his protective instincts, and the need to have her fought with his inclination to protect her. Her brown eyes seemed to grow bigger as she looked at him.

He heard, "Honey. Honey, what's the matter? You look so miserable," and his fences fell as he pulled her into his arms.

"Ginger, honey, I need you. *Baby, I need you!*"

Did he imagine that her fingers caressed his cheeks before she squeezed him to her? He felt her gentle hands at the back of his head, and told himself that he'd begun to hallucinate.

"Ginger. I don't want us to start anything, because I couldn't stop. I don't *want* to stop. I want to make love with you."

"Shh, darling. I haven't asked you to stop."

He moved back and looked into her eyes and at the sweet lips that trembled in anticipation of his kiss, and shudders raced through his body. When she dampened her lips and parted them, he primed himself for the loving she offered. He sat her in his lap, rested her head against his shoulder, and bent to her mouth. She took his tongue eagerly, aggressively, begging for all he could give her. He dipped into her sweet mouth and explored the nectar that was there for him. When he thought he could stand no more, she took his hand and placed it on her breast.

He rolled its tip between his fingers until she moaned, broke the kiss, and asked for more. He hadn't noticed that she'd changed into a sundress until, with ease, he reached inside of it and, for the first time, felt the warmth of her woman's flesh. Her hand pressed the back of his head and he pulled her flesh into his mouth and suckled her until she shifted in his lap. Another minute of it, and he knew he'd explode.

"Where's your bedroom, Honey?"

She nodded to her right and he picked her up, sped down the short hallway to her room and lay her on her bed. He leaned over, unwrapped the sundress, and threw it on a chair. He pulled his T–shirt over his head, turned back to her and jumped to full readiness when he saw that she wore only bikini panties and that her full breasts lay bare for him. He slipped out of his clothes and stared down at her.

Ginger gulped at the sight of him, big and proudly erect. Moisture accumulated in her mouth as she gazed at him, and marvelled at the look of wonder on his face. Her arms opened to him. "Come hold me."

Even in her frantic desire, she could see the vulnerability in him. "Are you sure, Ginger? If you take me, there's no turning back for me. I love you, and right now I need you like I need air. But if it's not the same with you, say it this second, and I'm out of here. I don't want a taste. I want you."

Didn't he know what he meant to her? "Jason, Darling, don't you know I love you?"

In seconds she had him in her arms, and he was holding her, squeezing her, loving her. At last she could feel his masculine hardness against her body. Her head emptied of all thoughts but him, and the frissons of heat in which he enveloped her as he took his time kissing every part of her, teasing her breast with his tongue and sucking it until she thought she would lose consciousness. He moved to the other breast and let his fingers trail down her body until he reached the seat of her desire. Overcome with a passion she'd never known before, she begged for relief, but he ignored her and worked his magic at her lover's gate. Heat spiraled in her, and she undulated helplessly against him until frantic for relief, she took him into her hands to lead him to her portal, but he stopped her and shielded himself to protect her. She shifted her hips wildly. Urging. Begging.

He rose above her and looked down into her face. "Will you take me in?"

She didn't answer. She couldn't. Her hands guided his entrance as though they'd done it forever. The feeling of him inside her sent her passion to fever heights. He filled her, heated her, and rocked her. Driving. Stroking. Branding her until every muscle of her body seemed to pound, pump and squeeze as he wrung a scream from her and hurtled her into ecstasy. Seconds passed, and she heard his lover's shout of triumph as he gave her the essence of himself.

They lay locked together for a long while before he said, "I've never had such a feeling. I think you're okay too, but I want you to tell me."

She kissed his neck. "Jason, if there's any more I don't think I could bear it. If I had to die ten minutes from now, I don't believe I'd complain."

That grin again. The man had a magic smile. "You mean you've had enough of me? You wouldn't be kicking and screaming to live, so you could make love with me night and day? Good Lord, I'm a flop."

She pinched his buttock. "Don't get cocky. I may get mean and see what you're made of."

Both of his eyebrows elevated as he braced himself on his elbows and looked at her. "Honey, as hungry as I was when you walked in there with that wine, you may have just talked yourself into trouble."

She hadn't been exactly overstuffed. "I can always holler uncle."

His white teeth flashed a grin. "Yeah, you'll holler, all right. Maybe we both will." He tucked both arms beneath her shoulders and began to move.

An hour later, still locked together, he looked into her face, kissed her eyelids, and whispered, "I meant what I said, Ginger. I love you. From now on, it's you and me together. Do you understand?"

She didn't need the urging, and she didn't want any misunderstandings. "What does that mean, exactly?"

He touched her lips lightly with his own. "It means you marry me. Okay?"

She let her nose rub the tip of his nose. "We don't ask, these days?"

His grin sent a pulsating spasm to the spot in her where he'd most likely feel it. "You already agreed that there'll be no turning back, but I'll get on my knees if it'll make you happy."

"I don't need that formality, Jason. You love me. That's all I want."

Her heart sang as he wrapped her in a lovers' euphoria, spinning dreams of the joys to come. "I love you, Baby, he whispered, his voice hoarse and unsteady. "You're my life."

She thought of the pain that had gripped her when she'd walked away from him in Zimbabwe because it was the right thing to do, said a silent prayer of thanks that, after she'd despaired of ever seeing him again, Providence had given them another chance.

"I love you, too, Jason. I think I have from the moment I met you."

He pulled the cover over them. "Let's go to sleep."

"What about the wine?"

"Wine? Baby, I'm drunk as it is."

* * *

As the week went by, Jason didn't think he'd ever known such happiness. They spoke by phone several times during each day, and saw each other every evening—dinner, movies, concerts, or walks along the river on Roosevelt Island. He had even pulled weeds in her garden and enjoyed it. He made up his mind to ask her for a wedding date, because he hated leaving her every night.

Sunday night, a week after their engagement, he asked her to meet him the next day at Tiffany's to choose their rings. It seemed to him that so simple a thing as discussing the date and the rings had brought them even closer together. He chose a two carat round diamond flanked by single baguettes, and watched her eyes sparkle with approval. They left the store hand in hand, and he didn't think he could contain his joy. He kissed her at the corner of Broadway and Houston, and took a taxi back to his office.

Ginger read and reread the papers in front of her. Peppard and Lowe were her first and best corporate clients, and she valued them, but she didn't much like the idea of representing a landlord against a tenant, especially not in an eviction suit. She knew landlords used all kinds of trumped–up reasons to get rid of tenants in rent controlled buildings. The eviction would allow her client to raise the rent on the next tenant, or to get the apartment decontrolled. It was the slickest real estate game in New York. She got to work polishing her brief for Thursday's court appearance, though the job made her uncomfortable.

The light on her intercom blinked, and she flicked the button. "What is it, Edna?"

"Mr. Calhoun on line two, Ms. Hinds."

Her pulse plunged into a wild gallop as she anticipated the sound of his voice. "Hello, Jason."

"Ginger, what the hell do you mean by arguing for Peppard and Lowe to get my brother kicked out of his loft?"

"Your brother?"

"Don't tell me you couldn't have guessed it. How many E.E. Calhouns who make a living as a sculptor do you think there are?"

"Hold on there, Jason. You're assuming a lot. I didn't know you had a brother. And even if I *had* known it, you don't have the right to speak to me this way. I can argue for anybody I please."

He didn't relent. "We're talking about my brother, my flesh and blood. Don't you understand that? Eric's been in that loft for nine years, and he has some rights."

"He doesn't have the right to cast those molds and drive all the other tenants mad with that hammering. If you can't apologize, I want you to hang up."

"All right. Good—bye, Ginger."

She sat there stunned as the dial tone irritated her eardrum. When at last she was able to manage it, she buzzed her secretary. "Edna, who is E.E. Calhoun's lawyer?"

"Asa McKenzie."

She thought of calling Jason and asking why he hadn't taken the case for his brother, thought better of it, leaned back in her chair, and asked herself whether going on with that case was worth losing Jason. But she realized that he hadn't given her a choice.

She read the relevant statutes for the third time and decided that she could represent her client and maintain her integrity without implicating Eric unduly, but the weight in her heart nearly robbed her of her breath. Her private phone rang.

"If you go through with this, Ginger, you'll destroy any chance we may have of a future together."

"You're a lawyer, too, Jason, and you know this case is

registered for day after tomorrow. If I back out now, my client will sue me. I wouldn't ask you to do what you're requesting of me—please kick your career right down the drain, Ginger."

"So you won't do it? I'm sorry. Good–bye."

Jason hung up, walked to the window, and looked down at the people who rushed along Madison Avenue like ants busily collecting sugar. He didn't want a life without Ginger, but if she could put his own brother out in the street for a client who meant nothing to her but money, could he go ahead with their marriage? He loved his younger brother, and he refused to take sides against him. If that's the way she planned to play it, too bad. At least he'd found out before he said those fateful words.

If she'd made it through the past two days, she could do anything, Ginger told herself as she walked into Civil Court at 60 Center Street in lower Manhattan. She hadn't argued before that judge, and didn't know what to expect. And the jury for which she'd had to settle wasn't what she wanted, but she could work with it. She kept her glance on the door until she saw Jason enter with Asa McKenzie and another man who was obviously Jason's brother.

Without looking in the direction of the man she loved, she outlined her client's complaint and his demands, adding that as a tenant she sympathized with renters, but that landlords had rights that the courts were bound to uphold. Asa McKenzie followed with a rebuttal that seemed to sway the jury, but in the end it found in favor of Peppard and Lowe. No one would ever know the measure of her relief when McKenzie failed to put Eric on the stand, relieving her of the responsibility of cross–examining him. It was only upon hearing the verdict that she realized how badly she had wanted to lose.

* * *

Wooden legs propelled her into her apartment that evening. She'd sat in her office until after seven o'clock, mulling over the events of her life. Jason had to have known that he'd sandwiched her between a rock and a hard place when he'd suggested she drop the case. If there was a profession in which reputation was one's only passport, it was that of a lawyer, and you didn't desert your client at the last minute unless you'd just won the lottery and had planned to retire, anyway. She changed into a peasant skirt and blouse and went to Andy's Place. She had no appetite, but being among familiar faces beat the emptiness of her apartment.

She stopped short at the sight of Amos Logan and her friend, Clarice, in what appeared to be an intimate huddle. She'd hoped to find at least one of them there alone and anxious for company. Amos saw her and waved her over to the table.

"Haven't seen you in here lately, Ginger. Pull up a chair."

She leaned over and kissed Clarice on the cheek. "You're looking good, Girl. Want to let me in on the secret?" When Clarice blushed, Ginger found Amos from the corner of her eye and caught a grin on his usually straight face. Her head snapped around, and she stared at him until he laughed aloud and told her. "Don't look so shocked, Ginger. After all, it's June—Lovers' Month. That case been to trial yet?"

She nodded. "This morning."

"What's the matter? You lose it?"

She shook her head and looked away from them as she gathered her composure.

"Well if you won it, why're you in the dumps?"

"Oh. Oh," Clarice said. "You're not even warm, Amos. Ginger, why aren't you celebrating with Jason?"

Amos sipped his brandy. "Good question. Where is he?"

Ginger got up, "You two stay here and enjoy yourselves. I . . . I'm going to turn in. Call you tomorrow, Clarice."

She left hurriedly, bumping into the Reverend Armstrong. " 'Scuse me, Reverend," she said, and hurried on without waiting to hear his reply. She loved the neighborliness on Roosevelt Island, but that same warmth and friendliness sometimes deprived you of your privacy. Inside her apartment, she turned the radio on and raised the volume high, as though loud music could banish her thoughts and drown out her pain.

Jason sat on the edge of a desk in his brother's loft. "The engagement's off, Eric. I can't marry a woman who'd take this kind of case against my brother when I begged her not to do it."

Eric got up from the lotus position he'd taken on the floor and walked over to Jason. "What are you talking about? What's this got to do with Ginger?"

"I didn't tell you? Ginger is G.A. Hinds, Peppard and Lowe's attorney."

Eric sat down. "Well, I'll be. She's a good lawyer and a beauty, too. She took the case for one of my friends against his landlord, and won. Don't you think you should have introduced us?"

"No, I don't. I was too mad. Anyway, it's too late now. The water's under the bridge."

The heat of Eric's stare gave him an uneasy feeling. "You mean that after what you went through before you found that woman, you'd give her up for something this stupid? Look here, Jason, she was easy on me, and you know it. There's a clause in my lease that's written in bold, capital letters specifying that the property cannot be used for commercial purposes. I've been getting away with it for nine years. If I stay here it means the rent will be doubled, but I can easily afford that now, because my pieces are selling well."

Jason jumped from the desk. "You're telling me that landlord wasn't out to get you?"

Eric shrugged. "No. In fact, he'd warned me several times. You didn't ask to see the lease, and I didn't think to show it to you. McKenzie knew I was wrong, and he said he doubted I'd win. Man, you'd better go mend your fences."

Jason's breath was slow coming. "Yeah. You can say that again."

He didn't think calling her would help, but he phoned, anyway. No answer, so he left a message. "Ginger, I need to talk with you. Please call me."

Repeated calls with the same message on her answering machine brought no response. He took a taxi home, showered, changed his clothes, and left. If she was in New York, he'd find her.

Hadn't she told Clarice she'd call her tomorrow? Annoyed, she jerked upon the door without looking through the peephole and released an audible gasp. *"Jason!"*

"Do you mind if I come in?" He held a calla lily loosely wrapped in clear plastic that was tied with a white satin ribbon.

She moved aside to let him enter, but left the door open and leaned against the wall, her arms folded in front of her.

"Can we talk, Ginger?"

She closed the door and followed him to her living room. "About what, Jason? Do you want me to find your brother a place to stay? Or maybe rent a studio for him? Why are you here? Just say it, and I'll listen. I don't have the energy to hassle with you."

"Is that why you didn't take my calls?"

"You could say that."

"I realize you're angry with me, and—?"

She stood toe–to–toe with him. "Angry? You think I'm angry? Jason, don't use the word angry to me. *I hurt!*"

He reached for her and slowly withdrew his hand. "I know, and I'm hurting too. I made one of the biggest mistakes of my life when I asked you to drop that case. I don't exonerate myself, either—I'd probably still be fuming if Eric hadn't told me he'd been warned about breaking his lease, which specifically said the loft couldn't be used for commercial purposes, and he'd broken it every day for nine years. His landlord had a right to redress."

She placed her hand on her hips, laid her head to the side, and studied him. "I didn't think that was the problem. You said I was working against your brother, and asked me to drop the case."

"I know I did, but looking back, I know that didn't make sense. I've always been too protective of Eric, and he's never needed that. I came here to ask you to forgive me. I just don't see how I'm going to be happy apart from you, Ginger. I can't begin to envisage life without you."

The heaviness eased away from her chest, and her mind seemed to swirl as she gazed into the warmth of his eyes, saw the love there, and felt the scraps of her soul begin to fit themselves together again.

"How do I know it won't happen again, that you won't expect me to give up what is so dear to me if it suits you to do that?"

He held out his arms to her. "If we work together, it won't be necessary."

She looked at those arms, open and full of the love and sweetness that she adored, but she didn't move. "Work together, how?"

"Calhoun and Hinds, Attorneys at Law. What do you say?"

She tried not to show her reaction, but she knew the smile on her face had never been wider. "You'd better be glad C comes before H or it would be—"

He offered her the calla lily, and when she took it, he

swooped her into his arms. Joy suffused her as his scent, strength, and whole being wrapped her in his love, and his taste once more filled her mouth and heated her blood. She took his hand and led him to that place where love abounded, where they loosed their bodies into each other, swept away in a vortex of unearthly rapture.

Friends and relatives filled the chairs in the rose garden of Brooklyn's Botanical Garden. Wearing a yellow organdy dress and matching wide–brimmed hat and carrying yellow roses, Linda Jenkins walked up the aisle to the altar, faced the minister, and glanced back at her sister. In a white organdy dress and hat identical in style to her sister's and carrying Jason's calla lilies, Ginger glided on satin–slippered feet over the tiny yellow roses that Jason had given the flower girls to spread in his bride's path. She inhaled the many–hued roses that perfumed the garden with their June freshness, and thought how fortunate she was. She knew that a bride didn't wear white for a second marriage, but it was *her* wedding, and she wanted Jason to know that her life began anew with him. She tried to hold back the tears of joy when she saw him standing there beside Eric, so unorthodox, with his back to the altar looking at her. She grinned, because she knew that if he thought her unhappy he would chuck tradition and come to meet her.

When she reached him, he gave her hand a gentle squeeze and whispered, "I love you. Love you. I think I'll take wings and fly."

"Don't forget to carry me with you," she whispered back.

The minister cleared her throat, "Dearly beloved . . ."

Ginger heard no more as Jason turned fully to her, love shining in his eyes, and pledged his being to her. She heard herself repeat the words that made her his wife, felt the arms she loved so dearly wrap around her and the sweetness of his mouth skim over hers. She looked up at him and saw that special grin that always mesmerized her, and her pounding heart sent the blood speeding through her body.

"Love me?" he asked.

"Oh, yes," she said. " 'Til the end of time."

Dear Readers,

I hope you have taken Ginger and Jason to your hearts, and that you have enjoyed their rocky journey to happiness as much as I enjoyed writing it. Chance often plays a great part in what we get out of life, and so it was with these two lovers. In real life, few of us are blessed with that perfect mate, but our lives and those of our mates will be richer, more romantic, and fulfilling if we invest more of ourselves in our relationships. Neither Ginger nor Jason hit the jackpot on the first try, but both understood themselves, knew their needs, and could open themselves to true love when it found them. In that respect, we could take a lesson from them.

I must take this opportunity to thank you for your wonderful response to *BEYOND DESIRE* and *OBSESSION*. You've kept me busy on Sunday afternoons answering the hundreds of letters that pour into my mail box, and I have enjoyed every minute of it. My thanks also to Karen Thomas, my editor, for this opportunity to be in touch with you, and to the sellers and distributors who carry my books.

I love to hear from you, so don't forget to write. If you'll send me a self–addressed, legal–size envelope, I'll send you a bookmark and information on what I'm doing. Write me at P.O. Box 45, New York, N. Y. 10044-0045 . My web pages are http://www.infokart.com/gwynneforster and http://www.tlt.com/authors/gforster/dara.htm

My thanks for your continued support.

Sincerely yours,
Gwynne Forster

A LOVE MADE IN HEAVEN

FRANCINE CRAFT

CHAPTER ONE

"If Washington, DC, had nothing except the cherry blossoms in full bloom to offer, it would still be a great place."

Margo Hilliard looked at a gorgeous sunrise coming onto the horizon as she stood by the guardrail at Hains Point with Ron Hyman. The cherry blossoms were at the sides and back of them, resplendent in pre–peak, white blossom time.

Ron squeezed her hand lightly and smiled. "Actually," he said, "you outdo the cherry blossoms, sweetheart."

Margo laughed merrily. "You're a shameless flatterer, my good man, but keep it up."

For a long while they continued to watch the sunrise before Ron said, "Let's go right into the middle of this spring wonderland. Maybe we should be getting married in April."

"That would be beautiful," Margo said, "but I've had my hands full getting our wedding together for May."

"Any old time," Ron answered. "I wish we were already married." He sounded wistful, and Margo was touched.

They walked into the midst of the blossoming cherry

trees and looked with awe at all that beauty. A surprisingly large number of people were out at that early hour, but it was far from crowded. Later, this section of southwest DC would be jammed with traffic and people with cameras at the ready.

Ron, a photographer, was seldom without his cameras.

"You're not shooting much today," Margo said.

"I decided I'll concentrate on my wife today."

Margo looked up, startled at his grave face. "I'm not your wife quite yet," she said.

"You are, you know. I knew I'd marry you right from the beginning."

He was so sweet, Margo thought, but it wasn't as simple as that. Ron had been married before—to a perfect 10—and their love was said to have been the stuff of legends.

As they walked along, obviously in love with each other, bystanders saw a fairly tall, lovely woman with skin the color of strong tea and dark brown hair and obsidian eyes. She had an oval face, a high, square forehead, and a full mouth. Her nose was nondescript, and her expression was soft, vulnerable. Ron liked the way she seemed both sensual and fresh.

Glancing at Ron, Margo liked the fact that he was several inches taller than she, lean and sinewy, fit as much from his hectic schedule as from working out. His hair was coarse, and sooty black. He had dark, olive skin and big, white teeth in a wide, sensual mouth. He could be a model.

Now, looking at him, Margo asked, "Did you really feel you'd marry me from the first?"

"In my bone marrow, I *knew*," he said quietly. "You're what I've looked for all my life."

"What about Jill? You two had a splendid love, Ron."

He nodded, stopping by a bench. "Let's sit down," he said as a small, brown boy with a whistle ran up and smiled at them. They both smiled back. The boy ran back to his parents.

"My love for Jill was completely different," he said. "We

grew up together. Neither of us had ever known anybody else. Our parents were friends. We had pretty much the same friends. Oh, one day there are many things I'll tell you, but I have to ask you to wait. It tears me up to talk about Jill. But never doubt that I love you, Margo, more than you'll ever know."

He moved closer to her, tipped her chin up with his finger, and kissed her lightly on the lips. His body was tense, and she wondered now, as she often did, if she was being foolish to marry a man who had been so much in love with his first wife and obviously was still so hurt by her death in an accident that he couldn't talk about her.

"People say we all have one great love," Margo said softly. "You're mine, Ron."

"You were going to marry Tony Willis."

"Tony and I were young. We had a lot of fun together. I wonder now if we were ever in love. But you were very much in love with Jill."

"I'd never deny it," he said gently, "but my love for you is so different. We think of men as being so damned strong, able to fashion our own security, but I never felt secure with Jill the way I feel with you."

As she looked at him with her sloe-eyed gaze he felt his heart turn over. One day they *had* to talk about his marriage to Jill, but when? The very hounds of hell seemed hard on his heels when he thought about his dead first wife, an automobile accident victim. He would talk with Margo in the near future, but it couldn't be now. He needed time, and the two years that had passed since Jill's death didn't begin to be enough time.

A petal blew off a nearby pink Southern magnolia tree and onto Margo's lap. She picked it up.

"I need a whole batch of these to play he loves me, he loves me not."

"What do *you* think?"

Without hesitation she answered, "I think you do, or I wouldn't be marrying you."

"That's my girl. You'll have me when everything and everybody else has gone."

Margo grew silent. He didn't stint in declaring his love, and yes, he *acted* as if he loved her, but so had Tony, right up until he told her they wouldn't be getting married because he had fallen in love with someone else. He'd been cheating even as they were engaged. The woman he left her to marry had been pregnant.

"Penny for your thoughts."

"I was thinking about Tony."

"I'm not Tony. I'd never pull what he pulled, never hurt you that way."

"No, I don't believe you would. We have something rare, Ron. Let's nurture it. I think we're honest with each other. Let's value that."

Ron expelled a harsh sigh. "I'm not completely honest with you, my love. I can't be just yet. There are things I have to talk with you about one day, but I can't talk about those things now. Can you, will you, bear with me?"

Margo paused a moment before she said, "Yes, darling, of course I will. I want to hear what you have to tell me, but I'll wait."

His voice had been urgent, passionate. Margo was certain it had to do with Jill. Jill—the 10.

The April air was warmer than usual, and an even warmer day had been forecast. Margo's navy knit slacks and jacket and her navy–and–white striped silk blouse were all good seasonal garb. Ron's even more informal gray Dockers slacks, darker gray jacket, and his gray–and–white striped cotton shirt had all been selected for him by Margo.

"Jill was your model," she said. "You must have come here often?" The words came to her lips quite unbidden. She hadn't meant to ask.

He nodded. "Actually, in the end Jill wasn't doing as much modeling for me. She was really making it as a runway model, and she was gone often. But yes, we came here to Hains Point a lot. Does that bother you?"

Margo shrugged. "It shouldn't, but I do think you loved her so much that I wonder if anyone else could ever come close."

There, she'd said what she hadn't said in the two years she'd known him.

Ron looked at her a long moment. He was climbing the walls with wanting her at that very instant, yet he'd be lying if he said that he hadn't thought of Jill like that at times. Hell, he couldn't answer her statement, but he knew he'd try.

"Just *anybody* couldn't come close," he said. "You don't just come close with me, Margo. You're about as close to me as I am to myself."

"Thank you for saying that," Margo said. She felt better, but she knew the doubts would linger, and she talked to herself about this. She had to be confident of his love. He would talk to her about what he and Jill had shared, and she would understand. One day. It needed to be soon.

Driving up Sixteenth Street, Northwest, in Ron's navy Catera Cadillac, Margo listened to the smooth purr of the heavy engine and leaned back in comfort on the beige leather upholstery. Ron was already a highly successful photographer. He put a hand on her knee and stroked it.

They were on the way to his house on upper Seventeenth Street, a house he had shared with Jill. Ron drove at a leisurely speed. Few people were about. In just a couple of hours the streets would be fairly full of churchgoers and others. She opened the window of the car and let the sharp breeze in.

Ron's house was a two–story buff brick, with massed evergreens and azaleas in front. He pulled up in front of the house and cut the engine, got out, and came around to let her out.

"You're such a gentleman," she told him.

"Guarding treasure," he said evenly.

Margo laughed. Even if she did come in second best to his first wife, she loved this man. It hurt, she admitted, that she wasn't first in his heart. She didn't think she was, and others had hinted that he'd never love anyone the way he'd loved Jill. He acted with love, though, and they were getting married. This wasn't a perfect world, she thought now. And yes, she'd take it. She'd *take* it.

They paused in Ron's large living room, which was furnished with Spanish decor. Ron had first brought her there when they'd begun dating, not quite a year prior.

"Orange juice? Coffee?" he asked.

Margo shook her head. "I drank orange juice before I left home. I'm cutting back on coffee, and we'll be having breakfast at your parents' house in less than an hour."

"Or a little longer," he said, grinning.

Margo smiled. "Along with that silver tongue, you have a wicked leer, too," she teased.

"Lady," he said, "with what you pack, a saint might leer—"

"And you're no saint," she finished for him.

He drew her close and kissed her long and deep, and her heart fluttered and she felt herself melting in his arms. He was so dear. Ron pressed her lissome body into his, feeling her lush outlines, and he was close to crying inside because he held back feelings he didn't want to hold back. He loved her as much as he could love, but he thought now that was the problem. Margo deserved the best there was, the absolute best he had to offer. When was he going to be able to give her that?

"You have that glint in your eyes," she said. "It might not be a bad idea for us to go to your parents' house early. I seem to be very effective at getting you stalled in certain places."

"Love makes the world go round, sweetie," Ron said,

laughing. "I'll stop anything I'm doing to make love to you any old time."

"But not this morning," she said. "Right now I'm interested in getting my breakfast."

"Frigid," he said, smiling. "I'll fix your breakfast. My parents will understand. Dad, anyway."

"There's nothing to understand, because we're going to be there a bit early."

"Spoilsport. Dominating. Cruel." He ran a hand over his coarse, black, close–cropped hair. "Okay, you win. I was going to beat your socks off in a game of Scrabble, but I'll be kind. What I want to do is make some shots of you. Willing?"

She nodded. She liked the photos he took of her. Margo knew she was very attractive when she set out to be, but hers was the type of beauty that many possessed. It came from good care and hard work and a loving heart—not to mention soul.

Ron had photographic equipment all over the house. "What're your favorite cameras?" she asked. "You're so broad in your shooting range."

Ron thought for a moment. "Far and away the Leica you gave me. I'm a genius with that in my hands. Minolta runs second. Hell, several cameras run second. You know my father saw fit to put a lot of money into cameras for me when I was just beginning. "Reach for the best,' he said, 'and you'll always come out ahead. And boy, that means the best that's in *you.*' "

Ron had married the beauteous Jillian Wentworth, a Maryland state senator's daughter, and they had had four years of storybook happiness. Then she had died. Poor Ron.

They sat on a long, beige sofa and she stroked his face, thinking she wished she could make it all up to him. She certainly intended to do what she could.

Now he said, "You'll never know what your having that Leica made up for me meant to me."

"I'm glad," she murmured.

Looking around her as Ron set up his lens angles, Margo saw with pleased surprise that he was using the camera she had given him.

Margo was an editor for *Wedding Belles*, a Rockville–based magazine, and Jeff, one of their photographers, had told her about the camera and helped her have it equipped. It had cost a fortune, but Ron had already asked her to marry him and she was floating in her love for him, and he absolutely loved that camera.

Ron turned the heat up and removed her jacket. He posed her on a high stool and took the barrette and pins that fastened her moderately long, dark brown, chemically straightened hair so that it fell to her shoulders.

"Give me some pizzazz, lady," he drawled lazily. "Show me what you've got."

At times like this, Margo forgot that she wasn't beautiful. She certainly felt that she was with Ron's eyes on her as if she were the most important woman in the world.

Another thing she kept thinking as he took her from different angles was that there were few mementos and photos around the house now. When she had begun to come here, there had been many. A stunning painting of Jill had been over the living room fireplace. It wasn't there any longer.

They had shot for a good half hour when Ron came to her and lifted her off the stool. "At least shooting you keeps my mind off making love to you. Today, you're the essence of glamour."

She started to ask him about the painting, but thought better of it. It really touched her that he would be kind enough to remove signs of Jill from his house, probably for her comfort.

He went to the window and stood looking out. After a few minutes she went and stood by his side.

"Penny for your thoughts," she said.

He clasped his hands behind his back for a moment, then touched her face. "I've been thinking about this a lot, Margo. I want to build us a new house, or maybe we can find one we like, but I don't think I want to live here. What do you think?"

He'd never mentioned this before. Margo thought a moment. "It's a lovely house. Homey."

"Would you mind if I wanted terribly to move out of here?"

Margo looked at his somber face. "Why no, darling. Of course not. We can build, or find another place."

She felt an unexpected relief that he no longer wanted to live in this house he'd shared with Jill. His face was pained now, the way it often got if anyone spoke of his first wife. He had put away the mementos of her, and now he wanted to put away the house they'd lived in.

There's something strange here, Margo thought, and she needed to know what it was.

"One more month," he said, drawing her close again, "and we'll be man and wife. I can't tell you how much I want us to be married."

"As I do," she said slowly, "but it's getting hectic. I'm about to propose that we elope."

"The people who've already sent gifts would surely kill us."

"The wedding's going to leave me disabled with exhaustion."

"I'll do whatever more I can to give you a hand," he said, a quick concern on his face.

"Pay me no mind," she answered. "I just want to make certain you know these are some of the happiest days of my life."

Ron got her jacket, helped her into it, and slipped his on.

"Well, we're off to my beloved parents' house," he said, "where we've been promised a great breakfast. Ready?"

Margo nodded. She was as ready as she'd ever be. Dr. Hyman was a wonderful man, and he clearly liked her. Mrs. Hyman was another kettle of fish. She and Jill had been soulmates, and she didn't let Margo forget it.

Ron's parents, Laurette and Wallace, lived in Rockville, Maryland, in a spacious, white colonial house. Ron let Margo and himself in with his key. Dr. Hyman was a retired dean of the dental school at Howard University. Mrs. Hyman was a retired chemistry professor from the same school.

"It's good to see you again, Margo," said Dr. Hyman, a dark chocolate, silver–haired bear of a man. "It won't be long now before you're a member of this family."

Margo smiled. He always made her feel so welcome. Mrs. Hyman was a pale, reserved woman with white silk hair and Margo understood quite well that she would never take Jill's place in this family so far as Laurette Hyman was concerned.

The house was formally furnished, with mauve and pale blues and violet in the living room and carefully color coordinated decor in the rest of the house.

"Breakfast in just a little while," Mrs. Hyman said. "Mrs. Allen is giving it her best."

Nora Allen was their maid, and Mrs. Hyman was careful to keep a maid–mistress division in place. She was courteous and pleasant, and she called Nora Mrs. Allen, but something in her manner revealed that she didn't consider her on the same level of humanity.

"Let's wait in the library, shall we?" Mrs. Hyman said, as they walked down the first floor hallway that was lushly carpeted in deep mauve and violet.

Laurette flung the door open, and Margo suppressed a gasp of surprise. Facing them was the splendid painting of Jill that she had seen at Ron's house when she had first visited him. Then the painting had disappeared. Margo had not asked about it.

"Mother, I thought you were going to put that painting in your office upstairs," Ron said.

"That's what I suggested," Dr. Hyman said.

Mrs. Hyman shrugged. "It's such a beautiful portrait. Why hide it? Besides, it keeps me close to Jill. You don't mind, do you, dear?" she asked, turning to Margo.

Margo shook her head, taking in the painting—A full-length rendition of Jill in a yellow silk ball gown, with a diamond tiara atop her pale brown hair that spilled over her shoulders. She looked the young queen she had been. Jill Wentworth was one of two daughters of state Senator Marley Wentworth, a real estate mogul in the Washington area. They, too, lived in Rockville.

"I don't mind at all," Margo said, but she found that she did mind. She wanted Laurette Hyman to like her, and in the year she had been Ron's friend, then his fiancée, she had come to believe that that wouldn't happen.

Laurette patted her hand. "I didn't think you would."

"I still think a better place for it would be your office," Ron said stubbornly.

It was Laurette's turn to shrug. "When you have something that gorgeous, you want the world to see it," she said staunchly.

The library was pine–panelled, lined with books, many of which were handbound, teakwood furniture, deep–cushioned, black leather chairs, and a black leather sofa. They settled into a conversational circle

"Well, you have the man, never mind the picture," Dr. Hyman told Margo. "We loved Jill, no question about it, but we love you now. You can't know how happy you've made our son. He went through a year of hell after Jill died. Then he met you."

A warm look passed between father and son.

"I'm happy to know that," Margo said. "He's certainly made me very happy."

It seemed to Margo that Laurette sighed, but she couldn't be sure.

"You're looking well, Margo," Laurette finally said. "If you've been out to see the cherry blossoms as Ron said you would, you've been basking in glory. But so early. My goodness, don't tell me you're a romantic like my son."

"I'm afraid I am," Margo said.

"Without romance, mother, life wouldn't be worth living," Ron said.

"You're absolutely right, son." Ron's father looked quietly thoughtful.

Laurette looked at Ron fondly, then nodded at the portrait. "You and Jill had something I believe few people in this world ever know," she said. "Your romance, your wedding, was a sensation. Soon, you would have had children, I believe." She brushed a tear from her eye with a snow–white, linen handkerchief.

"Mother!" Ron said sternly. "This is not the time nor the place to talk about Jill. She's dead, and let her rest in peace."

Laurette sat perfectly still as her husband and her son held her in a steady gaze. She looked at Margo, her face gone suddenly somber, and said, "I'm sorry, Margo. Please understand how much I loved her. I can hardly be held accountable for that. Like his father, I'm glad you've made Ron so happy. For a while, I thought we'd lose him. I'm grateful to you, and will you forgive me?"

"There's nothing to forgive," Margo said easily. "I know a love like theirs isn't easy to get over, if you ever can. I can only hope that the love I have for Ron, and his for me, will help him to get over Jill in time."

"Well put," Dr. Hyman cut in. "I think you two are going to have a good, solid, healthy marriage. I just hope we won't lose any time before hearing the patter of little feet."

Margo blushed, and Ron grinned from ear to ear.

Mrs. Allen came in and announced that breakfast was served. Laurette rose. "You'll want to freshen up," she said to Margo.

Margo got up and went out into the hall, where she found Russell, Ron's brother, in his wheelchair.

"Margo!" He held out his arms and she bent and hugged him.

"Where've you been keeping yourself?" she asked.

"Well, I've been hitting the law books pretty hard, and I'm actually thinking of moving out of this antiquated mansion. I believe I've found a condo I can live in and with."

Margo's eyes twinkled. "Now find a woman you can love, and your life is perfect."

To her chagrin, Russ's face went somber. "In time, maybe," he murmured, "and maybe never. Let's take it one step at a time."

"Russ, you're such a good guy."

Russ grimaced. "I hardly think my dear brother would agree with you on that."

"He's never said anything to *me* against you. Oh, I notice tension between you two, but there's often tension between siblings. You're seven years older than he is."

"Yeah, but there's more to it than that. I think it's time we opened up to you and included you in our family pain as well as the good stuff. Did you know I was driving drunk when Jill was killed?"

"No, only that you were driving."

"Well, I was, but I haven't touched a drop since it happened. Oh God, I—"

He was suddenly perspiring profusely. "I should have kept my mouth shut, at least for the moment," he said. "I have no right to burden you with this, at least until you're married. I'm sorry, Margo."

Two apologies from members of the Hyman family in the span of a half hour, both having to do with Ron's first wife—his first wife, whose presence had enchanted the Hyman family, and whose death seemed to have shattered it.

"Don't be sorry," she said huskily, her heart aching for Russ. "You're paying a heavy price for the accident. Russ, others must have told you before—you have to forgive yourself."

"Would that I could, sister—in—law. And even better, why couldn't it have been me instead of Jill?"

"Don't talk like that!"

"You think my brother doesn't wish it?"

"I don't believe that. No one of us does. The accident happened the way it happened. Forgive yourself, Russ," she pleaded. "There's so much good you do. You work with inner city youth, many of whom you've been able to help greatly. Think what their lives would be without you. Don't talk like this. And come have breakfast with us."

Russ sighed heavily and shook his head. "I'd like to because you'll be there, but I have somewhere to go now, and I hardly think my beloved brother would welcome my presence."

Margo stood looking down at Russ. "There's still so much feeling between you and Ron. You're brothers for all time to come."

"And you're a sweetheart. Give me another hug, and I'm off. You've fortified and uplifted me for this day, anyway."

Margo bent, kissed his cheek, and hugged him again.

"Hey, I wondered if you'd gotten lost," Ron said, coming out the hall. He nodded coolly at Russ.

"How's it going?" he asked.

"I don't complain since it never helps," Russ answered. "Well, I'm off to the inner city. I'd like to snatch every kid I'm mentoring out of there and bring them home with me."

"You're helping them greatly, even if you can't do that," Margo told him.

"Take care," Ron said, his voice breaking a little. No

matter what Russ had done, there were bonds between them, but he would not, could not, stop hating him for what he had done. They both watched as Russ wheeled himself to the front door, out onto the porch, and down the ramp and to his specially equipped car. Then, silently, they went to join Laurette and Dr. Hyman at the breakfast table.

Laurette Hyman was known the city over as a gracious hostess. Her ego wouldn't let her do less for Margo just because she didn't really care for her. Margo was nice enough, she supposed, but Ron deserved the woman he'd first married. They were a prince and a princess. *Margo*, Laurette mused. *Attractive. Successful.* She certainly seemed to love Ron and he her, but Laurette couldn't imagine that he loved her as he'd loved Jill. She brought her attention back to the present.

Breakfast began with freshly squeezed orange juice and varied melon balls, then fresh, broiled salmon, eggs Benedict, and flaky croissants. An array of blueberry, strawberry, and raspberry Danish pastries wafted a mouthwatering aroma from the buffet.

Mrs. Allen served well. Margo found her dignity so compelling. She was a small, brown wren of a woman, seemingly compassionate, smart. Margo had often wondered with the visits she had made here what the woman's story was.

"I see Russ didn't choose to have breakfast with us," Dr. Hyman said. "He's off to help those kids he's so crazy about. I love my son for that."

"Maybe the accident did some good," Ron said. "God knows he caused enough damage."

"Ron," Laurette said crisply, "dear, I do wish you could find it in your heart to be kinder to your brother. He suffers, too. And I'm proud that he's not letting that accident destroy him. I don't think you could have loved Jill more than I did, and I've forgiven him."

"He's your son, mother. Of course you've forgiven him."

"And he's your brother."

Dr. Hyman held up a hand. "This conversation has got to be pretty awkward and uncomfortable for Margo. Let's let it rest, could we? I'd say Margo understands about Russ not having breakfast with us this morning."

"Yes," Margo murmured. "I do understand."

Margo had often marvelled at the chameleon qualities that Laurette possessed. Now she gave them all her sunniest smile.

"How are the wedding plans progressing, my dear? Everything on schedule?"

"Well, I've had a six-month wedding planner in place from the beginning," Margo said, switching moods herself. "So far, so good. I'm down to my one-month section, and my boss is being great about it."

"It's so fascinating that you work for *Wedding Belles*. I've always thought your job is the next best thing to being an artist," Laurette said.

"I like it very much."

"I never dreamed a wedding could be so much hard work," Ron commented.

"Well, with Jill—"

Dr. Hyman put his foot down with a glance at his wife. She flushed and looked down, then gave Margo a bright smile. "I'd love to address and mail your announcements."

Margo gave her a warm smile. "Well, thank you, and I appreciate your offer, but Jimilu, my best friend, has already started. There are other things I'd be proud for you to do, like sending the wedding announcements to the newspapers. Oh, thank Heaven we're making this semi–formal."

"Oh yes," Laurette began, and it was plain she wanted to say something about the high fashion wedding of Ron and Jill—a wedding held at the National Cathedral, with many dignitaries as guests, with a United States senator's daughter as flower girl and the son of an African country's prime minister as ring bearer. A glance from her husband silenced her again. Margo was beginning to appreciate Dr. Hyman more and more.

CHAPTER TWO

On the way to Margo's home, Ron felt downcast. These days he could hardly bear to be around his mother with her constant chatter about Jill. He felt she'd have to like Margo if she'd let herself know her, but she stubbornly resisted.

Sitting close to him, Margo commented, "You're so quiet. That was a lovely breakfast, and it was nice of your mother to ask us."

"Yeah," Ron said, "the old girl sometimes does some things right." He picked up her hand and squeezed it. "Dad's crazy about you."

"That makes us even, because I love your father, and my grandpa is sold on you as a husband for me."

"What about *your* feelings on the subject?"

"I'm hooked on you, angel, for good. I know where home is for me."

"You're sweet."

"No, I'm just honest."

It seemed a short trip from Rockville to upper Sixteenth Street, where Margo lived with her grandfather. She let

them in with her key and was pleasantly surprised to find
that he had two guests, her best friend Jimilu Worley and
Grace Smith, his longtime lady friend.

Margo kissed Grace's cheek as Jimilu, a deep chocolate,
satin–skinned woman, got up and hugged her.

"Oh, but we're putting it on today, aren't we? Girlfriend,
you look mah–vel–ous!"

"Plain old navy knit suit," Margo said. "Plain old striped
blouse. Plain old me."

"Nothing plain about any of you good–looking women
here," Ron said gallantly.

Jimilu hugged him. "If Margo ever tries to leave you,"
she said to Ron, "I'll personally take her to have her head
examined. For my money, you're the best thing I've ever
seen in husband material." She stopped and looked at
Ron, smiling.

"I ran into your brother, Russ, yesterday. We both work
with inner city children in a tutoring and mentoring pro-
gram. He's quite a guy."

It struck Margo that Ron seemed to close up at the
mention of his brother.

"Yes, he is quite a guy," he said drily. Jimilu and Margo
exchanged puzzled looks.

Gramps Summerlin—Jesse Roy Summerlin—Margo's
grandfather, a tall, pecan–brown, silver–haired man, had
been headed for the kitchen, but he came back in to hug
Margo and greet Ron.

"Well, I see you've got your Sunday–go–to–meeting
clothes on," Margo said. "Are you and Grace going out?"

"A little later," Grace said. She was a pleasantly plump,
ginger–colored, never married woman with a merry, round
face and the voice of a much younger woman.

"Don't let us stop you," Ron said.

"We won't," Gramps said, laughing. "We're aware that
you two are all the company each other needs."

"Look," Jimilu said, "even though I knew you two would
be having breakfast at your folks' house, I made shrimp

and crab gumbo too good to keep just for myself. I made
a lot, and I brought some for you all."

"I may be full now, but before I leave I'll certainly eat
my share. Thanks, Jimilu," Ron said.

"Yes, and I'll eat right along with him, but I am stuffed
now," Margo added.

"Well, we've eaten our share, too, Jesse and I, and I'd
guess part of yours, too," Grace said.

"You'd better not have, because you'll find yourself making new batch of gumbo. You wouldn't know that Jimilu
has never been to Louisiana." Margo looked at Grace with
mock sternness.

Jimilu laughed. "Good cookbooks are wonderful friends
to have."

"Yes," Margo said, "and people who *own* good cookbooks are wonderful friends to have."

"You look as if you're on your way somewhere special,"
Ron said to Jimilu, who was dressed in a cranberry red suit
with matching cranberry pumps.

Margo whistled at her, and the very attractive Jimilu—
who never really believed in her attractiveness—blushed.

"Well, I love compliments," Jimilu said, "even if I see
myself as part mud hen. I had a mean grandmother who
never failed to tell me, 'Pretty is as pretty does, missy.' I
guess it sank in to the bone."

Margo reflected that there was something wonderfully
warm and giving about Jimilu, but she often bore an aura
of sadness. *She's thirty,* Margo thought, *and should have three
or four kids and a great husband by now.* She and Margo were
close enough to be sisters, the way Ron and Russ should
be as brothers.

Her mind amended, *Close, the way Ron and Russ once had
been.*

Jimilu seemed nervous. "I guess I'd better be getting
on to my meeting," she said.

"Would you consider it nosy if I asked where?" Margo
smiled at her friend. "You're more jittery than I've seen

you lately, yet you're positively glowing. Would this meeting have to do with your inner city group?"

Jimilu nodded. "Yes, We're having a church meeting concerning these kids, and we're getting so much cooperation from church members." A nurse, Jimilu loved helping others.

"Hmmm," Margo said, grinning. "And would a certain man who shall remain nameless be slated for that same meeting?"

Jimilu chuckled. "He's the chief speaker, and one of our best workers."

They looked at each other in happy conspiracy, causing Ron to look from one to the other.

"What're you two up to?" he demanded. "Out to lead some guy a merry chase?"

Jimilu looked a little less happy. "I wish," she said shortly.

Ron looked bothered at Jimilu's apparent consternation. "Look, Jimilu, I certainly didn't mean that in a negative way. Any man you're interested in ought to consider himself a lucky dude." He caught Jimilu's hand, pressed it, and let it go.

"Thank you," Jimilu said. "I've really got to scoot. You two have fun. And look, the wedding stuff I'm doing is coming along fine. Rehearsal is set up, and I'm checking everything off day by day."

Gramps and Grace went out, saying that they would be back late and not to wait up for them.

After they had gone, Jimilu shook her head. "Boy, the life in today's senior citizens. Gramps at seventy–five, Grace at sixty–nine. They're having a ball. Make no mistake about that."

Margo raised her eyebrows. "Glow like that a few days longer," she said, "and you're going to find yourself having a ball, too."

"Then I'll glow harder," Jimilu came back. She looked

wistfully at the table that went the length of one wall, set up for displaying wedding gifts.

"What do you think about showing them so early?" Margo asked. "I've opened them all, but I don't think I want to put them out before a week or so ahead. No point in going out of our way to attract thieves. And some of these presents are *expensive*. I got extra insurance."

"That sounds about right to me," Jimilu said, getting up. "You have good security, but even with the best of security . . . we'd better not leave too much out until the last moment." She paused, then added, "I'm working hard to have you bright–eyed and raring to go on your wedding day. I'll see you two later. My fate awaits me."

When they were alone, Ron and Margo went up to her apartment, where she occupied the entire second floor. It was a wonderfully comfortable place, with big rooms and midnight blue carpeting. Margo had favored a decor of navy and other shades of blue, with aqua and shocking pink accents. She and Ron settled on the couch.

"Could I make you a drink?" Margo asked. "Or red wine?"

Ron shook his head.

"You really are quiet, darling. What's wrong?"

For a moment he hunched his shoulders. "Somehow a drink is the last thing I want when I see Russ," he said. His eyes looked bleak.

Margo placed her hand on Ron's face. "Can you just not forgive him for the accident?" she asked.

Ron was silent for a long moment. "God, I wish I could. You don't know how *much* I wish it."

"It's still hurting you so inside, my darling. Perhaps with your forgiving him, you'd be letting go of at least some of the pain."

In answer, Ron pulled her close and kissed her, his tongue going deep into her mouth. *And yes*, she thought, *this takes away thoughts of all else, but I don't want him to answer*

*my deepest questions with passionate kisses, as much as I crave
them.*

"Ron," she began.

"Let it go, Margo," he said with more sharpness than
he had intended. "I wish to God I *could* talk about it, but
I can't. One day I'll be able to talk, and you'll know, but
not now."

Margo knew that he walked close to some perilous emotional ledge, and she dared not cause him to lose his
footing.

"I'm sorry," she said contritely.

"No, *I'm* sorry. You deserve the best I have to offer, not
ragged snatches of my past. Am I hurting you, Margo,
when I tell you I have to wait until I can face this?"

Hurting her? Yes, he was hurting her, she thought, but
she knew that was not his intention. She was sure that he
loved her, as she loved him. But a part of him lay locked
in limbo, and more and more she was beginning to feel
she needed a whole love that held back nothing.

"You are hurting me a little, Ron," she said truthfully,
"but I know your heart is with me. I love you, darling, and
I can bear it. Especially when you say that you *will* tell me
what's in your heart."

"Count on it," he said.

He lay with his head in her lap, thinking how much he
loved her. Yet he couldn't deny that his past had this
terrible hold on him. He had been through hell when Jill
died. Could he take that kind of pain again? Even if he
forgave his brother, could he wipe out or heal from the
merciless emotional plunder of his very soul?

He and Margo had been drawn together when they'd
talked about hurt and past loves. They'd both been volun-
teers at Arena Stage—she as an usher, he as a stagehand
helper, handling some of the publicity photography. He'd
admired her laid back style, her warmth and generosity of
spirit. He felt good when he was with her, felt there was
nothing he couldn't do with her at his side.

The old pain never let him remember how much like this he'd felt with Jill.

"Do you know how much I love you?" Margo asked him.

"I think I do," he said, "but I don't think you *could* love me half as much as I love you. I'd follow you to hell if it became necessary," he said.

She lifted her face for his kiss, and her body was swept with liquid fire, wanting him. She felt completely relaxed, with a delicious warmth sweeping through her. He sat up and turned to her and she wound her arms around his neck, pulling him closer, felt the steady drum of his heartbeat against her own.

"Margo, my darling," he whispered, "don't let me lose you."

"You never could," she answered. "We'll be together, Ron. It's what I want, if it's what you want. Us raising kids, going to the heights, growing middle–aged, then old. The whole nine yards."

With a deep sigh, Ron said, "I have some film to run. Glamour shots of my last wedding shoot. They want them tomorrow morning, if possible."

Margo was disappointed. Was he pulling away? Did it have to do with him and Jill? Then he said, "I forgot to ask Gramps to give me his ideas on a new house for us. He has such good ideas on building. Remind me next time."

Margo grew thoughtful. "There's no rush, is there?"

Ron clenched his fists for a moment. "I'm beginning to think there *is* a rush, honey. I don't like the thought of living with you too long in my present house." He sat thinking for a while before he said, "I'm beginning to be afraid the poison of what happened with Jill's death will infect our life together, and I won't have that."

He was tense, and his voice was strained.

"Ron," she said, "don't worry about me. I think I see now, in ways I never have in the time I've known you, how very hurt you were." She hesitated. "Honey, should we perhaps delay the wedding a bit? I wouldn't mind."

"No. I want us to be married as soon as possible. I'd elope tonight if I didn't know you *want* this wedding."

His answer warmed her. She kissed him with a slow, lingering meeting of mouths and tongues, yet she sensed that he wanted to get away for the moment. How much she ached with wanting to help him heal the terrible pain he so plainly suffered.

"I'm going to go," he said then. "Are you going to be all right? We've built each other up on the prelude to lovemaking side a whole lot this afternoon. I feel as if I'm leaving you in the lurch."

"I'll manage," she said. "There's always tomorrow."

Margo went down to the kitchen and got the gumbo for him to take with him.

After he left, Margo stretched out on the couch, her mind in a semi–daze. Soon she would be Mrs. Ronald Elliott Hyman, with a man she adored, who showed that he adored her.

But some part of her man lay chained to his first wife, for whose death he couldn't seem to forgive his older brother—The brother he'd once hero–worshipped.

There was Dr. Hyman, who liked her very much. And Laurette, his wife, who much preferred her son's first wife.

Margo had to admit that doubt was beginning to creep in. What if Ron were forcing his love? She pondered it clearly, and didn't think so. When they came together, the passion was explosive. They liked so many of the same things, and they both wanted children secure in their parents' love.

Don't borrow trouble, she told herself. *Even love isn't perfect.* And a mocking voice came to her: *Oh yes, some love is perfect.* From what she had heard, hadn't Ron's and Jill's love been? She batted the thought away, but it wouldn't stay.

Slowly she walked into her bedroom where a silver coffee set, a gift, peeked up from its filmy covers. She thought of her wedding planner, which, she'd kept for six months. There were things to do at each month's interval. Then two weeks. Then one. Then the days down to the day of the wedding.

She decided to take a leisurely bath, ran the water, undressed, and lingered in a tub of warm water with powdered oatmeal and jasmine oil. She wished for Ron. They often bathed together in frolic and fun. She wished Ron hadn't had to leave early; she longed for the time when he wouldn't be leaving at all.

As Margo lounged in the tepid, soothing water, her mind wandered to Tony Willis, whom she had been engaged to marry three years ago. For a moment she tried to stave off the memories, but they rushed in, anyway

Tony was the scion of a publishing dynasty of the Willises of Washington, DC, and Baltimore—handsome, ruddy skinned and dashing. Margo couldn't believe her luck in landing him. They had met at a mutual friend's wedding, and he had rushed her with his constant presence, expensive gifts, a ten carat engagement ring, and trips to Aruba, Africa, and Europe.

Then, days before they were to be married, he had come to her to confess that he had gotten another woman pregnant and would marry that woman. It had never occurred to her not to trust him.

Now it was one month before her wedding to another man who sometimes seemed to be emotionally leaving her in his grief for a former wife.

A few goosebumps sprinkled her skin. Could she take it if something happened, and she lost Ron? "I'm strong," she murmured. "And Ron isn't like Tony at all."

Stepping out of the tub, drying off, Margo saw her reflection in the mirrored wall. She could be a bit thinner, but she was satisfied. Hers was a good, healthy, well-tended body, lissome. She was no fashion model, but she thought she'd do very well, thank you.

She went into her bedroom and slipped into a new white

crepe gown from her trousseau, using it to bolster her flagging spirits. Ron would tell her more about his love for Jill at some time, as he had promised. Until then, there was nothing to do but wait.

CHAPTER THREE

Sitting at her desk on Monday morning three weeks later, Margo felt good. Unlike Tony, Ron wasn't going to come up a new daddy with another woman at the last minute. She was sure of that.

She had dressed carefully in a close–fitting, beige knit dress and had put on a multicolored, long bead necklace and matching earrings. The dress was easy to get into and out of—she had had a wedding gown fitting.

Margo glanced around at her office, which was off white, with custom–fitted furniture and a curved desk. She had furnished it with many personal touches like a large, lapis lazuli vase and colorful Sierra Club posters. She also had added one gorgeous poster of Denzel Washington.

Helen Adams, her boss, managing editor of *Wedding Belles,* a magazine for brides, stuck her head in the door.

"Butterflies still staying in place?" she asked brightly.

"They'd better," Margo said, "because I don't have time to pamper them."

"That's my girl. May I come in?"

"Please do. I have a lot of questions to ask you."

Helen was a woman nearing fifty who had helped start *Wedding Belles* in her early forties. She often confessed that she was shocked at the speed with which the magazine had built up a loyal following.

"For a woman who's been married three times and made a failure of all three, it's remarkable that I hit the nail on the head with this magazine," she often said.

Big–boned and easygoing, with milk chocolate skin and close–cropped black hair, Margo had always found Helen a love to work for.

Helen came in, sat down and crossed her gorgeous legs. She always wore heels to show them off, along with her shapely feet. Margo smiled.

"One day," she said, "you're going to get a man who understands your drive and appreciates your success."

Helen laughed. "And one day we're going to find that the moon really is made of green cheese. Please don't forget we're having a bridal shower for you today, and you'll need Ron's help to take the loot home. By the way, how is he? Speaking of husbands, I'd forgo them if I could have a son like Ron."

"He loves it when you say that. You know how much he likes you."

"Then it's a mutual admiration society, I'd settle for you as a daughter, too."

"Thanks, Helen," Margo said, blushing. "You're the best. Jimilu is picking me up. Ron's busy."

Helen blew a stream of air, a holdover from the days when she had smoked. "This new edition ought to bring circulation way up," she said now. " 'Weddings In Other Worlds.' As good as they all are, the article on African weddings is a real winner. I wanted to make sure you did that one."

"I've been delighted to." Margo reached into a folder and drew out a sheaf of papers. "See, I've already done my research and made notations. Now I'm doing the final writing. I didn't want to overstep my bounds by going too far ahead."

"You're too balanced to do that. You're the best I have, and I don't mind telling you. Ask for any assignment you want, beginning now. Oh yes, Margo, will you continue to work? Ron's really successful, I know, but I need my senior editor. You're the greatest."

Margo nodded. "Yes, he is, but I'll keep working until I get pregnant." She felt a thrill sweep through her just thinking about that, and let her hand lay on her flat stomach.

Helen saw the gesture and smiled, her eyes nearly closing. She reflected silently that she had practically no family, but lord, she had made wonderful friends. Magazine friends. Church friends. Club friends. People like Margo and Ron. She had a good life, and was part of a great magazine. *Wedding Belles* was her treasured substitute for a child.

Helen had just left when Ron's mother called.

"Am I catching you at a bad time?" Laurette asked.

"No, your timing's about perfect. How are you?"

"Well, I suppose I could be better. I'd like to come by and get the material for thank–you notes for some of your presents. When is a convenient time for you?"

Margo thought a moment. "Tonight's not good," she said. "They're giving me a shower here, and I have got to pack up and then unpack, my presents. Jimilu's keeping up with them as they come in. Tomorrow night's good for you to pick up the material for the wedding announcement to be sent to the papers."

"That's fine for me. Margo, I've wanted to give you a shower, but I'm not feeling well. My husband has been testy with me because he feels I don't reach out to you enough."

"Laurette, it's all right—"

"No, please hear me out. I try to be honest about everything. You know how I felt about Jill and Ron. She was the daughter of one of my best friends, and I loved her like a daughter. Can you understand that?"

"Yes, of course."

"It may sound cruel, my dear, but in facing it you'll be far happier. Ron will always stand by you. He's that type. I raised him that way. But he'll always love Jill as he'll never love anyone else, I'm afraid. Theirs was a love made in heaven, and I hope you don't think I'm being mean in telling you this."

"I thank you for speaking your mind," Margo said. "I certainly don't hold it against you."

"It isn't that I don't like you. I do," Laurette continued. "You've made my son very happy. As happy as he can be. But I think you ought to know what you're up against. I wish you all the luck in the world."

"Thank you."

"Oh, and Margo, I wonder if I could ask you not to say anything to my husband or Ron about our conversation? I mean what I said about Ron and Jill."

"If that's your wish, I'll honor it."

"Good—bye, my dear, and I'll be keeping my fingers crossed for you and my son."

After she had hung up, Margo sat for a moment, slightly dazed. She had talked with Ron on the phone before she left home that morning. She knew he had a rush schedule that day, but he'd said he might drop by here at work. Her phone rang again. It was the secretary, Mavis.

"You have a visitor," the secretary said. "A Mr. Willis."

Tony Willis! *Oh, good lord!* Margo thought.

Having difficulty catching her breath, Margo said, "Please send him in, and thank you." She stood up.

Tony opened the door slowly. "Vandal creeping in," he said.

"Tony, how are you?" Forcing a heartiness she didn't feel, she decided that he was fine. He certainly *looked* great, with his ruddy skin more deeply tanned from the California sun, his sleek, brown curly hair and green eyes shining.

He looked like Mr. Movie Star Tony Willis. He and his family were rich, and he showed it.

Tony came to her swiftly, then took one of her hands in his.

"Damn, but you're looking great, girl," he said. "Don't I get a deep, prolonged kiss for old times sake?"

"For old times sake, Tony? Do you even remember what happened to us in old times?"

Tony's face grew somber. "You bet I remember, Margo. You *bet* I remember."

He leaned forward and kissed her on the mouth. "You smell wonderful, as always. I'd like a better kiss."

Margo shook her head. "I don't believe in kissing married men. They're dangerous to my health," she said, and backed away from him.

"Then I get my kiss. I'm a free man, Margo. No longer hitched."

"I'm sorry," Margo said.

"Why? I'm not sorry. I do think you owe me one since you're to blame, though."

"Why do you say that?"

"Because I couldn't get you out of my mind."

"I doubt that. Was your child a girl or a boy?"

Tony was silent a moment. "She miscarried in the sixth month. You and I would be husband and wife now if she hadn't gotten pregnant."

"Tony, Tony," Margo said, "don't blame her. She didn't get pregnant by herself. You were engaged to marry me. You shouldn't have been playing around."

Tony shrugged. "Yeah, I know, but it isn't easy the way women throw themselves at you nowadays."

"I never threw myself at you, but you're a handsome man. Maybe women are just caught up in their attraction to you."

"You're right. You never did throw yourself at me. You did everything just right. Go out with me, Margo. Have dinner with me."

"I'm getting married, Tony. I can't." Would she go out with him if she weren't getting married? She wondered.

"So I've heard. But I'm free now, and the reason I didn't stay with Ellen is that I realized I still love you. We can make it work this time. I know we can."

Margo sat down. Her knees were shaking. "Please have a seat," she said. "Don't you recognize any rules? Respect any boundaries?"

"Hell, no," he said, "not where you and I are concerned. We belong together, and I'm going to see that we stay together this time."

The phone rang again, and Margo picked it up.

"Ron's here," Mavis said.

"Please send him in.'

Still shaking nervously, Margo leaned back in her chair as Ron came in, crossed to her side, and kissed her briefly.

"I was in the area so I thought I might take you out to lunch if you're not too busy, and bring you something in if you are."

"I'm going to have to settle for your bringing something in. My schedule's hectic. Ron, I'd like you to meet Tony Willis."

Tony stood up. Ron towered half a head over him, and it seemed to Margo that he stiffened. The two men shook hands.

"I've seen you around."

"I'm glad to get to know you," Ron said gravely, thinking, *Like hell.* If he'd *never* met the louse who'd hurt Margo, that would have been too soon.

"Likewise," Tony said, the soul of informality.

"Well, I'm going to get you something to eat," Ron said, beginning to leave.

As he reached for her hand, Margo caught his. "Don't go," she said. "They're having a shower for me, and I don't really need any lunch. I'd like you to stay."

Ron looked happy. He couldn't resist a glance at Tony, who looked as if he might be settling in. Margo felt a giggle rising in her throat. The two men were trying not to glare at one another.

Then Tony sat up straight. "Well, I've certainly got to go. Dad's made me a vice-president of our company, and I'm being reassigned to DC. Congratulations again, Margo." He reached for her hand, but she withheld it. "I'll be in touch." His smile was deep and warm, as if he loved her.

As Tony stood up, went out, and closed the door, the giggles that had crowded Margo's throat since Ron came in spilled out.

"Well," Ron grumbled, "the son of a bitch has a lot of nerve. Doesn't he know we're getting married? And after what he did to you?"

Margo nodded. "Yes, on both counts. He knows we're getting married. On second thought, I don't think he realizes how much he hurt me. He's not a terribly sensitive person."

"Oh, but I'll bet he's thrilling. He's a good-looking bastard."

"And well aware of it." She noted that Ron had used rougher language twice in a few minutes where he rarely did.

"Margo?"

"Yes."

"You *have* gotten over him?"

Margo stood up and pressed her body against his. She held his face in her hands and kissed him, her tongue seeking honey as he so often sought it from her. It was a very long, impassioned kiss, and when it ended she leaned weakly against him, her heart beating hard.

"Does that answer your question?" she asked.

"Hmmm," Ron said. "When you give me one of those, I'll take my chances that you love me."

"You'd better."

Ron took her hands, raised them to his lips.

"I love you," he said gently. "Tomorrow night's our

wedding rehearsal. I've had a good time with this upcoming wedding—and we've had a good time from the day I met you. I want to thank you for giving me my life back.''

"You're welcome, my darling," she said. "You did the same for me.''

He left then, and she sat in a chair by her desk and picked up the papers for the piece on African weddings. Her mind skipped about merrily, and she still felt Ron's lips against hers.

She felt a certain sadness, because she knew what hurt and lingering love was like. And she still heard Laurette's words as plainly as if the woman were still saying them: *Ron and Jill. Theirs was a love made in heaven.*

CHAPTER FOUR

In his studio on Seventh and F Streets, Northwest, Ron tried to work, but his mind was on Margo. So Tony Willis was back. Tony was quite a competitor. Had Margo looked happier than usual? That kiss he and Margo had shared that morning was something, and he could still feel her lips scorching his. But he was hurting Margo where his memories of Jill were concerned, and he knew it.

He had dreamed of Jill again the night before. It was the dream he'd often had beginning with her funeral. *He* was driving the car, not Russ, and he was furious at her. A truck loomed, and he fought to slam on brakes that wouldn't hold. There were flames and chaos. He was thrown clear, but Jill was trapped inside and he was screaming and screaming her name, looking with horror at her blood. He always woke up in a cold sweat and couldn't get his breath.

"Dear God," he said softly. His father had told him he should get counseling, but he couldn't talk about the accident, not to anyone. He certainly wasn't about to talk with Russ. He still could hardly contain his anger at his brother, whom he thought should have gotten treatment for his drinking problem years ago.

Disconsolately, he sat down, his hands between his knees. Then, idly picking up the Leica camera Margo had had specially fitted for him, he ran his hands over the smooth mold. Jill hadn't been particularly interested in his career, though she had been his favorite model. Yes, she was beautiful, but he wasn't hooked on physical beauty. He was now held by soul, and Margo had that in spades, as well as her own kind of beauty.

The cameras had loved Jill, and had she lived she would have been one of the most famous models on the runway. They had married young, he at twenty–two, she at twenty. Four years. Then the accident.

He stood up, setting the camera aside.

"Margo," he said aloud to himself, going to the buzzing telephone.

"Hello, lover," Margo said.

"Sweetheart! I was just thinking about you."

"Guess where I am?"

"I don't know, but when I left your office this morning I know that I was—steaming."

Margo laughed throatily. "I'm right up the street from you at the new African Arts Museum. As I told you, we're doing a story on weddings in Africa, and I came over to pick up some photographs. Our photographer is busy, and I see some pieces I want shot. Can you do me a favor?"

"Anything."

"Well, grab your box and come up here and make a few shots for me to take back. That will make my work so much easier. Can you do that?"

"You've got it. But I have a better idea. Why don't you walk that couple of blocks here, and I'll walk you back?"

"Why? I'm a little pressed for time."

"Just pamper me, angel. I'll see that you get back on time if I have to hire a jet."

"Okay."

Margo told the woman helping her that she'd be back shortly and walked along the newly refurbished Seventh Street, once the bane of the city, now some of the most beautiful buildings imaginable.

Ron stood at the door waiting for her. His shop was a warm, homey hodgepodge of costumes and cameras. People came from miles around for his wedding photos, and as much of his trade came from Baltimore as from metropolitan Washington.

"Did I start something this morning?" Margo said, laughing. She thought she'd be damned if she was going to let his mother's words about a love made in heaven steal her thunder. This man was hers.

Ron locked the door and took her in his arms.

"You look so good today, and you know what you started," he said. "Now, I'm going to see that you finish it."

He was trailing kisses down the sleeves of her dress as he removed her coat and put it aside.

"Ron. Honey! There's just no time."

"No time like the present." He planted kisses on her face and throat while her body melted for him, all too aware of his hardness pressing against her. He took her face in his hands and kissed her long and hard. Then his tongue sought hers the way hers had sought his this morning. Predictably her knees went weak, but held a certain strength, too.

"Ron. Sweetheart. Please. Helen is waiting for these photos. She has an African historian in, and he has to go back to New York tonight. Darling, you know I'm just as wild for you, too, but I hate being rushed."

Ron groaned. "I must really love you to be giving up so easily." He gave her a quick kiss and released her slowly, stroking her back.

"Tonight, for sure," she said throatily.

"If I haven't died from longing by then."

"You'll survive. If I will, then you surely will."

"Listen," he said, "if Willis comes back, put him out. Remember, you belong to me."

She smiled at him.

"Not for one second will I forget."

Ron grabbed his cameras and helped Margo with her coat. He wore a heavy navy sweater.

"Are you working alone?" she asked.

"Yeah. Kyle's off today. He's going to be my best man."

Margo grew thoughtful. "You've ruled out Russ, then?'

"I ruled him out from the beginning. I'll let forgiving him take its own sweet time."

"Hatred poisons, Ron. You know that."

"I don't hate him. I just don't want him too close to me anymore."

"You told me you once worshipped him."

"I did."

"Then, can't you find it in your heart to—' "

"Margo, let it *go* I tell you."

Margo went close to him, took his face in her hands, and kissed him. "All right," she said.

At the African Art Museum he took the photos she wanted, saw her and the photos into her car, and went back to his studio. To his surprise Kyle, who worked with him, was there.

"Hey, buddy, I thought you were treating yourself to some high living today."

Kyle looked bothered. "I got to thinking about your wedding, man, and I wanted to talk a bit about it."

Ron looked at him. "Shoot."

"Well, I wonder if in your heart of hearts you don't want Russ for best man."

Ron hit the table with the palm of his hand. "Do you and Margo have a conspiracy going?" he asked. "She was just here. No. I asked you, and I want you. Got a problem with that?"

"You know I haven't. There's nothing I'd like better. But Russ has done a lot to pull his life together since that horrible accident. He doesn't drink anymore, and hasn't since then. As a friend of you both, I want to see you happy. Margo has done wonders for you, but you and Russ need each other. Don't you realize that?''

"You're making me get someone else to be my best man? I can tell you it won't be Russ."

Kyle shook his head. "Your stubbornness stands you in good stead a lot of times," he said. "The way you've gone full speed ahead with this place, Photography by Hyman." He drew a deep breath. "But your stubbornness is hurting you now."

"Are you saying you won't be my best man?"

"You know better." Kyle's dark chocolate skin flushed. "Hell, I'll always stand by you, Ron, but I'm Russ's friend too."

Ron's heart constricted. "If you're my friend, Kyle, then let it go. Just stand as my best man, and let what lies between Russ and me go. Maybe it will heal in time. Okay?"

"Yeah, man, I hear you loud and clear. But I've got to say this—I'm sorry. I'm really sorry."

Kyle began to putter about the studio, and Ron went up on the mezzanine. He didn't turn the light on but sat down in semi–darkness, and the dream washed over him. In reality he hadn't been driving. Russ had. Did Russ hear her screaming in his sleep?

After the accident, Ron had gone to England to visit a friend of his mother's, to try to heal. And he had asked himself again and again if he had failed Jill somehow. Had he been as good a husband as he could be? You didn't think about those things too much when you were with a loved one. He and his parents had been devastated, as had Jill's family. He had wanted to die for so long a time.

Then he had met Margo a year or so after Jill's death, and from the very beginning she had soothed his pain, brought him back into the land of the living, then later into the land of the loving.

Margo. Her image rose before him in his mind. He loved

her the way he'd thought he'd never love again. And it
hadn't taken long to happen. His father had been really
happy for him. His mother hadn't forgiven him for finding
someone else to replace Jill. And Russ? Well, he didn't
give a damn what Russ was feeling, even if he was pleased
that Russ had stopped drinking. He had stopped too late.

Suddenly Ron thought of something he wanted to do
for Margo, someplace he wanted to take her. They had
great things going on. He touched her and the world lit
up for him. She came into his arms and the heavens
opened. He had asked her to come to his studio this afternoon because her presence lent grace and beauty where
it had been dark and sere with old memories of Jill and
her death—and other memories he couldn't bring himself
to think about.

Ron got up. Two weeks to go, and Margo was his. They'd
taken care of blood tests and licenses. She was really his
now, but it would be formal, posted notice to the world
that they loved each other, wanted to be together for all
time.

His mother had called him to say she wanted to give a
shower for Margo. That had surprised him.

He was glad Margo had decided on a semi–formal wedding, because the glorious cathedral wedding he and Jill
had had was something he didn't want to go through again.
But he wanted to make sure that Margo was really satisfied.
In fact, for the rest of his life, he thought, running his
palm over his hair, he intended to see that Margo was
satisfied in any way he could make it happen.

When Margo got back to her office with the photos
Helen wanted, everybody was in a festive mood preparing
for her bridal shower that afternoon.

"You're a love to do this for me," Helen said, "but I'm
sure you'd look for opportunities to visit your beloved's
neighborhood. You're in top form, Margo."

Margo laughed. "I guess I am happy. Weddings are so much fun."

Helen shrugged. "I'll have to find out about that one day."

And Margo found that she really was happy, in spite of the shadow of Jill that hung over her engagement. Trust her luck to love a man who had lived with such a perfect wife. Well, Ron was who she wanted.

Seeing a pink telephone slip she'd missed, she turned it over, after checking her voicemail. It was from Tony, and the word urgent was written on it. Pursing her lips, she twirled long strands of curled hair that hung in front of her ear and dialed.

"Tony Willis," the deep, smooth voice said.

"You called me and said it was urgent."

"Yeah. We've got to talk."

"About what, Tony?"

"Us."

"There is no us anymore. I'm getting married, remember?"

"Well, I'm not, and if I could turn back time I would be engaged again—to marry you."

Margo cleared her throat. "We can't turn back time, Tony. We're old news. Ron and I love each other. There's no room in my life for you anymore."

"Ouch!"

"You're being unfair," she said. "I'm not trying to hurt you. I didn't say 'ouch' when you decided you loved someone else and left."

Tony was quiet a moment. "I guess I had that coming," he finally said. Then, "I'm not going to just give you up to Hyman," he said. "I was wrong. Don't make me pay for it forever. We loved each other once, and I still love you."

"But I belong heart and soul to Ron," she said.

"Question is, does *he* belong heart and soul to you?"

Margo felt her heart constrict. Did he?

"Don't be cruel, Tony," she said gently.

"I'm not being cruel, babe," he said. "It's just that it was no secret that Ron adored his wife. Worshipped her. She was one hell of a beautiful woman. You deserve someone who loves you the way he loved her. Me."

Without hesitation Margo said, "I'll take what I have, Tony, thank you. I have to go now."

"Have dinner with me. Lunch with me. Something. Seems I remember saying those same words recently. Don't make me beg. I have to see you."

"No you don't, and I want you to stop this."

"You wish I'd stop pursuing you?"

"Yes."

"Remember the old nursery rhyme? If wishes were horses, beggars could ride?"

"Tony, you're being juvenile. I do have to go now."

Tony sighed. "Okay, I'll let you go, but give Hyman notice that he has a rival who doesn't like losing."

"Good—bye, Tony."

Margo swivelled in her chair, thinking about Tony. What she had with Ron she'd never had with Tony, although she'd loved him. She and Ron had a level of trust between them that was wonderful. Ron said he loved her, and his actions proved it. It was, she thought without wanting to, a matter of degree.

Helen came to Margo's open door, her face wreathed in smiles.

"Your presence is required in another room," she said. Margo got up and joined her.

The conference room was festively decorated with balloons and streamers, in a pink and raspberry color combination. Lovely. A big pink coconut and walnut cake sat in the middle of the long side table, and the punch bowl was filled with pink champagne and strawberry punch.

Someone came up with a tray of champagne flutes filled with the punch. Margo and Helen took one each and sipped.

"Delicious!" Margo exclaimed, lifting and biting into a strawberry.

Work wasn't work at all, surrounded daily by people like her co-workers, Margo thought.

The office had ten employees, and it was through Helen that they all pulled together. She went out of her way to build a stable and pleasant work environment.

"You're not leaving us when you get married, are you?" one of the data entry women inquired.

"Looking at us all here," Margo said, "I'm thinking I'll never leave."

A junior editor patted her swelling stomach and declared, "If you have the kind of luck I have, before you can bat two eyelashes this will happen."

"I can't think of anything nicer," Margo said.

Looking at Helen then, Margo saw a shadow of pain cross her face, and felt deeply for her. She would have liked to be closer to Helen, but Helen was her boss, and she'd found close friendship with bosses seldom worked out.

Someone tapped her on the back. She turned to find Jimilu behind her. They hugged.

"Thanks for inviting me," Jimilu said to Helen.

"Well, best friends, that kind of thing," Helen said. "We're happy to have you. Let me get you some punch."

"It's the best punch I've tasted in a long time," Margo told her.

Jimilu glanced at her watch. "I can only stay a little while, but I'll be back early to help you get that stack of stuff home. I can come back and take you home. And Tom can bring your car, since he uses the bus."

"Tom sure can," said their office boy, a gangling youth. "Hey, Margo, you made out like gangbusters," he said, pointing to the stack of presents and envelopes.

There were presents in all shapes and sizes. *So many presents from so few people,* Margo thought. In the past she had been more than generous for office showers. Now her co–workers had gone all out for her.

"You'll be pleased, too, at what I've done for your bridal registry," Helen said. "Oh, by the way, please do leave early and get this stuff home."

They turned then to a leisurely buffet lunch of New England clam chowder, oyster–cheese crackers, ham and turkey club sandwiches, and crisp raw vegetables. Margo thought the food, like the champagne, tasted scrumptious.

"I'll call the hospital and be gone a little longer," Jimilu said, "since you can leave early. I'll take you home, then pick you up again tonight to take you for the wedding gown fitting. Okay with you? Then Ron can pick you up from Steve's."

"Super," Margo said. Steve was a young designer who was making a name for himself in bridal apparel.

Margo told Jimilu about Tony's call after she'd gotten back from Ron's studio and about him being there that morning.

"Pass the wealth around," Jimilu said, laughing. "I could use one of those guys."

"I don't think so," Margo said, grinning. "I kind of think you're hooked right now on Russ."

A slow smile spread over Jimilu's face. "He called me last night," she said. "I wanted to call you, but it was late. He's a nice guy. Deep. Smart."

"I certainly like him," Margo said. "He's been through some terrible pain, too."

"I know," Jimilu said. "He told me about his part in Ron's wife's death. It's a shame to have to bear up under so much pain."

"It's the way life is," Margo said slowly. "Sometimes I find Ron looking into space, and he looks haunted."

Jimilu nodded. "He loves you so much."

"And I love him."

* * *

By seven that evening Jimilu and Margo had pulled into
a parking lot that accommodated Margo's dress designer's
customers. Steve's Bridal Wonderland was on a quiet street
in Silver Spring, zoned for both residences and businesses.
Steve lived on one side of the house; his bridal salon occupied the other side. Margo buzzed and he greeted them
at the locked door, letting them in with his bright smile.
He was a small, agile man who found the world a wonderful
place.

"Ladies. I think you, Margo, will be overjoyed. Your
gown is nearly finished. It and you will be gorgeous."

"With you handling it, things couldn't be otherwise."

He led them to his large fitting room, and in a cubicle
Margo got into the undergarments she would wear on her
wedding day.

"Good," Steve said. "Now we begin."

With his pincushion fastened onto his wrist and his tape
measure draped around his neck, he began the measuring
from every angle. He was careful not to prick Margo's skin.

"But I forget—I get so engrossed," he said. "Coffee? I
have some excellent flavors, and I have some really good
cookies. Or tea? I seem to remember, Margo, that you're
presently off coffee."

"I drink it from time to time," Margo said, "but not
tonight. We had a fairly late lunch with my shower and
everything—" She broke off. "I put a piece of shower cake
in my tote for you, Steve."

"I'll get it," Jimilu said, going to the tote, rummaging,
and coming back with the aluminum foil covered cake on
a thick paper plate, with a plastic fork.

Steve stopped a minute, pulled aside the paper that
covered the cake, and lifted the fork.

After a moment he said, "It's not only my favorite, but

it's good, really good. My mother always says I'll turn to sugar one day."

"Well, watch out for too many sweets," Margo cautioned him. "We don't want you getting diabetes."

Steve sighed. "Would that we could have all the things we want, and never suffer for them."

"Well, what I want," Margo told him, "is you around for a very long time. I'm putting in my bid for you to make my first daughter's wedding dress, in fact, the wedding dresses for all my daughters."

"Careful, Girlfriend," Jimilu said, chuckling. "You may be slated to have all boys."

"Then I'll wangle orders from their fiancées."

Steve finished the last of the cake, saying, "I'd like to find out who they ordered from. I must have one like it for my next get–together."

Margo told him the name of the caterer Helen used, and he picked up a pad and pencil and wrote it down, wiped his hands with a moist wipe, and settled down again to fitting Margo's gown.

"I see you in my vision," he said, "standing beside your fiancé. No, first I see you coming up the aisle in your beautiful flower garden. Margo, I have seen your garden, and I know what it will be like. Marvelous!"

"There's just one thing about garden weddings," Margo said. "Sometimes it rains."

"In which case?" Steve asked.

"Our pastor has been sweet enough to say we can have the church on a moment's notice. He's saving that Saturday at eleven for us in case we need it. Everyone has gone along with him."

"This is going to be one beautiful wedding," Steve said.

"Yes," Jimilu added, "no less is deserved for a woman who is an editor of a bridal mag."

Steve was sober as he fitted carefully, taking a nip here, making a tuck there.

"There's no better time than now to wish you all the

luck in the world," he said, "as well as thank you for all the business you've sent my way."

"You're more than welcome," Margo answered. "You're such a sweet guy."

"So my doting mother always tells me," Steve said, laughing. "She always frets that I'm cheating some woman out of a good husband. One day."

The buzzer sounded, and after a moment Steve put aside his fitting paraphernalia.

"That should be Ron," Margo said, and in a few minutes they heard Ron's voice."

"I'm sorry, Ron," Steve was telling him. "I don't allow us men beyond this section, but I have magazines in here and a small refrigerator where you'll find juices, hot water, and coffee, cocoa, and tea. You probably read *Emerge, Jet, Ebony, Heart and Soul* etc."

"Thanks. Any idea how much longer?" Ron asked.

Steve shrugged. "About forty–five minutes, I'd gauge."

Margo came to the door and blew Ron a kiss. His eyes lit up. Her expression said she wanted to be in his arms. His expression said that was where he wanted her. Steve grinned, his eyes half–closed, thinking that there was nothing in this world he liked better than designing gowns for happy brides.

CHAPTER FIVE

That same night, riding up Connecticut Avenue on the way to Ron's parents' house in Rockville, Margo felt happiness spread through her.

"My gown is going to be beautiful," she told Ron.

"I don't doubt it. And you're going to be beautiful in it."

"Thank you, sweetie. I get more and more nervous as the days pass."

"Don't be. You've got me for life. And I'm going to be really good to you."

"Oh, Ron, you *are* good to me."

"The best for the best. And I guess I'd better keep that up. I had a visitor this afternoon."

"Oh?"

"Yeah. Willis."

"Tony? What did he want?" She felt a small start of alarm.

"To serve notice on me."

"Oh good lord, what kind of notice?"

In his mind's eye, Ron could still see the movie star

handsome Tony Willis standing in his studio that afternoon.

"He told me he still loves you, and he wants you back."

"Well, that will never happen," she said staunchly.

Ron reached for Margo's hand, stroked it, and turned to look at her pleasant profile.

"I hope you're right," he said, his voice catching. "He was your first love."

"That's true, but it is in the past," Margo assured him.

"We're both people with unhappy past loves," Ron said then. "You with Willis dumping you for another woman, and me with,"—he seemed to hesitate—"Jill's death."

Margo squeezed his hand. "We'll work hard to come out on top of the pain we've both suffered," she said.

"If you knew how much I love you."

"I think I do," Margo said softly, "and I hope you know how much I love you."

The Hymans weren't home. Ron let Margo and himself in.

The house was quiet, the black–and–white octagonal block tile foyer as slick as glass. It was a beautiful residence, but to Margo it seemed cold, too formal. She wouldn't want to live there.

"Get used to it," Ron said. "As my wife you'll be coming over more often."

Margo laughed a little nervously. "Okay," she said. "I'm kind of tired. Luckily I didn't open my gifts from the shower today, or I'd be exhausted."

Still standing in the foyer, Ron kissed her forehead. "Poor baby," he said, "she's already strung out from our wedding, and we have nearly two more weeks to go."

Margo chuckled, warmth spreading through her body.

She and Ron went into the library. As he snapped a light on, Margo was all too aware of the painting of Jill above the fireplace. For a moment she couldn't tear her eyes away, as much as she wanted to.

"Damn it," Ron said, "I almost forgot. I have to pick

up a camera from Kyle. It's about a ten minute drive. Want to come with me? I should be back in a half hour."

Margo thought a moment.

"I love that part of the library at the other end," she said. "I think I'll just stay here and rest until you get back."

He nodded. "Make yourself comfortable," He kissed her then with fervor that made her very toes feel good.

"We've got to get away together soon," he said. "I mean away from everything and everybody."

"Our honeymoon will do that for us."

"I can't wait that long."

"Impatient."

"You said it. Especially where you're concerned."

Margo smoothed his crisp, black hair. She loved him so, and she knew from experience how a fallout from such a love could come to haunt you.

But Margo didn't rest once Ron was gone. She walked the long length of the library, admiring the black leather furniture, studying the portrait of Jill each time she passed it. *Well, Ron belongs to me now,* she thought, *and if I die tonight, I have lived a love I dreamed of.*

Did Ron belong to her the way he had once belonged to Jill? *I won't let that matter,* she thought fiercely. *He's mine now, as I am his.*

The lower end of the library was truly lovely, with stained glass windows on the end and one side that let in varied plays of light at all hours. The few times she'd been in the library she had found it so soothing, so restful. She turned out the lights and sat in darkness behind a huge, potted rubber plant and an Oriental screen, kicked off her shoes, and tucked her legs under her. Not liking the darkness, she got up and turned the lights back on. She hadn't realized how tired she was, and she fell fast asleep.

Waking up when she heard a man's voice, she started to call to Ron, but she recognized the voices of the Hymans.

"I guess I forgot to turn out the lights in here," Laurette said.

Dr. Hyman shrugged. "We're both more forgetful nowadays," he said, "it may be a price we pay for living this great, long life. Why do you look worried, my dear?"

Laurette sighed. "I'm looking at that painting, and thinking about Jill, I suppose."

"Then don't. For God's sake, Laurette, isn't it enough that Ron refuses to forgive Russ for the accident? We're supposed to have more wisdom."

"I know, but I just can't forget. Russ is my son, and I have to forgive him. He's flesh of my flesh. And I'm sorry Ron can't. I will grieve Jill forever. She was perfect for Ron. She was what a son of mine deserves."

"You're saying, you know, that Margo isn't good enough for him. And she *is*. She's a lovely young woman, Laurette. I keep wondering how you can be blind enough not to see that."

Laurette cleared her throat. "You keep fussing at me, and that's all right. That's the way you feel. But Margo isn't in the same league that Jill moved in. It's not a matter of her not being good enough for him, although I don't think she is."

"Laurette, please."

But Laurette kept on. "Ron and Jill were going to found a dynasty, Wally. I'm as sure of it as I am that I'm standing here. They had a love made in heaven."

Margo gasped. Laurette had used those same words to her on the phone. It hurt then, and it hurt now.

Dr. Hyman went close to his wife and gripped her shoulders. "Listen," he said firmly, "I want you to stop this nonsense. Our son has found himself a worthwhile partner whom I very much admire. We—you and I—are going to present a solid front to them."

Laurette sighed deeply. "Oh, very well, but only because I care so much for you and for our whole family."

"Can't you see that our son is going on with his life? His engagement to Margo proves that. Snap out of it, Laurette."

Laurette sighed. "I'm not sure he is altogether going on with his life," she said. "I see him looking at that portrait of Jill furtively, almost as if he doesn't want to look but can't help himself."

Dr. Hyman cleared his throat. "You were wrong to hang that painting there where Margo is faced with it each time she comes over if she comes in here."

"Well, life isn't what we want it to be. It is what it *is*," Laurette said sanctimoniously.

Not until then could Margo bring herself to get up and come out from behind the screen.

She started toward the Hymans. "I'm sorry," she began, "but I was fast asleep when you came in, and frankly I couldn't pull myself together fast enough to come out before now."

"Oh lord," escaped Dr. Hyman. "I'm so sorry you had to overhear this."

Releasing his wife, he came to Margo.

"And I'm sorrier than you will ever know," Laurette said, extending her hand. "Can you find it in your heart to forgive me?"

For a moment words were frozen in Margo's throat, then she could say, "There's nothing to forgive. I don't expect you to stop loving Jill because I came into the picture. You loved her. You love her now. You're hardly responsible for that."

Margo took a deep breath as Dr. Hyman smiled at her. "Ron and I love each other," she said. "I just want to make sure you're well aware of that."

To Margo's surprise, Laurette took her in her arms. "Oh, my dear, if only you knew." She released Margo. "Now, if you really can forgive me—I left a message on your home phone asking that you call me. I want to give you a magnificent bridal shower. It won't make up for the coldness I've shown you, and I should have done this earlier, but at least it will let you know that I have a heart, and it's warming toward you."

Dr. Hyman reached over and kissed his wife's cheek. She smiled brightly at him.

"Well," she said to Margo. "What do you think about my giving you a shower?"

Margo nodded. Actually she had more gifts than she needed, but she didn't want to hurt Laurette's feelings, although Laurette had given little thought to hurting hers.

"I think that's fine," Margo said. "That's very nice of you."

"Hey, what's going on here, a midnight meeting?" Ron said as he came through the door.

"Hello, dear," Laurette said.

"I'd say there's a lot going on in the right direction," Dr. Hyman said.

Ron's face lit up. "I'm glad to hear it."

"Ron," Dr. Hyman said, "I wonder if you and I could talk a bit about something that's been on my mind? I won't keep you long."

"Well, sure Dad," Ron answered, "but Margo's had a long, tiring day and I've got to get her home."

"Sure thing." Ron and Dr. Hyman left the room.

Laurette turned to Margo. "I know you're tired if you've had a long day, but could we just briefly discuss my plans for your shower? It's hardly classy that I've waited this long, but I mentioned that I wasn't feeling well."

"Then you shouldn't plan on giving me a shower," Margo said. "You have to think of yourself first. I understand."

"No, my dear, you can't be expected to understand. I've simply been wrong about you. I'm going to have to live with my grief over Jill, and I refuse to let it ruin my life or my family's."

"Thank you very much," Margo said, her eyes misting. Incredibly, Laurette seemed entirely sincere.

"Let's sit down," Laurette said, "and I'll tell you what I'll need from you. And I won't ask for much, because I know I'm late, and you have your hands full."

The two women sat in the pool of lamplight as if they were lifelong friends, and Margo felt more relaxed than she had felt in days. Still, she was aware that the goddesslike aura of Jill as it was reflected in the painting shadowed their every move.

Dr. Hyman faced his son as they sat in deep, cushioned chairs in his study.

"Son, I wonder if you'd consider asking Russ to be your best man."

Ron shook his head without hesitation. "I long ago selected Kyle," he said. "We're best friends, co-workers, and he agreed. I can hardly go back on this."

Dr. Hyman signed heavily. "Once you and your brother were best friends."

"I remember, Dad. No need to remind me. Those days will never come again."

Dr. Hyman shook his head. "You sound too adamant, and that's not like you. I know you blame Russ for Jill's death—"

"He was drunk again. Russ was thirty-three years old when the—accident happened. He was hardly a child or teenager. He was aware his drinking was out of control."

"He hasn't had a drink since that morning."

"He was late getting to that point."

"Ron, life has never gone well for those of us who judge ourselves and others harshly."

"Damnit, Dad," Ron shot back, "my life was hell after that accident. Not until Margo came along did I want to go on living."

"But Margo did come along, and you're happy again now."

"Yes."

"Do you still love Jill?"

"I'll always love her."

"But you love Margo."

"I adore Margo. My love for Jill was wrapped up in our families, in the fact that we worked together—although not enough, since she wanted to branch out more and travel more than I wanted to. No, I can't compare the way I love Margo and the way I loved Jill."

Dr. Hyman nodded. "Getting back to Russ."

Ron shook his head. "It does no good to talk about it, Dad," Ron said sadly. "As far as I'm concerned, the bond that existed between Russ and me is severed forever."

Dr. Hyman leaned forward and looked at his son, a long and searching look. "Think it over carefully," he said. "Forever is a long, long time. To give up on what you and Russ once knew as brothers is a painful thing. As you know, your uncle—my brother, Alex—and I had a great relationship. When he died at forty and you two boys were youngsters, I thought I couldn't get over it, but it's better now. Russ isn't dead. He told me recently he'd always be there for you if you wanted him."

"It isn't going to work that way with Russ and me, Dad. As I said, I'm sorry, but that's the way it is. Now I'd better go back and pick up Margo and get her home."

"Will you think about what I've said?"

"Sure. And will you really listen to what I've been telling you?"

Dr. Hyman nodded. His two boys were his pride and joy, and the men they had grown up to be never stopped pleasing him. If only his brother, Alex, had lived to see them grow up. Alex had been an alcoholic, and had died of liver cirrhosis. He was as proud that Russ had not taken a drink since that horrible accident as he had ever been of anything.

At home with Gramps, who had sat up waiting for them, Margo and Ron opened and admired a few of the new presents from the office shower. Margo was pleased that they had beefed up their security system since the presents had begun coming in and were being put on display.

Gramps brought out his dandelion wine and some tea-cakes he had baked for Gracie and himself that afternoon.

"You're setting a bad example for me with your cooking," Ron said. "I can't boil water."

"Oh, don't worry. I'm a good cooking teacher," Margo said. "I'll have you doing Beef Wellington in short order."

Ron laughed. "We'll see about that. Breathing deeply, he said, "I'd better see you in. I have a long day tomorrow."

"See me in?" Margo asked, laughing. "You're forgetting that the stairs to my apartment are inside. I *am* in."

"I forget," Ron said grinning. His long, smoldering look left no question as to what he meant. Gramps looked fondly from one to the other. However happy Margo might be these days, she was no happier than he was. He was delighted for them, and he had his own special patch of happiness—with Gracie.

Arm in arm, Margo and Ron slowly climbed the stairs. Pausing for a moment outside the door, he slowly kissed her as he opened the door. With them inside, he closed it and pressed her against the door. She could feel the outlines of his body and the length of hard flesh that told her how he wanted her.

"You're so beautiful," he whispered. "When am I going to get used to having you for my own?"

"*Do* get used to it," she answered. "We're going to be together for a long, long time."

They stood there locked in each other's arms for warm, loving moments, and both were caught up in bliss and wonder at the passion they knew. When they finally drew apart, Ron placed a hand beside her face, asking, "Why don't we go up to Sunset Beach tomorrow evening?"

Without hesitation, Margo answered, "I think that's a lovely idea. The weatherman says it may rain, though."

Ron laughed. "A weatherman after my own heart. I love making love to you in the rain."

"You have a one–track mind."

"No, only with you."

"Never mind. I love having you on one track."

"I'm glad, because I really can't help it when I'm so crazy about you. If only you knew what you've done for my life."

"I know what you've done for mine."

Ron gave her a little squeeze. "Mom told me about the shower she's giving for you. Just give her a little time, and she'll be as much on your side as Dad is."

"I'd like that," Margo told him, but she doubted that Laurette would ever be on her side.

"Of course, Russ was sold on you from the beginning."

"He told you that?"

Ron nodded. "Yes. We're no longer close, but we do comment on things to each other."

"Russ is a nice guy."

Ron only shrugged in answer before he said, "I'm going to go now. Hurry, tomorrow!"

He pressed her to him again, feeling the outlines of her luscious, soft, and yielding body even as she felt the fit hardness of his.

Releasing her, he said, "I'm going to go now, so you can get some rest."

"I can rest in your arms."

"I wouldn't let you for long, not the way I feel tonight. I want you so much, but I know you're too tired."

She couldn't deny her fatigue from the long, active day. Their wedding day was drawing close, and her bridal consultant had suggested that she make all her preparations before the final week and rest that last week, see family and friends, and begin savoring what would be one of the most important days in her life.

With another long kiss and a light slap on her backside, Ron left, and Margo sank down on the midnight blue sofa.

Glancing around at her cream–colored living room, at the midnight–blue chair and sofa and the blue–and–white striped chair, she kicked off her shoes and dug her feet into the midnight–blue plush rug.

She was going to miss living here with Gramps, but anywhere Ron was, was home. She got up and pulled off her outfit and remembered to check for phone messages.

Jimilu's delighted voice came on. "Don't answer tonight, because I have too much to tell you, but I'll give you a clue. Russ and I had a wonderful time at the movies. And tomorrow night we're going to the special meeting for A Helping Hand—you know, that's the new inner city group I helped found."

"I'd never forget that," Margo murmured. "I'm going to have to find time to help out."

She would talk with Jimilu tomorrow, but she was going to be pushed for time. She hadn't gotten as much done on the African wedding piece as she'd wanted to. Helen's quietly sensitive face came before her. Helen was too good a woman to not have a good man waiting in the wings. She racked her brain, and could come up with no answers for that one.

Going into her bedroom with the garments she'd removed in the living room on her arm, she finished undressing and studied herself in the full–length triple mirror. Somehow her body always seemed to look better after she had been thoroughly kissed by Ron. She hugged herself. Drawing her bathwater, she thought again of Ron and her together. What they had, she hadn't known with Tony.

Lounging in the tub as the very warm water washed over her, releasing oil bubbles of French lavender scent, she gave herself up to fantasies. She had dreams of Ron so often it seemed she should be running out of dreams by now, but she never did.

Reluctantly getting out of the tub, she dried off with a blue bathsheet, slid into a cream terry cloth robe, and padded back to the bedroom. As she was getting into her shortie nightgown, she suddenly wanted to look into her hope chest. She walked over and opened it, and her eyes lit up at the sight of all the silk, satin, crepe, and tricot underwear. Her trousseau gown and peignoir lay on top of the other garments. She had searched a long time before finding just that shade of peach that highlighted her skin. Ron was going to love this.

As she turned the lights off, the phone rang. That would be Ron saying goodnight. She picked up the phone, her *hello* carrying a dulcet tone of love.

"Well, I certainly didn't expect this kind of greeting."

She started at the sound of his voice, then said coolly, "Hello, Tony."

"You sure changed your tune quickly enough."

"It is late, and I have a rough day tomorrow."

"Do you still remember when you were going to marry me, and you had the wedding all planned? God, Margo, how could I have been such a fool?"

Cruelly, Margo said, "Perhaps that's just one of your failings."

"Don't be mean. It isn't like you."

"Tony, it's late, and as I said I have a lot to do tomorrow." The delicious feeling of going to the shore with Ron leapt to mind and thrilled her.

"I know I made a mistake," he said, "but I'm not giving up on us. I want you to know that."

"There is no *us*, Tony. What we had was over long ago. And you know what? As it turned out, that was much for the better."

"Talk to me, doll. At least talk to me. You owe me that for loving you so much."

"You know very little about love, Tony."

Tony was silent for a moment. "I admit that was once true of me. I've grown up, Margo. Believe me, I've found pain can do that to you."

"Tony, I really have to go to bed."

"Okay. I don't want us to start off again with you mad at me. I'm now the man you thought I was when we were getting married. Give us a chance, Margo. I don't believe you love Hyman the way you loved me. I think you still love me. I can see it on your face, your body movements toward me."

Margo's laugh was short. "All I can say, Tony, is that if you are taking a course in body language, you'll fail.'

"And if you were taking a course in love you'd be graduating *summa cum laude.*"

"I'm going to hang up now," Margo said. "Goodnight, Tony."

"Goodnight, my love, and I'm not giving up. I wish I were there in bed with you."

Ignoring him, Margo suddenly remembered Tony's call to Ron, and she asked, "Why did you go to see Ron?"

"I didn't go to see him, I went to *warn* him that I'm not giving you up, just as I keep telling you."

"Tony, you're being ridiculous."

"No, I'm a man in love."

"Goodnight, Tony." This time her voice was crisply firm.

"Goodnight, my darling."

Margo pressed the phone into its cradle. Now she had gone past annoyance with Tony. He had always been indulged and spoiled by his family. Did Tony have the makings of a stalker? How dare he? He had left her for another woman. It didn't make sense. Was he all there? When they were engaged, the wild things he did had seemed simply whimsical and funny. Now, remembering the times he drove too fast, teased too hard, was less than kind to animals around him, she found herself wondering.

She dialed Ron's number. He picked up on the first ring.

"Had you called me?" she asked him.

"Yeah. I got a busy signal."

"I thought so. It was Tony."

"Hey, that guy doesn't quit."

"Oh, he's going to quit, all right."

"It's getting to you, isn't it?"

"Yes. I'm not sure you realize that Tony is a male *Lola*. You know the song, 'whatever Lola wants' "

"Shall I challenge him to a duel?"

"Don't joke about it, darling. I'm remembering things Tony used to do, and they seem less innocent now than they did then."

He asked, and she told him how Tony used to maliciously tease both the family cat and dog, once breaking a cat's leg in a fit of anger.

"H'mm," Ron said when she had finished. "He sounds emotionally immature if nothing else, but then I came to that conclusion when he was around today. You're sure you don't still care for him?"

"I'm positive. You're lodged in my heart too tightly, and there just isn't room for anyone else."

"My own sweetheart," Ron said. "I'm sending you a kiss over the telephone line, and I'm counting the minutes until I pick you up tomorrow evening for our ride to Sunset Beach."

CHAPTER SIX

It was nearly eight that evening and misting rain as Margo and Ron reached Sunset Beach and the Hyman beach house. As they drove up, Warren Hill, the husband of the family that lived in the next house some hundred and fifty yards away, came up.

"Long time no see," he greeted them. "I've missed you two."

"And we've missed coming up," Ron said, "but we've been in a pre–wedding bind, and you were away when we were here last."

"Thanks for the wedding invitation," Warren said. "We'll be there."

Ron got out and asked a few questions about what had been going on at Sunset Beach, and listened to Warren's comments. Warren kept a weather eye on the house when they were away. Margo still sat in the car, her heart racing with joy at the thought of being in Ron's arms in a few minutes.

It seemed far too long before they unlocked the door, with Ron holding her with one arm.

"We have some stuff to unpack for our time tonight," Margo said. "Are you forgetting that?"

"It's forgotten for right now," Ron said huskily. "I've been on edge all day and the time is now."

Once inside, Ron turned on the lights and pressed Margo against the door as he had the night before in her apartment.

"Why are you crushing me flat against doors?" Margo teased.

"I'm trying to meld you right into me," he said. "Margo, you'll never know how much I love you."

Then their hands were busy taking off each other's clothes, flinging the garments aside and ardently touching each other's bodies. Finally Ron held her naked against him, her satiny, warm, brown flesh turning him on to fever pitch.

His big hands caressed her, then he held her so tightly she thought she would break. Holding and stroking her, Ron thought they had never been so close as they were now.

Her fingers pressed into his shoulders and back. "Oh, my darling," she whispered, "if you only knew how much I love you."

"You couldn't love me more than I love you," he whispered back.

They were wild for each other as she rode on Ron's hips on the way to the king size bed in the room assigned to Ron when he and Russ were children. Ron laid her down, too full of desire to be as gentle as he wanted to be, but neither was she gentle then.

They were both hungry for each other and as he stroked her flesh it seemed as if she had been feeling his hands on her body all day. And with that span of time in mind, her flesh burned with passion and desire.

Ron felt himself already near the edge from desire held back from the night before. He rolled her over so that her lovely breasts peeked up at him and he stroked her, kissing her shoulders and breasts. Margo felt as if she would faint with desire.

"Darling, why are you waiting?" she asked, dimly mindful of how close he was to his edge.

For a moment, Ron didn't answer. "Tonight—and last night—the very sight of you sets me on fire." Gently she stroked the shaft of his manhood until he closed a hand over hers, then removed her hand from himself.

"You're driving me over the edge," he told her. "Be patient, and I'll give you what you're begging for."

Margo laughed softly. "And you're not begging for the same thing?"

"You bet I am. That and more. I want you, love, body and soul. I want us soul to soul as much as body to body. You know that."

"Yes, I want the same thing."

But neither had much time to think of what they wanted, so intense and driven did they feel.

A little cooler now, Ron arched above her, slowly entering her hotly avid body where she gripped him tightly, making him gasp with pleasure. His mouth found her nipples and sucked them gently, then patterned circular kisses over her breasts, so that she felt herself slipping into a blessed oblivion.

Motioning to him that she wanted to be above him, she felt him roll her over, and she bent and touched her tongue to his nipples, teasing them so that he groaned and in long and short masterful strokes began an ascent to a heavenly place that she never wanted to end.

"Margo, Margo," he whispered. "How can you make me feel the way you do?'

"I don't know, sweetheart," she murmured. "I'm too busy wondering how you sense just what to do to me."

Ron squeezed her tightly. "If I don't sense what to do, tell me, and it's yours."

He arched above her then with thrusts of glory that swept her very soul until she felt wave after wondrous wave shake her body and she was limp with a marvelous relaxation she had never known outside his arms.

Poised above her, Ron knew for certain he had not ever felt the way he always felt in Margo's arms. If he had any doubts about the two of them, those doubts vanished when he was with her. Now, deep inside her, he felt his loins like a volcano—like eruption of banked fires, and his whole body was rife with love and seduction, for he and Margo always seduced each other's souls. It was a beautiful seduction, in the best sense. Gentle, or more passionate. Breathless. Positive. And both felt it would last forever.

They lay still for a long time, side by side with his arm draped over her midsection, and fell asleep. Margo dreamed of glorious green forests with starbursts of light coming through the trees. What they had just experienced had filled her with awe. Ron slept deeply and dreamed of Margo still in his arms.

They slept a short while, and Margo wakened first. She looked at him as he slept, his face earnest and loving, the heavily muscled body relaxed now. For a moment he smiled in his sleep. *How dear he is,* Margo thought.

Ron stirred, reliving in his dreams the act of love they had just gone through. He came awake to find her propped up on one elbow, her fingers tracing his jawline.

"Satisfied?" he asked her.

"Almost. Are you?"

Grinning, he said, "I'm a long way off. That was just a prelude."

She was quick on the uptake. "I'm game if you are. What about the things in the car? We were going to take it slow and easy. Good music. Great food. What happened?"

Ron chuckled. *"We* happened to each other the way we often do. Margo?"

"Yes."

"Do you feel something different about us tonight? As if we're more a part of each other than usual? We're separate, sure, but we're even more *with* each other. Do you feel what I'm talking about?"

"Yes."

Margo put her head on his chest and he stroked her back.

"I'm so glad I found you."

"I'm glad we found each other."

A vagrant thought wormed its way to her mind. Had it been this good for Ron and Jill? Or better? Margo felt it didn't get any better than tonight for her. She and Tony had been wild young lovers intent on having fun. Their love had been nothing like this. She blocked all thoughts of Tony from her mind, but it wasn't as easy to block thoughts of Ron and Jill.

"Let's get the things out of the car," Margo said.

"I'll get them. I think it's raining a little."

He sat up abruptly, then. "No, wait, honey," he said, "I have something else in mind. I want to walk along the beach with you in the rain, or maybe by now it's still misting."

"Oh, I'd love that."

"Then we can unload the car."

They looked around after putting on their clothes and found a rain poncho for Ron in the hall closet and a raincoat and a sweater for Jill in his parents' bedroom.

"Aren't you going to need a sweater?" she asked.

"No. I'm a hot–blooded dude tonight," he answered.

"Well, be careful. I don't want a flu–ridden bride-groom."

"Trust me. With my brand of happiness, germs don't stand a chance."

It was still misting, cool. Not quite two weeks before their wedding, Margo had never felt so happy as she felt tonight. Walking along, they passed the long, stone ledge near the Chesapeake Bay, and passing it Margo stroked the rock with long, slender fingers.

"So in love with you, I feel as grounded as this rock,"

she said, "yet as light as a butterfly. How can I feel both
ways?"

"There's no explaining love," Ron told her.

They walked along, hugging each other, sides together.
Suddenly he stopped and swung her around, took her face
in his hands, and kissed her long and deeply. It was a quiet
kiss, unlike the ones they had shared a little while before.
Those had been raw, nearly savage, reaching out to probe
their deepest recesses, and neither would have given anything for it. But Margo valued the tender moments, too.
She and Tony had rarely had very tender moments.

The mist seemed to seal them in, bring them closer.
They moved in a world where there were just the two of
them together.

Ron realized that they had walked farther than they
intended to and said, "Let's go back. We've got a lot more
loving to do." He hugged her again.

"We can't top what we just had."

"I'd be satisfied just to measure up to that," he said.
"Lord, were we ever hungry for each other!"

"Yes," she murmured. "We're quite a pair."

Walking back slowly, they savored the mist and a world
that enhanced their love. Margo's skin felt pleasantly damp
from the mist. The raincoat hood covered her hair. Fiercely
drawn to him again, Margo thought about what Ron had
said about this night being different. She felt that, too. It
was if they had reached glorious new heights of ecstasy.

Back at the house, with loving glances at each other,
they went to the car and unloaded a picnic hamper and
many tapes for the tape deck. Margo began smiling.

"Tell me what's tickling your fancy?" Ron asked.

"Just that we were one intense pair coming in. We didn't
need the food or the music. We just needed each other."

Ron nodded.

Margo spread out steak and cheese club sandwiches, a
thermos of split pea soup, brightly crisp salads, and wild

berry yogurt. The rolls they put in the microwave were soon ready.

They ate quickly. She wanted little, but the food tasted sharply delicious. Ron ate slowly. "Gathering strength," he said.

"I hear you," Margo told him. "I'll stack the few dishes and we can get back to unfinished business."

"A woman after my own heart."

They decided to sleep for an hour or so on the sunporch with its wraparound windows and beige vertical blinds. Then they would drive back to DC. They dragged a filled air mattress out and spread on sheets and blankets, then settled down. For a long while after they got undressed and got into bed, Ron was silent. The sunporch was pleasantly heated from the furnace, which had kicked in. Ron turned out the lights and opened the blinds. The skies were clearing.

"Penny for your thoughts," Margo said.

"I just can't get away from how special I feel with you tonight. It's as if we belong to the earth itself in a way I never have."

"You can count me in on that."

"Yes. The whole world is a beautiful place tonight," he answered.

"I wish we didn't have to go back tonight," she said wistfully.

"But we do," he said. "We'll just make it as late as possible. Who needs sleep?"

His lips were in her hair as he kissed her temples and hairline. He pulled her above him, his hands catching her ponytail and holding her away from him as his hungry mouth sought and found her breasts. For long moments, Margo thought she was going mad with desire.

Finally she said to him fiercely, "Don't keep me waiting, sweetheart. I hurt with wanting you."

"Well, I'm not going to have that," he said. "I'll give the lady what she wants."

Then he was inside her again, swollen and pulsing. He felt her heart beat as his own, and felt the nectared sheath of her body close around him tightly.

He thought that this was as good as it got, ever, covering her as they came together in climactic wonder.

"I love you," Ron said.

"And I love *you,*" Margo said breathlessly. "Ron, we never played the tapes."

"We didn't need them," Ron said. "Tonight *we* are the music. Why are we feeling this way now? We've made great love before. Hell, it's always great, for me with you."

"Yes, I feel the same way. I think it's far, far more than making love. In less than two weeks we'll belong together. We'll be together if we work it right for all time. Ron, we've got a wonderful love, and I think love doesn't come to more people than it does."

"You're *quite* right. Margo, I love you, respect you, honor you. Margo don't ever leave me."

"I won't," she answered without hesitation, "and please make me the same promise. Or if you must leave, don't do it cruelly, abruptly. Give me time to get used to it."

He caught her in a bear hug. "I won't need to do that, because I won't be leaving."

He took her left hand with his emerald–cut diamond on the third finger and kissed it, his tongue darting kisses on the warm flesh of her fingers. Then he traced kisses up her arms, and onto her neck and face and body. When he pressed full–length to her side, she could feel the heat in him, feel the swollen length of him as he grew intense with wanting her. His lips on her thighs and hips, legs and feet, traced gentle, hot kisses that aroused her to fever pitch. Then, tracing back he reached her breasts, nibbled them. Then, as he moved up to her face, his tongue courted the corners of her mouth, where he felt he had never known such sweetness.

Their tongues interacted feverishly, hungrily seeking the best each had to offer.

They had been so intensely involved that they didn't notice through the open blinds when the sky cleared and a galaxy of stars, with a full moon, hung in the sky.

"My God, that's so beautiful," Margo said.

CHAPTER SEVEN

In spite of getting back to DC and to bed so late, Margo woke early. Slowly she got out of bed and padded over to open one set of blinds.

"What a glorious morning," she said, hugging herself, then she added, "What glorious whole *days.*"

She looked out on the three acre backyard that would be witness to her marriage vows very few days from then. Her one week countdown began the next two days, and she thought, *Hurry, next Saturday!*

Gardeners and Gramps had worked diligently and well to bring the yard to perfection.

The ringing telephone interrupted her reverie.

"Hello, sunshine!"

"Hello, yourself. Oh Ron, I've really begun to get the feel of this whole wedding."

Ron laughed, "I'm way ahead of you. From the beginning, I've had it."

"I guess I was a little afraid," she said truthfully, "that you would run away as Tony did."

"Pity he didn't stay gone."

"Yes. How are you feeling?"

"Super. I'm calling to ask how you feel this morning."

Margo got back into bed—stretched out and languid. "Sweetheart," she said, "I blush when I think of that love-making last night. It was memorable, don't you think?"

"Yes, that and more."

"Don't forget we see the minister tonight to discuss our marriage."

"I won't."

"Time's getting short."

"Not short enough."

"You're sweet."

"No, I'm just anxious to have you signed, sealed, and delivered—to my arms permanently."

"That's where I want to be, and I want the same thing for myself where you're concerned."

"Well, I'm shooting a wedding this morning. One of the Howard dean's sons. It's glitz personified."

"I'm glad ours will be quiet and simple."

A slip up, she thought quickly. She hadn't been consciously thinking of Ron's first wedding. It, too, had been like the wedding he would shoot today—high powered glitz personified.

"So am I, sunshine. So am I glad our wedding will be quiet." After a moment he added, "I've been through the glitz thing, and I'll take our way anytime. Listen, I've got to run. I have to finish synchronizing this wedding with Kyle."

"I wish every woman in the world had someone like you."

"You flatter me. You're the great one."

"Maybe we're both just lucky."

"Could be," he said, "but I think we both try to be loving to each other."

*   *   *

Bathed and dressed, Margo went downstairs to find Gramps waiting for her with waffles and maple syrup.

"Coffee," he asked, "or are you off it again? You're looking wonderful, Margo."

"Thank you, and no coffee, you sweet grandfather. I *feel* wonderful. How are you?"

"Things are looking up more and more every day."

"With you and Gracie?"

"Who else?"

"You two make a great pair."

"Well, I don't want to be too lonesome when you move out."

"Why don't you and Gracie get married? You've courted more than ten years."

"Now you mind your business," Gramps said, smiling. "We'll get around to it one day."

"The world's coming to an end one day," Margo grumbled. She knew how much Gracie wanted to get married.

"Now, now, we'll get to it before then."

Gramps always put thin—sliced bacon on top of his waffle batter which made the bacon sink into the waffle. The result, especially with the maple syrup, was crisply delectable.

Finishing her scrambled eggs with shrimp, orange juice, and waffle, Margo kissed Gramps on the cheek.

"Now, I don't want you rushing around too much," he said. "Remember what Ron said the bridal consultant told you. Save the last week, which is next week, for yourself, family, and friends."

"Oh, I'm remembering," she said. "Gramps, this is the most marvelous time of my life. Do I deserve a man like Ron?"

"Do you deserve?" Gramps scoffed. "You deserve the best there is, pumpkin. The best ever offered is what you deserve."

Margo felt her eyes fill with tears, and she brushed them away. "You've been there for me, always," she said softly.

"I just wish your parents could see you married. They'd be proud."

Margo nodded. Her parents had been very close to each other, but she had not been close to them. Gramps had always been her champion. Still she said, "So do I wish they could see me married. Yes, I think they'd be proud. Meanwhile, I can't tell you how glad I am that you're here. I want you to know that I'll always be there for you."

"I'm glad," he said simply. "You're a remarkable young woman, Margo."

In her office, Margo sat still for a moment. She didn't feel today as she had yesterday. Yesterday had been great enough, but today she felt buoyant and full of joy. She couldn't help daydreaming of Ron and her the night before. She could almost feel his arms around her. Reluctantly putting the dream aside, she picked up the African wedding sheaf of papers. This was going to be one of her best.

She worked hard and well all morning, checking her manuscript. Then, on her relaxing break, her buzzer sounded. Answering, she found it was Helen.

"Can I talk with you for a few moments?"

"I'll be right there."

Margo stood up, smoothing her navy and small cream flower print miniskirt and cream short jacket.

"Well," Helen said as she entered. "I'd say you were out in the sun, and the sun fell in love with you. Girl, you're blinding me with your glow."

Margo laughed delightedly. "I'm not the only one. It looks, Helen, like there's something going on in your life that you're not talking about."

Helen closed her eyes a moment. "I'll never tell." She smiled broadly. "But yes, I will. An old friend, now a widower, called me last night and came over. He's in town for a few days—"

"And your happiness knows no bounds."

Helen sighed. "We were once everything to each other, but I had sick parents to take care of, and he felt he couldn't wait. I don't blame him. In spite of illness, my parents lived to be fairly old, and he wanted to get married."

"And I'll bet he's still smitten with you."

"Well, he had me pretty breathless, and he talked as if he's still interested."

"I'm happy for you."

"I know you are. Listen, Margo, take all the time you need for wedding preparations. You're doing a fantastic job on the African weddings, but it's almost done, and someone else could finish it."

"Thanks," Margo said, "but it's my baby. I'll finish it today, and someone else can put it to bed." She looked at her watch. "I'm meeting Ron for a quick lunch. Then we're going to talk to the bridal consultant at Madison's."

"It's wonderful to see you so happy like this," Helen said. "You were just beginning to work here when you were engaged before. I hated the way Tony hurt you. And I mention it because I saw him here."

"Yes. I don't know exactly what he's up to."

"Is he trying to get you back?"

"How did you guess?"

"A hunch. You've blossomed incredibly with Ron. Your job is going well, I don't mind telling you. I have big things to discuss with you later. You're a catch now."

"Why, thank you. I don't know what Tony is up to, but I intend to nip his dreams in the bud, if he truly has any. Tony's competitive. I think just the fact that someone else wants me is enough to turn him on."

The morning passed quickly. As Margo stood under the building awning waiting for Ron to pick her up, she felt lightheaded with happiness again. Monday was the day

Laurette would hold a bridal shower for her. She was pretty sure that Ron's mother was trying to make up for her mean–spirited comments about her inability to compete with Jill. She needn't have bothered. *The last thing,* Margo thought, *that I need is a wedding shower from Laurette.*

She had met only the family friends that Ron was especially close to, and that was enough.

"Wedding girl!"

Margo felt hands clasping her shoulders from behind as she stood there.

"You look great, lady! I mean, like you're living large and riding high."

"Tony, let go of me!"

"I was thinking about holding you tighter, like in my arms."

Had he been drinking? She couldn't smell anything on his breath. In a quick movement, he turned her around and hugged her tightly while she struggled to make him let go. His mouth crushed hers beneath his. She shut her teeth against him. A few passersby were gawking, and she finally elbowed him with a short jab to the ribs. He let her go. She expected Ron to drive up any minute, and anxiously looked in the direction he would come from.

"Hey, Miss Feminist! Don't knock the breath out of me."

"I'll do more than that if you don't behave yourself."

Tony stood back a moment and maliciously watched her. "Waiting for your hubby to be?"

"Yes, I am." It did no good to ignore him.

"I hope he saw me kiss you. Margo, listen to me. I'm desperate for what we had. I haven't had those feelings since I left you."

"I don't want to hear this nonsense," Margo hotly declared.

Tony got angry, then. "I'm seriously considering picketing your wedding, Margo. How would you like that?"

Margo stared at him, her mouth a little open.

For a moment she couldn't get her breath. Then she sputtered, "Oh Tony, for heaven's sake grow up, will you?"

"I mean it, Margo. I never had any dignity when it came to getting you for myself."

"May I remind you that you left me high and dry at the altar?"

"We had three days before we were to get married. You weren't at the altar."

"Three days isn't much time."

"I'm sorry. I've beaten myself raw, flagellating myself, to make it up to you. Margo, I'll get down on my knees. Crawl. Anything."

Ron tapped his horn then, and Margo turned to Tony, wanting to slap him.

"Cut out the foolishness, Tony. I mean it. I'm not going to have this."

"Sorry, love, I have to do what I've got to do." He turned from her and went into the building.

Angrily, Margo walked out to the car where Ron sat waiting.

As she got in he kissed her, then said, "Double question. How's it going? And wasn't that Willis? You look beautiful and bothered."

"I'm okay," Margo said. "I was very happy indeed until Tony came up behind me as I waited for you. He's gotten ridiculous."

"Well, I can't hold it against the man for wanting you."

"He forcefully tried to French kiss me," Margo said. "I would have slapped him, but I held myself in check."

"Next time, maybe you shouldn't. No, I amend that. Slapping him just wouldn't be your style."

"Don't be too sure. People change with necessity," Margo said glumly.

He patted her hand, squeezed it. "Do you want to eat before or after seeing the bridal consultant?"

"I think I'd rather see the bridal consultant first. After Tony, I want to let my stomach settle."

She looked at Ron's pleasant profile as he drove. "Remember," she said, "tonight is our meeting with our pastor. Monday, your mom's bridal shower for me."

"I remember both."

"How did the wedding you were going to photograph go?"

"Splendidly, so far, with the pre–wedding photos and the ceremony. I'm proud of Kyle and of myself. Kyle's going to be a master photographer one day."

"And you already are."

Ron shrugged. "Thanks. It seems I was born with a camera in my hand. Dad's a great amateur, and he bought me cameras all the years I was growing up."

"Russ was never interested in photography?"

"No. Law has always been Russ's love."

"From what I hear, he's one of the best. Is it true he may be appointed chairman of the Equal Employment Opportunity Commission?"

"It's true, all right, but he's got some stiff competition. Russ *is* keen on politics, and he's active. So, one day—"

Ron parked in the department store's parking garage and they took the elevator up to the eighth floor and the bridal department.

When they were seated in the bridal consultant's office, she faced them, smiling. "You two are my favorite couple for next wedding week," she said. "You just seem made for each other."

They both thanked her.

"Plus you're so pleasant to work with." She turned to Margo. "Now," she said, "you *are* getting everything shaped up so you can virtually take off next week? I always recommend this where it's possible, you know. And rest, rest, rest. We want a beautiful bride, and I'm sure that's what you'll be."

"I'll be mostly taking off," Margo said, "but I do have a project about weddings that I'm working on. I like it, so it will add to my happiness."

The bridal consultant nodded. "I'm sure you know best. Your registry is filling up beautifully. You have many good friends, my dear. And Wedding Band is a lovely china pattern."

The bridal consultant held out a laminated sheet with a photograph of the place setting. The cream china with the wide gold band bordering it had been hers and Ron's favorite from the beginning.

They chatted about the wedding for nearly a half hour, seeking additional ways to make this a day Ron and Margo would remember with ultimate pleasure.

When they were leaving, the bridal consultant wistfully said, "I'd make time to come to this wedding, if you'd like that."

They both assured her that they would, and she kissed Margo's cheek.

"It's people like you," she said, "who keep me in this business.

Walking to the tearoom in Madison's Department Store, Margo took Ron's arm.

"Nervous?" he asked. "The day you'll belong to me fast approacheth. Scared?"

"A little of both," she said, her face solemn. Not until then did she tell him what Tony had said about picketing their wedding.

He seemed nonplussed. "Sounds crazy, but crazy things are happening these days. I can take it if you can."

"But your parents would be scandalized. Isn't there an anti-picketing law, whereby you can't picket within so many yards of a person's house?"

"Call Russ and ask him," Ron said. "My guess is that Willis will do nothing. He has a big family that prides itself on maintaining decorum. But if he's there until the cops have to take him away, don't worry about my family. Dad and Russ will understand. As for mother ..." Ron shrugged. "We'll cross that bridge when we come to it."

Margo squeezed his arm. "You're one wonderful man all the way through," she said.

"With a woman like you, what man wouldn't be?"

The older woman hostess met them at the entrance to the tearoom and seated them. She smiled broadly at their obvious happiness. Checking fingers, she saw the engagement ring on Margo's hand, but not a wedding band on either his or her hand. Aha, she thought, so they were engaged, and if her penchant for reading lives held up, they were soon to be married.

Back in her office that afternoon Margo put the finishing touches on her African wedding piece. She would pass it on to Gloria, the production assistant. It would be the lead article for their August issue.

She said, "Come in," to a light tap, and Jimilu came in with Jeff, their freelance photographer.

"I'll only be a second," Jeff said. "Just checking in to see if you have any more ideas for special shots for the August issue."

Margo shook her head. "I really haven't had the time, but I'll do some thinking this weekend and get back to you."

Jeff saluted her. "I want that glow you've had lately to last at least through the ceremonies," he said. "Promise me?"

"I promise," Margo said, and he left.

Jimilu hugged Margo and sat down in a chair by the desk.

"What's up?" Margo asked. "You look a bit bothered."

"Make that a lot bothered, and you'd be right."

"Tell me what's wrong."

Jimilu tapped her well–manicured fingers on the desktop. "It's Russ," she said. "We *were* doing fine."

"I'll say you were."

"He's eaten up with guilt, Margo."

"Guilt over Jill's death and his drunk driving?"

"Yes. First of all, we're finding out from studies that some people crave alcohol as a physical craving. It's not a matter of will power, so they can't help it. This could happen to any one of us."

Margo nodded. "Yes, I've read about those studies. But he's not drinking anymore. Do you think he should see a therapist?"

"I've suggested that. He's adamantly against it. I think the accident shocked him out of drinking. He's afraid of starting back up."

"You've talked about this lately?"

"Last night. He told me he's really drawn to me, but he's backing away. He feels I deserve more than he can give me."

"Not 'can,' but 'will' give you?" Margo said.

"Yes. I think I've fallen in love with him, Margo. He's such a great guy."

"I don't want to see you hurt again," Margo said. "Why don't you just stay friends and continue talking about how things stand between you?"

"That's what I want to do, but he keeps saying he's falling in love with me, and he can't have that. He's punishing himself terribly for Jill's death, I think."

"Yes, I think so, too. I like Russ, and I've had such high hopes for a relationship between you two."

"He feels guilt, too, he told me, for the hell he's put Ron through. My God, Margo, these things happen. We have to go on when they happen."

Margo patted Jimilu's hand. "I know. We have to convince Russ of that. It would certainly help if Ron forgave him."

"Yes," she said. Then Jimilu brightened a little. "I'm off for the afternoon. This two weeks I've pulled an early shift. I'm going to try to get some rest. I certainly didn't get much last night."

"I don't wonder," Margo said compassionately.

"I started not to come by. You deserve all the happiness you can find for yourself. I certainly don't want to rain on your parade."

Margo thought a moment when she said, "We're friends, Jimilu, and we've been friends for a long while. That's what friends are for. To be with us when we need them. I pray for your happiness as well as my own."

"You're a true friend, Margo," Jimilu said, the tension in her easing. "I'm going to go home and sleep." She paused for a moment. "Two questions! Any more trouble out of Tony? And how did the visit to the bridal consultant go?"

Margo took the last question first. "My bridal registry is coming along swimmingly," she said. "I've got a lot of good stuff, more than I'll ever need. Friends of Ron's family have chipped in. Oh yes, Laurette's giving me a bridal shower Monday afternoon."

"She's coming around."

"No, I don't really think so. Remember, I told you about her telling me that Ron and Jill had a love made in heaven."

Jimilu nodded. "I remember. I'm sorry. That must have hurt."

"It did, but I'll survive." She stopped talking for a moment. "About Tony." She told her what had happened in the lobby of the building during the noon hour.

"Is he going off his rocker?" Jimilu said. "Picketing a wedding would be something only a crazy juvenile would do."

"Oh, I don't think he'd do it, but Tony has changed so much. I wonder if he's on some kind of drug. He always was wild. I was young, and just didn't realize how wild. I just thought it came from the way his parents had spoiled him. They had so much money, so much clout. I was in love, and frankly I didn't think too much about that side of him."

"Well," Jimilu said, "you hang in there. The stunt he's trying to pull would be harassment. That's what law enforcement is for."

"Ron wants me to talk with Russ about it. He says he'll also mention it. Lord, I wish the two of them could be close again."

"So do I," Jimilu said fervently. "Russ told me that they were once bosom buddies. And he almost cried when he spoke of how much he misses Ron."

"We have to work to get those two back together," Margo said.

Jimilu got up. "I'm going now. Keep a weather eye out for Tony. So many of our 'best people' are dabbling in drugs nowadays. Nothing I saw in the past with Tony prepared me for what I'm seeing now. He's way out of line."

"Right now you need him like you need a headache. I hope he straightens up, and I certainly hope he's not on drugs."

Margo held her hand up, crossing her fingers.

"Come out of the darkroom. You have very important people company."

Ron continued studying his film negatives for a few minutes, in the wet section of his darkroom, recognizing Kyle's voice. His film was super sharp, and a thrill of pleasure swept through him. This was going to be some of the best work he and Kyle had done lately.

Stepping out into the studio, he was surprised to see Russ sitting in his wheelchair.

"Russ, what brings you here?" Ron asked, acknowledging his brother's presence and smiling at Kyle.

"Let him tell you." Russ motioned toward Kyle.

"I have bad news," Kyle said. "My mom's had a heart attack, and I'm going home to be with her. She had flu last winter, and I didn't go. I've been thinking how much I want to see her."

"I'm really sorry to hear that. You know I want you to go."

"We don't have anything truly hot going for the next two weeks, which is the length of time I'd want to stay."

"You're right."

"Except for your wedding, and that's a big except. You know how much I was looking forward to being your best man."

"And we were looking forward to it, too, but first things first."

Russ cleared his throat. "I'll get right to the point, Ron. I'd be proud if you'd let me be your best man. We were tight once. I'd give anything for us to be like that again."

Ron wet his lips, his body constricting.

He wasn't going to beat around the bush. "I don't think so, Russ."

"It would mean everything to me. Maybe you never can forgive me, but if you think about it you know that I'd forgive you if what happened had been the other way around. If we can't forgive others, we can't forgive ourselves."

"I don't need a sermon," Ron said, "and God knows I don't need your psychological wisdom. I just don't think it would work."

Still Russ kept on, glancing down at his disabled legs. "I've suffered, but my physical suffering is nothing compared to hating myself for what I did to you."

Ron started to say something, but Kyle cut across him. "You're happy, man," he said evenly. "You're riding high on happy juice. You're in love. How can you *not* forgive Russ?"

His voice taut, Ron said, "Don't get too deeply involved in this, Kyle. You don't know the whole story."

"Ron, for God's sake," Russ begged.

"No, Russ. One day for my own sake I hope I *can* forgive you, but not now, not even when I'm as happy as I am, and in love."

Russ's voice was heavy. "Okay," he said. "I understand, but I had to try. I'll be at the wedding. You don't mind that?"

"No, I expect you to come. Margo wants you there."

"And you, brother?"

Ron was silent a long moment. "I want you there, too, but not as best man."

"Two years is a long time to hate, Ron. Hatred eats you alive," Russ said.

"So does the pain of things others do to us," Ron shot back. Russ blanched.

Ron thought again before he said, "As you're telling me, Russ, two years is a long time to hate. I keep praying I will get over what you did to me, the things you robbed me of, but it will take longer than the time that's passed."

Kyle looked from one to the other. "I'm sorry." he finally said. "You're both great guys, and the time and love you're losing is sad."

"I'll be going now," Russ said. "I'm glad you included me in your wedding in some way. At least you didn't cut me out entirely."

Inexplicably Ron felt cruel, and he said, "Thank Margo. She's the one who wants the world to shape up right. I gave up on that two years ago."

"Who will you get for best man?" Kyle asked.

"I have someone in mind," Ron said. "Jeff Taylor at *Wedding Belles* is a good bet. I've been talking to him a lot lately. He'll be my choice if he isn't busy. Otherwise, I guess I'll have to *rent* a best man."

Ron wanted to bite his tongue after his last remark. He

didn't always hate Russ so much. It just flared at times when he least expected it.

"Strike that last statement," Ron said. "I apologize. Russ, I'm sorry, but I think you understand."

"Yes," Russ said, "I understand, and I really am sorry. I'm older than you are, and I know how hatred can strip you."

"And I know how *hurt* can strip you," Ron said shortly. Then, "Believe me, Russ, I'm sorry too."

That night Margo and Ron had an appointment to see their minister. They smiled and looked at each other while sitting in their minister's study with his charming wife.

"One more week," Margo said, leaning forward in her chair to clasp Ron's hand.

"We're going to have a great life," Ron said somberly. "I'm anxious to get the having kids show on the road."

"Me, too. Sometimes I can almost feel the press of little bodies inside me first, then against me."

Ron grinned roguishly. "Not to mention the first steps we take to get them started."

"Oh yes," Margo said breathlessly.

"I'm glad you're here," the Reverend Zack Carpenter said, coming into the room. "I'm so looking forward to talking with you."

He shook their hands and settled his slight frame into a chair opposite them, with one chair vacant.

"You both look very happy," he said, "and as two of my best parishioners, I want to wish you all the world's best wedding bliss. Your wedding rehearsal the other night went splendidly."

"I'm really looking forward to being married," Margo said.

"And I'm looking forward to the whole enchilada," Ron said.

"For some reason, your wedding plans bring back memories of my own marriage," Reverend Carpenter told them. "I guess it's your obvious joy in this. It's the way Lois and I felt."

"And you're both still very happy," Margo said.

"Very. After ten years. Our children just make the happiness deeper."

They talked at length about what each expected of the marriage and of what each wanted.

Then Reverend Carpenter got up and got three slender, beautifully bound white silk *moire* books from his desk drawer. He came back and handed each one a book, keeping another for himself.

"Lois and I have put this together from the love and aspirations of the couples we've counseled. She'll be in shortly. One of the kids fell and hurt herself, but not too severely."

At his lead, they opened the books with heavy, ivory, gold–edged pages and began reading. Reverend Carpenter suggested that they each read a section. The borders were very wide, the black print large, and easily read.

"Let us begin with you, my dear," Reverend Carpenter said to Margo. She breathed deeply and read aloud.

"We are husband and wife.

Friends.

Lovers.

Fellow life travelers."

Ron read next.

"We come together with honor.

We adore each other.

We will be there for each other

For always we belong to each other."

And for the better part of a half hour they read the soothing words of love and hope. Lois came in quietly and took a seat in the chair that completed the circle.

"I would only wish," she said, "that you know the kind of happiness Zack and I have had. And I believe you do."

"Yes, we do know that kind of happiness," Ron said. "And we'll do everything in our power to see that it lasts."

"May I ask if there are things between you that bother you that you care to talk about?" Reverend Carpenter asked.

Yes, Margo thought quickly. *His love for Jill.* But under no circumstances could she talk about that. It was just something she had to learn to live with.

Instead she said, "I worry about being the best wife I can be to Ron."

Ron nodded slowly, "And that is one of my biggest worries—being a superb husband to Margo."

The minister grew pensive before he said, "Believe me, one of the most admirable ambitions you two can possess is wanting the success of this marriage. Of course it requires some of the world's hardest work. Next to parenting, it is, I think about the hardest."

"Life is hard, at least at times," Mrs. Carpenter said, "but it is so rewarding, as well."

"Love is the rose among the thorns of our lives," Reverend Carpenter added. "You both know the beauty of love and how to sustain it, so you are blessed."

The session lasted a little over an hour, and on leaving they made plans with the Carpenters to have additional sessions to get their marriage on the right track. Leaving there, Margo felt the peace of heaven inside her. As they walked down the walk of the Carpenter's red brick house, Margo thought she was going to be able to bear what hurt Jill's memory caused her very well. Ron had been so helpful there, moving Jill's pictures from view once she, Margo, had begun visiting him. He seldom spoke of Jill at all unless she brought up the subject. Immediately in her mind, there was Tony in the picture. Would he carry out his threat to picket her wedding?

"What're you thinking?" Ron asked. "You're so quiet."

Reaching his car, he unlocked the door and helped her in.

She was less than truthful. "Just how good it feels to be getting married," she said, then added, "to the man I love so much."

With the door still open, he bent and kissed her. "We're going to have it all, Margo," he said, "if there is any way I can swing it, we're going to have it all."

CHAPTER EIGHT

Laurette and Margo had decided on Monday for her bridal shower for Margo, because Margo would be off that week and better able to handle the many presents that shower would bring.

It had been a calm, peaceful weekend, with her working on displaying her wedding presents and spending time with Ron and Gramps, Gracie, and Jimilu. Margo woke up that Monday morning bursting with life. Soon she and Ron would be man and wife. Friends. Lovers. Fellow life travelers. Yes, and future parents. They had talked with the minister and his wife at length about that, and parenting had figured large in the lovely book the Carpenters had given them.

In spite of a few distractions, she felt that she and Ron were going to have a wonderful life. Getting up, she did a few deep knee bends and prepared to pull on jogging togs and go around the block a few times. First, she'd call Ron. As her hand went out to dial, the phone rang.

"Margo." Tony's voice was hoarse, breathy.

"I thought I asked you not to call me."

"I had to call."

"No, you don't have to badger me like this. And don't talk about loving me, Tony. You don't know the meaning of love."

"Margo, please hear me out. Will you?"

He sounded different. "All right," she said evenly.

"I had a mild stroke after I left you yesterday."

"A stroke?" She felt alarmed.

"Yes. I've been on drugs, babe. Couldn't you tell?"

"No, not really. I did wonder, just a bit. You were always pretty highly charged."

"I was more than that. I did drugs once in a while when we were going to get married, but not like this. At least I'm smart enough to know when I'm in trouble."

Margo was silent, not knowing what to say.

"Are you there?" he asked.

"I'm here. I guess I'm too shocked to say anything. How are you doing?"

"You couldn't care—not after the way I've acted."

"I have to admit I've been pretty angry at you."

"With good reason. My mind is working now, and I can look back at the way I've behaved with you lately and cringe. I'm asking that you forgive me. I won't be causing you any more trouble."

"Of course I forgive you, and I hope you can stay off drugs. I'm truly sorry about your stroke."

Tony sighed. "The doctors say it was minor, but it has scared the hell out of me. It twisted my face a bit, but they say they can straighten that out. Otherwise, I have a great chance to recover completely."

"I'm glad about that."

"I have to add that I wasn't lying when I've talked with you. One of the reasons my marriage didn't work out is that I was haunted by my love for you, and the way I knew I had hurt you. Even when you use them lightly, Margo, drugs don't just destroy your body. They destroy your mind and your soul."

"At least you know that now, before it's too late."

"Yes. I want you to be happy, and I wish you all the best. I'm going to a drug rehab center in New York as soon as I get out of the hospital and treatment for my stroke. Margo?"

"Yes."

"I'm sorrier than you'll ever know."

"Your calling me makes up for a lot," she said. "It's a classy thing for you to do."

"Thank you. You'd know about that. You're a classy lady."

He hung up then, and Margo sat on the side of the bed for a long time before she dialed Ron and told him about Tony's call.

"Lady Luck," he said, "is flashing sunshine on us non-stop. It looks as if she loves us as much as we love each other."

Time dragged a bit after that. Margo wanted the day and Laurette's shower to be over.

"You're a bit edgy," Gramps said, near time for her to be leaving. "I'll bet you're dreading Laurette's to–do."

Margo sighed. "More than you know. Her crowd is so uptight, so cold, and insensitive."

"You can handle it," he said. "I raised you to handle anything."

Margo pinched his cheek. "I couldn't have been raised by a nicer man."

Gramps' smile was wide and charming.

Laurette's shower had a theme—Wedding Wonderland—and she meant it to live up to her expectations. It didn't matter that she didn't particularly care for Margo. She didn't dislike her. It was simply that she wasn't Jill, the daughter she'd never had.

Margo arrived a little before the three o'clock time set for the shower. Many guests were already there, and Laurette glanced around her with pride at the decor that was coordinated in blues with touches of fuchsia, turquoise, and cream. Balloons and flowers were everywhere. It was a very expensive room, and it showed. Margo didn't know a lot of people who had cream silk living room walls.

Laurette hugged Margo as she let her in, something she seldom did.

"You're looking very well," Laurette said, "I'm proud of you."

Margo's eyebrows raised a bit. Had she expected her to turn up in jeans and an old jersey?

"Thank you," Margo said. "So do you always, of course."

Margo was dressed in a pearl gray, silk jersey jacket dress with bone buttons and a truly beautiful fuchsia, green, and pink scarf that had cost her far more than she wanted to pay. Today she was glad she'd bought it.

Laurette wore mocha crepe with beige and pale orange touches, and the fabulous gold and diamond brooch given to her as a Christmas present by her husband.

"I never see your brooch but what I marvel at Dr. Hyman's good taste," Margo said.

"Yes, my husband is as tasteful a man as you'll find, all right," Laurette said. "Call him Wally. He loves it when you do."

"Very well."

Normally Margo would have been nervous, but she felt very relaxed and at ease. She guessed Tony's call had a lot to do with it.

She felt even happier when Jimilu came in, all gentle confidence.

"What a marvelous home you have," Jimilu said to Laurette.

"Thank you," Laurette said quietly. "I'm so glad you could come."

Laurette moved away and Jimilu winked at Margo. "Your reinforcement of one party is here," she said. "You can relax."

There were twenty to thirty women there of all ages, friends of the Hymans. Wealthy women. Well dressed. Well educated. As Laurette introduced her, Margo mused that no one would know that Laurette didn't especially like her. She was a woman who always put on a magnificent front.

It didn't matter that Margo had come from a family unlike theirs, although rich in love and honor. By marrying Ron Hyman, she would become a part of their clan.

The presents were awe–inspiring. A beautiful chest of silver. Waterford crystal. Royal Doulton china. Gift certificates. Cards in thick, cream envelopes that told her they had responded to her bridal registry.

Their buffet lunch had all the good food imaginable. Baked turkey, ham, shaved beef, and rich beef rib roast. The most delicious potato salads—German, Southern, and Mexican. There was a wide array of raw vegetables. Desserts were bountiful and rich, but those on a diet were not forgotten, so there were several varieties of yogurt and a beautiful rainbow jello mold.

Circulating and thoroughly enjoying herself, Margo smiled when a young woman came up to her.

"Margo, how are you?"

"Fine, thank you, Stella. How are you?"

"Okay. I guess I really shouldn't be here."

"Why do you say that?"

"Well, I *am* Jill's sister. But then, Laurette is *my* godmother. I long ago got used to the idea that she vastly preferred Jill."

Margo made no further comment. She and Stella were both ushers at Arena Stage, and so were fairly well acquainted.

Now Stella spoke. "I haven't seen you around much at Arena."

"I've been really busy."

"With the marriage thing?"

"That, and my job."

"I know the feeling." Stella was a lawyer. Now she showed no inclination to move along. When ushering, Margo had had little to say to Stella, who was noted for her sharp wit and sharper tongue.

"I'll say this in friendly warning," Stella said. "My sister is going to be a hard act to follow."

Margo's heart constricted a little.

"I'm sure of that," Margo said, "but I'm game to try. I think Ron and I love each other enough to come out ahead."

Stella looked at her long and hard, her eyes unfathomable. "I wish you luck," she said, "but you're going to need more than love. There was something between my sister and Ron that was deeper than love. Those two belonged together. I'm sorry if I sound cruel, but it's true. He'll never get over her."

Standing there near the library door, Margo thought she could turn and see Jill's portrait through the open door, but she didn't turn. Instead, she saw Ron in her mind's eye. In just a few hours she would see Ron. She and Jimilu would load her car with the shower presents and take them to her house. Then she would go to Ron's house. Avid for each other, she and Ron would leave no time for her to think about others like Laurette and Jill's sister, Stella. No time at all.

That night at Ron's house Margo walked around, having changed to a light blue, velour jumpsuit with a matching headband. In Ron's bedroom she sat on the side of the bed, thinking about the times when Ron had spoken of his desire to build her another house. Now she knew that that was what she wanted, too, because she wanted no shadows over their life from his first marriage.

The bed looked inviting, and she was tired from the bridal shower, getting the presents home, with Jimilu's help, and unwrapping and displaying a few of them. Her eyes sparkled at the thought of all the gifts she'd gotten, and how pleasantly the shower had gone. Laurette had been friendlier than she'd ever been.

Getting up and wandering restlessly again, she went to the bar, mixed a pitcher of piña coladas, and sipped one slowly as she waited for Ron, who was photographing a dance recital.

Her cell phone rang and she picked it up, set it for talking.

"You're there waiting for me," Ron said. "I can't tell you how happy that makes me. How was the shower?"

"Splendid, Darling, as you might imagine. Your mother was really lovely to me today."

Ron was silent a moment before he said, "I'm happy to hear that. Mother can be charming when she sets out to be."

"Ron, you wouldn't believe the presents we got."

"I'm glad, but we don't really need presents. We're our presents to each other."

"You're right about that. When will you be coming home?"

"Within two hours or so. He glanced at his watch. Seven P.M. The dance school owner decided she wanted individual photos of her dancers, and that's going to take some time. I gave her a great contract."

"Have you eaten?"

"They have a loaded buffet here, so don't fix anything. Just rest and be ready for my hot kisses when I come. I've got to go now. I see the head lady coming in my direction. Bye, love."

With the connection broken, Margo pushed the antenna down and hung up the phone.

This was going to be a swift week, she decided. She had selected Jimilu's gift, a pearl butterfly pin. Tuesday was the wedding rehearsal. Wednesday she would have guests–to–be view the gifts. Thursday, the informal dinner for the wedding party. And Friday night she and Ron would have a candlelight dinner together. All in all, the restful week the bridal consultant had recommended. Smiling, Margo thought she was in a constant state of excitement. She was in love with life.

Busily photographing the young teen ballet dancers, Ron was in his element. He intended to branch out more and more into the arts, but he would always specialize in weddings. Thinking about weddings brought his mind to Kyle, his photographic aide, who would be with his mother by now.

His brother's sad face came before him. For over two years he had tried to forgive Russ, and it just hadn't worked. It wasn't going to work now. Jeff Taylor would make a good substitute best man, and he had agreed to Ron's plan.

The thought of Margo waiting for him made the blood quicken in his veins. They had so much together. He had an urge to look at Margo's photo in his wallet, but Mrs. Smith, the ballet school owner and a sweet woman, was upon him.

"I know I can expect the best from you," she said. "Did you enjoy the recital?"

"I loved it, and watching has given me a lot of ideas for angles to shoot from."

The woman was plainly overjoyed at her success. "There was a reporter here from the *Post,*" she said, "and also the *Washington Informer.*"

"Great. I noticed them both."

"Yes, the *Informer* photographer is coming by tomorrow to take more intimate shots. I do want to thank you for the very good price you gave me. I can tell you, we're having some financial difficulty. Had you heard about it?"

Ron nodded. "I had. I want to do what I can to help. Your school's been open for decades now, and I'll do what I can to see that it stays open."

Impulsively, the older woman caught his hand and pressed it.

"Whenever I hear about Generation X and how young

folks have gone bad these days, I think of people like you, Mr. Hyman. You help make life more worth living."

Ron grinned. "Just do me a favor. When the children my future bride and I will have reach dancing age, just stay open to teach them."

"Count on it."

A lissome thirteen–year–old came up. "May I be next?" she asked. "I have to leave early. My mom's picking me up."

"Sure," Ron said, thinking that one day he'd have a kid like this. His heart filled with joy at the prospect. Margo had taken dancing lessons as a youngster, he remembered her saying. He thought she had probably looked and been a lot like this young girl.

Margo fell fast asleep on Ron's bed and didn't awaken until she felt Ron shake her and stroke her back.

"Wake up, honey. I'm here, and the fun begins." Margo roused. She had been dreaming about her wedding— beautiful dreams. But there had been fairies there and one malevolent one—Stella, Jill's sister. The sister had been about to put a curse on Margo when Ron awakened her. She turned over to lie on her back and pulled him down to her.

"I had a beautiful dream about our wedding," she told him, "but it turned bad when Stella came in."

Ron grimaced. "That's about par for the course with Stella. That one's a dysfunctional family all by herself."

Margo began to laugh, but the laughter caught in her throat. "Let's not talk about negative things tonight," she said. "Just about weddings and love, and you and me."

"It's a deal," he said, drawing her close.

"I made piña coladas, your favorite next to brandy and milk. Would you like me to get you one?"

"No. Stay right where you are, lying here close to me. At this moment, you're all I want." He kissed her lightly, his tongue teasing the silken skin of her face and throat. She closed her eyes and let the glory of their love wash over her. When she opened them and looked at him, he seemed deeply bothered for a few fleeting seconds.

"Ron, what is it?" she asked with a start of alarm.

"It's nothing," he said. "I thought of something that happened some time ago, and shooting the kids this afternoon and tonight brought it all back."

He didn't offer to tell her what the bad scene was that had him gripped in pain now. His expression had cleared as he nibbled at her neck, but somehow she was sure he spoke less than the truth.

"I think I will have a piña colada," he said. "Shall I get you one?"

"No. It was the first one that put me to sleep."

He left the bed and went into the living room, and after a minute she got up to join him. She moved quietly, and when he turned from the bar to face her his expression was full of tenderness and love.

"Do you know something?" he asked her.

"No, but I want to know whatever it is you want to tell me."

"I want to dance with you. That shoot has left me wanting to hold you. And I want the music we had the other night at Sunset Beach."

Going to the tape deck he switched it on, and music from Mariah Carey's *Butterfly* album swirled around them. He held out his arms to her, and she went into them.

Pressed close to him with her head on his shoulder, she snuggled closer. The lines of his hard, lean body awakened the deepest passion she knew, and she closed her eyes and experienced the full glory of the moment.

"I love you, sweetheart," he said. "I'll always love you."

"No more than I love you," she whispered. "I want to bring you joy from now on."

"You do bring me joy," he said. "And I think you always will. That's why I love you so."

The fires kindled quickly in their blood, surprising both of them in its intensity. He leaned back, causing her to lean more heavily on him, and she felt his abiding love.

After a little while they stopped dancing and each removed the clothes from the other. He took her on the wide sofabed, and each knew the thrill of that moment. Her nakedness made him thrill with desire, and his nakedness energized her to hold him close and stroke the length of his body, then welcome him into her body, into the deepest recesses of her heart and soul.

It was late when they slept, in his bedroom. Margo dreamed the same dream she had dreamed earlier of Stella, who had said that Jill would be a hard act to follow.

She was surprised that she didn't dream at all of Laurette. For it was Laurette's words that had crushed her, that she remembered. It was Laurette who had said that *Ron and Jill had a love made in heaven.* Well, she thought staunchly, she wasn't going to let that ruin what she felt for Ron. They were getting married. He wanted to build her a house. He had removed the photographs of Jill from display in his house. He wasn't clinging to his first wife. He had made himself whole again. But a small inner voice taunted her. Ron still couldn't talk about his first marriage.

Coming fully awake, Margo simultaneously looked at the radio clock's luminous dial and reached for Ron. His side of the bed was empty. It was one o'clock in the morning.

Sitting up on the side of the bed, she listened for sounds from the bathroom. There were none. Softly she got up and padded about the house looking for Ron. A sliver of light shone from his den. The door was closed.

Making no sound, she opened the door a little way. Ron sat in a deep chair several feet into the room, his back to her. And in his hands he held a large photograph she had seen when she first began visiting—a photo of Ron, Jill, and Russ, their arms around each other. It was a stunning photograph taken by Ron's father.

Now Ron studied that photo, and it took a full minute

for Margo to realize that he was crying bitter tears. Then she heard him say softly, "Why did it have to happen this way?"

Stunned, Margo turned, silently pulling the door not quite shut behind her. Sadly, she thought she wouldn't intrude on grief like this. No wonder Ron no longer wanted to stay in this house, with its memories of Jill.

Ask him, she told herself. And she knew she wouldn't because it wasn't that he was unwilling to tell her—he simply couldn't bear to face the truth.

Going into the bedroom, feeling as if her life's blood was draining away, Margo switched on the bed lamp, quickly got into her clothes with trembling hands and left the house, closing the front door softly. She felt now that Ron was a man she no longer knew.

She couldn't go home. Gramps would want to know what was going on, and what could she tell him? She couldn't bear his warm compassion. What she wanted was Ron, not sympathy.

Her head was spinning as she walked along, and she hardly knew how she got into her car, parked a block away. She only knew she wasn't going home. She crossed over to and drove down Sixteenth Street, Northwest, to Pennsylvania Avenue, driving by rote, seeing little that appeared before her. Gramps would worry, and she didn't want him to, but she had left her cell phone at Ron's.

Out on the Washington–Baltimore Parkway, going toward the road that cut off and led to Sunset Beach, she didn't know she would go there until she was nearly there.

Jimilu would be worried. And Ron? When would he stop his tears of anguish over Jill long enough to miss her?

For a long moment, she wanted nothing so much as to die. Traffic was light. As she started to pass a truck, she realized she was climbing a hill. Only when an oncoming van came into view on her side did she pull back behind the truck and realize how close she had come to an accident.

She laughed shakily, hysterically. *If I'm going to die,* she thought, *I have no wish to take someone else with me, especially a stranger.*

By some miracle she pulled up in the Sunset Beach house driveway. Ron had had a set of keys made for her. She had no business here, she thought. This was the Hymans' house, not hers. *Ron,* she thought, her heart breaking, *I could have stood the truth if you'd told me you could never love another woman as you loved Jill. But would I marry you, knowing that?* She knew the answer was no. She deserved a love free of past encumbrances. She didn't believe she could live in a present dragged down by the unreleased loves of the past.

She sat in the car a long time with the lights on. Warren Hill's light came on in his house up the street. She knew he'd recognize her car when he walked nearer, as he was certain to do.

After a little while he turned on his porch light and came down his walk and toward the car. On shaky legs she got out of the car when he was about twenty feet away and called, "It's me, Warren. I drove up here to think."

He walked faster and peered at her in the headlights of the car.

"Margo, what the hell are you doing up here at this time of the morning?"

"I need to think," she said, "and I need to get away. Please don't tell anybody I'm here."

"They'll worry about you," he said. "Doesn't anybody know you're here? Do you have a key? I can let you in."

"I have a key. Will you please say nothing to anyone about my being here? I'm in a bad way, Warren, I have to think something through."

"Is something wrong between you and Ron?"

"Yes. I'm not going to marry him."

"Now what kind of nonsense is that?" he asked. "You two love each other as much as I've ever seen it happen."

"I can't talk about it. Please don't ask me to."

He let her in the house and she put her keys back into

her purse. *At least,* she thought, *the weather is cooperating.* It had been warm since the first of May.

"Now, you're sure you'll be all right?" he asked. "This is the damnedest thing I've come across lately."

"I won't stay," she said. "I'll go back in the morning. Please don't call anyone. Let me have this little time to myself."

Warren nodded. It wasn't something he wanted to do, but Margo was in a bad way and she'd been great to him. He wanted to do what he could to help.

"Well," he said, "tell you what I'm going to do. I'll sit out here on the porch for at least an hour or two. You want to spill some beans, come on out. Frankly, I don't think you're in any condition for me to leave you alone completely."

"Thanks, Warren," Margo said, her voice gone sad and helpless. "That will be just fine with me."

Margo pulled the dustcover back from the sofa and sat down, only to get up again, seized by agitation. She had not cried, and her throat was dry, constricted and aching. She would call Ron and Gramps first thing in the morning and let them know she was okay. But for right now she wanted to be alone.

She went to the window, opened the blinds, and saw Warren sitting on the porch as he'd said he would be. Her heart felt like lead in her breast. It was true, she thought, hearts really did break. Even when Tony had abandoned her to marry another woman, it had not hurt like this. Yet, being Margo, she hurt for Ron, too. He couldn't help loving the woman he loved. He had tried hard to put her, Margo, first, but the heart makes its own rules, follows its own directions.

She paced the length of the room, the way Ron did sometimes when he was thinking. But she wasn't thinking so much as feeling a pain so shattering it was dangerous.

She sat on the sofa then, and put her head on her knees. It wasn't as if she had lost Ron. He had said nothing about

their not being married. They had made love that night
and it had been great, as usual, though not like the night
when they had come here. That had been a meeting of
souls. Last night he had held her with tender ardor. Nothing in his manner had said anything other than that he
loved her devotedly.

But nothing erased that searing vision of Ron holding
the photograph of Russ, Jill, and him and crying as if his
heart would break. The Ron she had gotten to know cried,
but not easily, so his pain must have been truly terrible.

Softly she said to him in absentia, "I won't marry you,
my darling. You're chained to the past, a past so blessed
with love that you can't let go no matter how much you
want to. You've tried, Ron. Lord, how you've tried.. And
you love me. I can feel your love. But you can't come out
of the shadows of the past. Maybe time will heal your pain.
I'll wait a long while, because I've never felt for anyone
else what I feel for you. My age, twenty–five, is young, but
when it comes to the depths of passion, twenty–five is
ageless."

She got up again and slowly traversed the length of
the long, big room. A photograph album in one of the
bookcases caught her eye. It was thick and had an ivory
leather cover. Feeling masochistic, she took it down and
began to leaf through it. They were all there, mostly in
pictures taken on Sunset Beach of the Hymans and Jill
and her birth family.

After a few pages, her breath caught. A replica of the
photo Ron had been holding at his house tonight leapt
out at her, and she could see it far more clearly than she
had when Ron was holding it and crying. Ron. Jill. And
Russ. They were happy in these photographs. They
belonged together, in a setting she would never know. Ron
loved her, Margo, but like his mother he worshiped his
first wife.

Some people, some animals, she thought, died when
their mates died. Ron hadn't died, nor would she without

him, but she felt a gaping hole in her life, and knew that she would never be the same. The night seemed interminable.

She got up, turned off the lights, and was lost in thought when she saw the headlights of a car pull into the driveway. She heard Warren and Ron's voices. Then she heard his keys in the lock and heard him call, "Margo! Where are you?" as he turned the lights on.

He came to her swiftly and sat on the couch beside her.

"Warren called you," she said. "I asked him not to."

"No, he didn't."

Looking at the clock, she saw that there had hardly been enough time for him to realize that she was gone. It was less than an hour since she had arrived here.

"It's so soon after I left," she said. "How did you know I was here? It's your family house and I'm still a guest in it, but I had to have somewhere to be alone."

He took both her hands in his. "Margo, we have to talk."

"I'm not sure there's anything to talk about."

"Yes, there is. I should have taken you more into my confidence. I should have told you everything. Now I'm going to."

"It's all right, Ron," she said. "I think I understand. We can't help loving who we love. I didn't tell you, but talking to Laurette one day when she called me at the office—"

"Go on. What happened?"

"Laurette said that your love for Jill, and hers for you, was a love made in heaven."

Ron's harsh laugh was between a laugh and a sob.

"A love made in heaven? Dear God," he said. "Please listen to me, my darling. Listen while I tell you what happened between Jill and Russ and me. Will you listen?"

Margo nodded, unable to speak because her throat was so tight.

He caught her hands with both of his and continued to hold them. Her hands were cold, and he rubbed them. He began to talk.

"By the time Jill died and Russ was so badly injured, all the love was on my side," he said. "The accident happened one morning about nine in the crush of thick traffic. I'm going to be blunt about this. They were headed for New York, then Toronto. They were running away together, to be married when Jill could divorce me. She told me that she was pregnant with his child. She'd held me off with excuses for several months."

Margo drew a quick, surprised breath, but said nothing. Ron continued. "I knew she was changing in her feelings toward me, but we had been married four years and I just thought it was the passing of time. My mother and father were never overly demonstrative."

He cleared his throat, telling himself to get the whole miserable story out as soon as possible, but dear Lord, it still hurt so much. Would Margo understand? How could she not? She had to, or he was done for. He couldn't let her go.

"At first we were really in love," he continued," more than anyone I knew. But I'm telling you about the beginning, and it's the end that you must know."

Margo took her hands from his and touched his face. "Take your time, my darling," she said, "and we can talk later if you need more time to talk about this."

Because she sensed that Ron was coming apart from reliving the pain he'd suffered, she couldn't rush him.

"No," he said, "I have to tell you now." His voice was hoarse, strained.

"Jill said they'd planned to just go away and leave a note for me, but she thought she owed it to me to tell me face–to–face, so they came to our house, Jill's and mine. They didn't want to hurt Mother and Dad, or her parents. They would write to both sets of parents a little later, begging them to understand.

"Russ had been drinking, as usual. When I'd mentioned this to him many times before that he always said he could handle it. And it came to seem that he was right, that he could—"

Pain made his voice ragged now, and Margo stroked his face and shoulders.

"I was crazy with pain, Margo, and I'd had no preparation to get used to this. My emotional world had been pretty safe until then. No shocks that I remember.

"They asked me to forgive them. Russ was drunk, too drunk to be driving. We were all sitting down and Jill got up, came to my chair and kissed me. Then she pleaded with me to divorce her, and asked me again to forgive them. They didn't want our parents to know for a little while. They wanted me to say they were going to separate places after they reached New York. Later, they would tell them.

"I went crazy with anger, then. You know I'm not quick to lose my temper, but I yelled, *'Go* away together. I'll give you the damned divorce.' As wild as I felt, I had the presence of mind to look at both of them, and their eyes were shining with love for each other. I lost it, then.

"I lashed out at them. 'Go on together! Toronto. New York. Europe. What the hell difference does it make? Now get out, and may God damn the two of you. I hope you both rot in hell!' I've felt sick with guilt about those words, Margo."

"Because you wanted them both dead?"

"Yes. Oh God, yes. Since then I've felt that my words may have helped to hasten her death and his injuries. Russ and I had been close all our lives."

Stroking his back, Margo said, "They were adults, Ron. They were in love, and your words couldn't have affected them that much. They were wrapped up in each other. I'm sure you wanted to kill them. You were in love with Jill, and Russ had taken her away from you."

He caught her to him fiercely. "Margo. Margo, no wonder I love you so."

"The way I love you," she said, "it would be strange if you didn't return at least some of that love."

Ron hugged her again, still needing to talk. "When I saw Jill's mangled body and Russ's crushed legs, I felt sick with guilt. The accident happened within an hour of their leaving me. They had gotten no farther than a few miles out on the Baltimore–Washington Parkway. When I look at Russ now in his wheelchair—"

"Your wanting it to happen couldn't make it happen," Margo soothed him. "Sweetheart, you're punishing yourself unnecessarily. It was an accident. Forgive yourself, and forgive them. God would want you to. And ask His forgiveness."

Ron shuddered. "I couldn't talk about it. I knew you were getting a lot of flak about Jill's and my love, our *perfect* marriage, but I couldn't face the fact that I had wanted them both dead.

"If you had known Russ before the accident. He was an athlete. A football quarterback in college. He was never still. Now—"

"It was his choice to be drinking when the accident happened."

Ron felt a little easier then in his mind. "If only I could have talked with you about it, or with someone, before you came into my life, I could have spared you this grief."

"Ron," Margo told him, "let's just be happy that you told me now. You came up here so quickly. When did you realize I had gone, and how did you know I would come here?"

Ron thought a moment. "I pulled myself together and I knew I had to talk with you right then, but you had left. I realized you'd almost surely seen me crying and suspected the worst, that my love for Jill was pushing you out.

"And how did I know you'd come here? I didn't, but I thought about the night recently we drove up here and how we both felt that night was so special to us. In my twenty–eight years on this earth, I've never felt anything like it. Not with Jill. Not with anyone.

"I didn't want to disturb your Gramps. I just didn't think you'd go to Gracie or to Jimilu feeling the way you must have felt. I just felt in the deepest part of my heart that you'd come here, trying to regain something we found here.

"And you wouldn't have come here if you hadn't felt close to me still, in spite of the pain. Margo, forgive me."

"You know I forgive you. But from this moment on, let's be open with each other, sweetheart. Please."

He lifted her and turned her legs across his body as they sat there, locked in a tender embrace. Their hands could not press each other close enough. He teased the corners of her mouth with his tongue, and she opened to him. Her breasts came alive with wanting him.

Pausing, he said huskily, "We're the ones, you and I, who have the love made in heaven."

Margo laughed throatily. "And you know something, my love," she said, "it's a love that's going to last forever."

CHAPTER NINE

On the morning of her wedding day, Margo thought it was the most beautiful day she had ever seen. She lay back on the bed for a few moments, remembering Ron's face the night he had told her the truth about Jill and his marriage. She still hurt a little at his having borne all that pain for the two years since that accident. She breathed deeply. It was over now, and something far more precious had begun. She and Ron felt so close now, so open.

She took a leisurely bath with jasmine bubbles, then dried off and got into a big, pink terry cloth robe.

Sitting at her vanity, she deftly put up her dark brown hair into a French twist. The day before, her hairdresser had shown her just how to make it look professional. The wedding would be at eleven o'clock. She wanted nothing to eat save a tall glass of orange juice and half a strawberry Danish. A knock sounded and she answered it to find Gramps standing there, a big smile on his face.

"I thought I'd bring you what you like to eat when you don't want much to eat."

Margo laughed, took the tray, and set it on her night table. "You know me so well," she said.

"And I'm going to miss you, my girl, but I couldn't be happier for you and Ron."

Margo kissed his cheek and took a raisin muffin, orange juice, and half a Danish.

As Gramps stood looking out the window Margo said, "I hope you and Gracie have serious plans for a wedding of your own one day."

Turning, he grinned from ear to ear. "As a matter of fact," he said, "we're thinking about September, on her birthday."

"Oh, that's wonderful," Margo said, happily hugging him.

The door chimes sounded, and Gramps went downstairs to answer them. Margo opened her door to listen, expecting Jimilu; she was not disappointed. In a few moments her friend and maid of honor had bounced up the stairs and into Margo's room.

"Well bride to be, I'm here to help you get the show on the road," she said.

"Have you had breakfast?" Margo asked.

"I have, but I'm actually full on love."

"Russ?"

"Who else? We're hitting on all eight cylinders again. He's such a great guy."

"And all yours."

"I certainly hope so." Jimilu went to the closet, brought out Margo's wedding gown in its wrap, and laid it on the bed. "I'm so glad Ron told you the whole story."

Margo nodded in agreement.

"We have two and a half hours," Jimilu said, "to get ready for what has to be one of the loveliest weddings of the season."

* * *

The big backyard of Gramps's house, where the wedding was to take place, had been trimmed and planted to excellence. Azaleas and rose bushes in bud and light bloom were massed at a spot that would serve as the point of ceremony. And Ron waited for her there, pleased the way he had seldom been in his life. He could hardly believe the joy he had known since talking to Margo a few nights ago about Jill, Russ, and him.

And in his wheelchair Russ sat by his brother's side, happy for him. For the first time in two years, he felt surges of happiness, and looked forward to those surges continuing with Jimilu now firmly in his life.

The many guests were seated on folding chairs as the orchestra struck up the wedding march, giving Margo and Gramps their cue to come up the dark green nylon carpeted aisle of the emerald green backyard.

Margo's gown was heavy cream lace over cream silk satin, off the shoulder, with long sleeves, ending in lacy points over her hands. She held a bouquet of creamy white baby's breath and full-size orchids.

A hush swept over the guests as she walked along with Gramps, who could not have been prouder. A mist of tears stood in his eyes. His granddaughter had known so much heartache, and he felt this was the beginning of far happier times for her. And thinking of his own coming marriage, catching Gracie's eye as she sat on a chair near the aisle turned halfway to watch them, he knew a rush of happiness himself.

From the time she had begun to step forward toward him, Ron had looked at his beloved, drinking her in. Lord, she was beautiful! When she reached him, both trembled with love and passion. This was a holy day for them, surrounded by friends and relatives.

Steve, the wedding dress designer, sat with the other guests, his eyes shining. This was one of the most beautiful gowns he had ever fashioned, and he felt that Margo's own inner beauty had inspired him to do his best work.

The bridal consultant was there, beaming her happiness for them.

From Reverend Carpenter's "Dearly beloved, we are gathered here today . . ."—to his final intonation—"You may kiss the bride," Margo felt as if she floated on a cloud. She was radiant, lightheaded with joy and exultation.

Ron took her in his arms and kissed her, his tongue searching hers for new meaning.

"I love you," he whispered, then deepened the kiss while Reverend Carpenter looked on, smiling.

"And I love you," she said, her eyes misting.

As the kiss ended, Margo looked around to see Jimilu standing by Russ's wheelchair. Margo bent and kissed him. "For my new brother—in—law," she said.

Ron took his brother's hand. "With love and forgiveness," he said.

And Russ responded in a choked voice, "Thanks, Ron. You'll never know how much your forgiveness has meant to me."

Margo's boss, Helen, came up, a distinguished gray—haired man in tow. Introducing him to them, she was as starry—eyed as a bride.

"I'm in love with weddings," he said. "I hope to have one of my own just a little later." He gave Helen a long, loving look. Helen caught her breath, and her face was wreathed in smiles.

The caterers were beginning to circulate among the guests, and the six—tiered wedding cake sat on the elevated, white damask—covered table.

Ron's parents came to them. They had spoken for a few minutes with Margo before the wedding, and wished them well. Now Dr. Hyman kissed Margo.

"You're a daughter—in—law after my own heart," he told her.

Laurette nodded. "I am so sorry for the misery I put you through," she said. "Now that I know the whole story,

I'm ashamed of myself. I haven't dared ask for your forgiveness."

"Of course I forgive you," Margo said.

"Thank you for the largeness of your heart, and I promise you things will be different between you and me from now on."

Margo smiled as the older woman leaned forward and kissed her cheek.

Friends of the Hymans Margo had invited at Laurette's request let her know that she was welcome in their circle.

Walking among the guests with Ron, Margo knew that she had never been so happy. Suddenly he said, "What if I kissed you yet again?"

"What do you think?"

He kissed her lightly this time, his glance going over her like a blessing. "Know what I'm thinking?" she asked.

"No. Tell me."

"That I can't wait to get you on that plane to Alaska. When does the plane leave?"

"Surprise. We're going on a private jet. A man here in town that I've done a lot of work for has let me use it. Of course, I'll do some work for him at no charge."

"Oh, sweetheart, I don't know what to say."

"Say nothing, my darling, I can see how you feel about this. As I said, it's my surprise for you, just for being the wonderful woman you are."

"I hope I deserve you," she told him, her face glowing with joy, "because I'm going to spend the rest of my life trying to."

Nestled in the Coast Mountains—back a ways from Juneau and extending farther in both directions—Coast Dream Lodge's cottages were very cool. Margo and Ron sat in front of a fieldstone fireplace in their private cottage.

Across from them, reflected in the big picture window, they saw a splendid yellow, gold, and coral sunrise.

"Alaska is such a beautiful place," Margo murmured. "It was made to order for us."

"We've got glory on our minds, all right," Ron said as he turned Margo's face to him and kissed her full on the mouth. Her lips parted, and their tongues slowly and lazily went into a dance of love. She drew back, somber for a moment. "Ron, I shudder when I think how close we came to not getting married. I was so certain you didn't love me enough for it to last."

"I should have been more open. Believe me, I won't make that mistake again. I love you, sweetheart. I'm always going to love you."

Margo stroked his cheek, kissing the other cheek as she did so.

"I'm glad our friends Val and Del Craig told us about this place," she said.

"It's all we could ask for, and we're going to make the best of it, believe me," he responded.

In the distance, a blue haze lay over the mountains and they felt sealed in by the massed trees and the mountain scenery.

"Do you want to go out and explore?" she asked him.

His glance lingered on the peach lace, silk–lined nightgown she wore. He pulled the fabric's wide straps down from her shoulders and began a torrent of kisses over her body.

"You didn't answer my question," she said, laughing.

"What do you think?" he asked, laughing with her. He stood, pulling her up with him. Then he picked her up and walked into their bedroom where he put her on the fur–covered king–size bed and stood looking down at her before he sat down and took her in his arms.

"Maybe day after tomorrow, or the next day," he said, "I'll want to explore the mountainside. Right now, I intend to explore the marvelous woman I married yesterday. Will you go along with me?"

Margo looked sober for a moment before she said, "Fair

enough, because I intend to explore the love of my life all my life.''

"Now do you believe me?" he asked. "I told you it is *our* love that was made in heaven."

"With all my heart," she answered, and kissed him again.

Dear Readers:

I hope you enjoy reading about the wedding woes and wonders of Margo Hilliard and Ron Hyman as much as I enjoyed writing about them.

Thank you for your kindness and support in writing about my past books—*Devoted, The Black Pearl,* the anthology *A Mother's Love,* and recently *Lyrics of Love* and *Still in Love.*

Writing takes on a new dimension with the wonderfully supportive comments you send me. Keep them coming. Each one will be answered with care.

As always, I wish you good health, success, love and romance to fill your long and happy life.

Cordially
Francine Craft

CHAMPAGNE WISHES

NIQUI STANHOPE

CHAPTER ONE

"Are you sure about this, Rob?" Summer Stevens gave the donkey an uncertain glance. "It doesn't seem to want me on its back."

The tall, lanky boy gave her a look of teenage exasperation. "Come on, man, all you have to do is swing yuh leg up and climb on so—" He pulled himself onto the animal's back with a certain amount of practiced ease.

Summer looked around at the small crowd of people who had gathered to watch. She knew that she was in serious danger of making a complete fool of herself. Riding barnyard animals at fairs had never been her cup of tea, but, she had promised Rob that she would take part in the race, and there was no backing out of it now. She had to do it.

Before making another attempt to get onto the animal's back, she let her eyes wander through the thickening crowd again. Why weren't Gavin and Nicholas back yet? They had both gone off in the direction of the greasy pig area. She had elected, quite willingly, to stay behind with Rob, since chasing slippery pigs around filthy, muddy pens was definitely not her idea of how to spend a fun afternoon. But now she was beginning to wish that she had gone along.

"OK," she said, taking a large breath, "here goes nothing." She stepped onto the rather shaky mounting stone, uttered a brief prayer that the animal would stand still while she attempted this most difficult maneuver, then swung her right leg across the broad width of its back.

Before she could get herself properly settled the animal threw back its head and released a hee hawing bellow that almost caused Summer to lose her precarious balance astride its back.

"Oh my God," she said, making a wild lunge at the rudimentary reins hanging from the bridle, "I don't think he likes this at all."

"Give him a little kick with your heels," Rob volunteered helpfully.

"With my heels?"

The boy nodded. "Just a little tap."

Summer turned her heels inward, giving the animal a tiny nudge in the side. The donkey started forward a couple of paces, then came to an abrupt stop.

"What now?" Summer called to Rob, who had managed to spur his mount into some semblance of a canter.

"Tap him again," the boy called, "a little harder this time."

Summer tapped again, without much success. Her second and third tries were also answered with small steps forward.

"How am I gonna get him to run if he won't even walk for me?"

"You want to switch donkeys, then?" Rob asked.

Summer shook her head. "Let me try him again.

She tapped. This time much harder. Almost without warning, the animal broke into a startling, completely uncontrolled gallop.

"You're going the wrong way, man!" Rob shouted as

Summer took off in the direction of a row of very colorful food stands.

The crowd parted as she tore by, hair streaming behind her like a banner.

"Pull up on the reins!" Rob bellowed somewhere off to her rear. "No . . . no. Pull up! What're you doing?" he shouted in exasperation.

"What am I doing?" Summer panted. "I'm not doing anything at all. This . . . this beast is running the entire show."

Rob spurred his mount on with a jab in the side. "Look out for that tree," he bellowed as Summer came dangerously close to an overhanging branch. "Don't knock over de people jerk chicken stand!"

The donkey narrowly avoided the long row of food stands directly in its path, and Summer just managed to keep her seat on its back as the animal veered from its current course. A crowd was now running somewhere behind, and out of the corner of an eye she could see several vendors making hasty attempts to remove their wares from her path.

Her heart quickened with relief at the sound of another voice. Gavin was back. *Thank God.*

She clung to the braying donkey as though her life depended on it. And, in a moment of sudden clarity, she realized that it quite probably did.

"Take your toes out of his side!" Gavin bellowed.

"I can't get him to stop!" she shouted. Then, as though to further demonstrate exactly who was in control of the situation, the animal veered off again, and attempted to vault a huge plant pot as it did so.

Gavin repeated the instruction, but Summer gave a very determined shake of her head. "I'll fall off if I do."

Gavin brought his donkey abreast of hers, and Summer gave him a wide-eyed stare. If it weren't for the fact that she was in a very desperate situation indeed, she would have broken into gales of uncontrollable laughter. The sight of such a big man on the back of an animal of that size was priceless.

He reached out an arm to grab the reins away from her, and within seconds, he had managed to somehow bring both animals to a shuddering stop. He pulled her into his arms as soon as they were both standing on firm ground. His heart thundered beneath her ear, and Summer looked up at him, a shaky little smile playing around the corners of her mouth. "What is *wrong* with that donkey?"

Gavin stroked a few tendrils back from her face. "Why do you let Rob talk you into doing these things? You could've broken your neck."

"I'm part of the turnabout donkey race. I had to get some practice in, before things started."

Gavin raised an eyebrow. "You mean you intend to get back on that animal?"

"I won't if you agree to ride in my place," she said, giving him a hopeful look. "You were kinda good up there. How did you catch up to me so fast, anyway?"

The black eyes swept over her face and settled briefly on her lips. "Fear."

Summer held his gaze for a moment. "You mean you'd care if something happened to me?"

"You are a silly thing," he said softly, his eyes beginning to fill with humor.

"Hmm. Sometimes . . . maybe," she agreed. "Where's Nicky?"

Gavin grinned. "Still wrestling in the mud with the pig. Not sure yet who's winning." He wrapped an arm about her, gathered up the reins, and began leading both animals back toward the tiny, fenced in area where the other donkeys were penned. The sun was quite hot now, and a steady throng of people continued to fill the large fairgrounds.

Summer raised a hand to shield her eyes. "You know," she said. "I just love Jamaica. The people, the food, the music . . . even the air. It all seems different, somehow."

Gavin looked down at her, and for a moment there was

a flicker of uncertainty in his eyes. "How long are you going to stay with me . . . once you're finished decorating my cottage—?"

Summer gave him a quick glance. "For a while . . . yet."

He seemed dissatisfied with her response. "How long? A few more weeks? Months, maybe?"

Summer plucked a long, slender reed, and played with the stem. He wanted her to stay with him until he tired of her. That, she knew. She was also aware that he certainly did not love her, although he might desire her. And the knowledge of this hurt, hurt a good deal, since she felt such deep and turbulent emotion for him.

"Well? Don't I get an answer, then?"

She sighed. "I don't know how much longer I'll stay."

She turned honey–gold eyes to him, and Gavin felt his groin tighten. She was so beautiful. Whenever she looked at him in that special way of hers, there was little that he wouldn't do for her. How very far they had come since their first meeting several months before, in that parking lot in Los Angeles. He never would have guessed then that she would be the one to take such a strong hold on his heart. She was exactly the kind of woman he had vowed never to get involved with—an independent career girl, a savvy designer with no obvious domestic proclivities. Definitely not the kind of girl he wanted to marry. Yet, she had taken his senses in a manner no one before her had managed to do.

He was glad they had finally reached a compromise on the sleeping arrangements, though. For weeks he had been unable to get adequate rest, knowing that she slept in his house, mere rooms away, on the floor just beneath him. It had taken quite a bit of doing to get her to agree to share his bed. She had been worried about what his brothers might think if she suddenly took up residence in his bedroom. He had managed to convince her that none of his brothers, Nicky, Rob, or Mik, would be aware of who slept where on Friday nights, since more often than not they were too busy with their own activities.

So, it had been agreed. Friday nights would be theirs. And, how he found himself looking forward to those nights. All week, sometimes during the most delicate of business negotiations, his mind suddenly drifted to her, and to thoughts of Friday. He was almost addicted to the sweet, soft, scent of her. To the warm feel of her legs as they wrapped around him. To the tiny mewling cries she made deep in the night as she clung to him, head thrown back, soul exposed. At those times, with the waves crashing against the powder–white sands, the wind whispering through the leaves, soft and rough limbs intertwined, he was as close to heaven as he'd ever been.

He wanted her to stay in Jamaica for at least another six months. She had no job to return to in Los Angeles, after all, so why shouldn't she stay? They could enjoy each other for a while longer.

"Hey, you two." Nicholas waved at them as he emerged from the teeming crowd. "I caught my pig," he said, holding up a blue ribbon.

"Are you sure you caught the pig ... or did the pig catch you?" Summer grinned up at him. "You're absolutely filthy."

"Don't I deserve a hug?" he asked, walking threateningly in her direction.

Summer warded him off with a hand. "Later. Don't you *dare* hug me now."

"So where's the youngster?" Nicholas asked, looking around.

Gavin nodded in the general direction of the donkey pen and Rob. "Over there putting his steed through its paces. He almost got Summer killed a while ago."

"Oh, nothing that serious," Summer interjected hurriedly. "I got stuck with a wayward animal, that's all."

"Ah," Nicholas nodded. "The turnabout race. Who won?"

Summer shielded her eyes and took a look in the direction of the field. "It hasn't started yet. Gavin's riding in my place."

Nicholas turned to give his brother a speculative stare. "You're riding in the race? I thought you vowed never to take part in it. You thought it too—what was the word again—juvenile?"

Gavin gave Nicholas a heavy frown. "If I don't ride, Summer will probably end up in the hospital with several very painful fractures."

Summer laughed. "Come on, now, I don't think I'm that bad."

Gavin laced her fingers through his. "Believe me, you're worse than that. If I hadn't come along when I did a while back, you'd be on your way to the emergency room right now."

Before she could formulate a suitable response, Summer spied a woman walking rapidly in their general direction. *Janet.* A wave of anger rippled through her. What was *she* doing here? Surely Gavin hadn't invited her?

In a few paces, the other woman was upon them. "Hello," she said cheerfully. "Isn't this funny, running into you like this?" She gave Summer a flicker of a glance. "You've still got your designer in tow, I see."

Summer gritted her teeth. "Hello, Janet. It's been a while since we've seen you. Months, isn't it?" Her voice was pleasant, revealing none of the bubbling anger that seethed just beneath the surface.

Janet nodded at her. "Yes. I've been out of the country—had to do some runway modeling in Paris. You know how that is? But now I'm back." She turned a hundred watt smile in Gavin's direction. "Aren't you going to give me a hug, darling?"

Gavin released Summer's hand with marked reluctance. He wasn't at all keen on giving Janet any kind of hug. It had been his suspicion for a while now that the two women had not taken well to each other.

"Welcome back, Janet." He enveloped her in a brief bear hug. "Nice to see you again." In answer, Janet's arms wrapped around the broad expanse of his back, shapely fingers clinging for a lot longer than was really necessary.

"Gavin," she said softly, "I've missed you."

Summer exchanged a glance with Nicholas, who had been observing the unfolding drama through slitted eyes.

"Well, don't I get a hug, too?" Nicholas asked when Gavin had put Janet firmly from him. She wrinkled her nose at him. "What have you been doing? Rolling around in the mud?" Nicholas laughed, and drew her hand through the nook of his arm.

"Let's leave these two lovebirds to themselves. We'll go and have a look at the reggae stage. Maybe you can show me some of your moves."

"I'd really prefer—" Janet protested, swinging her head back to look at Gavin, but Nicholas swept her away, turning to wink in a conspiratorial manner at Summer.

When they were alone again, Summer managed to take a normal breath. She had been holding unto herself so very tightly for the last several minutes that the simple rise and fall of her chest actually pained her. It was so obvious to her and to anyone else with half a brain, that Janet was interested in Gavin, that it was hard to believe he could be unaware of it. That he should think her intentions were strictly friendly was nothing short of ridiculous.

"I don't care about her," Gavin said, interrupting the volcanic thoughts coursing through her.

Summer half–turned to him. "Well, why do you let her touch you like that?"

"I was just being polite. She has been a sort of . . . friend of mine for several years now."

"Was she ever the same sort of friend to you, as I am now?"

"No," he said, and the black eyes looking down at her were sincere.

She nodded. "OK."

His lips twisted into a little smile. "OK? Are you completely certain about that?"

"Yes. If you say you never—"

A thumb stroked across the back of her hand. "I never." And, in the middle of the fair grounds, with people milling all around, he turned her completely into his arms, and kissed her.

"I want you," he said when he raised his head again. "Only you."

Summer met his eyes, and she tried desperately to hide the questions in hers. She had heard these very words before. Granted, Gavin was nothing at all like her ex-fiancé but he *was* a man, and she wasn't at all sure how much she should trust him. She was very aware of the quicksilver emotional ability of members of the opposite sex. They were deeply in love with someone one minute, and the next they were off gallivanting with hordes of other women.

Sure, he might want her now. But, how long would he feel the way he did? And, what would she do when he decided that he no longer needed her?

CHAPTER TWO

Nicholas returned alone about two hours later. He came
to sit next to Summer, who had seated herself beneath a
leafy mango tree in preparation for the start of the turnabout race. "I got rid of her," he said, leaning back onto
his elbows.

Summer fanned herself vigorously with a straw hat.
"Where is she now?"

He gave her a grin. "Probably on her way home. She
had a little . . . accident."

Summer turned to him, her eyes widening. "What did
you do?"

The big shoulders shrugged. "It's amazing how much
damage red punch can do to the front of a dress."

"You didn't." she said, and an unwilling smile flickered
about her lips.

"I did. But not deliberately, of course."

Summer gave his shoulder a little shove. "Of course."
Her eyes sparkled down at him. "Nicky, why do you, Mik,
and Rob seem to like me so much?"

Nicholas raised both eyebrows. "Mik and Rob? They don't like you at all—"

Summer chortled. "Oh shaddup. They *love* me."

"All right, all right," he conceded, "we all like you. Very much. Actually, when baby Amber grows up, if she turns out just like you, I'll be happy."

Summer reached down to hold his hand. "I'm really going to miss you all when I go."

Nicholas sat up. "Go? Go where?" All hints of playfulness had left his eyes.

Summer drew an aimless little circle in the grass. "Well, I can't stay here forever. I came to Jamaica to do a design job, remember? And the cottage is nearly finished now. It'll take me maybe another week to finish up the internal design effects. After that, there'll be no real reason for me to stay on."

"No real reason? What about Gavin?"

Summer lowered her head and plucked insistently at a blade of grass. After several minutes, she raised turbid eyes. "Well, it's going to end anyway, isn't it? Maybe now's the time to go, when neither of us is that involved emotionally with the other."

Nicholas turned her chin, and Summer cringed from the inspection. "You love him," he said after a moment, "and if you deny it, I'll call you a liar."

Summer snatched her face away. "Sometimes, Nicky, you have absolutely no tact at all. What if I do care about him? He doesn't about me, at least not in the same way. So, why should I stay and watch him slowly drift away from me—maybe into the arms of someone like that . . . that Janet person?"

Nicholas flopped back onto the grass again, and he appeared to be in deep thought for several minutes. "Why do you think Gavin doesn't feel the same way you do?" he finally asked.

"Trust me," Summer said, squishing the straw hat onto her head again, and retying the cotton straps beneath her chin. "I know. They're ways for a woman to tell. You wouldn't understand."

A frown crinkled his brow. "Well, you'd be silly to run away from him now—leaving him to the devices of our friend, Janet."

"So, I wasn't wrong about her, then? She is interested in Gavin?"

Nicholas nodded. "She has been for years."

"And Gavin doesn't know it?"

"Oh, he knows. He just hasn't done much, if anything, about it."

"So he lied to me, then? About them being just friends?"

Nicholas shrugged. "No. For him, that's all they are. But, Janet still continues to hope. I guess, since he hasn't really pushed her away."

Summer reached down to muss his curly black hair affectionately. "Why couldn't I have chosen you, Nicky? You're so . . . uncomplicated."

He grinned. "I'm fickle, remember? I play with women's hearts without any concern given to the carnage I leave behind. I'm irresponsible . . . unreliable . . . wild . . . ?"

Summer smiled. "You don't fool me, Nicholas Champagne." she said. "You're more like Gavin than you'd like everyone to think."

He gave her a thoughtful, "Hmm," and picked up her hand to study the lines crisscrossing the flat of her palm. "Maybe that's why I like you. You saw right through me from the start. I'll have to have a talk with my brother."

Summer directed a look at him that was almost fierce. "If you mention a word of any of this to him, I'll never speak to you again. I mean it, Nicky," she said when it seemed clear that he was about to raise some form of objection.

He lifted both hands in mock surrender. "OK. I won't say a word."

"Promise me."

"I promise." The handsome face that was so like his

brother's yet so different turned toward her. She met the black eyes for a long moment.

"All right," she finally said. "But, believe me, I'll know it if you do."

Nicholas gave an exaggerated sigh. "There's no trust in you at all, Summer Stevens. Who was responsible for bringing you to Jamaica in the first place? I ask you."

She leaned down to press a kiss to the side of his face. "Sometimes I forget. Let's watch the race. I think it's about to start."

Nicholas raised a hand to shield his eyes. All around them, people were camped on the grass. Some sat on large towels, others on colorful blankets. The wonderful aroma of jerk chicken, peas and rice, and curry goat drifted across from dozens of food stands just a few feet away.

Summer turned to look at the jagged array of donkeys. "Can you see Gavin yet?

Nicholas pointed. "There's Rob, near the end, but I don't see—oh, there he is."

Summer smothered a laugh. "He's so tall. His feet almost touch the ground."

"And you say he doesn't care about you, " Nicholas said with the hint of a smile in his voice. "Look at him. He's even willing to make a fool of himself, just so you won't get hurt."

Summer flicked a long swatch of black hair behind a shoulder. "That's just the kinda guy he is. I don't think it means anything one way or the other."

Nicholas got to his feet in one fluid movement. "Come on, let's go closer." He extended a hand to pull her up.

Summer got to her feet and spent a minute dusting the seat of her pants. "So, how do you win this race, anyway?"

Nicholas reached out to pluck a bit of grass from her hair. "The last donkey that crosses the finish line wins."

Summer's brow wrinkled. "The last one?"

"Yep. That's why it's called a turnabout race."

"Strange. Is this a national thing, or—"

"I think it's only popular in certain parts of Ocho Rios."

Summer climbed onto the wooden fence bordering the field where the participants were gathered. She raised a hand to give Gavin an exuberant wave. He raised something that looked very much like a riding crop, in brief salute. Summer pulled her straw hat down a bit further. "Does Rob understand that he has to come in last to win?"

Nicholas nodded. "He knows the rules, but I think he still wants to come in first. That boy is so competitive. He's like Gavin all over again."

"You know," Summer said, turning to give him a look, "you should be grateful that you grew up with so many siblings. I was kinda lonely as a kid."

Nicholas shrugged. "At least you had your parents. I didn't."

"You had Gavin . . . and he was almost like a parent to you all."

"True," Nicholas conceded. "That's why—" Whatever it was he was about to say stalled somewhere in the back of his throat. He muttered a heated expletive under his breath.

"What's the matter with—?" Summer began.

"She's back," Nicholas said.

"Janet?" Summer asked, swinging about and very nearly managing to throw herself completely off the fence.

Nicholas nodded. "How did she manage to get home and back so quickly?"

Summer pulled out a pair of sunglasses and fitted them snugly on her nose. "Maybe she carries a change of clothes in her car."

"Maybe if we hide—" Nicholas began.

Summer shook her head. "Too late. She's seen us."

Within seconds, Janet was upon them. She was now dressed in a sporty denim halter top, a pair of skintight denim shorts, and matching tennis shoes. Her hair was swept up into a soft bun, and a pair of designer sunglasses sat jauntily atop her head. "Didn't want to miss the race," she said as soon as she was close enough. "Is there room for me on the fence?"

Summer gave Nicholas a prod in the side, and whispered: "You'll have to give her your seat, Nicky."

"Like hell I will," he whispered back.

"Shh," Summer giggled. "She'll hear you."

"OK," he said, sliding from his perch. "But you and Gavin had better name your firstborn after me." His words sent an involuntary thrill through Summer. How wonderful it would be to have Gavin Pagne's child. The very thought of it was enough to send a rush of warm blood to her face. Maybe Nicholas was right. Maybe she should remain in Jamaica and fight for the man she wanted. After all, which man had ever gone willingly to the altar?

A smile flickered across her face. Janet Carr would be no match for her once she put her mind to it. No match at all.

The remainder of the afternoon went by in a blur. The turnabout race was one of the most hilarious events Summer had ever witnessed. All of the participants had gathered at the starting line, and a man dressed in blue jeans and a white T–shirt counted down, then raised his hand and fired a starter pistol. The sudden explosion had thrown the animals into a braying panic. Several donkeys took off at a gallop in the wrong direction. This, Summer had to keep reminding herself, was a good thing, since the entire object of the race was to come in last. And, at some point in the ensuing excitement, Rob managed to be thrown from his mount into the low slung branches of a nearby tree.

Gavin's donkey, which at first had begun running toward the finish line, had suddenly decided to sit firmly in the deepest puddle of mud that could be found on the field, and, for the remainder of the race, could not be persuaded to budge.

The high point of the race though, was surely when the man with the starter pistol, who had enthusiastically set the entire melee in motion, was forced to take refuge in the very tree into which Rob had been summarily hoisted when one of the donkeys turned vicious.

At the end of it all, it was still unclear to Summer who had actually won the race. The entire crowd of people had piled onto the field, laughing and shouting good–naturedly at the bedraggled participants.

Summer made a beeline for Gavin, who was still attempting to remove his donkey from the puddle of mud. It was all she could do not to break into gales of uncontrollable laughter.

"Did you win?" she asked, her eyes sparkling with humor.

He lifted a mud–streaked face. "OK, funny girl. Here," he said, handing her a length of rope, "help me pull." Summer grabbed hold of the rope, and heaved. "What is *wrong* with this animal?" she grunted after an unsuccessful session of straining against the cord.

"Let's get Nicholas over here, and Rob. Where *is* that boy, anyhow?" he said, turning to quickly scan the crowd.

"Nicky!" Summer bellowed, lifting a hand and waving. "Over here." She gave a tight little sigh when Janet materialized at his side. There was no getting rid of the woman. Why didn't she take the hint and just go away?

Gavin gave Summer a hooded glance as the other woman approached. This just might be the way to get Summer to stay. With Janet around constantly, there was no chance at all that Summer would be leaving Jamaica anytime soon. He'd bet his life on that.

"Gavin, you're hurt," Janet said as soon as she was close enough.

"He's not hurt," Summer and Nicholas voiced almost in unison, and, Gavin did his utmost to prevent the smile he was feeling from showing.

"Give me a hand here, Nicky," he said, motioning to the rope. "Now I understand why people say 'as stubborn as a mule.' "

"Let me help Summer pull," Janet offered. "I grew up here in Jamaica, so I know how to handle animals."

"Thank you so much," Summer muttered heatedly under her breath.

Within minutes, with their combined efforts, the donkey was back on its feet and walking contentedly back toward the pen. Once it was neatly locked in the enclosure, Gavin walked across to wrap an arm about Summer. His eyes glinted down at her, dark and seductive.

"Ready to go?"

"I have to thank you first," she said.

"You mean for riding in your place?"

She nodded, and there was a tinge of mischief in her voice. "It looked like a lot of fun."

He pulled her into his arms. "What do you say we ditch the others and go back home. Then . . . you can thank me properly."

She raised an eyebrow. "Gavin Pagne," she said, using the family's shortened version of their name, "This is so unlike you. And it's not even Friday."

He bent his head to kiss the corner of her mouth. "This Friday thing . . . that was all your idea, remember?"

"Uhmm," she said, turning to present him with the full softness of her lips. "I'm beginning to regret that."

A hand came up to cradle the base of her skull. "We can always change our agreement to every day."

"No," she said, nipping at his mouth, "we can't. Not with Nicky, Rob, and Mik around all the time. Not to mention Janet."

"She's been watching us all day. I would guess she probably suspects there's something between us."

"Not enough to make her leave you alone, though. Why don't you just tell her?"

Gavin raised an eyebrow in the same manner she had done just moments before. "To leave me alone?"

"I don't like her," Summer said, "and the feeling's mutual."

"You want me to get rid of my friends?"

"Not all your friends, just her. She . . . she wants you."

Gavin threw back his head and laughed. And, the deep, husky sound of him caused the baby–soft hairs at the nape of Summer's neck to stand at attention.

"What are you laughing at?" she asked, a tinge of annoyance in her voice.

A flicker of a smile still played around his mouth. "It's really strange that you two don't get along. You have so much in common."

Summer frowned. "We do? You mean other than you?"

The comment earned her another grin. "You were both adopted."

A shadow came and went in Summer's eyes, and Gavin tilted her chin up. "Are you still bothered about all that?"

Summer shook her head. "No, not really. I was for a while. But, I love my parents too much for that to hurt our relationship. I just wish—"

"That your mom and dad were your real parents?"

She looked up at him, and the surprise showed in her eyes. "How did you know that?"

He stroked the side of her face with a finger. "It's what I would've wished for, too, if I'd had parents like yours."

"Gavin," she said softly? and there was a new tenderness in her eyes.

"What are you two whispering about?" Nicholas asked, coming to lean against a nearby tree.

Summer peered around him, her eyes searching the thinning crowd. "Where's Janet?"

Nicholas shrugged. "Gone, I guess."

Gavin gave his brother a long, speculative look. "Gone? So where were you all this time?"

"Leave him alone, Gavin," Summer intervened before Nicholas could reply. "Nicky can go off alone if he wants to."

Nicholas winked at her, a smile playing around his lips. "He forgets I'm over twenty–one."

Tolerant amusement came and went in Gavin's eyes. "Sometimes I think you forget it, too."

Summer looked from one to the other. In four short months, she had become so very attached to them both. It was becoming increasingly difficult to face the inevitable— the time when she would no longer have this closeness. No longer have Gavin. "Let's go home," she said, turning to grab hold of Nicholas's arm, too. "Where's Rob?"

"Riding the pigs in the greasy pit area," Nicholas said, grinning.

Summer gave a little shake of her head. "My God. First donkeys, now pigs. You Champagne men are really a crazy bunch."

Gavin laughed. "You hang around with us for a while, and before long you'll be just as crazy, too."

Summer gave him a little look. "And just imagine, a few short months ago, I thought you were—"

"You thought I was?"

She shrugged. "Well, you know. Kinda cold, and not at all the type who would ride a donkey, of all things."

A slow smile spread across his face. "Well, it just goes to show you how very wrong you can be."

With the beginnings of a pleasant breeze rolling in from off the ocean, arm in arm with two of the most important men in her life, such a reply seemed completely adequate. They walked in a leisurely manner back toward the large pigpen area. And, for that brief moment, with the sun beginning to set and a multicolored tapestry of pink and orange inching its way slowly across the sky, Summer felt a small measure of contentment steal into the corner of her heart.

How nice it would be if she could stay. For a long while she had thought it would have been enough to lie with Gavin Pagne. But, it wasn't enough. She needed him in a permanent way. And, one way or another, she was going to have him.

CHAPTER THREE

"What is that?" Summer asked, looking up from a bed of yellow roses.

Gavin extended the brown paper bag. "*Drops*. They're grated coconut cakes. Try one."

She stuck the little trowel into the soft soil, wiped a hand across the round of her forehead. "Coconut cakes? They're sweet, I guess?"

"Uhmm," Gavin said, taking a crunchy bite of his. "Open," he said, extending a hand.

Summer wrinkled her nose. "I don't know if I'll like it, though."

"You will. Open up."

Summer took the brown, sugary cake on her tongue, and after a moment's hesitation she chewed. "Umm, they're good." She opened her mouth again for another portion.

Gavin came to stoop beside her. After a moment of twirling a finger aimlessly in the soil, he asked, "Have you ever thought of having kids?"

A sizable portion of coconut somehow managed to make its way down the wrong passageway in her throat. For the next few minutes, she was subjected to the indignity of having to wrestle with huge, hacking coughs. Gavin banged her several times on the back, all the while enquiring quite solicitously whether or not she was OK. After additional moments of wheezing and wiping runny eyes, she was finally able to croak in a voice several shades more husky than usual, "Yes. I'm fine. You can stop banging me on the back now, thank you."

"Well?" he said when she went back to her digging. "Have you ever thought about it? I mean, are kids something that you want?"

She plowed the soil with the tool, churning up huge chunks of it and then conversely, patting the rich dirt back into place. Her mind was in a tailspin. Could it be that he was actually considering a permanent relationship with her? Men like Gavin Pagne did not suddenly, out of the blue, start questioning you about children and your plans regarding procreation. "I . . . I love children," she began, "you know that."

He sat back on his haunches. "And, they love you, too, if baby Amber is anything to go by."

"She's a beautiful baby. Anyone would love her. And Nicky is maturing so well in the role of daddy, isn't he?" She knew she was babbling, but she just could not seem to get anything too intelligent past her lips.

Gavin picked up a clump of earth and squeezed it into a tiny ball. "Does that mean you don't want children of your own?"

"No!" she said wildly. "I mean yes. Of course I want children. At least two, or even three, maybe."

He gave her a sidelong glance. "You're not worried about what it'll probably do to your figure?"

She dug again with the tool. "Do you think me that superficial?"

He stood up. "Let's go take a dip in the ocean. It is Sunday, after all. You'll have more than enough time this week to finish up your flower beds."

"I'm gonna run some climbing roses up the trellis work," she said, pointing to the intricate wraparound framework that ran around the sides of the cottage. "What do you think about yellow?"

Gavin gave this suggestion a moment of thought. "I know a guy in Kingston who's a magician with roses. He's a biologist, really. He's into genetic engineering. Maybe he might—hmm," he said, breaking off midthought. "Yellow is fine."

"Are you sure you like that color?" she gave him a doubtful look. He hadn't seemed at all certain for a minute there, talking about his friend and whatever it was he did with genetic engineering and roses when she'd just asked him a simple question about color.

"Very sure. I love yellow." He extended a hand to lock fingers with her. "Almost the color of your eyes . . . sometimes."

She lifted two neatly groomed eyebrows. "Yellow?"

"Well,"—he turned to give her a long, considering look—"maybe closer to gold. With brown flecks."

"Hmm," she said. Then, because she could no longer hold back the driving curiosity, "Why did you ask me about kids just now?" A certain calm had settled over her now, so she could ask the question without falling into a paroxysm of any sort.

He turned to lock eyes with her, and for the life of her she couldn't read him. She, who had prided herself for so many years on her ability to correctly ferret out the very soul of a man, could not ascertain a single thing from the silky depths of his black eyes.

"I was just curious."

Summer let out the tight breath that she had been holding. Curiosity. Was that really all that was behind the question? Or was there something more? She steeled herself. She would just have to get at the truth, even if he wouldn't give it to her willingly. "Gavin, remember what we both said about . . . about romantic love?"

They walked down the stone stairs leading to the beach.
"No," he said, "what did we say?"

A flush of embarrassment stained her cheeks. How could
he not remember something as fundamentally important
as that?

"In LA, when we had dinner for the first time?"

He laughed. "Yeah. You with your false teeth and shed-
ding wig. I never would've believed that you had the nerve
to go out in public looking like that."

She grinned at him. "You deserved everything you got.
You were so rude to me in that parking lot."

"Rude?" he said, looking down at her with laughter in
his eyes.

"Rude . . . you know you took my parking space deliberately . . . and I was late for my presentation . . . Let me see
if I can remember exactly what you said." And, she lowered
her voice in a remarkably poor imitation of his deep baritone. "You said, 'Step away from the car please, I'd like
to get out.' "

Amusement sparkled in his eyes. "Did I say that?"

She nodded. "You did."

He turned her in the warm sand, his hands reaching
down to cradle the small of her back.

"I'm sorry," he said, and without further preamble he
lowered his head and took her lips in such a slow and very
tender manner that when he raised his head again, silly
tears clamored at the backs of Summer's eyes.

Gavin stroked a finger down the smooth run of her
nose, then bent his head to softly kiss each eyelid. "Am I
forgiven?" he asked.

Words of love trembled on her lips. "I forgave you a
long while ago, babe." How wrong she had been to doubt
that this kind of emotion could ever truly exist between a
man and a woman. How very wrong. Maybe this was to be
her punishment—to be completely in love with a man
whose opinions on love were exactly as hers had once
been.

"I bought you something," he said after a long period of companionable walking. Foaming waves curled about their feet, and a salty breeze picked at the soft tendrils over hanging her face. Summer's heart pounded for a minute. Maybe this was it—the reason behind all of his questions about whether or not she wanted kids.

"Where is it? In your pocket?" she asked breathlessly. Her eyes hunted for the characteristic bulge of a ring box.

He laughed. "It's a little too big for my pocket," he said, and, he took her by both shoulders and pointed in the direction of a small wooden jetty. "See that?"

"What?" For a minute, her eyes were almost too blurry for her to see clearly. Was there a boat moored to the jetty, waiting to take her off to some secluded romantic spot, where he would then propose to her?

He ran his hands down her shoulders in a manner that stirred her blood. "You like water sports, don't you?"

She nodded stupidly. "Yes." But what did that have to do with rings, romantic proposals, and the like?

"Well," he continued. totally oblivious to her distress, "I got you a jet ski. It's a two seater, so we can go out together. He continued to talk about the water scooter, going into intricate detail on the power of the engine, the smooth lines of the body, the right techniques to use. When he was finally through, he looked down at her. "What's the matter? Don't you like it?"

She blinked and forced a cheerful note back into her voice. "Oh, I love it. It's . . . it's beautiful."

"Do you have your suit on under there?" he asked, giving her T-shirt a look.

She shook her head. "I'll have to go back up to the house to get one. Are you—" She paused midsentence. There was someone coming toward them. Someone with long brown legs, an impossibly skinny florescent green bikini, a huge straw hat, and fashionably sleek sunglasses.

"I think it's Janet," Gavin said, shielding his eyes against the sun. Summer gritted her teeth. The woman was relentless. There was no way in heaven that she was going to leave Gavin alone with her, not even for a minute.

"Going swimming?" Janet called, her voice tinkling across the short expanse of sand.

Gavin waved at her. "Summer's going to try out her new jet ski."

"Oh, what fun." She was upon them now, and the designer fragrance she wore very nearly overpowered the surrounding foliage.

"Hello, Janet," Summer said. And, for the life of her could not think of a single word more of polite frivolity to exchange with the other woman.

Janet nodded briefly in her direction, then proceeded to completely ignore her. "Gavin," she said, winding a hand about his arm, "you've been promising to show me how to dive." She gave him a tiny pout. "Aren't you ever going to find some time for me?"

Gavin unwound her clinging fingers, and Summer felt her spirits soar. If that wasn't a subtle brush off, then she didn't know what was. Surely she would go away now, and not try to hang around for the remainder of the afternoon.

"Summer is an expert diver," Gavin was saying while Summer's mind flickered over the problem at hand. "Aren't you, babe?" he asked, turning to give her an unreadable look.

Summer suppressed a sigh. "Yes. I dive a bit." She knew exactly what he was up to. He wanted them to spend some time together. He seemed to have the misguided impression that this would somehow make them like each other, but he was completely wrong on that account. She and Janet were like oil and water, and there was no way on earth they were ever going to become bosom friends.

"I'm sure she's not as good as you are, Gavin," Janet demurred before Summer could raise any particular objections to the blossoming idea.

A flicker of a smile played about his lips. "Actually, she's better."

Summer gave him a sharp glance. Did he really mean that? Or was he just having some twisted fun at her expense?

"Well," Janet began, "I'm sure Summer doesn't want to spend the rest of the day teaching me how to dive."

Summer's eyes flickered over the other woman. They were both of a similar height, both possessed of long, shapely limbs and lean, elegant features. Could it be that Gavin was actually interested in them both? Was that the real reason he had never told Janet to get lost in no uncertain terms? "I would love to," she said, and mentally gritted her teeth at the idea. "But Gavin and I need to spend some time together . . . alone. I'm sure you understand?" Since Gavin, for reasons known only to himself, was unwilling to take the bull by the horns, she would do it. She had run into women like Janet before—women who needed to be told the lay of the land in the most unequivocal manner.

Janet gave her a look of simmering dislike. "Well . . ." She turned to Gavin for support, her eyes soft and pleading.

Gavin shot a lightning glance in Summer's direction. From the set of her mouth and the tight way she held herself, he could tell that she was upset. Very upset. "I'll ask Nicky to come down," Gavin said. "He'd be more than happy to give you some instruction."

Janet took a moment to carefully spread her large beach towel down on the powder–fine sand. She removed the straw bag from her shoulder, and unbuttoned the remaining fastenings on her cover up cape. Once she was nicely situated on the towel, long limbs soft and gleaming in the afternoon sun, she said. "OK. If I can't have you— right now—I'll settle for Nicholas."

Gavin nodded. "Right. I'll go get him. Won't be a minute."

"Don't forget to bring back my suit. You know where it is," Summer said very deliberately.

Gavin met her eyes for an instant, and amusement danced in his. "I'll find it."

Once he was gone, Janet turned cold, black eyes in her direction. "If I were you, I wouldn't congratulate myself too much."

Hot blood rushed to Summer's head, and it was a long moment before she had herself adequately under control. She forced a level of calm into her voice that she was far from feeling. "I beg your pardon?"

Janet smiled. "Oh come, come," she said. "We're both women of the world, aren't we? There's no need for any pretense between us. You and I both want the same thing. One of us is going to get it, and the other isn't."

Summer's heartbeat thickened in her chest. What a completely brazen hussy. The ease with which she had just unburdened herself made it clear that she was well familiar with situations of this type. Well, she had chosen the wrong adversary this time.

"By 'thing,' I guess you must be referring to Gavin?"

Janet's laugh tinkled. "Let me tell you a couple of home truths, Summer dear. Men like Gavin Pagne don't marry women like you. They'll take whatever it is you give them— and from the looks of things, it's obvious that you've given him plenty. But, don't expect it to last. I've known him for a long while, and I've seen dozens of women come and go."

Summer took an even breath. She was just mere seconds away from slapping the smug expression from Janet's face. Never in her life had she ever run into anyone possessed of quite so much gall. "I'm going to say this to you just once. When you leave here today, don't come back. Gavin is too polite to let you know that you're not wanted here, but believe me when I tell you this—I'm not. So, let's keep things nice and friendly, shall we? When Gavin returns, you will make your excuses, and we'll both pretend that this never happened."

Janet sat up on the towel, pulling her legs up and wrapping her arms around them both. "Well," she said, "aren't you the lady of the manor?" Her eyes took on a diamond hard gleam. "Gavin spends Friday nights with you, doesn't he?" The laugh which Summer had come to despise tinkled again. "Where do you think he spends the other six?"

CHAPTER FOUR

The remainder of the day was completely ruined for Summer after that. She understood very well what Janet had managed to do. She had planted the seeds of doubt in her mind. Not that she really believed her outrageous suggestion for even a second. Gavin was too moral a person to engage in anything sleazy or underhanded. But, the entire quality of contentment which had filled her prior to Janet's arrival had been destroyed. And, when Gavin returned with Nicholas in tow she had to literally force herself to enjoy the beautiful new jet ski.

Later that evening as she was preparing for bed, there was a knock on her door. She put the hairbrush down, shook the heavy weight of black hair to her shoulders, and went to pull back the door. "Gavin." Her heartbeat quickened at the sight of him. He was dressed in a white muscle vest and black sweatpants. His hair was still damp from the shower.

"Let's go for a walk on the beach," he said.

Summer looked down at the thin cotton nightshirt she

was wearing. "Let me put a pair of jeans on. I'll be ready in a flash."

He lounged in the doorway, a smile flickering in his eyes. "Can I watch?"

Summer grinned. "No. You can't. Wait here."

He poked her playfully in the stomach. "Heartless woman."

She closed the door and leaned back against the wood. God, she loved him so much. Her mother had been completely right when she had said that there was a man out there especially for her. There was no doubt in her mind that Gavin Pagne was that man. Her engagement to Kevin Jones had been a piece of insanity, and she was so glad it had fallen through. How tragic it would have been to find herself married to the wrong man.

"Babe?" Gavin's voice spurred Summer into action. She yanked a pair of soft, well–faded jeans from the closet, pulled them on, wiggling a bit to get them over her hips, then stuck her feet into a pair of black thong sandals. She ran the brush through her thick head of hair one final time, took a quick glance at her reflection in the mirror, then ran to pull open the door. "Here I am," she said, and pressed an enthusiastic kiss to his lips.

He held her to him for a moment longer when she would have pulled away. She could feel the warm thud of his heart against her breast, and a thrill ran through her at the feel of him. "Do you love me?" he asked.

For a second, the breath completely left Summer's lungs. "What?" she stammered.

He repeated the question and she met his eyes, trembling inside at the thought of what havoc this particular disclosure might create in their relationship. He didn't love her, after all. So, what good would this particular piece of knowledge do him? It could only give him more power over her than he already had. And that would not be a good thing. Not a good thing at all.

"I . . . I . . ." Somehow, the right words were not there.

What could she say? She wouldn't tell him that she didn't love him. Because she did. Very much. Still—

He looked down at her, his black eyes shuttered. "Yes?"

"I . . . like you very much."

One of his hands slid beneath the cotton shirt to massage the soft skin of her back.

"You *like* me? Well, I guess that's better than nothing."

Summer lifted a finger to run it across the firm warmth of his lips. This opportunity was too good to miss. She had to ask him. Had to know. No matter what he said. "And what about you? Do you care about me?" At the last minute, she had avoided the word 'love.' Why was it so difficult for her to say?

He was silent for what seemed like several minutes, his expression hooded. "I care about you. Very much."

Excitement ran through Summer as she met his eyes. So, he cared about her. He didn't love her, but he cared. That was a start. It was certainly a far cry from the situation just a few months ago, when he had seemed to despise her at best. Most of that had been Nicholas's fault, of course. He had hired her to decorate the cottage, without Gavin's approval. More questions trembled on her lips, but before she could put the words into the right order he took her hand in his, and said, "Let's go down to the beach. There's something I want to talk to you about."

On the way down her mind churned at top speed, but she held her tongue until they were down on the sand. They walked hand in hand for a good stretch. Finally the silence was too much for her, and she had to know what it was.

"So, are you going to tell me?" Huge waves crashed hypnotically against the shoreline, and a soft breeze rustled around them, but the beauty of the evening was completely lost on Summer as she waited for his reply.

"Has Nicholas told you much about our mother?" For a minute, Summer blinked at him. "Your mother?" *What had she to do with things?*

He nodded. "Has he told you anything about her?"

"Well, not very much," she hedged. "Just little things here and there."

He turned to look out at the ocean, and in the darkness he appeared remote, very like the figure he had been just months before. When he spoke, it was as if the words were being torn from him at great cost. "She left us when we were kids."

Summer wrapped her arms around him. "I know. Nicky told me that."

"Did he tell you why she did?"

"She wanted to get married again, her fiancé didn't want a ready made family?"

He sighed. "That's the popular story. But, it's not true."

"You mean . . . Nicky doesn't know the truth?"

"No."

"Why?" It didn't make any sense at all. Why would the truth have been kept from Nicholas?

He shrugged. "Letting him think that she'd abandoned us was easier when he was younger. Just as your parents let you think that you were their biological child."

She stroked a soothing hand down the flat of his back, and waited for him to continue. "She suffers from a particular kind of mental condition that causes her to lose time. She also has a form of multiple personality disorder."

Summer's mouth popped open, and her tongue darted out to moisten her lips.

"Oh," was all she could manage.

"Did you ever wonder why I was spending all that money to fix up the cottage?"

"Well, I thought maybe you'd gotten tired of living together in the same house with Mik, Rob, and Nicky. Thought you wanted a place of your own. . . something that was still close enough for you to keep an eye on things."

He shook his head. "I'm bringing her home."

"To live in the cottage?"

"Yes. Her condition isn't dangerous to others. Just to herself. Most of the time, she doesn't even remember who she is, doesn't remember anything at all."

"Not even you, and Nicky?"

He shook his head, and Summer looked up at him. There was a hint of something very like tears in his eyes, and her heart tightened. She held him closer, trying to make him understand that it didn't matter about his mother. "It's all right, babe," she said, and there was a catch in her voice. "Your mom will be happy here. I'm almost through with the cottage now. All I have left are little artistic touches here and there. She's going to be really comfortable, I promise."

He looked down at her, and for the first time, she saw vulnerability in him. "You don't mind, then? About her condition?"

"Mind? You mean, will that scare me off?"

He nodded. "Mental illness is something most people feel uncomfortable with."

She smiled. "I'm not most people."

His lips twisted in a little smile, and she felt the tenderest of emotions tug at her heart. "You take care of everyone, Gavin. It's time to let someone take care of you."

He bent his head to gently take her lips. "I've never wanted anyone to take care of me before now."

"Let me," she said softly, and slid her hands up to hold the back of his neck.

They sat for the next hour on the beach, and Summer nestled snugly in Gavin's arms, her head resting somewhere just under his chin. The unceasing rhythm of the ocean was so soothing that Summer found herself struggling against sleep. How nice it was to be held by him, to know that this was where she belonged—that this was where she wanted to be for the rest of her life. With him. Anywhere at all, as long as he was there.

"Gavin?"

"Uhmm?" His voice was a husky rumble.

"When're you going to tell Nicky? About your mom, I mean."

"Soon."

"Do you think he'll understand?"

His chest rose and fell in a silent sigh. "I don't know."

She swept the thickness of her hair across one shoulder, and turned to look at him. "He loves you, you know. He wants you to be happy."

In the moonlight, his eyes were dark and mysterious. "I'm happy now," he said. He threaded his fingers through her hair until they were resting against her scalp. "I'd be happier still, though, if today were Friday."

Summer smiled up at him. "You are shameless."

He bent to rub his nose slowly back and forth against hers. "No, just hungry."

She pressed a kiss to the side of his face. "Well, if a man hungers, then he must eat."

CHAPTER FIVE

"Do you like it when I do that?" he asked, his voice several tones huskier than usual.

Summer's pupils dilated. "Uhmm," was all she could manage.

Gavin bent his head again, and this time he kissed her with a thoroughness that had her clinging to him, head thrown back, hands clasping the back of his neck. "Shh," he said, nipping at the side of her neck. "Someone's coming."

He maneuvered her onto the broad bed and lay above her, elbows propped on either side of her head. A smile flickered in his eyes. "We need our own place, don't we?"

Summer lifted a hand to stroke the side of his face. "You and me? Living in sin?"

He laughed. "Such old–fashioned views you have about such things. Doesn't everybody live together these days?"

She gave the question serious consideration. "Not everybody. Some people still believe in love and marriage, in having babies, and growing old together."

He bent his head to give her lips a quick kiss. "And that's what you want?"

She nodded. "That's what I want—but not for the reasons you might think."

"Hmm," he said, and ran a finger along the length of a neatly arched eyebrow. "Let's take a shower together?"

Summer gave him a long, considering look. So, he was going to change the subject on her again. And, just as they were closing in on making a major breakthrough, too.

"If we shower together it will have to be just that, nothing else."

He lifted an eyebrow, and a smile played around his lips. "God, I've created a monster. You mean you won't even let me—?"

"No. Not even that," she interrupted before he could finish.

"Why not? Because it's not Friday? The magical day?"

"You know why not. Mik is in the next room. The walls are very thin. And you make all sorts of noises."

"Uhmm," he said, rolling off her. "But, how can I help it? You're so"—his eyes took on a hint of serious intent— "soft, and—"

"Yes?" she said, sitting up.

"And beautiful. So right, for me."

Her heart thudded heavily against her ribs, and her lips rounded in a surprised "O." He turned toward her, his eyes seeking hers out. "You weren't part of my plan, you know."

She slid off the bed, extending a hand to pull him up. "Are you sorry you met me, then?"

"No. I can't imagine what my life would've been like if I hadn't met you."

"OK." She smiled. "Let's take that shower. Though,"— she paused to give him a considering look—"you may not be up to it."

He gave her a boyish grin. "Is that so?"

She nodded. "That's the way I see it."

"OK, missy," he said, crooking a finger at her. "Let's just see about that."

She walked the short distance to the window and pushed it wide open, so that a flood of sea breeze rolled into the room. Just outside, a huge mango tree rustled in the wind.

Gavin came up behind, placing a hand on either side of her. He kissed the back of her neck. "Have you decided that you're not up to the task, then?"

She turned, with mischief in her eyes. "Oh, no. You're not going to get out of it that easily."

He bent his head, pausing scant inches from her lips. "No?"

She undid the top button on her blouse. "No."

He watched as she slowly worked her way down the front of it, long, elegant fingers nimbly unfastening the pearl buttons. She left the final button in place, and gave him a saucy look.

"What do you think?"

He propped a hand under his chin. "Hmm. Not bad, not bad. But, what do you think about this?" He reached down to grab both sides of his T-shirt and yanked it up and over his head. The flat, well-defined,washboard stomach was nothing short of pure artistry. The smooth run of his arms, perfection itself. The hard pectorals, like twin sculptures formed in solid bronze.

Despite herself, she reached out a hand to touch him but he stepped back just out of reach. "No," he said, "these are your rules. Looking is allowed, but I'm sorry to say there can be no touching involved."

She nodded. "Ah *hah*. OK, Mister Pagne." Her fingers went to the final button on the blouse, making short work of it. She slid the cotton top slowly from her shoulders, exposing a smooth expanse of golden brown skin. She watched as his Adam's apple moved up, then down again. His eyes skimmed her lacy black bra and the hint of soft golden flesh beneath.

She lifted an eyebrow. "You were saying?"

His chest moved for several seconds, and with a fierce look in his eyes, he said, "I'm not through with you yet, sweetheart."

She watched as his fingers went to the fastenings of his jeans, plucking and pulling with the unstudied mastery of a Chippendale dancer. A soft sound escaped her as the denim slid from his hips to reveal his long, sinewy brown legs, and a pair of elastic black briefs. He was beautiful. There was no other word for it. And, there was not an ounce of fat on him anywhere at all, either. Everything was as it should be. Tight. Solid. She breathed again *God, what a body.* Her eyes darted up to find that he was watching her with the intensity of a caged tiger. She took a step toward him, and he met her halfway.

"Shall we call it a draw?" he asked huskily.

She nodded. *Yes, call it a draw. Call it anything at all.* Just as long as she could hold him. Touch him. Taste him . . .

Their lips met and clung. He dragged her in close, molding her body to his, devouring the softness of her lips, grunting in satisfaction when she matched him stroke for stroke.

"We've gotta stop," she panted, breathless minutes later.

"No," he said, tangling a hand in the thickness of her hair. "Not now. Not yet."

Her fingers ran gently across his chest. "Yes, now. We can't. Mik's next door studying. Remember?"

He groaned. "Good God, woman, what are you trying to do to me?"

She linked her fingers with his. "Let's take that shower."

He grimaced. "Cold. I hope."

In the bathroom she slid from her jeans, and was in the process of removing her remaining garments when he forestalled her. "I think you'd better leave those on."

A smile curved her lips. "I thought you were made of sterner stuff than that, Gavin Pagne."

He laughed. "You're always making incorrect assumptions about me, aren't you? Are there other fallacies about me milling around in that head of yours, I wonder?''

Summer slid back the shower door, reached in, and turned on the water. "Maybe. You'll never know.''

He came up behind her, pulling her back to rest against the flat of his chest. "I will, and sooner than you think.''

She gave a noncommittal "Umm," then asked him to pass her the thick bristled brush that was sitting on the side of the sink.

"Let me," he said, when she reached to take it from him.

She turned. "You want to brush my hair?''

He touched the tip of her nose. "There's a first time for everything.''

She grinned at him. "Are you sure you know what you're doing?''

"Stand still," he said, winding the thick pelt of gleaming black hair around the flat of his palm. He raised a hand and began stroking evenly from root to tip—long, slow, languorous movements that sent bolts of fire through her blood. "Turn this way," he said, tilting her head toward the left.

She followed his instructions like a sleepwalker. Her eyes were half–closed, her fingers curled around the warm thighs just behind. Never had she known that it could be like this, that such a simple act could be filled with such raw sensation. No man had ever brushed her hair before— or ever wanted to, for that matter.

"Turn," he said again, and she did, presenting him with the right side of her head, bending so that he might sweep the thick waves up and over the crown. After long moments of continued brushing, he finally paused to say, "How was that?''

She turned to face him again, and the love she felt for him was shining softly in her eyes. "Aren't you going to braid it, too?''

He placed the brush on the sink, and pulled her into his arms. "What do I get if I do?"

She giggled. "A shower?"

He turned her around and gave her rump a playful smack. "In you go, missy."

She stepped into the steaming cubicle, and peered out at him. "Aren't you coming in, too?"

His chest rose and fell. "No. I've changed my mind."

She settled her hands on her hips. "Gavin Pagne."

"OK, OK. Let me tell you, though, we're gonna have to get ourselves a larger shower very soon. There's no room at all in there for me."

She shifted a bit to give him more space, and a blast of deliciously warm water hit her full in the face. She sputtered, and swept her hair back in a smooth, black pelt.

He reached out and closed the shower door behind him. "Now what?"

Summer picked up a translucent bar of green soap which had a tropical flower suspended somewhere in the middle of it. "Turn around. I'll soap your back for you."

He turned. "Be gentle."

"Shaddup." She grinned. She moved the bar in slow circles across the flat of his back, massaging each inch of skin with a feather light touch.

He turned to look at her, and there was an expression in his eyes that she had never seen before. "Why haven't I ever done this before?"

"You mean, I'm the first? You've never taken a shower with anyone else, ever?"

He nodded. "Never wanted to."

She lathered the small of his back, pausing to massage the area just above his spine. "Not even with Janet?"

He turned, removing the bar from her hands. "Especially not with her."

"Umm," she said.

He bent his head to press a watery kiss to the side of her face. "Umm, indeed."

For the next half hour they luxuriated in the steamy shower cubicle, kissing, touching, holding. He lathered her hair with ample amounts of shampoo, and she did the same for him, laughing heartily at the sight of him standing there, his head covered with nothing but white foam.

When they were finally through and nicely wrapped in thick bath towels, Summer said, "You know, that's the most fun I've ever had."

Gavin unwrapped her towel and gently patted every inch of her dry. He lingered over the wet fabric clinging to her bosom, moving in slow circles across the center of each mound "You should get out of that," he said. "I don't want you to catch cold."

Summer moved closer, wrapping her arms about his middle, a long swatch of wet hair dribbling down the center of her back. "I'm made of very hardy stock, you know." She gave him a cheeky smile. " But can we say the same about you?"

The phone on the tiny bedside table rang before he could make a reply. Gavin walked across to lift the receiver "Yes?" His voice held a trace of impatience.

Summer listened as his tone went through a radical change. He spoke very pleasantly for several minutes, then turned with a hand placed across the receiver mouth. "Your mom," he said.

"Here she is now, Mrs. Stevens," he said, and beckoned her closer. "It was very nice talking to you."

Summer took the phone from him. "Hello, Mom," she said, smiling. For the next little while, she happily filled her mother in on the happenings of the past two weeks. She inquired about her father, and was well-satisfied when she was told that his bad hip had healed quite nicely. She tried to keep her voice neutral when her mother began to question her about the quality of her stay in Jamaica. "I'm having a great time," Summer assured her. "You were right. Coming here was just what I needed." She was acutely aware that Gavin was standing somewhere behind her, listening to her every word, so she spoke very briefly and hung up with the promise that she would call again in about a week.

She turned from the phone to find him dressed in a pair of striped pajamas. "I keep forgetting that this is really your room, and that most of your clothes are still in here," she said.

Gavin tied the drawstring about his waist in a slack bow. "Yeah," he said, and there was a hint of a smile in his eyes. "You and Nicky threw me out."

"Just Nicky. This was all his idea—to move me in here while you were still in the States. Remember?"

He grinned. "How could I forget? You bit me on the shoulder the night I returned, if my memory serves me correctly."

She closed the distance between them. "That's only because you climbed into my bed in the middle of the night, smacked me on the rump, and told me to get out. I thought I was being attacked."

Gavin threw back his head and released a loud guffaw. "You know I thought you were Mik."

She rubbed the spot on his shoulder through the cotton shirt. "Does it still hurt?"

He rotated the shoulder in question. "No. Actually, where you hit me in the head with your shoe, that," he said, fingering the area, "still hurts."

She kissed the shoulder, then the spot of skin on his forehead where she had clobbered him with the heel of her shoe. "I'm sorry," she said, and managed to look completely repentant.

He wrapped an arm about her. "How sorry are you?"

She gave him a slitted look, humor dancing somewhere in the depths of her eyes. "I think you must have the most one track mind of any man I've ever come across."

"Me?" He was all innocence. "I have no idea what you mean. I just wanted you to read to me for a while. That's all."

"Sure you did." She nodded and walked into the bathroom to finish drying her hair. When she emerged again she was clothed in a huge, cotton T–shirt, and her hair swung in silky waves about her shoulders.

Gavin was lying propped against the pillows on the neatly made bed, his head resting comfortably on his hands.

"Are you staying?" she asked, coming to sit on the edge.

He rolled unto his side, one hand propped against a temple. "Unless you say I have to go."

"Let me think," she said, unrolling a sock ball.

He pulled her back into his arms, growling in her ear. "Don't think too long, missy. I might give up on all of my noble intentions, and decide to convince you otherwise."

"OK, OK, you can stay," she said, stifling a shriek of laughter when his fingers went to her ribs and began to tickle.

"Good," he said. And he pressed a warm kiss to the side of her neck.

Summer turned to face him, and he touched the tip of her nose with a long finger. "It's still early yet—not even ten o'clock—what are we going to do?"

"Well, you did say you wanted me to read to you. Or—"

He pounced. "Or?"

"Or we could go downstairs and watch TV."

"No. I want you all to myself tonight. Nicky and Rob will probably be down there right now."

"A book, then?"

He sighed. "A book."

She stood and walked the short distance to the bookcase in the corner of the room. Most of the leather–bound volumes were classics of one kind or another. She spent a moment mentally sifting through various titles. "Alex Haley's *Roots?*" she finally asked, turning to give him a look.

He shifted into a sitting position. "OK."

Summer lifted the book from the shelf. It was a gorgeous first edition, nicely bound in sturdy black leather and made even more attractive by the golden sheen on its gilt–tipped pages.

She ran a finger down the thick spine. "Wow," she said, and there was a trace of reverence in her voice. "My copy at home looks nothing like this."

She returned to sit on the bed, and Gavin peeled back the blanket so that she might slide her feet under. When she was comfortably situated, he rested his head in her lap and said. "I'm ready for you." Summer reached back to prop two pillows behind her, shifted a bit to properly position his head, opened up the book cover, and began to read.

CHAPTER SIX

They fell asleep with Gavin's head cradled in Summer's lap, his arms wrapped about her lower half. At some point deep in the night, he had shifted to pull her fully into his arms, and then slept again.

The next morning, Summer awoke to the gentle crash of waves on the beach. She lay still for a moment, just listening to the soothing sound of it. The peace and utter quiet was remarkable. It was almost as though for just a tiny moment, time had frozen.

Gavin shifted beside her, and she reached down to stroke his curly black hair. In sleep, with his features completely relaxed, he appeared almost as angelic as baby Amber. It was hard to believe that he was actually the head of one of the most successful shipping concerns on the island. How completely wrong she had been about him. She had once thought him rude, cold, arrogant, but he was none of those things. In fact, she would be hard-pressed to find another man quite like him—a man with those certain qualities of kindness and generosity, a man who would give up a large portion of his own life so that he might adequately raise his younger siblings. There were not too many out there like him. Not too many at all.

She ran a finger down the bridge of his nose, pausing to gently trace the outline of his lips. He shifted in response, mumbled something unintelligible, and slung a long leg across her. Summer snuggled back into his arms and knew with a certainty that she would never be more content than she was at that very moment.

An hour later, Gavin was roused from sleep by the strident bellows of baby Amber. He looked down at Summer for a long while. Even in sleep, she was beautiful. A thoughtful expression ran across his face. What was he going to do about the state of things between them? He had fought against it for the longest time, and it was becoming increasingly clear that he was losing the battle—that, in fact, it wasn't even worth fighting at all. He was coming to need her more and more each day, so much that it was increasingly more difficult to imagine living without her. He loved the way she talked, the funny little gestures she often made with her hands when she was in earnest about making a particular point. He loved playing with her, laughing with her, kissing her. God, she made him happy. That's what she did. She made life fun. Fun, for heaven's sake. It had never been like that before, not with anyone.

He checked his watch. It was almost seven–thirty. He lingered a moment more, reluctant to leave her. His hand reached out to stroke the soft, golden skin of one arm. "What am I going to do about you, babe?" he muttered.

Summer opened one eye carefully. She had heard the soft question, even though it had not been meant for her ears. A smile curved the corners of her lips.

The baby released another volley of very strenuous bellows, and Summer turned with a hand across her eyes. "She's probably hungry."

Gavin leaned down to press a quick kiss against her lips. "I thought you were still asleep."

"I was," she said, sitting up. A long curtain of black hair

sloped silkily across one shoulder, and her eyes were a soft hazel in the early morning light. "I'll go prepare a bottle for the baby. I wonder where Nicky is."

Gavin stood, arching backward in a long, lazy stretch. "He's probably still asleep."

A frown wrinkled the smooth skin of Summer's forehead. "How could he possibly sleep through this?"

Gavin grinned. "Depending on what it was he was doing last night, he might be able to sleep through just about anything."

Summer made a noncommittal sound and went to the closet. "I'll go get her while you put on a pair of pants," Gavin said, and was gone before Summer could utter anything in response.

He was back moments later with the baby perched on his shoulder. "She's wet," he said.

Summer poked a head out of the bathroom. "Did you find out where Nicholas is?"

Gavin bounced the baby. "He's probably just where I said—asleep in bed."

"And Rob and Mik?" She was almost through dressing.

"Rob's left for school, and Mik was up late studying for his final exams, so he's also asleep."

Summer emerged from the bathroom fully clothed. Her abundant tresses were swept up and neatly pinned in a smooth chignon. She held out her arms for the baby. "Do you think Nicky's becoming more responsible?"

Gavin handed the infant over, and perched on the side of the bed to watch the diaper changing process. "He's improved over the last year, but he still has a long way to go. I think he still has some unresolved issues surrounding our mother."

Summer looked up. There was a splotch of baby powder on the right side of her face. "That's why you have to tell him the truth about your mom's condition. I don't think you should wait any longer."

Gavin rubbed the side of his jaw. "I know."

"Pass me her jumper," Summer said, nodding at the pretty pink–and–white item of baby apparel.

Gavin handed it over. "You do that well.

"Umm," Summer said, looking up at him. "Nothing like my cooking, though, huh?"

Gavin laughed. "I love you babe, but by no stretch of the imagination could I possibly say that you're a good cook."

Summer's hands went still, and an equal quality of silence settled over Gavin. He appeared just as shocked by the revelation as she. A few seconds ticked by, during which time they did little more than just stare at each other.

"What—what did you just say?" Summer finally managed.

His chest rose and fell, and Summer watched the movement with a certain amount of bemused fascination. "I didn't mean—" he began.

"To say you love me?" Summer interrupted.

He moved to stare out the window, his hands shoved deep into his pants pockets. "Well, not to tell you like that."

She came up behind him. The baby was in her arms, so she could do no more than rub her face against the side of his arm. "I won't use it against you, Gavin. And, my plans won't change, either. I'll stay for a while, but not forever. You don't need to feel trapped."

He turned, and the look he gave her was unreadable. "You mean it makes no difference that I love you? You still intend to go anyway, at some point?"

She gave the question very careful consideration before replying. "I don't think you want to feel whatever it is you feel for me, for whatever reason. Besides, it may not even be love, not the real kind, anyway. So, yes, I'll be going, anyway."

He frowned. "You're no authority on love, so don't try to tell me what it is I feel for you. And what about you? Do you have feelings of any kind for me? Or am I just a passing phase for you? Someone to fill in the gap with until the right man comes along."

Summer took a calming breath. The man she loved more than she had thought it possible to love anyone had just told her that he loved her, and they were now embroiled in some idiotic argument—about what, she wasn't even completely sure. "You're not a passing phase to me. I don't think you could be a passing anything to any woman in her right mind."

"That doesn't answer my question."

She clenched her teeth. Never before had she ever felt so very vulnerable. "Yes. I do. I care deeply about you." She turned about to hush the baby, who was beginning to make little cranky sounds again, and used this opportunity to hide her face from him. She hadn't wanted to tell him how she felt. Not yet, not until she was absolutely certain that he did indeed need and want her in a permanent way. Now, it was too late. If whatever it was he felt for her was not real, she would be left with nothing. Not even her pride.

"Summer, put the baby down for a minute and come here."

She turned to give him a look of defiance. Did he think he could order her about now? The expression on his face forestalled any hasty words she might have spoken. There was a quality of tenderness there, a hesitance she had not seen before.

She placed the baby carefully on the bed and walked to him, stopping just inches away, hands tightly clasped behind her back.

"Let's try this again," he said. "I'm kinda new at this, so forgive me if I don't get it right the first time." He drew her closer, reaching behind to link his fingers with hers. "I love you," he said. A flicker of a smile came and went in his eyes. "Now, your turn. It's not hard after the first time."

She blinked. Oh God, here it was. There would be no

turning back now. No opportunity to save face. The bald truth of it would be out in the open for all to see.

He tilted her chin up. "Trust me."

She turned her lips into his palm. "I . . . love you too," she mumbled. She looked up into his blazing, black eyes and experienced a sinking sensation. Triumph. It was written all over him. He knew he had her now. He hadn't been sure before, but now he knew it. "I'd better go fix a bottle for the baby," she said after a moment.

Gavin released her shoulders and gave a short bark of laughter. "We'll talk about whatever it is that's bothering you—tonight. I'll be in Kingston all day today, wrapping up some business with our office out there. I should be back by about eight."

She nodded. "Is Nicky going to be at home today, or is he going in to the office?"

Gavin shrugged. "He can have the day off. There's no reason why he can't keep an eye on things from home, just for today."

Summer propped the baby on her shoulder. "Good. He can help me at the cottage, then."

"You two aren't still trying to find Henry Morgan's gold, are you?" Gavin asked, leaning back against the window sill, his arms folded across his stomach.

Summer met the glinting, black eyes. It was completely clear that he did not believe that Henry Morgan's gold was buried somewhere on the property. In fact, she would be willing to bet that he regarded her secretive activities with Nicholas nothing short of amusing.

"The gold's there somewhere," she said. "It has to be. No one has ever found it since it was buried centuries ago."

"Well, babe," he said, straightening away from the window sill, "if it makes you happy to think so, go ahead with it. Just don't let Nicky make you do anything dangerous."

She smiled. "I'll be fine. You worry too much."

"You're even beginning to sound like Nicholas. I'm not

sure he's a good influence on you, at all," he said, running a hand through the tightly curled mop of hair atop his head.

"Go take your shower." Summer grinned. "I'll wake Nicky up."

She left the room with the baby now sleeping soundly against her shoulder. She walked down the long corridor to the door at the very end of it, taking great care not to wake the baby as she lifted an arm and knocked softly on the wood. "Nicky?" Her voice was barely above a whisper.

When there was no response, she banged a little harder. The baby shifted, churned its feet a bit, and uttered a disgruntled burble of sound. She turned the doorknob and was surprised when it offered no resistance. She pushed it open a crack, and peered inside.

"Nicky?" she said again. The bed was neatly made, the coverlet turned down as though in preparation for a night of very sound sleep. There was no evidence that the bed had been slept in.

A shard of alarm ran quickly through her. Where could he be? It was clear that he hadn't spent the night there, and he always did—regardless. Her brain shot straight into overdrive. Could he have gotten into trouble at one of the rough bars he loved to frequent? Maybe he was lying in a ditch somewhere right now, his life's blood pouring from numerous gaping wounds. Maybe he was broken and battered in some no name hospital. He had told her on any number of occasions that he wasn't a physically adept person, that he couldn't defend himself in a fight, that it was always Gavin who had fought all of his battles.

Unconsciously, she rubbed the baby's back. She had to calm herself. There was no point at all in working herself into a lather about something that probably had no basis in reality. She took a long deep breath, and backed slowly from the room.

A voice directly behind caused her to start so much that

she very nearly lost her grip on the infant. "Looking for me?"

She spun about, an expression of tremendous relief in her eyes. "Nicky! I thought—" She paused, and her eyes ran over him quickly. He was clothed in evening attire: A dark green, silk shirt, tapered black slacks, and the latest fashion in expensive men's footwear. His entire outfit screamed designer original; outrageously expensive.

She tilted her chin up and gave him a speculative little look. "And where have you *been?*"

The wicked grin that she had come to know and love so well flashed for a moment. "If I told you that, my girl, you'd probably blush all the way down to your toes."

Summer's lips curved in an answering smile. "Try me. I don't blush easily."

He came fully into the room. "Maybe later. How's the little munchkin?" he asked, nodding at the baby.

"Your daughter's hungry. She woke us—that is, me— up really early this morning.

Nicholas ran a hand through his hair in a gesture that made Summer think of Gavin. "Let me go change, and we'll get her something to eat. Is Mik up yet?" he asked, turning again to look at her.

"Nope. Unlike some people, he was up studying for half the night."

Nicholas threw back his head and let out a great guffaw of laughter. "I'm the black sheep of the family, or don't you remember?"

Summer batted him playfully with a hand. "I'll leave you to dress. Oh, by the way," she said, pausing at the door, "you have the day off today."

"Ahh," Nicholas said, smiling, "it definitely pays to be in the good books of the boss's lady."

Summer grinned. "Shaddap. I had nothing whatsoever to do with it."

She left the room in high spirits. Nicholas always had this strange, effervescent effect on her. He had the ability to pull her from the jaws of the doldrums. Gavin did, too, but in a completely different way. How fortunate she was to have taken this job in Jamaica. If she hadn't, she would never have met Gavin Pagne and his three wonderfully crazy siblings.

The formula was nicely prepared and bottled by the time Nicholas strolled into the kitchen. Summer tested the liquid on the inner side of her wrist. She spared Nicholas a quick glance as he settled himself on a stool. "Aren't you tired?"

He stretched. "Never felt better."

She fitted the nipple into the tiny mouth. "Make some breakfast, then."

Nicholas uncurled from the stool. "Man, you're bossy. Hasn't Gavin mellowed you at all?"

Summer sat. "I've mellowed him, I think."

Nicholas walked to one of the cupboards and began pulling out pots. "So, how are things going with my big brother?"

Summer shifted on the hard stool. "You know, we really should get some tie cushions for these stools. They're not very comfortable."

Nicholas turned from his busy activities at the cupboard, to give her a slitted look. "Umm," he said after a moment of intense staring, "something's happened. Tell me."

Summer played for time by cooing at Amber and generally making a large fuss over the infant, who was suckling greedily at the bottle.

"Yes?" he said after a long stretch of waiting.

She gave him a direct look. "Nothing's happened. Just . . . normal stuff. Nothing at all, really."

Nicholas placed a large saucepan on the stove, and turned to root about in the cupboard again. He emerged this time with a skillet, a cooking spoon, and a rack of some sort. He placed all of these on the kitchen table, then went to the fridge and began to stack eggs in a plastic bowl.

Summer watched him, and a puzzled frown crept in between her eyes. This was unlike him. "Aren't you going to ask more questions?"

He brought the eggs back to the table, and there was a diabolical light in his eyes. "Psychology is a wonderful thing. The silent treatment really works, doesn't it?"

Summer grinned at him. "You're a devil, Nicky."

Nicholas leaned down to press a quick kiss to her cheek. "And now for breakfast."

Summer pointed at the bowl of eggs. "Do you need help with those?"

"Lord, no. Keep her away from the eggs," Gavin said, coming through the door. He was dressed in formal business attire: A dark navy, pin–striped suit. Maroon tie. Black, patent leather shoes. His black hair curled about his head in glistening waves. If it were possible to describe a man as being beautiful, she would be well justified in that description now. He was nothing short of gorgeous, and for a long moment Summer found it difficult to remove the sudden dryness from her throat.

Nicholas grinned at his brother. "Come on, Gav. Give her another chance. I'm sure it was entirely unrelated to her cooking that you came down with a serious case of the runs after one of her meals."

Gavin patted his stomach. "I can't risk it today. If I get an attack in Kingston—well, I don't think I need say more than that."

Summer laughed at their gentle teasing. She was well aware that cooking was not up there on her list of strengths, but she would get better at it, even if she had to resort to culinary classes. She *would* get better. "Come and sit," she said to Gavin, and shifted to make room for him at the table. Gavin removed a stool from beneath the table with a tug of a foot. "Can you believe how she bosses me around?" he said to his brother.

Nicholas nodded in agreement. "What can we do about it, I wonder?"

Gavin gave Summer a slow, sexy smile. "I'll think of something—when I return."

Nicholas broke an egg neatly on the side of the bowl, and dropped the perfectly shaped yolk into the frying pan.

"How do you want yours, Summer?"

Just a few short months ago she would have declined breakfast entirely. Now she looked forward to the meal with great enthusiasm. "I'll take mine sunny side up."

"Mine, too," Gavin said.

Nicholas busied himself with frying eggs and toasting large quantities of bread.

"Have you done enough for Mik, too?" Summer asked. "He should be up soon."

Nicholas inserted the toasted slices of bread into the wire rack. "We've got enough food here to feed an entire army."

Summer stood. "I'll go put the baby down. She's asleep again." She left the kitchen with a "Don't start without me" comment floating on the air. When she returned, the shiny lacquer table in the dining room was nicely set, complete with side plates and rolled napkins.

"Wow, Nicky," she said in genuine admiration, "you've outdone yourself this time."

He pulled out a chair for her. "Sit," he said. "I'll bring the food out."

"Are you sure you don't need any help?"

He winked. "I've got it well in hand."

When he had left the dining room Summer turned to Gavin, who was now seated at the head of the table. "Have you bawled Nicky out recently? What's gotten into him?"

Gavin linked his fingers, resting his chin in the area between them. "I'm just waiting for the bomb to drop. He's probably totaled the Jeep, or something like that. I'll find out—eventually."

"Hmm," Summer allowed, and gave herself up to her own thoughts on the matter.

Nicholas returned with a heaping platter of fried eggs and another of nicely buttered, golden toast. He was back and forth after that, carrying jugs of ice cold milk, juice and water, soft slabs of creamy cheese, and a sizable hunk of fresh bread.

"Shouldn't we wait for Mik?" Summer asked when it became clear that the eating was about to begin.

"He'll come down when he's ready," Gavin said, reaching for the eggs. He helped himself to two of these, several slices of toast, and a tall glass of juice. Summer selected a single egg, two slices of toast, and a glass of milk. She waited until Nicholas had served himself before beginning to eat. Between mouthfuls, she asked, "What business are you doing in Kingston today, babe?"

Gavin placed a thick slice of cheese on a piece of toast, bit, and chewed with obvious enjoyment. "We're going to start shipping private party barrels between the US and Asia. Should be a very lucrative undertaking."

"Umm," Summer said, taking a sip of milk. "So, are you going to be opening up offices there? In Asia, I mean."

"Our first office will be in Beijing. Nicky's going to open that one. I'm worn out from all the traveling at the moment. Besides"—he turned to give her a look—"I have more important things to keep me at home now."

A pleased flush rushed to Summer's face and neck, and she refused to meet Nicholas's eyes. It was abundantly clear that he was going to give her a very hard time of it as soon as Gavin was gone.

"Are we going to have a tender moment?" Nicholas asked, wiggling his eyebrows in the most ridiculous fashion.

"No. No tender moments," Gavin said, standing. "I have to get going." He wiped his mouth with a napkin, bent to press a lightning kiss on Summer's lips. "Don't do anything crazy," he said to Nicholas. "I should be back by about eight." He winked at Summer. "Keep dinner warm for me—just don't cook it."

Summer chuckled. "OK, Mr. Pagne, sir. But one of these days you're going to beg me to do some cooking for you."

There was a smile in his eyes when he held out a hand and said, "Walk me to the car."

They said a long good–bye, and Summer stood in the circular courtyard and watched him drive off, waving until he was completely out of sight. She turned to find Nicholas standing in the doorway, a slice of crispy toast in one hand. He beckoned her in with the half–eaten bread. "Don't look so glum. He'll be back."

Summer forced a smile to her lips. "I'm not glum. I just wish I could've gone with him. He didn't even ask me if I wanted to."

Nicholas closed the door behind them, and drew her back to the dining room. "Have some more food," he said. "You still don't eat enough. Since you've been here, you *have* gained a pound or two, though."

"One or two too many," Summer agreed, patting her stomach.

Nicholas smiled. "Nonsense. You've filled out nicely. When you arrived here a few months ago, you were as skinny as a rail."

"Thank you very much," Summer said, "I'll just take my nicely filled out self off to the cottage. I have work to do today."

Nicholas stood. "Wait, and I'll go with you. I want to see what you've done lately. And if you've a bit of free time, we can always continue looking for Morgan's gold."

"Dish a plate for Mik," Summer said. She gave her watch a quick glance. "Shouldn't you go check on him, too? He has been sleeping for quite a long while now."

Nicholas reached for an empty plate. "You're going to make a great mother someday."

Summer bit back the information she longed to share. What would Nicholas have to say if he knew that his big brother had asked her whether she liked children, and had told her in no uncertain terms that he loved her.

"What? No reply," Nicholas was saying teasingly. "This has to be a first."

She grinned at him. "I'll go up and wake Mik, let him know we're leaving the baby with him."

"I'm awake," came the yawned reply from somewhere on the staircase.

Summer's eyes wandered over the sleep–tousled young man as he strolled into the room. He needed a haircut, she noted absently, and a shave. There were dark shadows beneath his eyes, and a sleep–deprived look about him.

"Even after all this time, I still can't get over how much you look like Gavin," she said as he seated himself at the table.

"Almost his double at this age, everyone tells me," Mik said, helping himself to a large quantity of eggs and toast.

"Umm," Summer agreed, and she had to fight against the urge to fondly ruffle a hand through his black hair.

"We're going up to the cottage," Nicholas said. "Keep an eye on the baby. The bottles are all prepared and in the fridge. All you have to do is warm them up. OK?"

"Mik gave his brother a patient look. "Haven't I done this all before?"

"Never while you were studying for your pre–med finals."

"He'll be fine. Won't you, Mik?" Summer intervened skillfully.

The young man nodded. "If I have any problems with her, I'll come get you."

"Come on, Nicky." With that, Summer hustled Nicholas out of the house.

They walked across the cobblestone courtyard, down the stone stairs leading to the beach, and onto the powder–fine white sand. The ocean was crystal blue, with nary a ripple to disturb the smoothness of its surface. Summer bent and scooped up a palmful of warm, golden sand. She shook it back and forth for a minute, playing with some tiny pink shells she had somehow managed to pick up.

"Beautiful, aren't they?"

Nicholas gave her a slightly distracted look. "What?"

"The shells—especially the tiny ones. The designs are so intricate."

The black eyes went to her hand, then up to her face. "Are you going to stay with us?"

It was her turn to utter a startled, "What?"

Nicholas gave her a frown. "Don't give me that 'what,' routine. You heard me."

Summer shook her head. "You are just incredible, do you know that? You've decided that I'm the one for Gavin, and whether he likes it or not you're going to try to push it through."

"What are you complaining about? You should be thanking me instead of pretending that you're upset."

"Geez," Summer said, "I think you'd better go back to the house and get some sleep. You're as ornery as a bear with a sore paw."

A rueful grin twisted the corners of his mouth. "Yeah. Sorry," he said. "It's not you. It's something else."

Summer gave him a sideways glance. "Something else?"

"Umm," he said. "Janet."

Summer turned to quickly glance behind them. For a split second she had actually thought that Janet had suddenly materialized from somewhere behind. "What about Janet? She's not coming here today, is she?"

Nicholas shrugged. "Who can tell?" He walked on for a few more paces, then said, "What do you think of her?"

"What do I think of her?" Summer was almost incredulous. "You know what I think of her. I can't stand her."

"I know," Nicholas said, and a frown gathered between his brows. "I can't stand her, either. Still——" He let the remainder of the thought hang for a moment on the air. "She's kinda cute though . . . don't you think?"

Summer gave him a startled look. "Oh my God, Nicky, please tell me you're not developing a thing for her."

He gave a sharp crack of laughter. "Maybe I should go after her, it would certainly keep her occupied . . . away from you and Gavin."

"Hmm," Summer said, "Janet isn't one of my favorite people, but not even she deserves such treatment."

He gave an exaggerated sigh. "OK. I'll stay away from her for the while, but only if you promise to stay on with us."

Summer hesitated. Even though she had told Gavin just that morning that she intended to leave not too long after the cottage was fully refurbished, she still had not completely come to terms with the crushing finality of it.

"I'd love to stay with you guys forever, but, I've got to get back to LA. Start over. Pick up my life where I left off."

"Pick it up here."

Summer sighed. "It's complicated."

Nicholas made a sound of disgust. "Maybe you're not the girl I thought you were, Summer Stevens."

A strong gust of ocean–scented air whipped a swatch of hair across Summer's face, and she took a moment to scrape the errant strands back behind her ears. "Your interesting psychological twists are not going to work on me this time, Nicky my friend. I know you a little too well for that now."

Amusement danced in his eyes. "Is that so?"

She nodded. "That's right."

"Well, we'll have to see about that," he said, and extended a hand to help her up the concrete stairs leading to the cottage. At the top, he came to an abrupt halt.

Summer looked up at him. "Now what?"

"There's one place we haven't looked yet."

She sighed. "What are you rambling about now?"

"Henry Morgan's buried gold. There's one place on the property we haven't even thought to look yet."

Her interest picked up. "Where's that?"

"Down in the catacombs—underneath the foundation of the house itself."

A frown wrinkled the smooth skin of her forehead. "The catacombs?"

Nicholas grabbed hold of her hand and hustled her up the front stairs to the cottage.

"Don't you want to see what I've done with the garden— the yellow roses?" she panted as he very nearly pushed her through the front door.

"Later, later," he said. "Let's go down to the caves right now. While there's plenty of natural light."

"Take it easy, Nicky," Summer said in an attempt to interject some modicum of reason into the proceedings. "Gavin's probably right, anyway, and there is no gold. Maybe someone found it centuries ago, and just never let on. You know—to keep the legend alive."

"Maybe. But it's worth a look, don't you think?"

"All right," she allowed, and followed him down the nicely painted stairs into the basement. She felt around blindly for a moment for the light switch. A shiver went through her. For some reason, this was the only part of the entire cottage of which she was not overly fond. "Didn't one of the owners of the cottage hang himself somewhere down here a couple of decades ago?"

Her voice held a note of unease, and Nicholas turned. "A Dutchman, back in the early part of the century. Hey, are you all right?"

She shivered again, prompting Nicholas to wrap a protective arm about her shoulders. "It's OK," he said, massaging the gooseflesh from her. "All of the stories about this cottage are just that—stories, long ago traces of the past. There's no truth to the legend of the curse. I'm sure."

She nodded. "I'm just being silly. Somehow, I've never

liked this room much. I feel as though something terrible happened here, at sometime."

"Hmm," Nicholas said, and he gave her a searching look before continuing. "There is another story that I never told you. Maybe I'd better not now."

"No," Summer demurred, "tell me. Maybe it'll help."

He nodded. "This cottage was used as a halfway house for runaway plantation bondsmen."

"Umm," she said. "I remember, . . . you told me."

"Well, the reason it was discontinued as a safe house was that a massacre took place right here, in this very basement, centuries ago."

Summer squinted at him. She wasn't certain whether or not he was completely serious. "Are you pulling my leg?"

He shook his head. "I wouldn't. Not about something like this."

"What happened?" She was almost afraid to hear it.

'Well, the story goes that it happened on a night when the sea was angry, and it was too dangerous to sail. There was a great storm, you see—not exactly a hurricane, but the winds were strong and wild enough to drive the hardiest of men to shelter. A rowdy group of plantation hands happened upon the cottage during the height of the gale, and they found twenty or more slaves hiding in and about the cottage."

"God," Summer said, "I can guess what happened next."

Nicholas nodded. "The plantation *men*—if you can call them that—rounded every last bondsman up, herded them into this basement, and slaughtered them all—like animals—torturing some before putting an end to their misery."

Summer ground her teeth. "Incredible. It's no wonder this place has a horrible aura about it."

"Yes," Nicholas agreed. He began walking the circumference of the room, stomping on the ground with the flat of his foot.

Summer watched him in silence for a while. Finally, all of the walking and stomping became too much for her. "What in the name of heaven are you doing?" she was forced to ask.

Nicholas paused in the stomping for a bit. "There's a hollow area somewhere about—a hidden trapdoor."

Her eyebrows came together. "There is no trap door down here."

"Trust me. There is."

Nicholas resumed the stomping, and after another stretch, he declared, "I've found it. He crouched and ran his fingers along the flat of the floor. Summer watched as he reached into a tiny hole and yanked upward.

"I had no idea that was there," she said, momentarily startled. "Are you sure it's safe?"

Nicholas peered down into the black hole. Dark water lapped somewhere at the end of the short run of stone stairs. "We'll need some light. Do you have a torch? Maybe two?"

"There's a lantern in the pantry. I'll get it," she said, and was climbing the stairs before he could suggest otherwise. She had no desire at all to be left alone in that basement.

When she returned, Nicholas was nowhere to be seen. Summer held the lantern before her, and peered down into the hole in the flooring. "Nicky?" Her voice echoed eerily, bouncing off the walls and recoiling to reverberate again. She called again, and was relieved when she heard his voice coming from somewhere in the belly of the cave.

"Come on down," he bellowed. "It's beautiful down here. Not what you'd expect at all."

Summer took a breath. "How do I get myself into these things?" she muttered under her breath. She tested the first stair, holding the lantern before her and mumbling all the while about being forced to ride pigs, donkeys, and all manner of creatures, and now this.

"Careful with the last stair," Nicholas called again. "It's a bit slippery. Moss I think."

Summer held on to the craggy stone wall, and gingerly felt her way downward. When she arrived at the bottom, she held the lantern out. The darkness was so complete that it appeared to press in on the light, dimming its glow. She raised a hand to her eyes. "Nicky, where are you?"

His voice came from a short distance off. "Around the corner. Walk in the direction of my voice."

She followed, as he had instructed, stumbling a bit over jutting parts on the ground. She came to a side of the cave, and followed it around and down a gentle slope. A gasp of wonderment escaped her as she rounded the final corner. Nothing in her life, up to that point, could possibly have prepared her for this. "Amazing," she mumbled, and her feet came to a very natural stop. "Everywhere's blue— even the rocks."

She put the lantern at her feet. There was no need for light now. The cave was filled with a white glow which appeared to be coming from a location which she couldn't quite pinpoint. Nicholas sat just a few feet away, legs dangling into the blue–green water lapping gently at the base of the rocks.

Summer walked across to sit. "Have you known of this place all along?"

He picked up a chunk of soft rock, curled his arm as far back as it would go, then flung it out toward the middle of the pool. He nodded. "How did you think the runaways made it out to sea without anyone seeing them?"

Summer's brow wrinkled. "I just assumed that they climbed down the face of the cliffs."

Nicholas threw another rock. "Nope. The cliffs would've been too risky. It was much safer to paddle a longboat into this cave, and to leave through the house."

Summer followed the water with her eyes. "You mean this little lagoon leads all the way out to the open sea?"

"Yup. Through the centuries, this inlet has been used by

just about everyone. Pirates. British privateers. Plantation runaways. People say that many a Spanish buccaneer lost his life on the rocks around here, spilling trunkloads of gold doubloons unto the ocean floor.''

"Wow," Summer said, "the place is just steeped in history, isn't it?"

Nicholas dusted the palm of a hand against his jeans. "See how smooth the wall is over there?" He pointed to a location on the craggy rock face obliquely opposite where they sat.

Summer looked, but could see nothing particularly outstanding about the spot. "I see it, but it looks like anywhere else to me."

Nicholas heaved a tiny pebble at the other wall, and watched with a narrowed gaze as it rebounded from the craggy surface. "Looks man–made to me."

Summer squinted. "You mean—"

"Uh huh." He nodded. "There's something sealed in the wall of the cave."

Summer looked again. "Now that you mention it, it does kinda look like that." Her voice rose in sudden excitement.

Nicholas pulled his T–shirt up over his head to reveal his long, lean torso. Summer's eyes flickered over the flat whipcord stomach. A smile curved her lips. "Now I completely understand."

"Understand what?" Black eyes locked with hers for an instant, before shifting away again to fasten on the wall.

"Understand why women hound you incessantly."

His sudden laughter echoed hollowly around the cave. "And why is that?"

She reached up a hand to pat the firm abdominal muscles. "For your body."

He pulled her to her feet, his eyes filled with dark amusement. "Gavin's going to have his hands full with you."

She gave him a little nudge with her shoulder. "Don't get too conceited about it, now. My interest was strictly clinical."

"Of course," he said, grinning. He shrugged out of his pants and dove cleanly into the water. He covered the short distance to the other side in a few measured strokes. With athletic ease, he hauled himself from the water to sit on the craggy ledge. "OK. You're next," he said.

Summer wrinkled her nose. "No. I'll stay on this side. I don't want to get all wet. Besides, I don't have on my swim suit."

He shook the water from his hair like a wet puppy. "All right. I guess I'll be claiming all the gold for myself—when I find it."

It was Summer's turn to laugh. "You mean you wouldn't share the spoils with me?"

Nicholas tested the wall with the flat of a thumb. "Nope."

"What about with Gavin and the rest of the boys?"

"Hmm." He considered her suggestion for a moment. "I'd give them ten percent."

She grinned. "Each?"

"No. Just ten percent."

She shook her head. "Geez, you're such a nice guy."

He picked up a rock, tapped the smooth spot, listened, tapped again.

"It sounds hollow," he said after a minute.

Summer's heart picked up a bit. "Can you break through the surface?"

Nicholas shook his head. "It's solid rock. I'm going to need special tools. We'll have to go back to the house—get a pick, maybe some rope."

"Why don't you wait until Gavin gets back? He'd be able to help you better than I could."

Nicholas gave this suggestion a moment's thought. "He won't be back until dark. It'll be too late, then—to start digging, I mean."

"If there's buried treasure in there, it's been in there for centuries. It can wait another day."

Nicholas slid back into the water. "OK, Miss practical."

Summer leaned over to haul him out, and gave a little shriek when the chain hanging about her neck fell without warning into the dark blue water. She grabbed ineffectually at it.

"My chain—Nicky grab it!" With lightning quickness, Nicholas was back in the water. He disappeared beneath the surface, then was back again, holding the silver chain in his hand.

Summer gave him a hand up again. "The locket's gone," she said, taking the chain from him, and peering again into the water. "Did you see a tiny, heart–shaped locket down there?"

Nicholas shook his head. "You're lucky I found the chain. Buy yourself a new locket," he said when she continued to look downcast. "There's lots of nice trinkets in the Ocho Rios market."

"It's a family heirloom," she said. "You can't buy that in a market. There was a picture of my mom and dad in there."

Nicholas picked up his T–shirt, hauling it back on with little regard for the fact that he was soaking wet. The fabric clung to his well–muscled chest like a second skin. He wrapped an arm about her. "I'll see if I can find it tomorrow, when the light is better."

"Do you think it might still be there? What about the tides?"

Nicholas shrugged. "You never know. The ocean is kinda peaceful around here. Not much of a current." He gave her a little squeeze. "Don't worry, I'll find it."

Summer followed him back along the rocky pathway, and up into the first cave. Again the light of the lantern failed to do much to penetrate the thick darkness. "My God, Nicky!" she was forced to exclaim at one point when he walked confidently ahead of her, "how can you see where you're going? Have you got cat eyes or something?"

"Or something," he said, and turned to flash sturdy white teeth at her. He removed the lantern from her hands and stood aside with a helpful, "Up you go," comment as she made her way up the stairs.

Nicholas followed her back through the basement and up into the tastefully appointed living room. There were soothing splashes of cream and blue everywhere. Huge, overstuffed cream sofas with blue throw cushions were nicely positioned about the space. Ornately fashioned blue vases sat on cream and gold end tables, and matching hand–crafted Jamaican throw rugs added just the right touch of warmth and hominess to the overall picture of cool elegance.

"Well?" Summer prompted after he continued to observe the room without comment. A smile lifted the corners of his lips. "Not bad. Not bad at all. I've been meaning to mention it for weeks now. This is nice, very nice. It's relaxing, somehow."

She gave him a long look. "Do you mean that?"

"Of course I do." He pulled back the French doors to let the ocean breeze roll into the room. "I could live here—and that says a lot right there."

Summer walked out onto the whitewashed, wraparound verandah. "The only thing left is the swing," she said, pointing to the wide, two seater that hung from two sturdy metal rings firmly affixed to the wooden ceiling. "I'm going to pad the seat, then cover it using the same cream and blue motif. It'll have to be a water–resistant type material, though, because of the ocean air."

Nicholas came to stand next to her, bending to lean on the railing. "This is what some nineteenth century novels would describe as an idyllic spot."

"Umm," Summer agreed. " Can you imagine waking to the crash of the waves every morning? How much better than that does it get?"

He gave her a sidelong glance. "That's why you should stay."

"My parents—I couldn't leave them to live here. They need me."

"Bring them here, then. The warm climate would be much better for them."

Summer considered this for a tempting moment. The idea did have some appeal. Her parents could sell the home they had at Mammoth, or perhaps rent it out. They could purchase a small villa along the beach, something nice and cozy. And she was certain that they would both love Jamaica. Her father had visited the island before, after all, and her mother was always in favor of trying new things.

"I don't know," she said after a good long while. "Gavin may feel crowded, pressured. You know what I mean?" She turned to give him a quick look.

The black eyes were serious. "He doesn't know how to ask you to stay. Why don't you help him?"

Summer picked up the hand closest to her, and held it. "Does your brother know how much you love him?"

The eyes shifted away from her to stare at the azure blue ocean. "Gavin raised me and the boys single-handedly. He fought our battles for us. Sometimes literally. He was always there. We want him to be happy. I want him to be happy." The eyes shifted back to hold hers. "If I didn't think you were the right one for him, I would've sent you on your way a long time ago." He squeezed her hand. "He needs you. Stay with him."

Summer's eyes misted over, and for a moment, her voice was nothing more than a thick croak in her throat. "I—" She struggled to find the right words. How could she adequately say how deeply he had moved her? How humbled she was by the kind of love he had for his brother? How grateful she was to be considered worthy of the love of a man like Gavin Pagne? "Are you suggesting that we . . . that we live together?"

Black eyebrows rose and became one smooth pelt. "Live together?" Laughter gleamed in his eyes. "Gavin would never live with anyone without the benefit of marriage. Don't you know that?"

"Don't be too sure about that," Summer demurred. "He asked me to . . . to be his—"

"His?"

"Mistress," she said after a brief hesitation over the word.

"And you said no, of course?"

Summer nodded. "Of course."

Nicholas gave her a wink. "Good. He was probably just testing you."

"Well, maybe," Summer said, and before she could stop herself the words were past her lips. "This morning he said he loved me."

Nicholas straightened, and there was triumph in his eyes. "And you weren't going to tell me this, I guess?"

"No" Summer frowned. "I probably shouldn't have told you now. Nicky," she said when a devilish smile began to twist his lips, "promise me you won't say anything to anyone. Anyone at all."

He wrapped her arm through the nook of his. "Summer—Champagne," he said, rolling the the two names around thoughtfully. His eyes had taken on a dark glitter. "I like the sound of that."

"Nicky," she said again, and endeavored to look several measures short of threatening. "Promise me."

"I promise you that—you and Gavin will be married before next August. That I promise."

Summer took a breath. He was like a runaway freight train. Once he'd made up his mind about something, there was no stopping him. No stopping him at all.

CHAPTER SEVEN

Gavin glanced at his watch. The day had been a lot more successful than he had dared hope. The Beijing deal was all sewn up, and he had even found enough time to visit with one of the island's best private detectives. For a long while now, he had wondered about Janet Carr. A month ago, he had decided to do something about it. Her background had always puzzled him. In many ways, she was as much an enigma to him now as she had been the first day they met. Over the years since then, he had gently handled her interest in him, keeping her at bay yet never completely sending her away. She was alone, and maybe this was the main reason he had allowed her free access to his home, and family.

But things were changing, and something needed to be done. He had never thought he'd ever consider shifting his life around for any woman, but that was before he had met Summer Stevens. She was that strange, intangible thing that had always been absent from his life. He looked forward to seeing her every day, to knowing that she would be there in the evenings when he got home. He needed

her. Wanted her. Would only struggle through life, without
her now.

On a sudden impulse he pulled over to the side of the
road, and got out. He had driven the Moneague Roadway
a thousand times, but had never before stopped to buy
anything from any of the vendors scattered along the
length of it. There were many selling water coconuts, juicy
golden patties, and trays of oven warm bulla, while others
hawked intricately carved and polished wooden carvings.

Gavin took a moment to remove his jacket and tie, then
unfastened the first several buttons on his shirt before
going over to inspect the wares of each vendor. "Give me
three bags of patties," he said, nodding at the wonderfully
flaky meat pastries. "Some bulla, too." He pointed at a
well–stacked pile of sweet breads.

"How about some nice jackfruit fe' you?" another vendor asked, reaching beneath her makeshift table, and holding up the fruit. Jackfruit was really not one of his favorites,
and Gavin was on the verge of turning the woman down.
But, before he could utter the right words, he caught sight
of the skinny child seated at her side. "How many jackfruit
do you have?" he asked.

The woman immediately dived beneath the table and
emerged with an entire box full. "OK." Gavin nodded,
"I'll take them all." She gave him a great smile, and went
about the process of quickly boxing the fruit.

"And what about your carvings?" Gavin asked, looking
at the gorgeous pieces of wooden artwork. "How are you
selling them?"

"Meh will g'you a good price, man," the woman said
with great enthusiasm. "Which one you like?"

After a moment's consideration, he said, "I'll take
them all."

It was close to an hour before Gavin could make it back
to the truck. The grateful vendor, with the sheen of tears
in her eyes, had insisted on inviting him back to a rather
ramshackle little house just behind, where she got great

pleasure from feeding him large quantities of bulla bread and tea, gracefully served on battered pieces of crockery. Finally, at a few minutes after seven, Gavin was forced to excuse himself The woman walked him back to the truck, followed by a legion of sons toting the many purchases he had made.

Once everything was nicely situated in the back, she handed Gavin a long knife and said, "Don't fe'get fe' stick de jackfruit."

It took Gavin a couple of seconds to completely understand what it was she was suggesting. Then, it dawned on him—the old Jamaican superstition about never traveling with jackfruit in the car unless you very carefully carved a slice into each one. It was a firmly held local belief that ill fortune would befall any traveler who neglected to have this done.

Gavin accepted the knife, and assured the woman that he would cut the jackfruit once he got to the next gas station. He gave them all a final wave, a toot of the horn, and pulled back onto the road to merge with the evening traffic.

Summer removed a card from the top of the pack and fitted it neatly into the seven held in her hand. "Hmm," she said, after a moment of long consideration.

"Play de game, man. Play de game," Rob said with a trace of youthful impatience.

Nicholas stretched back in his chair, linking long fingers behind his head. "Give her a moment."

Summer hesitated a while longer. Then she looked up to give the gathering a wide smile. "Well," she said, "I was thinking of taking it easy on you guys, but I couldn't make myself do it. She slapped a card onto the face of the table, then laid down the set in her hands. "Gin."

Rob tossed his cards into the air with a vehement exclamation. "Ten games in a row. You must be cheating, man."

Summer gave the boy a quick wink. "I'm just that good."

Nicholas gave her an amused look. "Is that right?"

Summer nodded. "You've seen me in action."

He leaned forward to whisper in her ear. "You know I let you win."

Summer snorted in disbelief. "Nonsense."

Nicholas turned to Rob. "Stack the cards up, boy. I'm going to teach this lady how to play cards."

The next hour was passed in a flurry of activity. At various points, cards were flung into the air, slapped with great enthusiasm onto the flat of the table, and even crumpled and heaved across the room during the most heated moments.

"Well, what do you think of that, Summer . . . Stevens . . . Champagne?" Nicholas asked with a lift of a cocky brow.

"You're a cardshark," Summer said, but there was a trace of humor in her eyes.

Nicholas stood and bowed at the waist. "Thank you, thank you very much." He held up both hands. "No applause please."

Summer shoved at him. "Oh, sit down," she said, grinning. "You're so conceited."

Nicholas sank back into his chair just moments before the clock on the wall chimed nine times. All eyes flashed to the smooth face of it.

"Gavin's late," Summer said, and she made a valiant attempt at hiding the niggle of worry which had been eating at her for the last hour or so.

Nicholas stood and went to the window to pull back the curtain. "He is sometimes—could be things in Kingston are taking a lot longer than he thought they would."

Summer's brow furrowed. "Could be."

Nicholas turned to Rob, who was now seated before the TV set. "Have you finished your homework?"

"Yeah," the boy said without shifting his eyes from the screen.

"I'll go take Mik his dinner on a tray—he hasn't eaten since lunch," Summer said.

Nicholas gave her a distracted look. "Yeah. OK."

Summer walked into the kitchen, and for the next several minutes went about the process of selecting a dinner tray, covering the silver sheen of it with a square of cream linen, positioning the cutlery and glasses and, finally, ladling huge quantities of peas and rice and jerk chicken onto a large plate. She toted the tray through the kitchen, and up the stairs to the second floor. It took a bit of doing to balance it on the flat of one leg and knock on the door at the same time, but she managed it, somehow, without any misadventures.

"Come," the voice said, and Summer entered. Her eyes quickly skimmed the disarray. There were stacks of books lying face down on the bed and the floor. Papers of various color and description were strewn about the desk and floor, and there was an explosion of clothing from an assortment of drawers and closets. Mik sat in the midst of this confusion, bent over a thick book of some sort.

Summer took a breath. "I brought your dinner," she said, and held on tightly to what it was she really wanted to say about the state of his room. Mik looked up, and Summer felt a surge of sudden sympathy. He was working himself to a frazzle over his exams. She had never felt the need to study this hard, had never put much effort at all into anything other than her design work.

Mik gestured with a hand. "Thanks. Could you put it over there?" He pointed at the only spot in the entire room that was not covered with an object of some sort.

Summer stood her ground. "Come and eat now," she said. "You won't be able to retain anything at all if your body runs low on nutrients."

"I can't," Mik mumbled, and peered at the book again.

"Come on," Summer coaxed. "A little break will do you good, anyway."

The struggle on the young man's face was apparent, and

Summer helped him by peeling back the linen to reveal the sumptuous meal beneath.

"Peas and rice," she said, "jerk chicken. Ice cold mango lemonade. Rocky road ice cream—" Mik closed the book. A tired grin lifted the corners of his lips. "OK. Maybe just a little."

Summer set the tray down. "I'm going to stay and make sure you—" The door suddenly pushed back and what she was about to say died in her throat. Nicholas beckoned her outside and she went, closing the door behind her.

"What is it, Nicky?" Summer asked, alarm bells already beginning to go off in her head.

Nicholas pulled her into his arms, and held on to her for a long moment. Summer's heart pounded She pulled back almost too afraid to ask. "Gavin?" she managed to say after a bit of stumbling.

Nicholas nodded. "There's been an accident up on the Moneague Roadway. Two minibuses . . . other vehicles . . . a head–on collision. A couple cars went over the side into the gully below—"

Summer forced herself to take a breath, then another one. The blood was pounding through her head, and a feeling of dizziness was beginning to overcome her. "Is he—?" Tears pooled in her eyes, and she couldn't get herself to actually formulate the question.

Nicholas held her tight. "We don't know. Rob thinks he saw a shot of the truck on TV. The front end of it,"— his voice broke—"the front end of it was all caved in."

Summer shook her head. "It . . . it can't be. Maybe Rob was mistaken. Maybe it wasn't his truck. Lots of vehicles look alike. We can call, find out," she said, her eyes wild with despair. "He can't be gone, Nicky. He can't be. I still feel him here. I still feel him." She opened and closed her hands, gripping convulsively at the fabric of his shirt.

Nicholas held her away, and wiped a gritty thumb against the soft skin beneath her eyes. "We won't tell Mik. Not yet. Not until we're sure."

"Maybe—" Her voice broke. "Maybe if, if we pray. He'll be all right if we pray."

"Pray?" Nicholas said. "I haven't prayed since our mother left us as kids. It does no good."

Summer gripped his hand. "It's all we have. If we believe and pray, he'll be all right. Come on, Nicky."

He looked down at her. "Now?"

She nodded. "Right now. Close your eyes. Hold my hand."

They stood together in the darkened hallway, heads bent, eyes closed. They were both so completely absorbed that when the light flicked on and a voice inquired, "What is this, some new ritual?" neither responded.

Gavin laid the bags in his hand at his feet. "Nicholas," he grated, "go down and help Rob unload the truck."

Nicholas and Summer turned in the direction of his voice, and for a long moment they just stared. Then Summer found her legs, and within seconds she was in his arms, plastering his face with kisses.

Gavin wrapped an arm about her. "What did I do to deserve this?" he asked, and tried to intercept some of the wild kisses with some of his own.

The next several minutes were a bit confused, during which time Nicholas pressed quite a few kisses of his own on both Summer's and Gavin's cheeks. It was a good long while before Summer was able to lead Gavin into her room, and close the door behind.

"Well," Gavin said, leaning back against the closed door, his eyes shining with latent humor, "what was that all about?"

Summer came to him again, wrapping her arms about his middle. "Haven't you heard?"

"Heard what?"

"The accident up on Moneague. Rob thought he saw a shot of your truck on television."

"So," he said, bending toward her, "you thought I was dead, then?"

She nodded, and he ran a thumb down the side of her face. "That would explain Nicky kissing me on the cheek. He hasn't done that since he was a little boy."

The words choked in Summer's throat. "We were praying just now. He loves you, you know?"

Gavin bent his head to softly kiss her lips. "And I love him—and you." His husky voice wrapped around her, and a shiver ran quickly across her skin.

"Gavin," she said, her heart beating in thick thumps against her ribs.

"Umm?"

"Remember when you asked me if I would stay in Jamaica? Live with you, sort of?"

He lifted his head to look down at her. "Are you saying yes, now?"

She nodded. "Yes. I don't seem to care too much what other people think anymore."

He pressed wandering kisses to the side of her neck, the fine line of her jaw, the tender skin just beneath her eyes. "Well," he said huskily, "*I* care what they think." He kissed the soft fullness of her bottom lip. "I want you to be respected by my brothers, by the people who work for Champagne Industries, and everyone else."

Summer blinked huge, golden eyes at him. "What else can we do, then? We can't live together, we can't live apart."

Gavin took her hand in his and led her across to the large bed. "Sit for a minute, babe," he said.

Summer sat, her hands primly crossed in her lap. Gavin stood before her for long minutes before he said anything more. "Years ago," he began, "after I'd grown through my wild years, I created the ideal picture of what the woman I would marry should be like. I've always wanted someone without experience, someone who's never known another man. It's been my thing—what I wanted for me. From the very beginning though, there's been something strong and good between us. And now it's gotten to the point where

I'm beginning to realize that the things I once thought were so important don't mean a thing, at all." He paused to inspect her face, then continued. "I've known you now for less than six months, and yet, it feels as if I've known you all my life."

He gave a rueful laugh. "You're the worst cook I've ever run into, but, it doesn't seem to make a difference." He came to sit next to her and reached out a hand to tilt her chin up. "I can't stand the thought of another man touching you, after me."

Summer swallowed audibly. Her heart was doing a merry jig in her chest. "Should I join a convent, then?" she asked, making a very feeble attempt at humor.

Gavin chuckled. "God," he grated, "then both of our lives would be nothing more than a daily hell. No, that's definitely not the answer."

"Well," Summer began, selecting her words with great care. "The only option left open to us is . . . marriage."

"Umm," Gavin said. "Marriage."

"But what about wanting to marry a virgin Cordon Blue chef? What about all that?"

Gavin ran a finger across her lips. "I did get a virgin cordon blue chef. You know nothing at all about cooking, after all. So, in that sense I guess I got the virgin I wanted."

Summer chuckled. "Sometimes life plays tricks on you." She took his face in her hands. "Besides, would an innocent know how to do this?" and she stretched to sample his lips. "Or this?" she asked, and slipped her tongue between his lips to softly stroke his.

He growled a response, and reached a hand to cup the back of her head. "Let's go to bed," he said, "we can tell everyone about things tomorrow."

"Umm," Summer agreed hazily. "We'll have to tell Nicky first, and my parents."

"And the boys—"

Summer nodded. "And the boys."

CHAPTER EIGHT

Summer was awakened from contented slumber the next morning by the shrill ringing of the doorbell. She turned in Gavin's arms, swept a cloud of heavy hair from her face, and checked her watch.

Gavin muttered a protest as she attempted to wiggle out from under the long thigh that trapped both of hers. The doorbell sounded again, and Gavin opened an eye. "Who could that be at this hour?"

Summer gave him a sleepy smile. "Hi," she said, and there was a hint of shyness in her voice.

Gavin gathered her in closer. "Hi, yourself. How do you feel?"

Summer gave herself up to the luxury of a long, very enjoyable stretch. "Wonderful." The bell sounded yet again, and she was finally forced to say, "Hadn't we better answer that? Whoever it is doesn't seem willing to go away."

Gavin shifted away from her, and spent a moment getting into a pair of sweats. He walked to the closet, selected a T-shirt, and yanked it on. "Don't go anywhere," he said, "I'll be back in a minute."

After fifteen minutes of waiting, Summer got out of bed and padded to the bedroom door. She pulled it open just a fraction, and listened. Male voices. She closed it again after only a moment, and went to the bathroom to run the water for her shower.

She emerged freshly bathed and dressed in white cotton shorts and a dark, maroon T-shirt. She spent a bit of time creaming her legs and arms, then sat before the mirror and began running a brush absently through her hair. There was such a feeling of deep contentment in her today that nothing, absolutely nothing at all, could possibly ruin it for her.

On a sudden impulse, she put down the brush, and padded on bare feet to Nicholas's room. She knocked softly, then entered. He was seated at a desk in the far corner of the room, bent over a stack of papers. Summer gave him a bright smile. "You're up early."

Nicholas turned toward her. "Hey, there," he said, and Summer was momentarily taken aback. He looked so very responsible in glasses. Not at all like the happy-go-lucky guy she had come to know and love over the past several months. She walked slowly toward him. "I didn't know you wore glasses."

He reached back to massage his neck. "I don't wear them a lot. They make me look too unapproachable."

Summer considered him for a moment, her head tilted to one side. "I dunno. I kinda like them."

"So," he said, "are you going to tell me, or what?"

Summer crossed her arms. "You know, you should've been a lawyer or something."

Nicholas removed the glasses, carefully folded the arms and placed them atop the pile of papers. "I am a lawyer or something."

Summer blinked. "What?" she asked after a minute.

"I have a doctorate. Didn't you know that?"

She stared some more. "You have a doctoral degree in law?"

He smiled. "I know you think I'm just a pretty face. But the dull, boring truth of it is, I'm actually kinda smart."

Summer grinned. "You're putting me on."

Nicholas reached into the bottom drawer of the desk, rooted around for a bit, then removed a mounted diploma. He handed it over with an, "I don't know whether to be insulted or not, but here it is in black and white."

Summer's eyes flickered over the document. "UCLA? You went there? My God, so did I, for a while."

"I know," he said.

Her eyes flashed back to him. "You know?"

"We're both around the same age, remember? We were there at the same time."

"You mean, you mean—" Summer stuttered, "I met you when I was there?"

Nicholas ran a hand down his jaw. "No. We never really met. That is to say, you never noticed me." He reached for the glasses again, and slid them back onto his face.

"Imagine me . . . several years ago . . . thirty pounds lighter . . . a bit shorter . . . glasses. You never would've noticed me."

Summer sank onto the side of the bed. "This is incredible." She looked down at the diploma again, as if to reassure herself that it was actually real. "So this entire plan to bring me here to Jamaica so that I would meet Gavin again was hatched way back then?"

He gave her a pleased smile. "I'm glad you think I'm that devious, but no, I hadn't thought of it then. It was only after I saw your portfolio with your picture that I remembered you. And since Gavin couldn't seem to stop talking about you, I decided to bring you here—to decorate the cottage."

Summer gave him a narrow-eyed look. "I don't know whether to punch you or kiss you," she said.

"And what will the best man look like if he turns up at the wedding all beaten and bruised?"

Summer turned to grab a pillow. "You were listening

outside the door last night," she said, and proceeded to
heave every pillow on the bed at him in rapid succession.

The door pushed open during the melee, and Gavin
stood on the threshold, arms folded, tolerant humor twin-
kling in his eyes. "I can't leave you two alone for a second,"
he said.

Summer grinned. "Your brother, Gavin—" The words
she was about to say stilled on her tongue at the expression
that flashed across Nicholas's face. "Look at this," she
said instead, holding up the diploma, "a lawyer—can you
believe it? Your brother is just amazing. I think he deserves
a promotion of some sort."

A flash of silent gratitude came and went in Nicholas's
eyes. Then he was grinning and saying, "Forget the promotion—I want a raise."

Gavin straightened away from the door. "Nicky, come
downstairs with me for a minute. There's something I want
to tell you."

A few hours later, Summer was standing before the
kitchen sink, apron tied neatly about her waist, her hands
busily scrubbing at a pile of baby bottles.

Gavin came up behind her, parted the thick curtain of
her black hair, and pressed a warm kiss to the nape of her
neck. Summer turned, hands dripping. "I'm going to get
you a housekeeper," he said. "I don't want you doing that
anymore."

Summer wound her arms about his neck, and kissed
him softly on the mouth.

"I thought you had something against housekeepers.
Remember what you said to me when I first got here
months ago?" She lowered her voice in a very poor attempt
at mimicry. "You said there is no one around here to fetch
and carry for you, so—"

Gavin kissed her into silence. "Don't remind me," he
said.

"How did Nicky take the news about your mother?" she asked, changing the subject.

Gavin's chest moved in a silent sigh. "Much better than I expected. He was shaken, I guess, but I think he'll be OK. What he needs now is a good woman." He kissed her again. "You know someone just right. Someone like you."

Summer beamed. "Like me?"

He nodded. "Promise me you won't tell him, but, I've the perfect candidate in mind."

The desire to chuckle bubbled to the surface, and Summer fought it back. "Here we go again," she said.

Gavin raised his head. "What?"

She pulled his head back down. "Never mind, babe, I'll tell you later."

Dear Readers,

I hope you enjoyed this brief visit with the Champagne family. I would like to invite you to read my new novel, *Made For Each Other,* which tells Gavin and Summer's entire story. I always love to hear from my readers, so don't forget to drop me a line!

Niqui Stanhope
P.O. Box 6852
Burbank, CA 91510

COMING IN JULY ...

FIRE AND DESIRE,   (1-58314-024-7, $4.99/$6.50)
by Brenda Jackson
Geologist Corithians Avery, and head foreman of Madaris Explor-
ations, Trevor Grant, are assigned the same business trip to South
America. Each has bittersweet memories of a night two years ago
when she walked in on him—Trevor half-naked and she wearing
nothing more than a black negligee. The hot climate is sure to
rouse suppressed desires.

HEART OF STONE,   (1-58314-025-5, $4.99/$6.50)
by Doris Johnson
Disillusioned with dating, wine shop manager Sydney Cox has
settled for her a mundane life of work and lonely nights. Then
unexpectedly, love knocks her down. Executive security manager
Adam Stone enters the restaurant and literally runs into Sydney.
The collision cracks the barriers surrounding their hearts ...
and allows love to creep in.

NIGHT HEAT,   (1-58314-026-3, $4.99/$6.50)
by Simona Taylor
When Trinidad tour guide Rhea De Silva is assigned a group of
American tourists at the last minute, things don't go too well.
Journalist Marcus Lucien is on tour to depict a true to life picture
of the island, even if the truth isn't always pretty. Rhea fears his
candid article may deflect tourism. But the night heat makes the
attraction between the two grow harder to resist.

UNDER YOUR SPELL,   (1-58314-027-1, $4.99/$6.50)
by Marcia King-Gamble
Marley Greaves returns to San Simone for a job as research
assistant to Dane Carmichael, anthropologist and author. Dane's
reputation on the island has been clouded, but Marley is drawn
to him entirely. So when strange things happen as they research
Obeah practices, Marley sticks by him to help dispel the rumors
... and the barrier around his heart.

*Available wherever paperbacks are sold, or order direct from the Pub-
lisher. Send cover price plus 50¢ per copy for mailing and handling
to BET Books, c/o Kensington Publishing Corp., Consumer Orders, or
call (toll free) 888-345-BOOK, to place your order using Mastercard
or Visa. Residents of New York, Washington D.C., and Tennessee must
include sales tax. DO NOT SEND CASH.*

WARMHEARTED AFRICAN-AMERICAN ROMANCES BY *FRANCIS RAY*

FOREVER YOURS   (0-7860-0483-5, $4.99/$6.50)
Victoria Chandler must find a husband or her grandparents will call in loans
that support her chain of lingerie boutiques. She fixes a mock marriage to
ranch owner Kane Taggert. The marriage will only last one year, and her
business will be secure. The only problem is that Kane has other plans for
Victoria. He'll cast a spell that will make her his forever.

HEART OF THE FALCON   (0-7860-0483-5, $4.99/$6.50)
A passionate night with millionaire Daniel Falcon, leaves Madelyn Taggert
enamored . . . and heartbroken. She never accepted that the long-time family
friend would fulfill her dreams, only to see him walk away without regrets.
After his parent's bitter marriage, the last thing Daniel expected was to be
consumed by the need to have her for a lifetime.

INCOGNITO   (0-7860-0364-2, $4.99/$6.50)
Owner of an advertising firm, Erin Cortland witnessed an awful crime and
lived to tell about it. Frightened, she runs into the arms of Jake Hunter, the
man sent to protect her. He doesn't want the job. He left the police force after
a similar assignment ended in tragedy. But when he learns not only one man
is after her and that he is falling in love, he will risk anything to protect her.

ONLY HERS   (07860-0255-7, $4.99/$6.50)
St. Louis R.N. Shannon Johnson recently inherited a parcel of Texas land.
She sought it as refuge until landowner Matt Taggart challenged her to prove
she's got what it takes to work a sprawling ranch. She, on the other hand,
soon challenges him to dare to love again.

SILKEN BETRAYAL   (0-7860-0426-6, $4.99/$6.50)
The only man executive secretary Lauren Bennett needed was her five-year-old
son Joshua. Her only intent was to keep Joshua away from powerful in-laws.
Then Jordan Hamilton entered her life. He sought her because of a personal
vendetta against her father-in-law. When Jordan develops strong feelings for
Lauren and Joshua, he must choose revenge or love.

UNDENIABLE   (07860-0125-9, $4.99/$6.50)
Wealthy Texas heiress Rachel Malone defied her powerful father and eloped
with Logan Williams. But a trump-up assault charge set the whole town and
Rachel against him and he fled Stanton with a heart full of pain. Eight years
later, he's back and he wants revenge . . . and Rachel.

*Available wherever paperbacks are sold, or order direct from the
Publisher. Send cover price plus 50¢ per copy for mailing and
handling to Kensington Publishing Corp., Consumer Orders,
or call (toll free) 888-345-BOOK, to place your order using
Mastercard or Visa. Residents of New York and Tennessee
must include sales tax. DO NOT SEND CASH.*